Love & War

Commander Hursey's Story

To Margaret-Ann

with all love &
affection,

from David
(The Author)

Feb: 5th 2013

Love & War

Commander Hursey's Story

By

David Arnold

Strategic Book Publishing and Rights Co.

Strategic Book Publishing and Rights Co.
12620 FM 1960, Suite A4-507
Houston TX 77065
www.sbpra.com

ISBN: 978-1-61897-672-7

DEDICATION

To my wife, Andrea Damita Arnold who patiently proofread
the whole thing for me.

This novel is entirely fictitious although largely based on actual ships, shore establishments, and events that took place during 1942. Senior commanders of Operation Torch such as General Eisenhower, Major-General Fredendall, Rear-Admiral Sir Harold Burrough RN, and Commodore (later Vice Admiral) Thomas Troubridge RN, mentioned in this book were real people. Otherwise all characters are imaginary and not based on any person, alive or dead. I have used the names of some of my erstwhile shipmates and friends here and there, but the characters given those names in this book bear no resemblance to them in real life.

INTRODUCTION

In the late autumn of 1942, three major actions altered the course of the war against Germany and the other Axis powers, and swung the balance irrevocably in favour of the Allies. The better known are the Battle of el Alamein and the siege and subsequent surrender of the German Sixth Army in Stalingrad on the River Volga. Operations Torch, the Allied landing on the coast of North and West Africa at Algiers, Oran, and Casablanca is less well remembered today. Yet when it took place, it was by far the largest amphibious landing in history, which took years of practice, and learning the new art of disembarking an army and its equipment on a hostile shore from specialised landing craft. It had the potential of a huge disaster if it failed. Training took place for some two years before the actual landing at the Scottish base at Inveraray on Loch Fyne. Operation Torch was the precursor of the landings at Anzio and the Normandy Invasion in June 1944, which opened up the second front in Europe.

The capitulation of Colonel-General, later Field Marshal von Paulus's Sixth Army in Stalingrad took place between their encirclement by the Russian Armies under Marshal Zukov on 19 November 1942, and the final surrender of von Paulus, twenty-six generals, and ninety thousand troops on 22 January 1943. The Axis casualties in the battle, killed, captured, or wounded are estimated to have been eight hundred and fifty thousand, of which four hundred thousand were German. Paradoxically, the air transport formation, Luftflotte 4, urgently needed to supply the encircled Sixth Army was detached on Hitler's personal orders, on 8 November 1942, in order to combat the Allied Army landed that day by the Operation Torch fleet.

The Second Battle of el Alamein, commanded by General Bernard Law Montgomery, took place from 23 October to 11 November 1942. Winston Churchill called it, "Not the beginning of the end [which is actually was, with hindsight] but the end of the beginning." Montgomery drove Field Marshall Rommel's Fifth Panzer Army plus numerous Italian formations inexorably to the west, along the North African coast. They were starved of fuel and supplies by the attacks carried out by allied surface ships and submarines operating out of Malta. Eventually the remaining Germans and Italians were sandwiched between General Eisenhower's forces landed by Operation Torch and Montgomery's forces, and surrendered at Tunis on 13May 1943, As well as many supply ships, all their tanks and equipment, an entire Italian army, and the loss of the dubious support of a hundred and twenty thousand Vichy French troops and personnel, two hundred and seventy five thousand German soldiers were killed or captured.

The Third Reich never recovered from these three, nearly concurrent defeats. I have told the story of part of Operation Torch and the build-up to it through the eyes of a young Merchant Navy officer, Warwick Hursey, who was hurriedly recruited to serve in the Royal Naval Reserve in late 1941.

CAST OF CHARACTERS

(In approximate order of appearance)

Warwick M. G. Hursey – Master Mariner, later Commander Royal Naval Reserve

Sarah Anne Hursey, nee Walker – Warwick Hursey's landlady in Newcastle and, later, his wife

SS FRESHWATER BAY

Jeremy Smythe – a Deputy Assistant Shipping Officer
Sam Rowing –Chief Engineer
Cyril Naismith –Chief Officer (known as "the Mate")
John Evered –Second Mate
Murdo McLeod –Third Mate
William Garthwaite –Second Engineer
Fred Carter –Third Engineer.
Bob Baker –Chief Steward
Ken Vernon –Wireless Operator (aka Sparks)
Eric Chalk –Boatswain (aka bos'n)
Chippie Somas –Carpenter
Shirley – Sarah Walker's friend and, later, her property manager in Newcastle
Captain Oliver Windle RN –Officer in charge of shipping, South Wales

GIBRALTAR

Madam Erica –Owner of the Red Shoes Bar and brothel

Sub-Lieutenant Price-Williams RN –Wardmaster, *HMS Raleigh*
Rear Admiral MacDonald RN –Flag Officer *Gibraltar* (later Vice Admiral)
Lieutenant Commander Jim Marsh RN –Base intelligence officer
Sub-Lieutenant David MacDonald RN – Admiral MacDonald's elder son (later Lieutenant).
John Francis –Able seaman interested in navigation
Esperanza –An attractive Spanish prostitute

ENGLAND

Edith Hursey – Warwick's mother
Captain Frank Hursey TA – Warwick's father, later Major, Royal Transport Corps.
Sally Hursey – Warwick's sister (a medical student, later a qualified doctor)
Major Giles – Retired landlord of the village pub and local Home Guard Commander
Commander Robin King RN – *HMS Victory's* Administrative Officer Portsmouth
Betty King – Commander King's wife
Canon Felix Farson-Smythe, DD – Vicar of St. Margaret's Church, Warnham
Mrs. Mary Johnson (nee Walker) - Sarah's mother
Captain Bertram-Franks RN- Captain Designate of *HMS Aurora*
Squadron Leader Archie Fowler –Anti-submarine Liberator pilot
Captain Francis William Bailey OBE – Captain of the *Aquitania*

HMS STRIKER

Lieutenant Jock Liddle RNR – First Lieutenant
Sub-Lieutenant Robin Wearn RNVR – Watchkeeper and gunnery officer

Sub-Lieutenant Jack Watson RNVR – Watchkeeper, communications, and anti-submarine officer (later Lieutenant)
Lieutenant Tony Mayley RN – Engineer Officer
Surgeon Lieutenant-Commander Fred Woods RNVR – Doctor
Peter Darley – Royal Navy Commissioned Supply Officer
CPO Fred Bates – Coxswain
Ashley Elliott –Leading Stoker
William Hill –Stoker, lover of Leading Stoker Elliott's wife
Lieutenant-Commander James Samson RN – Captain of *HMS Vindex*

BOSTON, MASSACHUSETTS

Captain David Shepherd RN –Naval Attaché, Washington
Rear Admiral David Wixon RN – Head of English equipment purchasing team, USA
Joseph Hegarty –Boss of Harvard Marine Electrics Inc.
Mr. Bristow – the Lloyds' Surveyor, Boston
Patrick Murphy –Manager, Charles River Shipyard
Captain John Osmond USN –Engineering specialist from the US Bureau of Ships

THE THAMES NAUTICAL TRAINING COLLEGE - *HMS WORCESTER*

Captain Gordon Steele VC, RNR –Captain Superintendent
Redvers Martin –Chief Cadet Captain in Warwick's first term

PORTSMOUTH AND HOME

Lieutenant Jones RN –SD electrical engineer attached to the base
Commander Perkins RN – Warwick's relief, *HMS Striker*
Vice-Admiral Christie RN –Flag Officer Southern Command
Mr. Pearson –Family solicitor based in Cheltenham

Commander Ken Mills RN –Officer on the Senior Officers' Command Course

Bert Alfrey – Gardener/handyman/chauffeur at West Lodge

Ethel Alfrey – Bert Alfrey's wife; cook-housekeeper at West Lodge

The Reverend Christopher Lovell MA –Village vicar

Doctor Ian Williams –Local GP

Mrs. Betty Williams – Doctor William's wife

HMS Quebec– INVERARAY – LOCH FYNE

Lieutenant-Commander Parker RN –Captain, *HMS Bruiser*, whom Warwick relieved

Commodore Thomas Troubridge RN – Navy commander, Oran landings

US Major General Lloyd Fredendall – Military commander, Oran landing troops

Heimlich Zeigler –Danish banker and refugee, leasing Morag House

Anne Zeigler – Zeigler's wife

Monika Zeigler – Zeiglers' elder daughter (later Monika MacDonald)

Brigitte Zeigler – Ziegler's younger daughter

Karl Zeigler – Zeigler's son, an SS Haupsturmfuher attached to the German Sixth Army

Captain Marc Andrew-Jones QC RNR –Base's Judge Advocate

Jeanie Cameron – Daughter of the landlord of the Prince Charles pub

HMS BRUISER AND THE LANDING CRAFT TASK UNIT

Lieutenant Bill Browne RN –First Lieutenant

PO Morton –Wardroom steward

Second Lieutenant Josiah Crowthorne –Black US Army Lieutenant on liaison duties

Colonel James Wolfe – US Army Colonel; First Engineer Amphibious Brigade

US Major Robert Brightman – Colonel Wolfe's deputy

Lieutenant-Colonel Tim Street – British First Armoured Division

Lieutenant Jerry Collins USNR –Commander of a large US landing craft

Lieutenant Alan Royle USNR – Commander of a large US landing craft; Collins's friend

Lieutenant-Commander Fred Harden USN – Warwick's deputy

Surgeon Lieutenant Ian Mitchell RNVR –Ship's doctor

Surgeon Sub-Lieutenant Jim Agnew RNVR – Mitchell's newly qualified assistant

Rear Admiral Sir Harold Burrough RN –Operational Fleet Commander

Midshipman Rodwick RN- Trainee navigating officer and Captain's Secretary

CPO Blessed –Ship's Coxswain and Master at Arms

Lieutenant Eddie Freeland RNR – *HMS Bruiser's* engineer officer

LONDON BRIEFING AND CLARIDGES HOTEL

Commander James C Williamson III USN –Task group commander

General Dwight D. Eisenhower – US Army General in overall command

Vice-Admiral Sir Bertram Ramsey RN – General Eisenhower's deputy

Major General James Doolittle USAF – Air commander for the operation

Lieutenant-General Kenneth Anderson –British land commander

Rear Admiral Ken Hewett USN – American operational fleet commander

Captain Kay Summersby – General Eisenhower's female driver

DAVID ARNOLD

GIBRALTAR AND *HM HOSPITAL SHIP OXFORDSHIRE*

Josianne –French nurse in Gibraltar Military Hospital
William Strong –Second Officer of the Oxfordshire
Captain "Annie" Lawrie – Master of the hospital ship Oxfordshire
Roger Holmes –Chief Officer
Nick Childs ACA –Accountant Sarah retained to advise her
Bert Wicks –Live-in handyman and gardener for West Lodge
Lilly Wicks – Bert Wicks' wife; cook/housekeeper for West Lodge

CHAPTER ONE

She was a very old ship and owed her continued existence only to the general depression and the fact that no one had thought it worthwhile to scrap her. An iron Black Sea tramp dating from the end of the last century, she had been laid up in a muddy creek in a backwater of the River Tyne about ten miles upstream of Newcastle in the great shipping slump of the 1930s, her working days apparently over for good. There she remained, abandoned, listing to port, with paint blistering and most of her brass fittings removed by night visitors, while many finer and newer ships went to the shipbreakers. The plentiful population of grain-fed rats gradually died out as their food supply dwindled to nothing, and their little carcasses dried and ceased to smell, hidden away in the cabin bulkheads and deckhead linings. Then came the outbreak of war and the formation of the War Emergency Transport Board, known as WETB and usually referred to as the "Wet-B." Losses of British merchant ships to German aircraft and submarines reached critical levels, and all the backwaters of harbours and creeks were scoured for replacement tonnage. Eventually the Board's eye fell on the old *Freshwater Bay*.

A local tug was engaged to pull her out of the mud at high tide and move her to a local yard. A schedule of refit and reconditioning was drawn up and the work commenced. She spent a week or so in dry dock, while the years of accumulated molluscs and weed was removed from her hull, new zinc anodes were fitted to the rudder and propeller boss, and her hull was given two coats of anti-corrosive paint and an anti-fouling coat. She was re-launched and put alongside the refitting dock. At that time of the war, only minimum effort and material could be spared to make her reasonably seaworthy. She was not expected to have much of a future, being old and slow and a coal-burner, always steaming with a plume of black smoke issuing from her tall funnel and thus visible for miles at sea in the daytime, especially in calm conditions.

The perennial problem arose of crewing her. She was not a very attractive berth for anyone, and firemen and trimmers were in short supply, the modern trend being for oil-fired or motor ships. Qualified officers were hard to come by in both the navigating and engineering departments. War losses of personnel were high, and additional vessels of all shapes and sizes were being hastily mobilised. Many of the better-qualified Merchant Marine officers had been members of the Royal Naval Reserve in peace time and were quickly subsumed as highly trained personnel into the rapidly expanding Royal Navy. Temporary watch keeping certificates were issued to young and green cadets who had a few voyages to their credit, to fill the gaps. The Board of Trade got less and less particular in their statutory manning requirements in these emergency conditions. Overall it was felt that if a small ship had a competent and fully qualified captain and chief engineer on board, there was a reasonable chance that she would keep going for the voyage and arrive where she was supposed to in due course. That is if the U-boats didn't get her first.

CHAPTER TWO

Warwick Hursey was Junior Second Officer of a large P&O passenger ship which had just docked in London that morning in late October 1941 with several battalions of Australian troops embarked. Promotion in the company was slow, but he hoped to rise to be in command before he was fifty. He had spent three years as a cadet on the Thames Nautical Training College, *HMS Worcester*, between the ages of fourteen and seventeen, and then another three years as an apprentice with P&O. When he obtained a Second-Mates' Certificate, he was invited back by the company's marine superintendent as a junior fourth officer. He was a tall, dark, well-built man now, clever and competent and popular with his senior officers, the Indian crew, and the passengers. He remained with the company while he obtained promotion and his certificates, the last of which, that of Master of a Foreign-Going Steamship; he had passed in London just before the voyage that had just ended. He was now twenty-six and unmarried; the officers on the passenger ships of those times lived well while afloat, but after they had invested in the required smart uniforms and tropical kit, they tended to have little or nothing at the bank and a large, overdue account at the marine tailor's. Few of them married before their mid-thirties as a consequence; they simply couldn't afford to set up a home ashore with a wife and children.

His relief arrived; he handed over to him in his cabin, packed his kit, changed into civilian clothes, and made his way to the gangway to await the taxi to take him to the railway station. He rang his mother from the gangway telephone to warn her he'd be home in a few hours for a fortnight's leave. She seemed very happy at the prospect. With his father away, she had little to do in the Sussex countryside but worry about submarines and torpedoes and starving castaways drifting in the ocean in lifeboats; the papers were full of such stories.

Just as he was about to leave the ship, the gangway quartermaster called him aside. He had a small man with a neat moustache, thick glasses, a bowler hat, and a slightly shiny black jacket in tow. The latter introduced himself as a Mr. Jeremy Smyth and proffered his card, which showed him to be a Deputy Assistant Shipping Officer employed by the WETB.

"Mr. Hursey?" he enquired.

"Yes, I'm Hursey and I'm just about to go on leave. My relieving officer is up top if you need anything – I'm off now. I've been away for three months and I'm very keen to get home now for a couple of weeks' rest. My taxi's due any minute."

"Doubtless you realise there's a war on, Mr. Hursey, being in the shipping business and things are pretty tight here." So saying, he handed over a buff envelope marked "Movement and Appointment Order." Warwick opened it hurriedly. It was on official WETB notepaper, and addressed to Captain W. M. G. Hursey, which brought him up with a start.

Under the powers vested in the War Emergency Transport Board (hereinafter referred to as "the Board") by virtue of the Emergency Powers Act 1940, you are now to consider yourself as employed by the Board as Ship Master at a rate of £85 10s per calendar month plus approved expenses and subsistence.

You are hereby requested and required to proceed forthwith to the Newcastle Shipyard of Hebburn & Co to stand by the refit of, and subsequently take command of the Board's commandeered steam ship *Freshwater Bay*, now lying at that yard. A transport warrant is enclosed.

I remain, your obedient servant,

Andrew Mains
A Principal Deputy Secretary to the Board.

He looked around him. The world paused; the sounds of the gulls and dockside cranes were stilled and the daylight seemed to have darkened a little. Bright points like stars danced around his peripheral vision. He sat down on the quartermaster's chair, afraid he might actually pass out, which gave him the opportunity to recover his thoughts. Mr. Smyth tapped his fingers on the teak rail and looked rather pointedly at his watch.

"Tell me about this *Freshwater Bay* ship. What exactly is she and why am I involved? I have a three year contract with P&O and can't just swan off to some other ship, you know! Besides, I'm due some leave and I've just rung my mother to tell her I'll soon be home."

"Captain Hursey," said Smyth, emphasising the title somewhat, "you are qualified to command a ship; you have a foreign-going masters' ticket. We are at our wits end to feed this country. Every bit of spare tonnage available has to be put into service, and there is a desperate shortage of qualified navigating and engineer officers to man these ships. War losses and the demands of the Admiralty have exacerbated the situation."

From an inside pocket he drew out a long, white, unsealed envelope and handed it to Warwick. "There's your fine ship, sir! Not quite what you're used to, but she can carry three thousand tons of food and other vital supplies to us from the States. That's what's important!"

Warwick opened the envelope and drew out several sheets of typed foolscap, a large, black and white photograph, and a deck plan and elevation, all of which he glanced through quickly.

He discovered that his first command was to be an iron ship built on the Tyne in 1895, and that she had been in the Black Sea grain trade for many years. She was a coal-burner with two, single ended Scotch boilers and a triple expansion steam engine, all of the same vintage as the ship. She had a deadweight tonnage of thirty-five hundred– the maximum weight of cargo she could carry – spread over four hatches with two steam winches and two derricks to each hatch. She was certainly not the sort of ship he was used to; he'd only been on P&O cargo ships in his career, and they was modern and fast motor ships with twelve passengers and run to passenger ship standards.

"What about my company contract? I can't just walk out without head office's permission, Mr. Smyth."

"Head office has already been informed and so has your captain. My boss is up there now," said Smyth. "The fact is that these big passenger ships can no longer be allowed to run with eight qualified watchkeepers, and have two people with masters' tickets on the bridge for each four-hour watch at sea. The chief officers will have to keep watch now, instead of swanning about on the passenger decks, and their maximum complement of deck officers in the future will be the master, three navigating officers, and four cadets. The same applies to the engineers. Besides, there'll be no more passengers for the duration of this war. Troop carrying is what it's about now. I'm afraid you're surplus to requirements and so the WETB is your new employer. Welcome to the club!"

Smyth was obviously enjoying himself. For a man whose life was devoted to getting ancient ships manned and into productive use, the rich lode of qualified officers and seamen that the newly arrived passenger ship would provide was a matter of great satisfaction. Never being in a position financially to travel on them himself, he imagined that their officers led a life of bacchanalian pleasure, and deep down and not even to be admitted to himself, he thought that a spell coaxing an ancient tramp ship over the North Atlantic in winter, with U-boats aplenty, would do young Warwick Hursey good. His desk in a warm corner of the Board's London offices, with the heavy china mugs of hot ministry tea and buns coming round on a trolley at regular intervals during the morning and afternoon had never seemed such a fair prospect.

"You'd best ring your mother quickly; your rail warrant expires at midnight and there's a train to Newcastle from Saint Pancras at one-twenty you ought to catch."

CHAPTER THREE

There was a keen and biting east wind blowing across the open spaces of Hebburn's refitting dock. It was early evening that day. Cranes were stilled as the day shift was finishing up. Cloth-capped men, wrapped in ancient coats and carrying small parcels, were making their way through the dock gate and to their homes on the streets of little back-to-back houses outside. Street lights shone through the damp and misty air. It was drizzling intermittently, and the sheets of droplets blew across the dock and the berthed ships in waves. Several ships in various states of disrepair and refitting were moored alongside. There was a modern tanker having her deck guns and communication masts fitted and being painted grey. Behind her was a big, two-funnelled passenger ship with an old-fashioned counter stern being converted into an armed merchant cruiser. There were a couple of other nondescript merchant ships undergoing major surgery and, at the end of the row, the unmistakable shape of a small, steam driven, three-island tramp ship. Warwick pulled his mac more tightly around him and made his way across the puddles, oily mud, bits of timber, rusty lumps of metal, and stray bits of wire rope to her rudimentary gangway. The ship's power was obviously not connected, and strings of low-wattage bulbs lighted the decks and alleyways. Someone was welding on the foredeck and there were a couple of workers securing the single-barrelled Bofors gun that had been placed on the poop.

"That will really frighten them if we meet the Scharnhorst!" muttered Warwick to himself as he climbed the rusty iron ladder to the bridge. He noted that a proper wheelhouse providing shelter for the officer of the watch had been fabricated in front of the chart room. Even the stingy surveyors from WETB had realised that the North Atlantic in winter was no place for an open bridge and a canvass dodger to protect the helmsman and watchkeeper for four hours. The new wheelhouse had recently been painted out in eau-de-nil with new wiring and a wheel, two brass engine room telegraphs to port and starboard, and a compass binnacle as its main furnishings. There was a heating radiator next to the helmsman (trust an old steam ship to have good heating) and new teak doors to the bridge wings. A door had been cut into the aft bulkhead that had formed the front of the old chart room. This room contained little else but a chart table with several chart drawers under it, a bookcase with *Admiralty Pilot Books* and a set of *Norrie's Nautical Tables*, and a dusty looking settee. There were a couple of unwound chronometers in their little glass boxes protected by a Perspex sheet on top, like incubating ostrich eggs. Warwick viewed these arrangements with some satisfaction. Navigating this vessel would be basic, but the basics were there. With a sextant, tables, and rated chronometers, he could get this ship anywhere he had charts for, even if he had to rely on the old sailing ship "lead, line, and lookout" routine.

Through the darkening gloom he saw a figure below on the boat deck in a fairly clean white boiler suit and an old peaked cap, talking to a couple of dockyard workers by the port lifeboat. He went down the bridge ladder and introduced himself. The figure introduced himself to Warwick in turn.

"I'm Sam Rowing, chief engineer." He was about thirty years old, balding, and of middle height, but broad and muscular. He had a twinkle in his blue eyes as if the whole thing was some kind of joke being played out, or perhaps a difficult dream from which he was convinced he would soon awake. His friendly, outgoing manner endeared him to Warwick from the start.

"When did you get your Chief's ticket, Sam?" asked Warwick.

"Now let me think back, captain. It must have been all of three days ago. I got two letters in the post that day, one registered, with my Chief's ticket enclosed, and the other from WETB ordering me to stand by as chief of this old bucket."

"You've a steam ticket?" asked Warwick.

"Yes; I was with Blue Star Line for most of my time at sea, and their ships are mostly steam turbine driven, although some are motor, so I've a combined steam and motor ticket now. I must say, though, I've never been with an old, triple expansion engine like this one before. If you go down below, it looks like a Victorian print of the bowels of the Great Eastern."

"What sort of shape is she in below?"

"Not as bad as I feared. These old brass con-rod and casting steam engines are pretty indestructible, and the boilers and pipework seem reasonable, although some valves and pipes are being replaced now. She was pretty well run in her time and then sealed up from the wind and weather when she was laid up. I have high hopes of her working up to nine knots or so when we're up and running."

The two men took to each other. They had both served their time in the regular liners but were young, highly qualified, well trained, unattached, and up for adventure. Paradoxically, their rapid promotion to the old *Freshwater Bay* was something to look forward to, something they missed as junior officers on a large ship where everything ran to a rigid and pre-ordained plan. There was no crusty old captain or chief engineer of vast seniority laying down the law and issuing edicts to concern them. Sam had booked in at a small private guest house a few streets away.

"It's a comfortable place; the landlady owns it. She bought it from money she was left by some old boy who was her lover for a few years; a real-life sugar daddy. Anyway she's a young redhead with a bosom to die for, so you'd better watch yourself!"

Warwick took a taxi to the station to collect his luggage and then, with darkened headlights, drove through the drizzle and blacked-out streets to the address Sam had given him.

Sam was right about the landlady, he thought to himself. She turned out to be in her early thirties, not tall but with a very attractive, full figure and a startling head of naturally auburn hair that gleamed in the light. That and her lightly freckled face and lovely green eyes were what he first noticed. She had a welcoming smile that somehow made him feel he was at home; it seemed to be just for him. She exuded warmth and fun to be had.

"My name is Sarah Anne Walker," she said. She had a low, pleasant voice with no trace of a Geordie accent. He could smell the faint scent of a subtle and probably expensive perfume. Later he found out she was born in Chelmsford and had moved up to Newcastle to be with her elderly lover when she was nineteen. She said she still had one room vacant, so Warwick paid her a month's rent in advance and was shown to his room. It had an old-fashioned double bed and a window onto the street with strips of anti-blast brown paper tape across it. There was a decent carpet on the floor, and bedside lights, with the bathroom next door. Above all, it was warm; Warwick had not realised how cold he had got standing around in the shipyard in the rain and wind.

After he had unpacked, he knocked on Sam's door and they went down together to the small, cosy parlour. There, they spread out the plans and written material concerning their new ship and began working through the main tasks yet to be undertaken to bring the ship up to a reasonably seaworthy condition. Both had been warned that the refitting and deployment of British merchant ships was classified, but they didn't think that Admiral Donitz or, for that matter Adolf Hitler, would have much of an interest in the progress of *S. S. Freshwater Bay's* refit, so they carried on when Sarah joined them with a pot of tea and some biscuits on a plate with a fancy doily.

"What would you chaps like for dinner? I've some pork chops which I can fry up and roast a couple of potatoes to go with them. The yard has block-booked all my other rooms, but you two are the only game in town at the moment."

"That would be fine, love; even better if you had a couple of bottles of beer to wash it down," Warwick replied. "Tell me, do you fancy coming out with us afterward for a drink? I'm sure you know all the best places around here."

"As I said, you two are the only ones in the house tonight. I could do with a break. What with all these new ships in the yard, I am full up most of the time and I only have a girl in the daytime coming in to help out. Yes, I'd love to come for a drink after supper."

Later that evening, they found themselves in a smoky bar near the centre of town. It was full of service men in uniform, mainly soldiers, but with a smattering of navy and merchant navy sailors as well as some young local civilians. It was Friday night and the crowd was busy getting drunk, having received their week's pay that afternoon. A three-piece band was playing old Hollywood tunes on a raised platform opposite the bar. A young and over-made up girl with a dress that was a just a little too low cut came on stage at intervals and sang Vera Lynn songs in a husky, pleasant voice.

Sam had excused himself earlier, saying that he had a big day on tomorrow. Sarah and Warwick were left alone with their drinks at a small side-table at the back of the room. They found conversation flowed naturally and easily, and they warmed to each other. Sarah told him her life story. They were a happy family of three until her father lost his job as the production manager of a West Country engineering firm in the general depression that followed the Great War. He never really recovered from that shock; he'd worked there for thirty years, man and boy. He died when she was twelve and her mother married again the following year, more out of financial necessity than love. Sarah resented her new stepfather, especially as he began to show more and more interest in her and less in her mother. Sarah was entering puberty and beginning to develop her lovely figure.

One night when her mother was out for some reason, the step-father tried to rape her, breaking into the bathroom while she was in the bath. She managed to fight him off but suffered some big and obvious bruises in the process. She escaped mainly because her mother arrived home early. When she told her mother what had happened, she was greeted with incredulity. Her step-father accused her of trying to seduce him and that was what her mother at least pretended to believe.

She moved in with her grandmother nearby after the subsequent huge and bitter family row. There she remained until she was eighteen, when her grandmother died and her house was put on the market. She was on her own then, and lucky to get a job as housekeeper and general help to the widowed owner of a local investment advisory business. He was in his late fifties, still an active, handsome man. The job provided her with a little money and a roof over her head, as she was required to live in.

After some months, the inevitable happened and she became his mistress. That lasted for twelve years, until he died and left her the house and £12,500. She sold the house and moved up to the North East where the great depression of the 1930s had made property cheap. She bought her own large house and three other, smaller ones, and lived on the rents, renting rooms in her house and, the income from £5,000 of 2% Government Stock.

Warwick's life seemed rather banal in contrast. First son of a happy family in West Sussex, his father ran the local garage. He had a sister five years younger, who was at medical school. He told her of the Warnham village school, his time at Collyers Grammar School in the nearby town of Horsham, and his joining the training ship *HMS Worcester* moored off Greenhithe in Kent when he was thirteen. He dwelt longer on his time on the Worcester, his love of the sea, the ships passing down the river to his continual interest, sleeping in hammocks, scrubbing the decks of the old clipper *Cutty Sark*, moored alongside, and of his eventual promotion to senior cadet captain and acceptance as an apprentice by the P&O Company. His unremarkable if successful career to date, culminating in his ship's docking only that morning, his sudden promotion to captain, and his subsequent arrival at his new command.

"Let's get out of here," said Warwick. "I have a big day tomorrow, too, and I just can't stand all this smoke." Unusually for those days, neither of them smoked and the atmosphere had gotten thicker and thicker. "Besides, there's going to be a fight in here before the evening's out, and I really want to be clear of it. Some of those roughnecks over there might actually end up being my crew, and it wouldn't help much if they remembered punching me in the ear a little while back."

When they got outside, the drizzle had stopped and the sky had cleared. Although the wind had gone, it was still quite cold. The town was completely blacked out, and as they walked, Warwick put a protective arm around Sarah's waist. Eventually they managed to hail a passing taxi. They sat together in the back, snuggled up together. He put his arm around her again. He couldn't resist caressing her face and neck, and she turned toward him. The kissed, at first chastely and then with increasing urgency.

"What's that lovely perfume you're wearing?" he asked her when they paused.

"Chanel Number 5," she replied. "My old man gave me a lot of it before the war, and I still have some left, which is just as well; it's impossible to get now."

They got out at Sarah's house and went up the stairs together after she had locked up and switched out the lights. Sam was fast asleep, and they were the only others in the house. Sarah led him to her bedroom. She undressed in front of him, without concealment or shame or self-consciousness, and after a while, he undressed too and slid in between the sheets. She sat naked at her dressing table, her arms upraised while she brushed out her long, auburn-red hair. She was in profile to him and he thought how beautiful the line of her upraised, soft, freckled white arm over her left breast was with the light shining behind her.

He thought that some poet like Shelly ought to have written a sonnet about that so feminine beauty of line. He felt a surge throughout his whole body; a combination of lust, love, and huge affection for this glorious woman who had surmounted so much in her life, yet remained such a beautiful and loving person. He didn't care that she had been an old man's mistress, nor if she had had hundreds of lovers in the past. Nothing like that mattered; she was Sarah, and she was his now. She walked over to the bed and turned off the bedside light. He felt the warmth of her as she cuddled up to him, her searching hands already reaching down his body. His last semi-subconscious thought before they made love for the first of several times that night was that it had really been one hell of a day.

CHAPTER FOUR

It was a clear, crisp morning at the fitting out dock. Sam and Warwick had arrived on the ship after a full fried breakfast, cooked by Sarah for both of them. They both tried to behave normally in front of Sam, but their sudden intense attraction and obvious feelings toward each other must have been unmistakable. The little pat on Sarah's bottom as she poured the tea, a ruffle of Warwick's hair on his neck as he looked up at her; it was inevitable and very easy to deduce what had happened. Sam was an experienced man and no fool, but if he guessed what Warwick's new-found relationship was with their hostess, he didn't see fit to bring it up.

They had discovered their respective cabins, had the shipyard cleaners put them into some kind of habitable state, moved some of their kit into them, and established their office in the tiny officers' dining saloon, forward on the main deck. They spread out their plans and notes on the saloon tables and adjacent sideboards and serving tables. The yard had lent them a typewriter and installed a telephone line, and the ship's foreman and engineers were instructed to report to them there. Gradually the schedule of outstanding items was drawn up and agreed, and the necessary work orders issued. They were frequently called away to inspect the lower holds, winches, steering engine pipework, and various items that needed servicing or replacement. All kinds of equipment kept arriving at the quayside – four Carley floats and crates of new radio room equipment to replace the ancient transmitters in situ, dating from

WWI and untouched from the years the ship was laid up. There was a new radio direction finding set complete with goniometer and RDF loop, and an echo sounder for the chartroom. There were also cases of engineering spares for Sam to sort out, covering not only the engine room but also the cargo winches, windlass, capstans aft, and the steering engine. Eight new steel derricks came mid-morning on a long, articulated lorry. The old wooden ones had warped and cracked in the sun over the years, and were completely unfit for load carrying now. Warwick, after consulting with Sam, reckoned it would be at least two weeks before the ship was ready for sea.

Around mid-morning, the rest of the WETB-employed officers arrived: three mates, two engineers, and a Chief Steward. They were a mixed bunch. The mate, Cyril Naismith, was about seventy and hadn't been to sea for fifteen years. He held a master's ticket in steam dated 1897 and wore wire-rimmed glasses. He was a small, grey-haired man, his wrinkled skin nut-brown with years of exposure to all types of weather. He had served in sail as an apprentice and held a deep-sea second mates' certificate for a square-rigged ship. He had been managing a boatyard in Devon since he left the sea in 1926. Warwick sized him up immediately as a tough little nut and a real seaman. The second mate, John Evered, a big, pleasant, open and obliging young man of twenty, had just passed his second mates' ticket; previously he had been an apprentice in the Commonwealth and Dominion Line on refrigerated cargo passenger ships trading to Australia and New Zealand. He had had good training but lacked any experience as an officer. The third mate, Murdo McLeod, was a forty-year-old ex-fishing skipper from the Western Isles with a temporary licence from the Board of Trade. He had spent all his adult life in deep-sea trawlers. He was to prove an exceptionally fine and reliable seaman.

Both the engineers had served their apprenticeship in Doxford's works. William Doxford & Co. built big marine diesel engines which were used throughout the shipping world. Both were local boys from Newcastle. Neither had any experience with steam reciprocating machinery. The elder, William Garthwaite, was twenty-eight and had a temporary second engineer's licence. The younger, Fred Carter was straight out of his apprenticeship and had never been to sea before. The horizons of them both seemed to be bound by crossheads, Newcastle United's results in the league, and the quantity and quality of the local brew, Newcastle Brown Ale. Bob Baker, the Chief Steward was around fifty and had been a second purser in the big Cunard liners in his time and said he had held that position on the old *Mauritania*. Prematurely bald, and with a worried, furtive look, he had been at sea longer than anyone else except the mate, and knew all the ropes. He went to work straight away sorting out the catering department stores and organising things – it was what he had spent his whole life doing.

Things went faster that afternoon with all the new officers working through the lists that Warwick and Sam had made out. The mate and third mate worked together uncoiling the new wires, greasing them, and rigging them from the winches, through steel blocks and to swivels on the derricks. The engineers helped rig a pressurised steam hose from the boiler in the yard, so that the deck machinery could be serviced, run, and tested. The second mate took delivery of several chart folios, Notices to Mariners, and war operational paperwork dealing with routing, general convoy instructions, and secret charts of minefield locations. He busied himself bringing charts up to date and winding and adjusting the chronometers.

It was obvious that they would be working late, so Warwick phoned both Sarah and his mother, in that order. To Sarah, he said that Sam and he would get something to eat brought in and be home around ten o'clock. She said there were a couple of other shipyard officials in the house now, but she was longing to see him and sent him much, much love and tons of kisses. Taking a deep breath, he rang his mother. He told her about the ship, what they had been doing, and that he was comfortably settled in a boarding house with the chief engineer, and that they had a nice, kind landlady who looked after them well. He felt that he need describe Sarah no further. His mother, born in the reign of Queen Victoria, would not have approved at all his doings of the previous night. She was in a very happy state of mind, anyway; his father had been granted leave from his position as a captain in the Transport Corps in Northern Ireland and was coming home to Sussex for a few days. He had occupied the same position in the army at the end of WWI. In spite of his being fifty-five years old, he had been asked to re-join at his old rank soon after the outbreak of this war, as he was a knowledgeable and experienced motor engineer and a good organiser. He had also served as an acting major in the Territorial Army during the intervening twenty-one years of peace.

Sam and Warwick shared a taxi and got home at ten thirty that night. They drank a bottle of beer each in the kitchen, said goodnight, and went to their rooms. Warwick had a quick bath, changed into a pair of clean pyjamas, and, with his heart thumping and the adrenalin surging, tip-toed along the passageway and tapped on Sarah's door, hoping against hope she hadn't given him up for lost and gone to sleep. She hadn't; the door opened quite quickly, to reveal Sarah in a translucent night dress. But only for the brief instant it took for her to pull him inside and shut the door.

CHAPTER FIVE

The next morning, the rest of the crew assembled in the long room of the Newcastle Shipping Office, were read the Articles and signed on for a two-year, foreign-going voyage on the *S. S. Freshwater Bay*. There was a wireless operator employed by Marconi on contract; Ken Vernon, a small, eager young man with horn-rimmed glasses. He was known to all as Sparks, and it was his first trip to sea. The bos'n, Eric Chalk, a middle aged cockney with a lot of sea time in his career, the carpenter, Chippie Somas, three ABs, three ordinary seamen, and two deck boys made up the on-deck crowd. The engine room storekeeper, the donkey man, four trimmers, four firemen, and three greasers were the engine room team. There was a cook, a steward, and a pantry boy. Finally, there were two army gunners and one a corporal to handle the Bofors gun on the poop. The corporal told Warwick that the ship was lucky to have a 40mm Mark III Bofors gun that could fire 120 rounds of two-pound shells a minute; they could penetrate Panzer tank armour and would certainly discourage surfaced U-boats. Most of the old merchant ships had been allocated pre-WWI three-inch guns that had lain in the armaments stores for years, and, with untrained crews, would be lucky to get three rounds off over open sights within two minutes. The soldiers also had two Sten guns with five hundred rounds of ammunition under their care. That, with the captain's revolver and fifty rounds in his cabin safe, made up the ship's armament. Totting them up, Warwick discovered he had thirty-five souls under his command, not counting himself.

The work rate doubled with the dockyard workers completing their specified refit jobs, and the crew, cleaning, painting, oiling, greasing, and cleaning out the holds. The funnel and upper works were painted naval grey, while the hull remained black with a red boot-topping line. They had painted over the varnish work on the rail capping around the bridge and woodwork under the wheelhouse windows, much to Warwick's disgust. He resolved to have a word with the mate and have that scraped off and re-varnished as soon as they got clear of the yard. On the funnel was painted a white shield with blue edging, and the letters *WET B* on the shield in red.

After ten days, the ship was just about ready to sail. Sam and Warwick ticked off the few remaining items on their respective lists. Bob Baker checked aboard the last of the catering stores. Steam was raised on both boilers and the main engine was run slowly ahead and astern after additional warps had been secured to ensure that the ship did not break free from the quay. The ship's steam generators took over from the shore electricity supply, and the steam hose was disconnected.

Warwick was summoned to a WETB planning meeting at the shipping office. There he discovered he was to proceed to the coal staithes at Swansea unescorted, leaving the next day at 0630. The old ship was to load there a hundred and fifty tons of bunker coal and twelve hundred tons of best steam coal as cargo in the lower holds for the navy coaling station at Gibraltar, plus approximately nine hundred and fifty tons of general supplies for the garrison in the tween decks; mainly ammunition, tinned food, spare parts, and a couple of Jeeps. They were scheduled to join convoy GR 16 in ten days' time.

He came away with his routing and latest minefield location details, realising with a sudden pang that this would be the last night for some time he would spend with Sarah. Over the past few weeks, they had become closer both physically and as friends and companions. Warwick had had affairs before, but they were hurried things taken in the brief leave times between voyages, and mostly unconsummated. He had had the odd one night stand in his apprenticeship, but he had never really been close to a woman and shared his life with hers as he had with Sarah. She had become a major factor in his life, he realised. What started as an exciting affair with a beautiful and demanding woman had grown into a great surge of love made all the more intense because he knew she felt the same way about him.

One night, her friend Shirley, whom she had fixed up for a blind date with Sam, had confided in Warwick. "You are the man she has always wanted. Look after her, and she will care for you and love and adore you for the rest of her life."

Sam was in on the secret now, and had, in fact, started a somewhat less intense relationship with Shirley.

Because he was still young, nearly seven years younger than Sarah, he did not realise how attractive he actually was, especially in his uniform with the broad four gold stripes on his arm and the gold scrambled egg on his cap. He was tall and dark and handsome, and so pleasant in his manner as to attract almost any eligible woman. He went home early that night, having arranged for a taxi at 0500 and alerted Cyril and the bos'n that they would be singling up at 0600 and the ship should have steam up and be secured for sea by then.

It was his last night with Sarah for several months; possibly forever, what with the enemy submarines at sea and the blitz ashore. Her boarding house was too near the shipyard to be safe from bombs, and his slow old ship was a sitting duck if she were to be caught in the wrong place at the wrong time. They had an hour before dinner, and the maid was in the kitchen tending to the roast and peeling the potatoes for the night's dinner, so they went to bed together by mutual consent. There was desperation in their love making that both of them felt. Warwick held her tight and was more forceful and violent than usual. When it was over, they laid on their backs, side by side, exhausted, hot and wet. All too soon, Sarah had to get up, shower, and go down to attend to her other boarders. Warwick was left lying in her bed on damp sheets and pillows, with only the faint residual trace of Chanel No. 5 to remember her by, feeling lost and miserable. He had never experienced the joy and desolation of real love, and it alarmed him that, with his first command due to sail tomorrow, his mind was all Sarah. Sarah, Sarah, Sarah. Nothing else seemed to signify and when he tried to think about the ship and his responsibilities, he couldn't concentrate no matter how vital it was to plan the voyage and assess his officers and crew.

After dinner, the two of them walked round the corner to a nearby pub and had a few joyless drinks. They didn't have much to say to each other for once. They just sat and sipped their drinks and held hands and felt mutual misery. When they got outside at about ten o'clock, it was very cold and the sky looked overcast and threatening. Warwick wondered if they were in for some early winter snow. They walked back through the blackout to the boarding house and kissed briefly, then went unhappily to their separate rooms to try to sleep. Warwick and Sam had an 0400 call arranged.

CHAPTER SIX

There was no wind at five a. m. when they got aboard, but a gentle but dense snowfall restricted visibility to about fifty yards. It was bitterly cold. Warwick wore his long johns, a thick, slightly yellow, woollen vest, a couple of heavy sweaters, one over the other, sea boots, a uniform jacket, a duffel coat, a cap, and thick gloves. Murdo reported in his soft, Western Isles' burr that all the crew were on board, although some were more sober than others. He didn't specify further, and Warwick was content to let the ex-fishing skipper deal with the matter; he must have had similar problems, time without number, on the Scottish fishing boats when they left port.

Sam arrived on the bridge to say they had a full head of steam and the main engine was ready to move. Cyril, wrapped up like an elderly gnome, went forward and John went aft to single up the ropes to a line and a spring at each end.

The steam windlass forward and capstans aft rattled away as the deck crew handled the mooring lines. The iron decks and hatches were covered in a thick, white cloth of wet snow, with bare patches where the warm winches exuded little squirts of escaping steam. From below came the sound of a fireman's shovel clanging on the plates; a signal, understood from the time of the first steamships a hundred years before that he needed the trimmers to dump more coal into the stokehold. Everyone was always sorry for the sufferings of the black gang down below in the Red Sea or the tropics, but on a bitter, snowy morning in Newcastle in December, they were warm, dry, and stripped to their vests; they had the best of it down there that morning.

At 0615, the pilot came aboard, a big, bluff, red-faced Geordie well past retirement age, who had been called back for emergency service. He was so wrapped up he looked like a cross between a grizzly bear and the Michelin man.

"All ready to go, captain?" he asked.

"We're all singled up and there's a full head of steam to the main engine."

"She's an old one, this one, to be sure!' said the pilot. 'I used to take these Baltic grain ships in and out when I was an apprentice pilot here, around the turn of the century."

"She's been laid up half her life. She seems in pretty good shape for all of that. This will be her first voyage under her own power for nearly eleven years."

"Well, let's see how she goes. Let go the head rope, stern rope, and after spring, please. Dead slow ahead. Hard a-starboard."

There was a puff of black smoke and the old engine burst into life. The stern swung out and she backed away from the wharf and then steamed slowly ahead out of the refit dock. Warwick had never experienced the thump, thump of a ship's steam reciprocating engine under way before. It was so different from the remote hum he was used to on the big passenger ships, overlaid by the noises of various ventilation and forced draft fans.

If anything, the snow was thicker as they steamed down the river past the wharves and yards that lined the banks. These appeared only dimly through the murk when the ship was abeam of them. As they cleared the entrance, the pilot ordered full speed ahead for the fairway buoy.

Cyril came up to the bridge, as the four to eight was his watch. John went aft with an AB to the taffrail to set up the towed log, their only indication of distance run and consequent calculated speed through the water. The fairway buoy came into sight ahead and the pilot stopped the ship opposite the pilot boat, which was close by.

"The compass seems about right, at least on an easterly course," said Warwick to Cyril. The ship had been swung and both the steering and standard compasses adjusted before Warwick had joined her to oversee the process. In this clag, he would have to rely on the magnetic compass and the distance log reading for his navigation, although the new DF set had been calibrated and checked as working correctly. However, with no shore stations active around the coast (as they would aid friend and foe alike), this would be of very limited use on the coastal passage to Swansea. It might pick up the BBC Home Service and thus give an approximate bearing of Broadcasting House in London, but not much more.

The pilot strode forward to number two hatch in the waist of the ship, where a pilot ladder had been rigged, and climbed ponderously down into his launch, which had come alongside.

"Full ahead; come to starboard to 155 degrees!" ordered Warwick. "Do not sound the whistle; bad visibility or not, I don't want to call attention to us at this stage of the war." With the loss of the old, experienced pilot, he suddenly realised he was on his own, in command of a ship, in bad visibility, and in enemy infested waters; all for the first time in his seagoing life. He had a sinking, slightly panicky feeling in the pit of his stomach, but his years of training came to aid him. He knew what he had to do.

"Cyril, are you happy to take over? I'll lie down on the chartroom settee until it clears a bit."

The mate took up his position on the wing of the bridge. The lookout had been posted above on the monkey island. The spare hand streamed the log aft, set it to zero, and the mate noted the time it was set in the scrap log. The old ship steamed south-east into the murk.

After an hour or so, Warwick got up. It was as thick as ever, but a grey light was beginning to suffuse the darkness to the east.

"At least we are safe from submarines, aircraft, and Erich Bey's destroyers in this clag," he said to Cyril, who was in process of handing over the watch to Murdo, the third mate, it being just before eight o'clock.

Commander Bey was in the habit of leading a surprise raid with three or four big German destroyers into adjacent British east coast waters and picking off any coastal traffic he came across, as well as shelling coastal towns and generally causing as much mayhem as he could.

The thought struck Warwick that Erich Bey's flotilla might have been fitted with radar, but he put it aside. Certainly England was ahead in that respect; Professors Randal and Boot of Birmingham University had invented the cavity magnetron a couple of years back, making compact radar sets possible for ships and even aeroplanes to carry. Of course, with wartime priorities being what they were, it was too much to expect an old tramp ship like *Freshwater Bay* to be allocated a set as yet.

They continued south-west and then south and the snow eventually stopped. Visibility improved to half a mile, then a mile, and they were able to get some bearings off lighthouses and churches on the low-lying Suffolk coast. With a little wind behind them, they were making nearly ten knots, being in ballast and thus light. The log readings agreed, and both the steering and standard compasses seemed to be close to the deviation cards that the shipyard compass adjuster had provided. Warwick decided he could go down to his cabin and clear up some paperwork. It was still thickly overcast; too much so for any aircraft to worry them, and in the shallow waters off the Happisburgh shoals, there was little danger of U-boat activity.

The next morning, having crossed the mouth of the Thames Estuary without incident, they were off the Dover Strait, flying their identifying code flags and signalling with their Aldis lamp as they went close in to the reporting station on the North Foreland. Sparks listened in to the broadcast detailing enemy activity in the vicinity and reported that there were no known hazards that day for their passage in the Dover to Isle of Wight section of the coast. Some twenty Dornier bombers flew over them at high altitude, escorted by fighters and harried by Spitfires and Hurricanes, but they were bound for London and ignored the lonely old steam ship far below. They proceeded west without further incident and picked up the Swansea pilot on the afternoon of the third day at sea. A tug eased her into her berth under the coal staithes and the loading of her bunker and cargo coal began straight away. The mates were kept busy supervising the shifting of coal chutes from hatch to hatch, but after Warwick had dealt with the inevitable paperwork, always part of shipmasters' business, and after the local officer of WETB had eventually departed, having finished his third pink gin ensconced in Warwick's only easy chair, Sam and he could relax in his cabin with a whisky and talk over their first voyage together.

Sam said that things below had gone reasonably well, considering. They had had their problems, both with the stokers, a couple of whom seemed particularly obtuse and workshy, and with the machinery, with all kinds of small, unnoticed problems manifesting themselves. The latter was only to be expected in a ship that had been laid up for many years. Ideally, she should have run acceptance trials and been signed off from the yard as ready, but peacetime rules no longer applied; everything was done to get cargoes moving and ships to sea as soon as possible. On deck, Warwick was very satisfied. He had good officers and a good crew; possibly better than an old, worn out ship like his deserved.

He sent for Cyril to join them for a drink and to hear his opinions, and after an interval, Cyril arrived, dressed in an old blue boiler suit and covered in coal dust, his remaining grey hair temporarily turned a youthful black.

"We should be clear of the coal berth by tomorrow afternoon when we are due to shift across to the other side of the harbour and load our general cargo, Cyril. Make sure the lower holds are all trimmed off level and the tween-deck hatches are on. You'll need to order some dunnage for the general cargo. And give the lads some overtime washing her down. Everything is thick with coal dust! It's getting into the cabins and floating on the mugs of tea."

"Aye, aye, sir," said Cyril. "We used to carry a lot of Welsh coal in the old sailing ships. It's all right if it's dry like this lot; if it's loaded wet, you're liable to get a fire down below when it heats up on passage. Many a good ship lost that way."

Warwick considered this prospect without enthusiasm. He'd never carried coal in bulk before. It wasn't the sort of cargo that P&O ships even considered. Still, Cyril seemed to know his stuff. "Tell us about your time in sail, Cyril."

"Well, sir, I served my time in sailing ships out of the Port of London in the eighties. We used to be in the grain trade to Australia, mainly. When I was just a young deckboy, I fell in love with an Aussie lass while we were loading in Melbourne. Over fifty years ago, it was, but I remember her so clearly to this day. Met her at a church social they invited us sailor boys to. Long blonde hair and lovely, long brown legs, right up to the thighs. Didn't think I could live without her. I wonder where she is now. Some bent and wrinkled old grandmother in Australia, I suppose. I married a good Devon girl when I was a second mate, and we were happy for over thirty years, until she died. No kids, unfortunately. But I never forgot that Aussie girl. Isobel was her name; I can see here now as if it was yesterday." The whisky had loosened his tongue a little; he proved delightful company with a fund of ancient sea stories.

Later, Warwick went ashore to the dock office telephone for a short call to his mother and a longer one to Sarah. Mother was happy; her husband was home safe and sound and her son was on the phone. He talked to his father briefly, and heard all about the tribulations of running the army transport pool in Londonderry. His father was obviously proud and impressed that Warwick had a ship to command at only twenty-six. His voice indicated a new level of respect for his firstborn's achievement; he didn't know how little Warwick had had to do with his rapid promotion. Warwick thought he would leave Sarah out of the conversation at this stage. No need for further complications and debate on that subject. He still had his own feelings and long-term plans to sort out in his head before he started explaining that he was suddenly and hopelessly in love with a woman seven years older than he was to his parents.

He then rang Sarah. The telephone was in her kitchen and it was dinner time. He could hear the talk in the background and the clattering of utensils and plates as the maid and evening cook prepared the meal. Sarah said that the boarding house was full; every room was taken. She also said that she was lonely and missed him and loved him and was praying, for the first time in several years, that he would be kept safe and return to her soon. The hopeless, sad longing was all too clear in her voice. He told her where they were and that they were loading, but not where they were bound. The big poster opposite the dockside phone box was clear on the situation. "CARELESS TALK COSTS LIVES!" it said in big, red letters.

The next day, they completed loading coal, washed down, secured the lower hold hatches, and shifted across to the general cargo berth. There they began to fill the tween decks with general cargo, supplies, food in cans, other stores, and ammunition for Gibraltar. Warwick and Cyril were called to the naval port captain's office for their convoy briefing.

Captain Oliver Windle RN held forth in his clipped, beautifully correct, English voice. "You will proceed at 1200 the day after tomorrow, December 23, to position Able, Able on the confidential chart in front of you, which you must take with you and keep secure on your ship. At an average of eight knots, you should join Convoy GR 16 presently assembling off Lynas Point to the west of Liverpool. In your confidential folders, you will find the recognition signals to be sent in Morse on the Aldis lamp when you sight the lead destroyer. The convoy will proceed out into the Atlantic, well clear of the French coast and especially Lorient where there is a significant U-boat presence, to point Baker, Baker on your chart. From there, it will zigzag its way south at a VMG of around eight knots to point Charlie, Charlie, approximately three hundred miles west of the Straits of Gibraltar. There, with the prior permission of the convoy commodore, you will break off and proceed unescorted to Gibraltar Harbour to unload and await further orders. Is that all quite clear?"

"Quite clear; thank you sir," said Warwick, thinking that they'd be at sea for Christmas Day and that he must remind Bill Baker to lay on some kind of a treat for the crew for Christmas lunch.

"Then it only remains for me to wish you the best of luck and God's speed," said Captain Windle, beginning to gather up his papers by way of their dismissal. Warwick had the passing thought that he said that to all the merchant shipmasters at the end of every briefing, but he was grateful for the sentiment nonetheless.

CHAPTER SEVEN

They sailed down the Bristol Channel and out into the Atlantic the following day. There was a moderate north-easterly breeze, around force four, and the sea was relatively calm. It was still very cold, but there was an invigorating freshness to the air which was welcome after the heavy Swansea smog. The sea sparkled as the old ship ploughed through it. Visibility was reasonable, with patchy cloud overhead and occasional glimpses of the sun. It was good weather for the U-boats that had their patrol area around Cape Clear, off Southern Ireland, some two hundred miles ahead of them.

Warwick resolved to give Ireland a wide berth, even if it did mean deviating from the direct course to the rendezvous point with the convoy. The ship was not fully loaded and had the best quality Welsh steam coal in the bunkers. The stokers and trimmers seemed to have settled down to the routine of their work. The old brass telegraphs were still set to full ahead but the engine and propeller revolutions had increased from a stately sixty-five per minute to seventy-two, with a consequent increase in speed to just over ten knots. The last of the coal dust had been washed away, and an ordinary seaman was scraping the varnish off the teak rails around the bridge, preparatory to rubbing them down and putting on a first coat of half-and-half varnish. The old ship seemed to be getting into her stride. They might even get around to polishing some of the remaining brass work at this rate!

Murdo had the morning watch, and Warwick came up to the bridge to chat. There were no ships around, and a brief glimpse of the sun had allowed Murdo to take an azimuth bearing and ascertain the standard compass error. Comparing that with the steering compass down in the wheelhouse gave them an accurate compass course, all chalked up on the blackboard in the front of the wheelhouse: Standard Course, Steering Course, Variation, Deviation, and True Course.

Warwick felt he ought to get to know his third mate better. "Did you ever go deep sea, Murdo?"

"Aye, sir; I was in the Navy during the First World War, a year or so in destroyers on the East Coast, and then submarines for three years. The pay was better, and I was a young lad then and money in my pocket mattered to me. When I went home to Stornaway, I cut a bonny dash with the local lassies."

"Where did you go – while you were at sea, I mean?"

"We were mostly around the English and Scottish coasts, but when I was in the old L26, we did do a few months in the Med. Navigator's Yeoman I was, an acting petty officer in the Reserve."

"That's interesting that you have submarine training, Murdo. It might just come in useful sometime. What happened after the war?"

"Weel, sir, there was one bonny lass too many and she got pregnant. We got married quickly and all was well. She's made me a fine wife and we have a couple of lads now, one nearly sixteen, the other nine. Her father was a fishing skipper, and I took over the boat from him when he got too old. Then this war came along, and after a wee while, the Admiralty commandeered the bigger fishing boats, mine included, and I was offered a temporary deep sea licence after a couple of months' training in Glasgow, and ended up on here."

Warwick took out his sextant. The sun was peeping through, and he wanted to get a sight while he had the opportunity.

"I'm afraid I have nae skill with that thing, sir," said Murdo.

"I'll teach you when I've time; it was my main job on the passenger ships. I was the navigator. Six star sights in the morning and evening, and sun/run/sun in the daytime. That was every day on passage while there was no land in sight, and every so often, the captain would ask to see my sight book to check through my calculations."

Cyril had taken a couple of star sights at morning twilight. He was rusty and slow working out the necessary spherical trigonometric calculations, but he knew his stuff and it all began to come back to him. Warwick had given him the old vernier sextant that the ship had originally been issued with during the refit, after correcting it. John would have to borrow one of the two sextants on board to take his sights and keep his hand in.

There was no sign of submarines or aircraft that night, as they passed eighty miles south of Cape Clear and headed out in the Atlantic toward the rendezvous point. The next day was Christmas Eve, and at 1700 that evening, smoke was visible to the south west. They closed what turned out to be their convoy maintaining radio silence as instructed, and identified the lead destroyer, which approached them at thirty knots and acknowledged their recognition signal on their Aldis lamp with a flurry of rapid dots and dashes, sent at a speed far in excess of the standard Merchant Navy requirement of eight words a minute. Fortunately, Warwick had had the prescience to get Ken the Sparks up on the bridge wing and he could read the fastest Morse ever likely to be encountered – thirty words a minute and more wouldn't faze him; far in excess of the speed anyone could send by lamp. So they were able to acknowledge their orders, their position in the convoy, and the zigzag patterns in operation without undue delay. Warwick felt very satisfied that this particular exercise had gone well; he guessed that the Navy signalmen had not expected the ancient old tramp ship to be able to cope with their smart, fast signals and had probably flashed them their orders all the faster just to enjoy the anticipated confusion on *S. S. Freshwater Bay's* bridge.

One up to the old MN, he thought to himself.

It was a clear night with a light north-westerly breeze. They were steaming at a fraction under ten knots and zigzagging fifty degrees either side of the base course line every twenty minutes for an hour, then every fifteen minutes, then back to the twenty minute pattern. It took a while to sort out position keeping and the course change alarms, but all the officers soon got the hang of it. Warwick wrote his night orders and went down to his cabin to sleep fitfully on his bed, dressed in trousers, socks, vest, and shirt. He wanted to be ready for any emergency.

Christmas morning dawned without any incident other than a tanker at the front of the second column suddenly deciding they'd seen a periscope and opening up on it with their three-inch gun, all without so much as a warning signal or any permission from the convoy commodore. This served only to wake up everyone in the twenty-six ships and five escorts at 0330 on Christmas morning. Some fairly unchristian thoughts were bandied about the convoy concerning the said tanker and its trigger-happy watchkeepers and gunners.

Bob Baker and his team did well with the Christmas dinner. There were typed menus on the tables, minestrone soup, roast Norfolk turkey with roast potatoes, chipolatas, stuffing and parsnips with cranberry sauce; plum duff and custard to follow. All hands were issued two bottles of beer from the ship's store. Warwick and Sam had laid in a couple of cases of slightly dubious Maltese red wine bought in a dockside store in Swansea for the officers, and they made free use of the South African brandy from the medical chest to finish their meal. Warwick carried out the time-honoured custom of serving the boy seamen and stewards their dinners in his uniform jacket with his captain's hat on. He got the impression that the crew were a contented lot and his command a happy one, in spite of the ancient and sub-standard accommodation when compared with modern ships.

They reached point Baker, Baker on the evening of the day of 1941 and Warwick requested permission to proceed independently to Gibraltar. The convoy commodore signalled back that he had intelligence that there were U-boats reported off the Straits. Warwick thought this was rather like reporting that whores had been sighted in Piccadilly in the evenings, but kept his musings to himself. Further signals indicated that an armed tug with an asdic and depth charges would come out of Gibraltar to escort them when they were a hundred miles off, and that a maritime Wellington bomber would fly patrols on the morrow over their route in. Three hundred miles, thirty hours steaming, twenty of them unescorted. The next day, New Year's Day 1942, would be the dangerous time. Warwick resolved to leave the crew at partial action stations and go into watch and watch routine; four hours on, four hours off. He would set a zigzag pattern, the lookouts would be doubled up, and the gun's crew would be dressed and close by, with the gun loaded for immediate action, and a full load of ammunition for it in the ready-use lockers. They would all get plenty of rest after the ship had come alongside. John was taken out of the deck watch list and appointed damage control officer with the Chippy, a couple of ordinary seamen, and as many of the off-watch crew as he could round up to drill and organise. Fire and steam hoses were rigged and individual tin helmets and lifejackets kept at the ready. There was not much more he could do but say a silent prayer (in which he was covertly joined by most of the rest of the crew).

The next day, it was unusually calm and clear for the Atlantic in winter and much warmer now they were in the southern latitudes of the Mediterranean. The barometer had been going up for several days. They were obviously in an area of high pressure, confirmed by a glance at the barometer. The black smoke rose vertically from the tall funnel like a huge, towering, blackened mill chimney; it was a beacon for any submarine for miles around. Coupled with the unmistakable sound of a steam reciprocating engine beating out a steady seventy RPM, the old ship must have been audible to U-boat hydrophones for a hundred and fifty miles and her smoke visible for at least twenty.

It was just before the change of watch at ten to twelve when it happened.

"Torpedoes on the starboard beam!" screamed the lookout on the monkey island.

"Hard a-port; emergency full ahead! Sound the alarm!" shouted Warwick.

Four tracks of bubbles approached the ship at forty-five knots as she turned away to parallel their tracks. Murdo pressed the alarm button and gave a double ring on the telegraph. The helmsman swung the wheel over to its full extent. The ship shuddered and emitted even thicker smoke, heeling slightly as she turned. Warwick and Murdo watched the approaching torpedoes with horrid fascination as the alarm bell clattered loudly in the wheelhouse behind them. Everything seemed to be happening in slow motion, just like a car crash Warwick remembered; he had once been in one as a passenger.

The ship was turning too slowly! Two tracks passed astern and one ahead, but the remaining torpedo slammed into the ship's side abreast of number two hatch with a resounding CLANG. It reared up out of the water looking evil and black for an instant, forever etched on the watchers' memories. Then it ricocheted off to port, alternately diving and surfacing. Warwick had a passing thought about a physics lesson on light beams long ago. "The angle of incidence equals the angle of refraction," the grammar school teacher had drummed into them then. It seemed to hold good with German torpedoes, too. It took a moment for it to dawn on them all that the thing had actually failed to explode. It was a dud!

They had been saved by a rare case of German incompetence, unknown both to them and to British intelligence at that time. In the years before the war, the Germans had developed a magnetic proximity fuse for their torpedoes which was meant, with gyroscopic depth and course controls, to explode by the magnetic signature of a ship, just under the target's bottom, thus avoiding side armour plating and breaking the target ship's back with her inevitable loss. Grossly insufficient tests of the new torpedoes in the Baltic were carried out by the Torpedo-Verschs-Ansalt (TVA) in the summer of 1937, firing two or three of them at a vertical steel plates or steel nets, suspended in the water. The tests were by no means all successful and the conclusions drawn from them were overly optimistic, but the German Navy captain in charge of the test programme, Oskar Wehr, passed both the new and revolutionary magnetic proximity fuse and the gyroscopic depth and course controls as fully fit for service. He was promptly promoted to Rear Admiral for his efforts. The old and well proved direct contact system was retired in favour of this new magnetic device, as were the old manual course and depth mechanisms. Many Allied ships owed their continued existence to Oskar Wehr. U47 had even hit the old British battleship *Warspite* with three torpedoes during the Norwegian campaign in 1940; a beautiful and competent manoeuvre and a credit to her commander, the submarine ace, Lieutenant Gunther Prien, but to no avail. All failed to explode, and two of them porpoised in and out of the water, warning the battleship and her escorts of the U-boat's presence. The U47 received a thorough depth charging for her temerity and was lucky to survive. By the end of 1941, most of the dud torpedoes had been replaced by the old direct contact types, as the high casualties of Allied merchant and warships in the North Atlantic testified, but there were still a few of the magnetic proximity type still at sea.

"She'll surface now, sir," said Murdo. "She can't chase us at ten knots submerged; she'd run out her main batteries, grouped-up, within forty minutes at that speed. Anyway, she needs time to reload; she only has four forward tubes. She'll try to sink us with her four point five inch gun. She can do fifteen knots on her diesels while she's surfaced, and she'll rely on her speed to catch us and finish us off at close range."

Sure enough, after a delay of three or four minutes, the U-boat surfaced in a flurry of foam, around two miles astern. Almost before the casing was above water, the gun crew came on deck through the forward hatch and began to train and load the gun. Officers in white caps appeared on the conning tower under the periscopes. The U-boat speeded up and began the chase. Being four or five knots faster, she visibly closed the gap between her and *Freshwater Bay*. After less than two minutes, the first shell from the U-boat passed close over the bridge with a loud whirring noise that made them all duck down under the bridge railings.

Meanwhile, the gun crew aft had not been idle. They fired a ranging, three second blast and six, two-pound shells took off at twenty three hundred feet per second in the direction of the pursuing submarine. The Bofors had a range of nine miles or eighteen thousand yards when elevated to 45 degrees; the U-boat was only four thousand yards away and the gun was only a little elevated. The shells described an almost horizontal path as they straddled the submarine's conning tower.

The U-boat's gun crew were a smart and well-drilled team. They had obviously practiced what the British called "Gun Action, Surface!" to perfection. Some thirty seconds after their first round, the second arrived, hitting to port side of the midship house just forward of number three hatch, some fifteen feet below the bridge level and well aft of it, with a flash, a loud explosion, and gout of flame. The port lifeboat was flung into the air and the aft two-thirds of it dissolved into its component planks. The aft davit disappeared over the side; the forward one leaned drunkenly outboard with the splintered remains of the bow of the boat swinging from it. The port boat was the one with the little, two cylinder Lister engine in it. The petrol tank tore loose and fell into the wrecked cabins and flames below and exploded. The smell of cordite hung heavy in the air.

The ship's gunners aft now had their range and bearing, and fired ten more shells in a five-second burst. Some of these shells from the Bofors now found their mark. One shell hit the periscope staff just above the officers' heads on the conning tower. There was an orange flash and two pounds of high velocity, semi-armour piercing shell met precision Zeiss optics, with the result that the attack periscope was completely sheared off, and the search periscope behind it bent over on the deck and onto the heads of the officers and gun crew alike.

The second shell hit the U-boat's casing abreast of the gun and lifted the wooden covered deck, sending splinters and shrapnel in all directions and wounding two of the gun's crew slightly. The third and last shell to hit passed through the free-flood space in the casing just aft of the conning tower, severed a pipe, destroyed a couple of valves, and came out the other side, leaving a jagged exit hole, but didn't explode. The kaptain-lieutenant in command pressed the klaxon twice; the signal for a crash dive. Both officers and gun crew disappeared below; there was a series of huge air bubbles from her ballast tanks as the Kingston valves opened and the U-boat broke off the action and dived, never to trouble *SS Freshwater Bay* further.

The ship still had problems however. Most of the damage control party led by the Chippy had been on the starboard side of number three hatch. The second mate and a couple of seamen had been on the port side where the shell struck. Now the remaining team, aided by the gun crew, ran forward, pulled the rigged hoses across the deck, and rapidly brought two seawater jets to play on the fire. Cyril arrived within a few seconds and took charge of the operation. Some of the off-watch engine room team came up and joined in the work. Cyril organised a party with asbestos gloves to direct the metal steam hose on the seat of the fire, just under where the lifeboat had rested in her chocks a few moments before. In five or six minutes, they had the fire under control.

Warwick ordered the original course and zigzag pattern resumed and left Murdo with the watch. He came down to the main deck to take stock of the damage. The exploding shell had lifted the port side of the boat deck and crumpled it. The adjacent lifeboat and davits were destroyed, along with several cowl ventilators. About five stokers' and trimmers' double cabins had been burned out, along with their messroom amidships aft and their heads and shower compartment. The iron main deck below had warped and rippled with the heat, but had remained intact. The port gangway bulwarks had been bent outwards, and some vent and filler pipes were sheared off. The damage was bad but containable. John Evered, Second Mate, and two ordinary seamen were missing. Chippy began to plug the broken vent pipes with soft wood plugs.

Eric Chalk, the bos'n, led a party into the wrecked area, sweeping out, washing down and throwing burnt debris over the side. Warwick and Cyril followed them in. It was still very hot and there was a horrid smell that reminded him of partially cooked meat. Warwick walked past a leg with a black shoe on its foot, fragments of a blue uniformed trouser leg, and a blackened thigh at the other end, burned brown in places and still oozing blood.

"Poor John," he said to Cyril. "He's done his last trip, I'm afraid." He suddenly felt sick. He moved outside quickly and sat on an adjacent bollard looking out to sea, taking great gulps of fresh sea air. He was white and sweating and he belched loudly. He felt a reflux of food in the back of his throat and tasted bile on his breath. He swallowed hard several times.

I mustn't show this in front of the crew; I must be strong, he thought to himself. He tried to distract his thoughts from the sight of that horrible, half burned leg. He remembered Hilaire Belloc's tribute to an old sailing friend who had died. *He was my constant and brave companion on the sea and now he will sail no more.* Poor John, just twenty and at the beginning his life.

Cyril appeared at his side. "You best sort out the radio enemy contact report message, sir. I'll stay here and handle this and bag up the bodies in canvass. I was mate of a troop ship in the first war, and we were hit by a shell right in the troop deck. We lost fifteen that day, and a couple with their legs and arms blown off as well. It don't affect me that much; leave it now, sir, please."

Up on the bridge, he felt better. He took the signal pad and wrote a brief account of the engagement, including the last known position of the wounded U-boat, the damage suffered by his ship, and the names and ranks of the three dead. He handed the pad to Ken to code and transmit to COMGIB. He sent for the two army gunners and took them down to his cabin to congratulate them personally on their excellent performance with their beloved gun. After drinking a tot of rum with them, he settled down to write letters to the next of kin, to his parents, and to Sarah.

He had never written a letter to a bereaved parent of one of the crew under his care before. Some captains reached the retirement age of sixty-five without ever having to do it, but that was before the war. He had been less than three months in command, and had already lost three of his young men.

He began to write.

S. S. Freshwater Bay, At Sea,
January 1, 1942

Dear Mr. and Mrs. Evered,

Today we suffered a torpedo and gun attack from a German U-boat during which my ship was badly damaged. Your son John, my Second Officer, was in charge of the damage control party aft when the second shell from the U-boat hit us and, along with two of his men, he was killed instantly while steadfastly carrying out his duty for his ship, his country, and his King.

In the short time I knew him, I developed a great admiration for John, in that he was a fine shipmate, a good seaman, and a highly competent watch keeping officer. I am writing this less than an hour after it all happened. I cannot tell you how bitterly sorry I am that we have lost John and his men, but my loss is as nothing when compared with yours.

Please accept my sincere and heartfelt sympathy. Please feel free to contact me at any time.

I will ensure that John's remains are buried in the British Service Cemetery at Gibraltar with full military honours.

Warwick M. G. Hursey
Master in Command

He signed it, addressed the envelope, and sealed it. Then he wrote two similar letters to the parents of the young seamen who died with John. He went back up on the bridge again; he felt he'd written enough letters for the time being. His enthusiasm for writing to his parents and above all Sarah had evaporated. His heart just wasn't in it.

CHAPTER EIGHT

They rendezvoused with the armed tug, *HMS Buster*, the following morning. The *Wellington* turned up and flew out past them, looking for the U-boat. They steamed the last hundred miles in the tug's company without incident. Warwick promoted Murdo to Second Officer and entered his promotion in the log to justify the increase in his monthly salary. They arrived off the Gibraltar breakwater in the evening of January 2, and were ordered to follow the tug in through the opened boom, past the duty boom defence vessel, and then berth behind the three-funnelled cruiser *HMS Sussex* on the South Mole, port side to, without the assistance of any harbour tugs or a pilot. It was Warwick's first experience of ship handling, and he discovered that he had a knack for it. He put the old and battered ship alongside gently and they tied up.

It was Friday night and he granted shore leave for all hands except the duty officer (Murdo), the duty engineer (Fred Carter), the bos'n (Eric) who didn't want to go ashore anyway, and two deck boys who guarded the gangway in the company of a Marine sentry, four on, four off, and had no say in the matter. Warwick went back to his cabin to deal with ship's business, his letters, and official correspondence. There were four letters from Sarah, two from his parents, and one from the Junior First Officer of his last ship, who was a close friend. These made him feel guilty, as he had yet to begin writing to Sarah, or anyone else for that matter. There was an invitation from *HMS Raleigh*, the Royal Navy base in Gibraltar for himself and his officers, to join the mess and asking for names and ranks by return. There was a note from the stevedore about unloading the general cargo and stores the next day; apparently some of it was urgently required. He passed that on to Cyril to organise. There was a note from the local surveyor requesting an appointment to inspect the battle damage and make arrangements for repairs after the cargo had been discharged. He passed that on to Sam to sort out. There was a polite invitation from the Flag Officer Gibraltar (FOGIB) to attend his private office for coffee the next morning at 1030 sharp, in order to brief him on the recent action with the U-boat.

There was an invitation to spend money gambling at the casino with a dozen free passes enclosed for the captain and his officers. There was another to meet Madame Erica and her clean and (medically certified) healthy young ladies at the Red Shoes Bar in High Street, both in the bar downstairs and in her sumptuous private rooms upstairs (all with tiled bathrooms en-suite). Warwick pinned the latter two invitations on the crew notice board.

Finally, there was a peremptory command to the Master of *SS Freshwater Bay* to attend the base medical centre in person immediately upon the ships' arrival alongside, to arrange with Wardmaster Sub-Lieutenant Price-Williams Royal Navy for the removal and burial of the ship's deceased in action. The tone of this latter missive had the effect of irritating and annoying Warwick with every pompous word. He thought of sending Murdo or the bos'n in his place. He thought of issuing a counter-order to Wardmaster Sub-Lieutenant Price-Williams, instructing him to repair on board immediately and report to the captain in his cabin to deal with the necessary formalities. In the end, he decided that the three pathetic bundles of human scraps which Cyril and the bos'n had managed to salvage, sort as best they could, sew up in approximately equal amounts, each in a canvas tube and wrap with two-yard red ensigns, could wait until the morning to be dealt with.

He began to write to Sarah, backdating the letter at the top by two days, and leaving hers that he had just received unopened for the time being. He told her all he could about the voyage and about the subsequent action and of John's death, and two of his men. Sarah had met John in Newcastle while they were refitting and thought him a fine young man. She would undoubtedly be very upset. He revealed his sadness and bitter thoughts about losing some of his crew. His tone cheered up a bit as he described the hits on the U-boat, forcing her to break off the action and dive. He told her he loved her and missed her and was longing to be cuddled up to her again in her big, warm bed. At that he paused, musing that he hadn't actually thought of her very much during their time at sea, what with looking out for enemy planes, U-boats, navigating the ship, convoy orders, zigzagging, Christmas at sea, and the multiplicity of other things that had occupied his mind. He pressed on with the letter regardless, thinking that running a boarding house in a back street of Newcastle was a very different life to being a captain of a ship in wartime.

Then he read her letters in date order. As he had guessed, not much had changed for her and they were mostly about her huge love for him and her longing for them to be back together. She thought about him so much and so often, out there in the Atlantic. The constant news of convoys attacked and ships sunk served to frighten and depress her. There were several pages enlarging on those sentiments in her neat script. There had been a couple of air raids on the yard, and some of the bombs had fallen on a house in the next street. Some of her windows had been shattered and had to be boarded up. It was hard to get glass and harder to get a glazier to fit it. The gas pipe had been severed and the gas supply had been off for several days, making cooking all but impossible. She mentioned a few more minor domestic problems; the sub-text of which Warwick deduced was that Sarah subconsciously needed a man about the house to help out and to lean on in times of crisis.

He wrote a comforting, single-page answer with the current date on it, mentioning that they were alongside and relatively safe, and including sympathetic mention of her problems at the boarding house and enclosed it in the same envelope. He then wrote a short answer to his parents' letter; not much had happened in deepest Sussex and his father had now returned to his transport unit. Then he went to bed.

There was an air-raid warning overnight but no bombs fell nearby, and Warwick's sleep was only partially disturbed by the sirens. He was dog tired and he slept soundly for a good seven hours. The next morning, he felt on top of the world as he shaved and selected his smartest uniform with its four, new gold stripes and the entwined diamond between the middle two. A stiff collar, new black tie, and highly polished shoes, plus his new uniform cap with its gold scrambled egg around its peak and a Merchant Navy standard cap badge affixed. After eggs and bacon in the saloon, he was ready to meet the admiral. But first he must deal with the question of the bodies and Wardmaster Sub-Lieutenant Price-Williams, Royal Navy.

He found Sub-Lieutenant Price-Williams' office at the back of the naval hospital and was shown into the anteroom by a portly, middle-aged Wren petty officer sitting in a glass reception box at the doorway. She didn't seem to have very much to occupy her, and spent most of her time watching him through narrowed eyes, only looking away at a sheaf of papers on her little desk when he gazed directly back at her. He wondered if she imagined he might be a new type of German spy.

He waited for twenty minutes, getting more and more impatient. He thought that the "immediately" in the original order of last night must have a very one-sided meaning. His mood darkened. This was not the way to treat a British ship captain! He rose suddenly, walked across the room, knocked hard on the office door, opened it, and went inside, deftly avoiding the overweight Wren's hurried dash to intercept him. Price-Williams was sitting at his desk reading a copy of the *Gibraltar Forces' Times*.

He looked up in alarm as the large, uniformed figure of Captain Hursey momentarily blocked his light. He was a small, plump man in his mid-thirties. His uniform was immaculate, with its single stripe and salmon-coloured strip under it, which identified his speciality as a Wardmaster. He wore big glasses with light coloured, almost translucent frames, a knitted black tie, and a very white handkerchief protruding from his left sleeve. His plump, pink hands were carefully manicured, and he was smoking a cigarette in a long, amber cigarette holder. His voice was high pitched and his accent was what Warwick would normally call 'posh/affected.'

"How dare you burst into my office like that? Who the hell told you that you could come in? Don't you know I'm very busy here? Get outside right away and damn well wait outside until I'm free!"

Now Warwick normally the most good-natured of men, kind to children and small animals, and the recipient of much favourable comment for his calm, polite bearing and friendly conversation from previous captains and passengers alike. On the other hand, he was six feet and three inches tall, two hundred and twenty pounds, fit, strong, the captain of a British ship with a long tradition to uphold, as well as once being the star performer of *HMS Worcester's* boxing team. Fellow cadets still talked of the Worcester verses Gravesend Police boxing tournament of 1932, where seventeen-year-old cadets were matched against beefy policemen in their mid-twenties. Warwick had knocked out a large, weathered, and extremely tough looking sergeant early in the second round of the heavyweight contest to salvage some honour for his ship.

Braver men than Price-Williams would have hesitated before provoking Warwick's wrath. A red mist passed before his eyes. The adrenalin ran hot in his veins. He leaned over the desk and grabbed Price-Williams' immaculate lapels. With a contraction of his biceps, he lifted him clean out of his chair so that his pudgy face was only an inch or so from his own. Price-Williams' glasses were knocked askew, giving him a peculiarly childlike look. He dropped his cigarette in its holder into the waste paper basket by his desk, where it smouldered away, unnoticed by both of them.

"Listen, my precious little arsehole," began Warwick in a conversational tone. "If you ever fuck me about again, I'll personally pull your unpleasant and overfed little face off and stuff it up your freckle. I've been shot at, torpedoed, and had half my crew killed, and I'm going to tell you exactly what you're going to do about it. Don't even think of arguing unless you're in a big hurry to meet your maker!"

Price-Williams gave a strangulated squeak, which Warwick took to be by way of assent, so he dropped him back in his chair. His face was almost touching the little Wardmaster's nose as he spoke. "You will go down to my ship, *SS Freshwater Bay*, berthed on the south mole, within the hour. You will report to my Chief Officer, by name Cyril Naismith. Please don't try to mess with him; he was sailing around the Horn in a four-master before the unfortunate occasion of your birth. You will arrange to be collected the three canvas hammocks containing all we could scrape up of my second officer and two of his men, take them to the morgue, and put them into coffins. You will further arrange for their burial at a time to be agreed with me, with full military honours. You will do this personally and not delegate any of it to Two Ton Tessie outside."

There was an audible intake of breath from outside the door. Warwick brought his fist down on Price-Williams' desk with a crash further to emphasise his instructions. The receiver of the red telephone fell off and Price-Williams, the inkstand, and its associated pens and pencils jumped violently.

"Do I make myself clear?" asked Warwick. "A simple assent will do."

"Yes, yes," breathed Price-Williams, white and shaking, with his uniform all disarranged and his glasses lodged at fifty degrees to his face.

Warwick threw open the door dramatically on his way out. There was a crash as the large Wren PO, who had been close up to the other side of it, was propelled rapidly backward onto the easy chair in the corner of the anteroom.

Warwick felt a glow of pure satisfaction. "Now for Rear Admiral MacDonald," he said to himself.

He arrived at the admiral's staff office at 1024. He was greeted somewhat deferentially by a tall, elegant young flag lieutenant complete with golden aiguillettes secured to his left shoulder. The news of his old ship beating off the U-boat attack had spread through the base, and he had become somewhat of a minor hero to its younger officers. He was shown into the admiral's large, airy office with its fine view of Gibraltar Bay.

"Please sit down, captain," said the admiral. He was a Scotsman in his early fifties, greying, small, and wiry. "You've met Robson, my flag lieutenant; this is Lieutenant-Commander Jim Marsh, the base intelligence officer. I want you to tell us exactly what happened the day before yesterday. Jim will be down to your ship later today to go through your log book and take down the fine details of times and positions, but I'd like to hear your account, in the first person, so to speak."

Warwick began the now familiar tale, omitting only his revulsion at the sight of the remains of the damage control party and his consequent need to sit down and recover. He ended the tale with that morning's arrangements for the funerals, rather mischievously telling the admiral that Sub-Lieutenant Price-Williams had generously agreed to take charge of them personally.

He fancied that Admiral MacDonald's face lost a little of its enthusiasm at the mention of Price-Williams and his funeral arrangements, but he soon got into his stride again.

"You'll be pleased to know that the *Wellington* found your submarine on the surface yesterday, some ten miles north-east of her last known position that you gave us. A large number of her crew were on deck, presumably engaged in some kind of emergency repairs. They dropped two depth charges as she crash-dived, leaving about ten of her men swimming around in the water. There was a great deal of oil and debris, and we think that she was probably destroyed. A Royal Navy corvette searched the area a few hours later and recovered both debris and bodies, and one man, miraculously still alive. He is in the base hospital and may recover. She turned out to be U168 on her second patrol, commanded by an experienced submariner. All in all a very satisfactory conclusion!"

"Thank you, sir," said Warwick.

"Now to move on to you and your ship. I want you to regard what I have to say to you as highly classified. You are not to discuss it with anyone except, possibly on a 'need to know' basis with your chief officer and chief engineer. For some time, we have been starved of supplies here in Gibraltar. This is partly to do with enemy submarines, surface raiders, and aircraft, and partly to the priority put on inbound cargoes from the USA. Some of the cargo presently being unloaded from your ship is vital to this base and is desperately needed.

"Your ship was built for the short-sea Mediterranean trades. She is old and slow and not really suited to the North Atlantic, especially in winter. You have been lucky with the weather so far, but you could be in some problems if you encountered a big Western Ocean storm. You need to carry too much of your capacity in fuel for crossing the Atlantic, and the USA is not really the best place to coal old ships; they mainly use oil fuel there now. I have therefore decided to detach you from WETB's operational command and attach you to mine here at COMGIB. You will be our dedicated supply ship and you will personally report to me or members of my staff.

"Now I am coming to the most secret part. For some time, in close cooperation with our American allies, we have been planning a major operation against the enemy in North Africa, to be known by the code name 'Operation Gymnast.' It requires months of planning and preparation and huge logistics. COMGIB will be its operational centre if it comes off. If so, I see you and your ship having a big part to play in this operation later in the year.

"For the time being, we will discharge your cargo, repair your battle damage as best we can, and load you up with various items which are needed in England. There is about fifteen hundred tons of salvaged equipment and scrap from an abandoned Italian light cruiser we managed to keep afloat and tow in. There are four of her six-inch guns complete with their mountings, as well as various items of reusable equipment we salvaged from her. There are crates of spent brass shell cases and miscellaneous items. Then there are the fruits of cross border transactions with our Spanish friends. General Franco may be a fascist and sympathise with Hitler and el Duce, but his people are only too pleased to trade. There is flour and corn in bags, and several hundred barrels containing wet hides, tallow, salt fish, and wine. There are a few tons of light wood boxes containing dried raisins and dates, plus anything more that we can get together before you are ready to sail. In all it amounts to about twenty five hundred tons; you won't be quite full on the way back, but you will be carrying a very much needed cargo to the old country, as you will appreciate."

Warwick mumbled his thanks to the admiral for all the detailed information. "Where are we bound for discharge, sir?" he enquired.

"Southampton; that will be your home port. It's convenient and the nearest major cargo port to us here. You won't have to run the gauntlet of the East Coast and the Dover Straits any more. You will be part of the regular and well escorted Mediterranean convoy system. We can provide some air cover for most of the way in cooperation with Coastal Command. Makes the U-boats keep their heads down. In any event, in that stretch of water, they are mainly concerned with getting out to their Atlantic patrol areas, or coming back to their home pens on the west coast of Brittany."

"Thank you so much, sir," said Warwick. "I am so grateful to you for taking me into your confidence like this."

"Ah, yes. That reminds me, captain. There's one more thing, I'm afraid. I appreciate that you are a British shipmaster with a huge amount of integrity and that you are a hundred percent patriotic and trustworthy, but you are still a civilian in the Navy's eyes. If you are to be made privy to our secret future strategy, you must be temporarily commissioned. I am, therefore, making arrangements with the Admiralty for you to be appointed as a Temporary Acting Lieutenant-Commander Royal Naval Reserve, and you will be employed by the Royal Navy in future and paid on that basis. May I suggest that you have at least one uniform and some epaulettes made up with your naval rank while you are here? Unless you have a large private income, you will find it considerably cheaper than going to Gieves in Portsmouth."

CHAPTER NINE

Warwick called in on the wardroom mess at *HMS Raleigh* and had a pre-lunch drink with some of the officers at the bar there. He was made very welcome and somewhat pestered both by offers of large pink gins and by requests to tell the story of his recent engagement with U168. There was no sign of Price-Williams; Warwick hoped that he was busy with the funeral arrangements.

After half an hour of so he went back to the ship, declining offers of lunch at the mess. The winches were rattling away and the general cargo was coming out of the tween decks. Stores were being loaded by hand up the gangway, superintended by Bob Baker. There were some cases of engineering requisites on the dock being checked by Bill Garthwaite, in a white boiler suit with his second engineer's epaulettes buttoned to the shoulders. Two dockyard workers with cutting equipment were working on the damaged area at the aft end of the midship housing, removing lumps of blackened metal and generally tidying up. Warwick wondered if the scrap they were removing would be returned to the ship as cargo in due course. He thought vaguely that it was a bit like the ship consuming herself.

After lunch, Jim Marsh came down. The rough and fair logs were laid out in the saloon and Jim set to work. He questioned Cyril, Murdo, the bos'n, Chippy, and the corporal of the gun. He took copious notes. Warwick went down to see all was well, and when Jim had finished, invited him up to his cabin for a drink.

"You know, Warwick, for someone who's only been here for twenty-four hours, you have gained yourself quite a reputation.

The old man was delighted about the U-boat business and really took to you this morning. I thought he was going to offer to make you a reserve lieutenant; the lieutenant-commander bit was a surprise to me. Even in wartime, twenty-six is very young for that rank, and you'll certainly be the youngest lieutenant-commander in the base."

"I suppose it was because I was in command of a ship and turned up in full uniform with four stripes and a captain's brass hat."

"Possibly, though the old man isn't usually swayed by uniforms and decorations. He tries to sort out the values that lie within the men serving under him, so that he knows how much to expect from each one. That business about Operation Gymnast is really top secret; I was surprised he mentioned it to you at all. Hitler only declared war on the USA three days after the Japanese attacked Pearl Harbour on December 7. It wouldn't do for it to become public knowledge that they have been planning joint operations with us against the Germans for several months before that.

"Talking about the values of the men under the COMGIB's command, there's a strange rumour going about that you gave the egregious Wardmaster a little shake-up this morning. I think it came from the wrennery, although I can't be sure. Tracing rumours is notoriously difficult even for me, the head of base intelligence."

"Err, yes; come to think of it, we did have a slight difference of opinion about the disposal of the bodies of my crew killed in action and their funeral arrangements, but I eventually managed to convince him of the logic of my arguments."

"Well I'll not question you further on it, but I will say that Joseph Price-Williams is pretty generally thought of as an obnoxious, stuck-up, overfed, over promoted, male matron who seems to have carved a little empire out for himself at the base hospital and seemed pretty untouchable; that is, until you came along. They've started calling him 'Mortuary Joe' in the mess,

55

much to his fury. When the rumour reached the old man, he burst out laughing and he's been in a good mood ever since."

"Thank the Lord for that!" said Warwick.

He fancied a quiet evening aboard, so he offered to keep ship that Saturday night. Cargo work finished at 1800 and Cyril and Murdo went ashore together to investigate the delights of High Street. Warwick wondered if they had taken the invitation to the Red Shoes Bar and Madam Erica and her girls with them. He decided that Cyril was probably a bit too old for that kind of thing and Murdo was happily married, anyway.

There was another letter from Sarah waiting him on his desk. He opened it and read it through quickly to make sure she was okay and then read it again slowly to catch up on the details. Newcastle had been bombed again. She was fed up with the difficulties and problems with running a boarding house in wartime next to a prime target for German bombers, even though every one of her bedrooms was occupied and she was taking in plenty of money. She had asked her friend Shirley to take over the business for half the income. She was coming south, not to Chelmsford where she had so many bad memories, but to somewhere in West Sussex or Hampshire.

She had an offer of a house in the country, in the Meon Valley, called West Lodge for £4,500, which she could well afford if she sold some of her government stock. It was late Georgian, had six bedrooms, three bathrooms, and a couple of acres of land. It needed some renovation. She enclosed a single black and white sheet of details with a poorly defined photograph at the top. She longed for him to come back to her and share her new house in the country. She had had enough of bombs and broken windows and war; she wanted to settle down with the man she loved. She repeated those desires and sentiments in several different variants for three neatly written pages. What did he think?

The Meon Valley was fairly close to Portsmouth and Southampton, and a comfortable but not impossible distance from his parents. He took up pen and paper and began to write back, showing his enthusiasm for her proposed purchase and plans for the two of them. Bound by strict confidentiality, he could not say that Southampton was to be their regular UK port in future, so he said that in future he was unlikely to be docked further north than London when the ship was in the United Kingdom. He wrote a page of endearments and told her several times how much he loved her and was missing her. He told her he had had a long meeting with the admiral and that he had been appointed a Lieutenant-Commander RNR. He was in process of signing off with much and fondest love and many kisses when there was a knock on the door.

It was a tall, slight young man, about twenty, who entered, wearing the uniform of a sub-lieutenant, with no colour insertion on his single stripe, meaning that he was in the executive branch.

He stood awkwardly, fingering his cap. "My name is David MacDonald, sir," he said. "I'm Admiral MacDonald's elder son."

"Well do sit down please," said Warwick. "What brings you down to my old ship on a Saturday night, David?"

"Sir, I was posted here to my father's command against his wishes after I had completed the last of my sub-lieutenants' courses at *HMS Vernon*. They put me in the hydrographic and navigational equipment section and there I have remained for nearly a year. It is a safe but boring and unadventurous posting. I want to play a big part in this war, not moulder away among musty manuals, charts, and metal boxes of valves and resistors. I have pestered my father for months for an active posting. I suppose he has a natural instinct to protect his firstborn, and if he hasn't, my mother back in England certainly has. All to no avail until today, sir. He sent for me this afternoon and said that he might have just the thing for me. He told me to report to you, sir. He said that your second mate had been killed in action and that you had a vacancy for a watchkeeping officer, sir. He said that one trip on this old steam ship would do more to make me a proper seaman than ten years shuffling charts here." He sat back, obviously nervous and trying not to tremble, waiting for Warwick's reaction.

"Now look, David," said Warwick after taking a moment to gather his thoughts, "this is not a comfortable billet. The ship is old and slow, and the accommodation is very poor by modern standards. We have already suffered personnel losses by enemy action. We are an unglamorous old tramp ship. A young man like you ought to be in destroyers or submarines or in the Fleet Air Arm, not steaming along in a clapped out old coal burner wondering when the inevitable torpedo will put an end to the voyage. It's all very well to have a sense of adventure, but war is absolutely not fun when you are being shot at or clearing up the aftermath." Warwick remembered all too clearly his own revulsion and necessary pause for recovery while sitting on the spring bollard, just after they'd put the fire out.

"My father said that you would say that. He said that I'd be at some risk, and that my mother would never forgive him if I was lost at sea, sir. He also said that he didn't know anyone who'd teach me more or look after me better that you would and that he would re-appoint me to an active post in a corvette or a frigate after this ship's next return here."

Warwick liked this frank and open young man immediately. He was also touched beyond belief that the admiral had entrusted his son to his care. He wondered if he had made his decision before or after he'd heard the rumour about the encounter with Mortuary Joe.

"Okay, David; you are hereby appointed Third Officer of *SS Freshwater Bay*. There's glory for you. Come back tomorrow and report to Cyril Naismith, the Chief Officer, who will put you to work and to Bob Baker, the Chief Steward, what you Navy chaps call a Pusser, so that your cabin may be cleaned out and your bunk made up with fresh linen. Make sure that you have white overalls and plenty of working shirts, blue or khaki; it doesn't matter. I think your normal Navy uniform will be perfectly adequate for one round voyage; don't spend money getting Merchant Navy kit. You'll find the routine a bit strange at first, but you'll soon get the hang of it. I'll take you down to the shipping office and sign you on foreign articles tomorrow at around 1100."

"Thank you, sir. Thank you so very much. It means a lot to me."

Warwick feared for a moment that the young man was about to burst into tears of gratitude, but he controlled himself and took his leave.

Warwick addressed the envelope to Sarah, put the finished letter inside it, sealed it up, and put it in the 'Post Out' tray. Then he went to bed.

The next day after breakfast, Sam came to him looking worried. The surveyor's preliminary report had arrived. The damage was more extensive than they had supposed. As well as the visible wreck of the midship cabins on the port side, the main deck and the ship's side adjacent to it had buckled, and some of the supporting frames were out of alignment. They would have to re-frame and re-plate the area, first removing the lubricating oil header tank and associated pipework underneath. The repairs would take at least six weeks, maybe more with the available labour and equipment, bearing in mind that unpredictable emergency warship repairs and refits took priority. They wouldn't be sailing until mid-March, as they would load their outbound cargo only after they left the local shipyard at Shepherd's Wharf.

Gradually over the next few days, the last of the general cargo came out and they started unloading the coal from the lower holds. On the following Friday, the funeral of John Evered and his two men was held in the Anglican Cathedral. It was beautifully organised. There was a gold-embossed, printed order of service, Warwick and Admiral MacDonald read the lessons, and the senior base padre told the congregation all he could about the deceased and how they came to die in the service of their country, in the very best traditions of the Merchant Navy. The ship's officers were there in full uniform. All the crew turned out in their Sunday best. A few wore bowler hats; the others Breton seamen's or flat cloth caps. Many of the officers and petty officers from the base were there, as well as some of the sailors. The three simple pine coffins were each draped with a three-yard red ensign. They were interred in the cemetery on the rock, overlooking the Straits of Gibraltar, with a Marine detachment firing a volley of shots over their graves. It was a fine, cool day with the soft Mediterranean sea breeze rustling the pines above. Price-Williams hovered in the background, choreographing the occasion, studiously ignoring Warwick, who had to admit that he'd done a fine job despite their little disagreement.

Warwick had arranged for the base photographer to take pictures of the funeral and of the graves to send to their parents with a little descriptive note from him.

Toward the end of January, the ship was clear of the last of the coal and shifted across to the repair dock at Shepherds Wharf. Work was sporadic, as there was a series of battle damaged ships coming in from the early Malta convoys to be patched up, which work had absolute priority. Cyril employed the crew sweeping and cleaning the last of the coal dust out of the holds, then cleaning the ship from top to bottom. After that, they were put over the side chipping, red-leading, and painting the hull grey, as she was now a naval auxiliary. Warwick had his woodwork in front and below the bridge windows scraped, sanded, and varnished, and the brasswork buffed up and protected from the weather by a light rub with a Vaseline-impregnated cloth. They hoisted the blue ensign in place of the red to show everyone that they were now a COMGIB unit commanded by a lieutenant-commander. After a few weeks of this treatment, the old ship began to look positively smart.

There was little for the deck officers to do, so, in consultation with Cyril, Warwick began afternoon classes in astro-navigation for Murdo and David and anyone else who was interested. One of the able seamen, John Francis by name, had ambitions to become an officer and joined in. David had been taught the

RN way to work out sights; he used a printed sight form and filled in the boxes, following the instructions beside them as to whether to add or subtract. He had no real understanding of the mathematics behind the spherical trigonometry involved. Warwick started from first principles.

"Now the first thing you must hoist in chaps is that we navigators imagine that there is a great sphere around the earth on which all the heavenly bodies lie. It is called the celestial sphere and has celestial poles to the north and south, positioned over the earth's poles. It is of no concern that the moon is only two hundred and fifty thousand miles from us, and yet some of the stars are millions of light years away. Since we are dealing with angles on the surface of this celestial sphere, their actual distance from us doesn't matter, just their angular distance from the celestial pole, the celestial equator, known as the equinoxial, and the point directly above our heads at our position on earth, known as our zenith."

Warwick got into his stride; he was enjoying himself. One day when the war was over, he had an ambition to take his Extras Masters' Certificate, a rare and difficult series of examinations that allowed one to become an Examiner of Masters and Mates, and represented the peak of the profession for those who remained at sea. He had done quite a bit of advanced studying of mathematics, navigation, physics, and metacentric stability while he was in his previous company and knew his subject inside out. He had some old charts pinned up in the saloon with their blank white backs outwards and, using a set of coloured pencils, drew the necessary diagrams on them in front of his little class. After several afternoons, he introduced them to the sextant and the chronometer.

"Don't forget, lads, that if you get a correct altitude and a correct time you took it, you have your sight. If either one is in error, it will not work out. It doesn't matter what sort of a balls-up you make of the ensuing calculations, if those two ingredients are correct, someone will be able to deduce a position line from what you have done, even if you can't! One position line from each sight; no more. Forget those films where the chap waves his sextant at the sun and reels off his latitude and longitude to the audience and his admiring crew. It doesn't happen in real life to anyone but Errol Flynn and the Black Pirate."

Later he took them out and made them take sights of the sun in the morning, work out the time of noon, take a meridian altitude, work out the time of transit of Venus and get a latitude from it, and take sights of stars and planets at morning and evening twilight. They used the harbour mole as a horizon. Warwick, knowing their exact position, had worked out a little additional correction to allow for the amount the top of the mole was above the visible horizon. He plotted their efforts on another chart back so that they could see how close their position lines were to the actual position of the ship. He was happy if they could get within a mile. When they eventually put to sea, he would have three more trained navigators, although they would all need to learn how to apply their new-found skills on a moving ship in a rough sea. The technique would come in due course; his job was to teach them the theory now.

The idea spread. Cyril began to take evening classes on sailing ship practice and coastal navigation with four-point bearings and running fixes. Murdo did a session on submarine practice. Jim Marsh came down and talked about intelligence gathering and codes. The base gunnery officer and the ship's gunners lectured on their specialities. The classes grew as some of the base personnel attended lectures they were particularly interested in. So the time passed until the repairs were complete with the exception of the minor fitting out of the cabins and some interior painting. The day after the new motor lifeboat was hoisted up on the new port davits, the old ship moved across to the scrap wharf and commenced loading the remains of one of Italy's less fortunate light cruisers into her lower holds.

CHAPTER TEN

The war went on. Great and historic events were in progress. In early March 1942, there were huge movements of German armies in Russia where Hitler prepared to renew his spring offensive after being checked a few miles from Moscow the previous December by a combination of the bitter Russian winter for which they were totally unprepared, and fresh troops drafted in by Stalin from Siberia, who were so conditioned by the extreme cold of their native territory that they thought minus thirty degrees Centigrade was relatively warm. On the North African coastal strip, General Auchinleck was fighting a see-saw battle with General Rommel. The British Eighth Army, reinforced by divisions of tough Australian, New Zealand, South African, and Indian troops, were pitted against the veterans of the German Afrika Korps and their supporting Italian armies.

Meanwhile, in Gibraltar, the cargo rattled into the old *Freshwater Bay's* holds and on March 8, it was Warwick's twenty-seventh birthday.

Cyril, Murdo, Sam, Bill Garthwaite, Ken the Sparks, and Jim Marsh invited him out to a celebratory dinner with a tour of the High Street hotspots to follow. They had a four-course dinner at the Rock Hotel, preceded by a couple of horses' necks in the mess as *HMS Raleigh*, accompanied by a few bottles of wine and completed by a two large glasses of vintage port each. Then they sallied forth to the clubs which were, at eleven thirty p. m., just warming up. By two the following morning, the survivors of the birthday bash were down to Jim Marsh, Sam, and Warwick.

They had fetched up in the Red Shoes Bar and were seated on rather wobbly bar stools with a young lady pleading for drinks next to each of them. Madam Erica was nowhere to be seen. It was a Tuesday night and there weren't many other customers.

Warwick's young lady was called Esperanza and was dark, Spanish, petite, pretty, and about twenty-five years old by external appearances in the rather subdued light of the establishment. She said she came from Madrid, where her father was a doctor with Republican sympathies. She had studied law at Madrid University, but the family had been forced to flee when Franco had won the Civil War, and now she earned her living in the Red Shoes, taking commission on the drinks the customers bought her. She also had a thirteen-year-old son to support.

Warwick felt a great surge of sympathy and affection for this lovely young woman and bought her a tall, greenish-blue drink with a small, paper umbrella stuck in the top, for an extortionate amount of his ready cash.

"What do you do, darling?" she asked in her delightful, low, accented voice.

"I'm a ship captain," said Warwick, making an effort to think about security and just how much he ought to tell her. For all he knew, she might be a German spy.

"I'm captain of a merchant ship." He emphasised the point; that wasn't a secret, anyway. "You're not a German spy, are you, my love?" he asked anxiously. He was keen to clear up that particular problem so that he could enjoy the evening without further security worries. He tried to focus on her breasts, about a foot below his eyes. Her light summer dress was very low cut and he could see the outline of her nipples. He considered them with some care and concluded that she probably wasn't wearing a bra. He was unduly pleased with this profound thought, as well as his powers of observation.

"You are a captain? How wonderful, and you so young! You must be very brave and clever. And you are so big and strong. Most women would die for a man like you!"

Warwick warmed further to the lovely Esperanza. How sweet and sensible and complimentary she was! Poor girl, stuck in this place with all the drunken, crude customers staring at her; always trying to get them to buy her drinks so she could care for her son. If Franco hadn't taken over, she might well be a high flying Madrid lawyer by now. He bought her another drink, careless of the diminishing number of notes in his pocket.

Jim had departed, whether to the gents or permanently, he didn't know, nor, for that matter, care very much. Sam was engaged in a deep conversation with his young lady and had his back to Warwick. *Best of luck, Sam*, thought Warwick.

"You're much too good for this sort of thing. Maybe you could resume your law studies, although I don't think Gibraltar has a law school. I might be able to help you get to England if you want."

"Are you married, captain? Your wife at home wouldn't like you looking after me, now, would she?"

"I'm not married. I'm abs-absolutely unattached," said Warwick, slurring the "absolutely" a little and resolutely thrusting thoughts of Sarah to the back of his mind and closing the lid on them. His passing thought was that 'absolutely unattached' was not an easy conjunction to attempt at this time of night.

"Would you like to come with me, my own big captain?" said Esperanza softly, stroking the back of his neck. She led him to a little curtained alcove off the main bar, where they sat down in a wooden booth. Esperanza pulled down the top of her dress, exposing two small and lovely breasts. She pulled Warwick's willing head down to nuzzle them. She smelled to Warwick of some remote and beautiful perfume overlaid by a waft of warm young woman. Further drinks seemed to have arrived from nowhere.

Warwick always prided himself on having total recall of events, even if, on rare occasions, he was a little drunk the previous evening. He vaguely remembered Esperanza leading him up the stairs at the back of the alcove to a small bedroom on the first floor. She dropped her dress to the floor and took off her shoes and panties, which comprised her simple costume, then lay back on the slightly grubby white counterpane. Warwick had a long-held belief, gleaned from pornographic, under-the-counter magazines which had been passed around when he was an apprentice that prostitutes only perform with their shoes on, and so took much comfort from the fact that Esperanza had taken hers off.

His muscles tightened in his stomach, and a delightful and overpowering feeling of barely controlled lust spread through his body. He stripped off and joined her. She was like an eel, kissing his face, then his stomach, then his thighs, and then the rest of him in that particular area. He had been deprived of female love and company for a couple of months, and, with the quantities of alcohol he had drunk, become aroused and uninhibited. They lay back in each other's arms afterward, both climaxed and contented. Warwick was so happy. This was the life! He had no thoughts of the morrow.

Warwick arrived back on the ship at 0850 the following morning. He had a painful ache at the back of his eyeballs and his mouth tasted like the bottom of a much worn Wellington boot. He knocked on Cyril's door to borrow some money to pay the cab driver. He ignored Cyril's rather knowing smile and polite enquiries after his health and that of his young lady. He looked at himself in his cabin mirror. He was unshaven and dishevelled, but not too bad, really; he only looked about ten years older than he actually was and that would pass. Hung-over young men, sick children, and cats recover quickly. He showered, shaved, and put on his uniform. He rang for the steward and ordered fried eggs on fried bread with crispy bacon, orange juice, and a large, black coffee served in his dayroom. After that he felt better, although he was conscious of a slight out-of-body feeling, which he correctly interpreted as the effects of a substantial amount of alcohol still circulating in his veins. He determined to have a little nap that afternoon, and not to see the lovely Esperanza again, despite his loving promises of a couple of hours back. That way was the road to dissipation, moral collapse, and ruin!

The four Italian six-inch guns were loaded, one on each side of number two hatch, and one on each side of number three, aft of the repaired midship housing. Cyril had had lugs welded to the deck to lash them down with wire strops. Their mountings were stowed on deck by numbers one and four hatches and similarly lashed. The rest of the general cargo was stowed in the tween decks and the hatches battened down, the derricks lowered and secured, and the ship made ready for sea. Warwick, Sam, and Cyril attended the convoy briefing, and on March 15, they joined a large, northbound convoy which included the battleship *HMS Malaya* and numerous escorting destroyers, frigates, and corvettes.

The following morning, well out in the Atlantic, they lost the sunshine of Gibraltar, and ran into a north-easterly gale caused by a big depression to the north. The wind was on the starboard bow, and the old ship ploughed up and down sluggishly into the great marching rows of seas, a quarter of a mile apart. The bitter wind blowing straight from the Arctic threw heavy clouds of spray across the decks and well above the bridge. Warwick was grateful that the ship wasn't fully loaded and that the crew accommodation in the foc'sle was still accessible. The low, black cumulo-nimbus clouds, with their bases at about two hundred feet, scudded overhead and there were icy periods of heavy sleet when the ship ahead became temporarily invisible and the convoy streamed fog buoys. There was no point in the convoy zigzagging; neither submarine nor aircraft could mount an attack on it in those conditions. Poor David was badly affected by sea sickness. He made a brave attempt to keep his eight to twelve watch with a bucket close to hand, but he was obviously incapable of handling convoy signals and the deployment of the fog buoy, as well as maintaining the concentration needed to take charge in an emergency in wartime at sea.

Warwick came up on the bridge to relieve him, but he refused to go below. "I can't sleep in these conditions; thank you sir. I'm happier outside in the fresh air on the wing of the bridge anyway. I'll put up with getting wet."

Warwick hoped that he was warmly wrapped up under his oilskins and sou'wester. He didn't want to add hyperthermia to David's woes. He carried his captain's chair out to the sheltered bridge wing cab and sat David in it with his bucket alongside. Then he went into the wheelhouse and slid the door shut. There were no hopes of getting any sight of the sun, so there was little for him to do but keep an eye on the convoy and think.

First of all, he thought of Sarah. She had bought the Georgian house in the Meon Valley and had moved into it. She would expect him to join her there for his leave period. He had written back assuring her that every moment he had spare he would spend with her.

Then there was his mother. She knew nothing of Sarah and would naturally expect him to spend his leave with her at home as he had always done in the past. It was about forty miles from Sarah's new house. He had written back without comment on that matter.

Then there was how to introduce the subject of Sarah to his parents. He couldn't very well say that he was sleeping with his moneyed ex-landlady who had moved south, and was considering marrying her in spite of the fact that she was nearly seven years older than he was. But if he wasn't engaged to her, how could he explain her to his rather Victorian parents?

He could say that he was deeply in love with her. He told himself that he was. That raised two more difficulties. Firstly, his time with her had been brief and he hadn't seen her for months. She was beginning to become a little remote in his memory. It was difficult to be passionate about someone you had difficulty remembering in detail. Second, there was the matter of Esperanza. Could he have been unfaithful to Sarah if he had really loved her, even if he was drunk at the time? How could he look Sarah in the face when they met? Should he confess all and risk her fury and rejection? He didn't want Sarah to reject him and throw him out, that was for sure. He thought of a little poetic snippet of sensual longing he had learned as a schoolchild, so appropriate at that moment:

Western wind when wilt thou blow,
The small down rain can rain?
Christ, if my love were in my arms,
And I in my bed again!

That seemed to sum up his feeling for Sarah perfectly at that moment.

The Esperanza affair led him to another unwelcome chain of thought. What if she had had gonorrhoea or syphilis or some other sexual disease? This was a serious matter in those pre-antibiotic days. Madame Erica advertised all her girls as healthy, but how much reliance could he place on that? Nine to ninety days for the signs of syphilis to appear, he remembered. It had hardly been nine days since his clandestine encounter so far. He inspected himself in the mirror every morning, but apart from the odd yellow pustule on his backside there was no sign of any infection.

He remembered telling a worried apprentice on a cargo ship with no doctor on board, "If you think you've got the clap, son, you haven't. It feels like pissing red hot fish hooks backward if you do get unlucky, so when you get it, you're in no doubts at all!" All very funny at the time, looking down at the worried little apprentice's face looking up at him. Not quite so funny now. Could he sleep with Sarah at all with this doubt hanging over him? If he did, what if he infected her? If he didn't, how could he explain it to her?

And so the watch passed, Warwick worried sick in the wheelhouse, and David wet, cold, physically sick and miserable in the port bridge wing cab. The convoy ploughed on into the murk regardless.

69

CHAPTER ELEVEN

The storm lasted forty-eight hours and then the weather reduced gradually to an eerie calm combined with thick fog and a big residual swell as the depression moved north-east over Finland and the Barents Sea. David resumed his watchkeeping duties the following day after eating a hearty breakfast. He seemed to have conquered his seasickness, as the ship was still rolling and pitching quite a lot in the cross swells.

The convoy was bound for Liverpool and as soon as it reached the latitude of the Bishop Rock lighthouse in the extreme south of the Scilly Isles, they were ordered to break away and proceed independently to Southampton. Warwick was pleased that the continued fog made it highly unlikely that they would be attacked by the enemy and thus made zigzagging unnecessary. However, they had not managed to get any kind of celestial sight for over two days, and their position was purely by estimation; a combination of the courses steered, the distance run by the patent log over the stern, plus Warwick and Cyril's estimate of the currents they had experienced, after consulting a huge book called *Ocean Currents of the World*. This had been printed as long ago as 1878, for the use of the deep-sea square-rigged ships of those days.

Warwick set a course to pass two miles south of the Bishop Rock, knowing that his estimated position could be anything up to twenty miles in error. The last position given by the Convoy Commodore was just under two miles north of their own estimate at the time. The Bishop Rock radio direction finding beacon was switched off to avoid aiding the enemy, but he understood that both the light which had a visibility in clear weather of twenty-four miles, and the fog signal were still operational.

They were due to be abeam of the rock at 0250, in the middle watch. During the first watch, Warwick paced up and down outside his cabin, on deck down from the bridge, peering into the fog and listening for the sound of a lighthouse foghorn. At midnight when Murdo came on watch they were, by his reckoning, some twenty-eight miles off. He moved up to the bridge.

Fog; thick, swirling, merciful fog. At least the ship was safe from torpedoes. Flat calm; an eerie silence broken only by the occasional softly spoken command, the regular thump of the engine, and the gentle swish of the bow wave. On the bridge, it was very cold and very dark; the only illumination was the light over the magnetic compass. The helmsman stood, an impassive figure at the back of the wheelhouse, silently turning the wheel a spoke or so this way and that.

"Should we slow down a bit and sound the foghorn, sir?" asked Murdo in his soft, Western Isles burr.

"No, I think not, Murdo. She's only doing ten knots as it is, and I don't want to advertise our presence to any surfaced U-boats nearby." He thought of the big P&O passenger ships in which he'd served until six months ago. They normally ran at twenty-two knots – in fog they might slow to a modest twelve knots or so.

"The big thing is to listen; the lookout on the foc'sle can hardly see us here on the bridge, let alone see the Bishop. Try to see if you can catch the sound of the lighthouse foghorn – that'll be our first warning."

Warwick felt a churning in his stomach. The echo sounder paper showed that they had crossed the continental shelf at midnight, which more or less tied in with their estimate. The Scillies were steep-to. Over the centuries, they had proved to be a graveyard of hundreds of ships. There was a real possibility that the old *Freshwater Bay*, his first command, would run up on the rocks before they heard or saw anything. A few miles out in their reckoning; an incorrect allowance for the swirling currents of the English Channel, and they would be well out of range of any sound from the shore.

He had been meticulous in his chart work, and Cyril had checked his workings when he plotted his estimated position. He had always been a precise and accurate navigator, but previously he had been demonstrating his skill and inviting his captain's trust. Now he was the captain, and there was no one else to rely on. Should he stop and wait until it cleared? That would expose him and his crew to danger as soon as his ship was visible to any passing U-boat. No, he must press on with all the speed Sam could squeeze out of the fifty-four-year-old engine.

The cold and damp were beginning to seep through his duffle coat. He found his hands shaking and put them into his pockets. He didn't want Murdo to realise how nervous he actually was. He walked to the back of the bridge and into the chartroom, and studied the neat pencilled lines on the chart again. No obvious errors or miscalculations. Three miles off now, two points on the port bow by his reckoning. He needed to be outside looking and listening. Maybe he'd hear breakers and have time to stop the ship before she hit. On a calm night, there wouldn't be a lot of sound around the rocks. He began to develop an unwonted respect for all the difficult and obtuse captains he'd silently criticised in the past. He didn't realise it was going to be quite like this!

"I can hear the Bishop!" shouted Murdo, at the same time as it was reported by the lookout. "Broad on the port bow, captain!" Now he could hear it, too, and see the glow of the light as well.

"Time the flashes, Murdo, and take a bearing," he ordered. "Must make sure it's the right lighthouse!" But he had no doubts; his navigation had been spot on. He felt a great surge of relief and silently gave up thanks to the god he had forgotten for some time.

They took running fixes from the light and established their position. The fog cleared during the morning and they arrived safely at the Needles the following evening. Warwick piloted his ship up the West Solent Channel, past the Solent Banks marker buoys, past the Prince Consort buoy off Cowes, and out into the Eastern Solent, finally anchoring her off Lee-on-Solent as directed by the Southampton Port Control.

The next morning, the pilot launch came alongside to put the pilot on board and they weighed anchor and moved slowly up the Itchen River to dock in the Port of Southampton. The officers and crew were paid off that morning, and a skeleton crew from the Royal Fleet Auxiliary headed up by an RFA chief officer arrived to take over and supervise the discharge and loading of the ship. The WETB employed everyone aboard except David MacDonald and Warwick, who were employed by the Royal Navy.

The ship emptied rapidly. Cargo plans, fuel remaining, and stability calculations being handed over, Warwick sent David on leave with a Second Class rail warrant to go comfort his worried mother who by now had been made aware her son was out in the Atlantic facing the U-boats and storms. He sent a telegram to Sarah to say he'd arrived safely in Southampton and would be with her as soon as he could.

He had decided to forget the Esperanza episode. As regards the possibility of any infection he might be carrying, he would trust to luck and the fact that she had seemed such a nice, fresh, clean girl. He'd never felt better; he was sure there were no horrible little medical wrigglers multiplying in his veins and arteries. He sent another telegram to his mother saying he'd be with her in a few hours. He drew up a rail warrant for Southampton Station to Horsham, packed, caught a taxi to the station, and arrived at his parents' home that evening.

CHAPTER TWELVE

His mother was obviously overjoyed to see him. He felt somewhat guilty, as his primary purpose in going home first was to borrow his father's 1936 Rover 12 saloon and scrounge sufficient petrol coupons so he could drive to Sarah's new house. Fortunately, for his father, head of a transport command, petrol coupons were in reasonable supply. Civilian pleasure driving was banned due to the country's chronic fuel shortage, but Warwick felt that with his lieutenant-commander's uniform on and his papers showing him to be captain of a large ship docked in Southampton, the police would not argue were he to be stopped and questioned.

"It's so lovely to have you home, Warwick, darling," said his mother that evening. They were seated in the old study sipping a pre-dinner sherry. "It's been so lonely here out in the country, and I have to rely on irregular deliveries from the local tradespeople, as well as the kindness of friends, to give me a lift into the village to do some shopping. It's over a month since I've managed to get to Horsham."

His mother had never learned to drive, which, considering his clandestine plans, was a mercy. The car was covered in a dust sheet in the garage, but had been used a month or so ago when his father had been home on leave so the battery should be okay.

"I met a girl called Sarah in Newcastle," began Warwick carefully. "She was in business there but has some time off and is back home in Hampshire for a while."

As he expected, his mother assumed that it was her parents' home that she had come back to.

"That's nice dear; I expect you'll want to take the car to go see her."

This was all proving too easy. "Yes, I thought I might drive over tomorrow and stay over for a few days if that's all right with you."

"You're young and unattached and away at sea a lot, Warwick. I was young once and it doesn't seem that long ago, whatever you think. I wouldn't begrudge you your chance of romance for all the world. You go to see your lady while you can. No one is more conscious than I am of the dangers you've been facing. We owe you and your mates a lot, we oldies, tucked away and safe here in the country. Only one thing, Warwick, do give me a ring when you can. If you feel like bringing Sarah over here to meet me, I'd make her very welcome."

Warwick felt a welling up of affection for his mother. What a kind, considerate, and wonderfully understanding woman she was. He ignored the thought that his mother expected him to be welcomed by Sarah's parents, whom she probably imagined to be much like herself and her husband.

In any event, she didn't ask any more questions about Sarah and the talk turned to his sister, Sally, who would graduate from the Middlesex Hospital's medical school that summer, provided she passed her final exams.

The following morning, he set off at about ten thirty, after sending a telegram from the local village post office to *HMS Victory*, the Royal Navy's shore base at Portsmouth, giving his contact address and emergency telephone number for the next few days.

After asking directions at the village post office to the address Sarah had sent him, he eventually located West Lodge in the deepest Hampshire countryside. It was a lovely early spring day with clear skies and a very light, warm, southerly breeze. Little lambs gambolled in the fields. Unidentified but obviously happy birds tweeted and chirruped away in the background. The trees were showing traces of that particular fresh light green tint only seen for a few weeks each year just before the leaves develop and turn darker. The smell of an early summer was in the air.

He found the drive, guarded by a dilapidated wooden gate, just about mounted on a rotten gatepost and festooned with convolvulus. Ahead, he saw a small, late Georgian country house, built in honey-coloured local stone, roofed in slate, and apparently unchanged externally for the hundred and fifty years since it was built. It was framed in the spreading lower branches of a glorious old cypress tree on the front lawn. There was some low, brick-built stabling behind the house with round topped, yellow brick arches over the doors and windows. Ladders were up against two first-floor windows; she was having the house painted.

As he pulled up, Sarah came running out of the tall front door, her long auburn hair streaming loose behind her. He drew in his breath; she was even lovelier than he remembered. Those brilliant green eyes; who could resist them? Some women are at their best at seventeen, some at fifty. Sarah was at her best in her mid-thirties, having lost the thin, hesitant, teenage look and her difficult past, and matured now into a fulfilled and experienced woman.

She threw her arms around him and covered his face with kisses. "God, you're back, you're safe, and you're mine – safe with me now. The man I will love and adore for all my life! Darling; so wonderful to see you and hold you. You've no idea how long I've waited for this moment. I've been so worried about you. Poor John, but for a few inches it might have so easily been you!"

Warwick wondered vaguely what all those kisses were doing to his uniform and his stiff collar before he let himself go and hugged and kissed her back. He had a huge feeling of satisfaction looking at Sarah in her floaty summer dress which showed off her magnificent figure so well. Christ, just to think he had been an obscure junior second officer, unloved and unattached just six short months ago. Now he was a captain, a lieutenant-commander; he had a beautiful and relatively rich woman who loved him, and the prospect of this idyllic house in the serene Hampshire countryside being his permanent home. He resolved to ask Sarah to marry him when the opportunity presented itself. Meanwhile, he carried his bags inside the front hall.

It was a tall room with black and white square tiles on the floor. Sparsely furnished, it was in process of being decorated, as the trestles and white cover sheets bore witness.

"The inside hadn't been redecorated for at least forty years," said Sarah, following his glance, "There were two old spinsters who lived here and when they died, the nephew inherited and put the place on the market. The central heating is coal fired and pretty shot. I don't know what we're going to do in the winter, with such a big house and coal rationed and so hard to get."

"We'll just have to huddle together for warmth," said Warwick happily. Sarah gave him a meaningful look with lowered eyes, clearly conveying to him that the huddling couldn't start too soon, as far as she was concerned.

"The house needs re-wiring, too. The electrical system must have been installed about 1910 by the look of it. Brass covered switches that they used to polish, and there's a dusty old DC generator in one of the outbuildings with teak racks for battery banks in the room next door. The whole area smells of battery acid, although they took out the glass cells before I bought the place. I suppose they needed the copper connecting strips and the battery acid for the war effort. We're on the mains now, but I worry about the wiring and fires in the roof. There's no hope of sorting it out at the moment; you can't get electricians or copper wire for love nor money. I've tried."

"How are you managing to get about, darling?" asked Warwick. "You're very remote here."

"You know I used to drive that little van about collecting the boarding house supplies in Newcastle. I left that for Shirley. When I came down here, after completing the purchase, I found a huge American Packard built in 1939 in the stable block, all covered in dust sheets. I don't know whose it was; possibly the old girls who lived here had a chauffeur. I'll ask in the village when I get a chance. Anyway, I registered it in my name and had the local garage man get it started and in running order. I've an old boy that lives down the road who has looked after the garden for years, and he washed, leathered, and polished it, and cleaned the inside for me. It looks very smart now and runs well. The only drawbacks are that it has a very big, American engine and guzzles petrol, and it's left-hand drive."

"I think I might be able to help out with a few extra petrol coupons, love," said Warwick. "In any case, I've got free use of my dad's car, that little Rover outside, so we ought to be okay for transport. I'll take you down to see the old ship one day this week."

Sarah showed him over the house. She hadn't much furniture yet, although she had attended a couple of local country house sales and bought a few useful and essential items such as a large, antique, four-poster bed with side curtains for their bedroom. The drawing room had been repainted, with the ceiling mouldings picked out in light blue, white, and gold. *There must be some local craftsman with an eye to the artistic*, thought Warwick.

The walls had been stripped and painted with plain magnolia wash. Sarah explained that it seemed simpler and cleaner than hunting around for diminishing and expensive stocks of suitable Georgian patterned wallpaper, and a lot quicker and less trouble. Eventually, when they re-wired and re-heated the house, they could spend time and money on decoration. For now, she wanted it to be clean, simple, and fresh. He left his gear in the master bedroom (*Or the mistress bedroom*, he thought slightly guiltily to himself), and they went downstairs to the kitchen for a cup of tea and some lunch.

The kitchen looked a little like a set for *Borley Rectory*, Scene Three; enter the evil poltergeist from stage left. It was exceedingly dark and gloomy in spite of the windows overlooking the stable block. There were hanging racks for drying clothes with lowering cords, now hoisted up near the high ceiling which was blackened with age and coal smoke. There were a couple of heavy-legged tables with scrubbed wood tops, and the room was dominated by a huge, black, coal-fired, cast iron cooking range.

"There's a woman from the village who comes in four days a week and cooks and cleans. She manages to get that thing going, although it smokes more than it cooks. When she's not here, I leave it well alone and either eat cold or take the Packard down to the Dog and Duck and they give me soup and bread and sometimes a roast on Sundays. I caused a bit of a sensation when I first took that bloody great black car down there. It was all polished and smart and I'd put a bit of a low-cut dress on for the occasion. I don't think much happens down there. It sure drew the yokels in. They arrived in droves; that's why the landlord always welcomes me now and goes out of his way to feed me if I give him a ring first. There's always a pheasant, hare, or rabbit hanging in his larder. They're off ration, you know."

The decorators arrived back after lunch, which put paid to any thoughts they might have had about an afternoon huddling together for warmth. Warwick changed into casual gear, unpacking into the master bedroom wardrobe and chest of drawers. He walked the grounds with Sarah, and inspected the outbuildings and their contents. In one, he found an old wooden sailing boat about eighteen feet long, with her mast, boom, and sails stowed up above across the roof beams. He felt that this had a lot of possibilities for after the war and he resolved to renovate it, rig it, and find a trailer for it so that he could take it down to the river to sail with Sarah.

That evening, Warwick drove them both down to the Dog and Duck in the Rover. It was a long, low, seventeenth century building in the middle of the village. The landlord, Giles, was a retired Army major from WWI, who commanded the local Home Guard unit. He was a tall, lean man with thinning grey hair, impressive, bushy eyebrows, a large, enquiring nose, and a pronounced Adam's apple. He was dressed in an old tweed suit with frayed cuffs and leather patches on the elbows, and he ran a taut pub: neat, tidy, with all the brass and copper objects brightly polished. There was an original stone inglenook with a lively log fire in it and an old, black Labrador warming himself in a basket nearby. Giles introduced himself to Warwick, made them both very welcome, and gave them a menu handwritten in his own neat script. On offer that night was vegetable soup with new bread and rabbit casserole to follow, with local cheese and some biscuits to finish.

Warwick bought Sarah a gin and tonic and a pint of draft bitter, drawn straight out of the spigot in the barrel behind the bar, for himself. While their food was being prepared, they began to circulate among the customers at the bar. There was the local doctor, the vicar sipping a small glass of amontillado, and a solicitor who practiced in Portsmouth, together with a couple of tenant farmers. They all admired Sarah and were obviously keen to make Warwick feel a member of the community. He told them stories of his time in P&O and of his more recent adventures with the U-boat and his ship. The time passed quickly with all that good and friendly company and plenty to drink, and it was ten thirty before they stepped outside into the frosty late-March air, slightly befuddled; as the Irish say, "Not drunk, but having drink taken."

The house was cold and dark. Without any discussion, they hurried upstairs to the master bedroom, undressed, and dived under the eiderdown and sheets on the big four-poster as quickly as they could. Warwick pulled the bed curtains closed, thinking vaguely that he could have been part of romantic film set in Elizabethan times, waiting for the villain suddenly to rip the curtains apart again from outside, with one slash of his rapier. They were both naked and covered in goose pimples. They cuddled up, as much for warmth as desire, pulling the eiderdown round their outer extremities and the bolster round their shoulders. Then the desire rose and the cold subsided in each of them; they began to feel warm flushes as the adrenalin kicked in, and their cuddles turned into caresses. Warwick tensed his muscles and stretched his legs in luxurious anticipation.

"My own darling, I love you so much. You don't know how long I've waited for this," whispered Sarah in his ear.

"My love, me too; so much," whispered Warwick tenderly, shutting his mind firmly on any stray thoughts that might pop up concerning the Red Shoes Bar and Esperanza.

Sarah was lying on her back. He rolled toward her and began to lift himself up between her legs, her knees bent up, wide open and inviting. Then the telephone rang loudly in the hall downstairs.

"Fuck!" said Warwick bitterly, frozen in mid-move.

"Don't answer it, darling" advised Sarah urgently.

"I must, love; this is the emergency number I gave them. It's nearly midnight. They wouldn't ring unless it's urgent."

So saying, Warwick pushed through the curtains, ran naked across the darkened bedroom, and rushed downstairs in the dark to the telephone, uttering an expletive as he stubbed his toe against the heavy hall table leg.

"This is Portsmouth Command's ops room; Lieutenant Warren speaking. Is that Lieutenant-Commander Hursey, please?"

"This is Hursey," said Warwick crossing his legs and wondering if his toe was bleeding.

"I'm afraid I've some rather bad news for you, sir. A large force of bombers raided Southampton docks tonight. We opened up with the Hayling Island anti-aircraft guns to fool them that they were over Portsea Island, which looks a lot like Hayling from the air, and scrambled the Tangmere-based fighters, but quite a few got through, and your ship was badly hit."

"You mean *Freshwater Bay?*"

Yes sir, she took a bomb just forward of the bridge and number two lower hold and the engine room flooded. There was no fire; the bomb went through two decks and exploded in the scrap in the lower hold, blowing out the engine room bulkhead.

She settled on the bottom, which is fairly uneven at that berth, and when the tide fell, she appears to have broken her back. I'm afraid she's a total loss, although we'll be able to get the cargo out and any valuable gear off."

"Can I do anything to help?" said Warwick, beginning to shiver. There was a sharp frost outside and the house was draughty and unheated.

"I don't think so, sir; certainly not tonight. The local salvage team and the stevedores will recover her cargo, and then they'll patch her up and tow her to the scrap berth at high tide to be dismantled. Could you ring us again in the morning, please, since you're unattached now, and on *HMS Victory's* books?"

Warwick slowly climbed back up the stairs, limping slightly. He had grown to love that old ship and felt an ineffable weight of sadness verging on despair come over him. Sarah had put on a nightgown and was sitting up in bed with the curtains open and the light on. He sat on the edge of the bed and told her the news. She cried a little; she knew how much he loved his ship. Neither of them felt much like making love now; the moment had passed for that night. They put on dressing gowns and went down to the kitchen to make tea. Eventually, they went back to bed at three a. m. and slept fitfully until wakened by the clatter of the decorators' ladders at eight thirty.

CHAPTER THIRTEEN

Warwick rang his mother and told her the news. He said that he would probably be redeployed in a week or so, but that his ship was beyond repair. He would bring Sarah home to meet her and return the car at the same time, and he would like some more petrol coupons if she could spare them. They fixed a date for the following Sunday, when his sister Sally would be home. Sarah would drive the Packard and he would take the Rover, and then they could go back together in the big car.

Warwick then rang *HMS Victory's* ops room. He arranged to drive down to Southampton docks that morning to collect his sextant, books, and the clothes he had left in his cabin. The duty officer asked him to come in to the base at 1100 on Monday next to meet Commander King, the Base Administrative Officer. He drove down to the docks alone for a last sight of his old ship. They were both a little edgy that morning with the frustrating and disturbed night they had suffered, as well as their natural depression over the loss of Warwick's first command.

Arriving at the docks, he caught sight of *SS Freshwater Bay*, well down by the head, a great hole in the deck between the base of the forward bridge structure and the aft end of number two hatch. There was a distinct sag in the deck with the side hull plates rippled and folded abreast of the damage, showing that she had broken her back. On the stern, the Bofors gun pointed silently skyward. Cargo was still being worked from the other hatches, and the salvage vessel was alongside, with divers down, patching her up and making her temporarily watertight so that she could be pumped out and towed clear when the cargo had been discharged. It was a tragic end to their role as a naval auxiliary and designated supply ship to COMGIB.

Warwick turned away sadly and went into the dock office. Here, the personal gear and other equipment salvaged from the ship was laid out. Little piles were separated on the concrete floor and labelled with handwritten sheets: Captain's Cabin, Bridge, First Mate's Cabin, etc. He put the former pile into his duffle bag and rescued his sextant from the Bridge pile, together with his almanac, star identifier, and set of Norrie's Tables. On his way out, he met Cyril, up from his Devon village on the same errand as he was.

"That's a sad sight after all the trouble we had getting her here, Cyril. I'm going to miss that old ship. Your gear's all laid out inside; you haven't lost any kit as far as I can see. What do you think you'll do next, or are you going to give it up and tend your garden?"

"They won't let me go, sir. Master's tickets are still as scarce as hen's teeth and as much in demand as ever. I'm off to Liverpool next week to join the Cunard liner *Sylvania* as a passenger, along with about thirty malcontents as my crew. When we get to New York, they are transporting us to Rhode Island where I will take command of a new Liberty ship built in Kaiser's Yard there."

"Congratulations, Cyril; that's really good news. You deserve it. What's the new ship called?" asked Warwick.

"I don't know; I don't think it's even built yet. They're all prefabricated in big sections and trucked to the yard, and then welded together in about ten days. Then they're named at the launch. Makes you think when they can build a ship in less time than it takes the crew to get to it!"

Warwick said goodbye to Cyril with regret. He'd come to respect the little old man as a fine and tough seaman, and as a good and loyal shipmate. He would miss him, wherever he was destined to be posted next.

He arrived home to find Sarah closeted with his host of the previous night, Major Giles, in his official role as the local billeting officer. He had inspected West Lodge, but agreed with Sarah that the unheated house in its present state of reconstruction, with the kitchen unable to cook hot food for most of the week, was manifestly incapable of taking in any children evacuated from London. The three of them had a warm gin and tonic together and they booked for dinner the following night at the pub.

When he had gone, they spent a happy afternoon wandering around the place, hand in hand, planning the decorations and refurbishments. As it got dark, they boiled up the kettle and heated some tomato soup by putting the open tin in boiling water in a saucepan. They followed this, after an interval, with hot tinned beef stew, tinned potatoes, and baked beans, all heated in the same way. They washed their feast down with a bottle of pre-war vintage red wine that Warwick had purloined from his father's wine rack the previous day. Then, by mutual agreement, they went to bed together at about eight thirty, before the house got too cold. They spent a wonderful and fulfilling night together. It was all they both had hoped for and anticipated for months on the previous night. For a while, they forgot the rest of the world, the sad old ship, half submerged, Warwick's family, bombs, and the war. There were only the two of them snuggled up behind the curtains of the old four-poster, deep in love, happy, and content.

The next day was a Saturday. They spent some time together in the drawing room, planning the strategy for their visit to Warwick's home on the following day. They agreed that Sarah would dress conservatively, and not put too much make-up on. Warwick felt that what looked so attractive when they spent the evening in the dim old village pub wouldn't really go down well on a visit to his mother and sister in a house deep in the Sussex countryside at lunchtime.

"I just have to use a certain amount of eye make-up," Sarah explained. "My red hair doesn't come out of a bottle, as you well know, and without some eyeliner and mascara I look like a blind mole coming out into the daylight; my eyebrows and eyelashes just don't show up at all. And a bit of green eyeliner makes all the difference, too."

They agreed that the arrival of Sarah separately in the big, black, shiny Packard might cause some initial problems and that Sarah would have to explain it away early on. Otherwise, Warwick's mother and sister might think he'd fallen in with a rich American heiress on a fishing trip. Also to be sorted out were the living arrangements at West Lodge. That brought up the matter of the exact nature of their relationship. They were living together but not married or engaged. It would soon become apparent that the house belonged to Sarah, and that her parents were not on hand to act as chaperones, as Warwick's mother had supposed. Both lapsed into awkward contemplation, and Sarah gradually developed a deep red blush; all the more visible on her on her lightly freckled skin.

Warwick was first to break the silence. "Sarah, I love you and I'm sure I always will. Why don't we become engaged today? I can't buy you a ring until next week, but you only have to change fingers with that sapphire one you're wearing for tomorrow."

"Is that supposed to be a proposal?" queried Sarah with some asperity. "It really does have the ring of haste and expediency without much sincerity to me!"

"Look, love; I'm twenty-seven now and captain of a ship, or at least I was. We can marry when we like. I earn enough to support a wife, and money's not short so far as you're concerned. The vicar would call the banns, and under the wartime arrangements for servicemen, we could marry before I am called back. We don't now have to wait for three Sundays to go by like they used to before the war."

"Down on your knees, Mr. Captain, and propose properly, bugger you!" said Sarah with a sharp edge to her voice.

Warwick sank to his knees slowly and rather clumsily, for he was a big, heavy man.

"Will you marry me, please, Sarah, darling?" he asked anxiously.

Sarah burst into tears, leaving Warwick kneeling uncomfortably on the uncarpeted and rather dusty wooden floor. He waited for thirty seconds or so, wondering if it was the done thing to get back on his feet, or if he ought to stay right where he was and wait for an answer. The thought crossed his mind that he'd be stuck in rather a ridiculous position if she refused him. He felt like someone doing an imitation of Toulouse Lautrec.

"Of course I'll marry you, you bloody old fool!" cried Sarah through her tears, throwing her arms around his head and pressing his nose into her stomach.

Warwick uttered muffled exclamations of joy and happiness from his position, pressed deep into the region of her navel.

The next day dawned fine, cool, and clear with a light south-westerly breeze. Little, puffy, cumulous clouds drifted across the sky like flocks of small, white-faced sheep. The spring sun shone brightly but without much intensity.

Warwick took the fine weather as a good omen. They set off together and Sarah followed Warwick, although Warwick had provided her with detailed directions on how to get there if they were separated enroute. They arrived around twelve-thirty, in good time for pre-lunch drinks. Warwick's mother and sister ran out to greet him as he pulled into the back yard. They were both in plain dresses, looking the typical village society ladies they were. They had both been born in the parish, and had not often travelled very far from it. He got out and hugged and kissed them just as the Packard drew up. It looked huge; even blacker, shinier, and longer than usual next to the little green Rover.

Sarah got out and walked toward them. She looked really stunning, but even Warwick had to admit, a little exotic in that setting, like a film star recently arrived from Hollywood, looking over the location for her subsequent role as Tess of the d'Urbervilles.

Warwick introduced her. "This is Sarah Walker; this is my mother Edith and my sister Sally, who's about to become a doctor."

The ladies shook hands guardedly.

Warwick blundered on with the vague notion that he ought to set the scene early on, before any preconceptions took root. "Sarah and I are engaged, and we plan to marry before I have to go back to sea."

His mother and sister looked somewhat taken aback at this intelligence.

"You weren't engaged to anyone a couple of days back when you borrowed the car, or at least I didn't think so," said his mother. "I really don't know what you father will think when I tell him! We welcome you to our home, Sarah, and it's lovely to meet you at last, but we really know very little about you. Warwick hasn't told us much except that he is very fond of you and that he wanted to go to your family house in Hampshire. What did your parents think of you two getting engaged? I suppose that's your father's car; is he an American?"

Sarah drew a deep and purposeful breath. "May we go inside, Mrs. Hursey and I'll tell you the whole story?"

She had that edge to her voice which Warwick had come to recognise as indicating her purposeful mood. He knew that her mind was made up on which course to adopt, so he hung back to let events take their course. Whatever happened, they'd be home together tonight when this ordeal was all over. They moved inside and accepted a glass of chilled white wine in silence.

Sarah began with her early family, the death of her father from despair, unemployed in the depression, the stepfather, the attempted rape, and her career as housekeeper and later mistress to the wealthy older man who had subsequently died and left her financially secure. She included the relevant dates, leaving no doubt as to her age and the fact that she was somewhat older than Warwick. She told them that she had left her business in Newcastle to be run by a friend, and that she had a significant income from that, government stock, and other houses she owned in the North East, which were let to long-term tenants. She told them how she had met Warwick and that they had fallen in love. She explained that she had recently bought West Lodge outright to be near him and that she was having it renovated as best she could, bearing in mind the wartime shortages of labour and materials.

She was absolutely honest and left nothing out. Nothing was omitted, nothing softened out of a sense of reticence or delicacy. She told it just as it was, in an unemotional, deadpan voice. When she'd finished, there was a moment's silence while Warwick, Sally, and his mother looked at their feet.

Then his mother spoke in calm and measured tones to him. "You're very lucky, Warwick; you always were. You've managed to persuade a very fine and exceptional young woman to be your wife. I only hope you'll both agree to have the wedding here, where my husband and I have lived for all our lives. I am sure Frank can get leave from Northern Ireland for his only son's wedding. If you give me permission, I can see the vicar and make the arrangements."

Warwick was amazed at his supposedly straight-laced, Victorian mother. He had not fully understood what she had said to him two days ago. What she had tried to say then was that she had been young and romantic once, remembered it all too well, and still felt the same way at times. Especially now it was wartime, where all their lives were in danger to a greater or lesser extent, he was entitled to follow his heart. She had read Chekhov and remembered what he had written. 'You live your life but once, and if you have not lived it, you have lost it forever; for it will never return.'

She had married Frank Hursey when she was only twenty. It had been a love match with her boyhood sweetheart. She was only forty-eight now, an attractive woman who didn't look her age, and she had warmed to Sarah's open, direct, and obvious honesty. She hated people who tried to soften facts by euphemisms and circumlocutions. She knew they would be friends and she could see how happy she had made her only son, which counted for so much to her.

Lunch went wonderfully well; so much better than they could have imagined beforehand. Mother had roasted a chicken to perfection and served it with parsnips, carrots, and asparagus grown in her own vegetable patch at the side of the house. Father's wine cellar took some punishment before and during the meal.

Sally entertained them with student and medical anecdotes and life in London during the blitz. She told of operations held by candlelight during an air raid, with little bits of plaster dropping from the ceiling of the operating theatre when there was a near miss, and of the students holding up a bed sheet over the patient on the table to prevent them dropping into the open wound, while the sister held a hurricane lamp underneath and the surgeon finished the operation by its light.

She mentioned the delicate and embarrassed young man who had come into Accident and Emergency with a light bulb lodged in his rectum. He asked to speak to a doctor in private and told him that he had been in a dark cupboard under the stairs with just a bath towel around his waist, when he tripped on something and sat down heavily on a box of bulbs. Sally left the description of how they managed to remove the bulb without breaking it as unsuitable for the lunch table.

Warwick had heard most of her stories before, but Sarah laughed out loud, genuinely amused, which endeared her to his sister. He thought there was nothing more flattering than to see someone obviously amused at your anecdotes. He laughed along, too, and the party overflowed with goodwill and mutual liking. They left together in the Packard at about four p. m. and got back to West Lodge just over an hour later.

CHAPTER FOURTEEN

The following morning, Warwick arrived at *HMS Victory's* main block in Portsmouth at 1045. He showed his ID card and pass, and made his way through the sentries at the gate, the piles of sandbags in front of the building, and identified himself to one of the two Marines guarding the main front doors. He was shown to Commander King's office and admitted after a brief wait.

Commander King was a tall, bluff Lancastrian in his late thirties, with a warm, welcoming smile, smoking a pipe. He shook hands with Warwick and offered him a chair in front of his large desk. His office windows overlooked the parade ground, the barracks, and the bare lower masts of *HMS Victory*, with her topmasts masts and yards removed and stored for the duration, snug in her dry dock.

Commander King followed his glance. "They nearly hit the old ship a couple of nights back, which would have been a disaster for morale; you know: Nelson's flagship at Trafalgar and all that. Bit of a symbol, really. Overcoming the tyrant against all odds, only this time it's Hitler, not Bonaparte. Anyway, I'm Robin King and very pleased to meet you. We've heard a lot about you from Admiral MacDonald in Gibraltar. It is really good to see you Royal Naval Reservists here as senior officers. Before I joined the RN in 1932, I was a sub-lieutenant RNR and a third officer in the Commonwealth & Dominion Line running to Australia and New Zealand and bringing frozen lamb and beef back to the UK. There was no future there for me in the depths of the great depression. They had a whole ship full of certificated officers, just to keep them employed. All the AB's on deck had mates' or second mates' tickets, and weren't getting in any allowable sea time for their next ticket nor any experience as officers, although they used to let them come up to the bridge and take sights on Sundays just to keep their hand in for better times. I volunteered for a temporary, short service commission, and as luck would have it, ended up here as a commander on the General List ten years later."

It was obvious to Warwick that Robin King had time on his hands and was glad to see another ex-Merchant Navy officer in his office to reminisce with.

"I sort of got dragooned into this, sir, but I am so glad I did. My future was very predictable in P&O unless we got torpedoed and I ended my career somewhat prematurely. I must say that I've lived half a lifetime in the last seven months since I got appointed as master of the old *Freshwater Bay*, now lying on the bottom of the River Itchen, unfortunately. I even met my future wife up in Newcastle; I proposed yesterday and we plan to tie the knot during this leave. Make an honest woman of her and all that."

"Ah, I see," said Commander King, taking a deep breath and poking around the bowl of his battered briar pipe with an old pair of brass dividers. "Getting married, eh? Well you'd better make it snappy, as you'll be off next Monday to Boston, Massachusetts. They are building escort carriers for us there from converted American merchant ships' hulls. They do all the steelwork and basic fitting out, you see, and then we send them across as part of a convoy as ferry carriers, full of lend-lease planes and equipment, and with a reduced crew. We complete their fitting out with our own RN kit; gunnery control radars, communications, electronics and flight control gear, either here in Portsmouth or up north in Dumbarton or Barrow-in-Furness. Then they go to Scotland for trials with a full crew and eventually join in protecting our convoys from U-boat packs. It's a particularly vital time for us; our present huge losses of our merchant ships are absolutely unsustainable. All we are left with in the mid-Atlantic, apart from the overworked and outnumbered escort vessels, is Hurricane fighters catapulted off the bows of specially fitted ships in the convoy called CAM ships; they can frighten the U-boats into diving and chase away the big Focke-Wulf Kondor reconnaissance planes. Then there's nowhere for them to go unless they are close to land and can find an airfield, otherwise they have to ditch alongside a destroyer. Then the pilot has an even chance at best of being rescued alive, depending upon the state of the weather. Very brave men, those pilots, but it really isn't an answer to the main threat."

Warwick considered for a moment. "Where do I fit into all this, sir?"

"You are appointed to take command of *HMS Striker*, the latest of the Archer Class of US escort carriers with a Royal Navy ferry crew of 195 in a fortnight and bring her back here in a fast convoy. You'll depart from Southampton in the Cunarder *Aquitania*, as will your crew, next Monday morning. Any questions?"

"I understand the ship is full of planes and tanks and things, and that lend-lease aircraft are lashed on deck, but what have we got to fight with if we are attacked?"

"I have details of the standard US Archer Class carriers here for you in this folder. They are big ships; they displace 14,500 tons when fully loaded with fuel and stores. They are powered by either diesel or steam turbine and can maintain seventeen knots in reasonable weather conditions. They have two, four-inch gun turrets, plus four single Bofors 40mm guns and two double Oerlikon 20mm AA guns. These will be manned by trained RN gunners who will form part of your crew. The only other anti-submarine equipment you have is a new instant direction finder called a Huff-Duff. This is a classified bit of kit which I'll explain to you over lunch. There are neither depth charges nor any asdic equipment."

"Do you think I could make a couple of phone calls before we go down to the wardroom, sir?" asked Warwick.

"Want to warn your fiancée and the guests, do you? No problem; use my phone. Tell the Wren on reception that the calls concern urgent operational matters, subject not to be disclosed. Use my name as authorisation if you need to."

Warwick phoned Sarah to tell her the news. She was initially somewhat upset, but became less so when he said he would ask his mother to get an emergency licence and schedule the great event for that Saturday.

"If we can't marry in Warnham Church, then we'll go to the registry office in Horsham. We can always have a proper celebration of our marriage in the local church when I get back and there's time to organise things properly."

He then rang his mother, who promised to warn the vicar and his father. There weren't many guests anyway, just Warwick's family, Sarah's friend Shirley, and some of the *Freshwater Bay* team and their ladies, if they were available.

He rang Sam, who was still on leave, to ask him if he'd be best man and he said he'd be honoured to. He also agreed to invite Bill Garthwaite, Fred Carter, and Bob Baker on Warwick's behalf, all of whom lived around the Newcastle area.

Warwick then telephoned Murdo and invited him and his wife.

"It's a long way from the Western Isles, but I'll do my best," said Murdo. "Sarah's a bonny lass and I'm sure she'll make you very happy."

Finally, he phoned David, who said he could make it and his new girlfriend could come, too, if that was okay.

He joined Robin King in the wardroom after about twenty minutes. They chatted about old times in the Merchant Navy and swapped yarns.

"This was the first wardroom I ever saw, all those years ago," Robin began after they had armed themselves with large pink gins. "I was a bit overawed, being only a Probationary Acting Sub-Lieutenant in the Reserve at the time. You can't get much lower on the officers' ladder than that. I remember there was a very snooty commander here then. He had a French wife and, being a fluent French speaker, spiced all his comments with French *bon-mots*. He looked me up and down and obviously didn't like what he saw very much. He reminded me of someone who'd just smelt a fart just under his nose. He made an obvious effort to address me in his annoying, fluty, high-pitched voice.

'We have a big mess dinner here next Thursday, young man. You are expected to attend. Since you are from the Merchant Service, I don't expect you to have mess undress, which is the correct rig, so I will be satisfied if you wear your normal number four uniform jacket with a wing collar and a bow tie. If you have problems tying a double-ended bow tie, you can obtain a single ended one from the mess canteen stores. Do not even consider wearing a made-up bow tie; if it is discovered, you will have to stand everyone present a glass of port, and that will cost you a month's pay at least!'

"I thought to myself, 'you patronising, stuck-up bastard'," continued Robin, "so I determined to wear mess dress just to show him what we chaps from the Merchant Navy were made of. Problem was that I was a bit short of available funds. Gieves was out, and anyway there wasn't time to have anything new made. So I went along to Ikey Goodes' second-hand uniform shop just down the road on the Hard. They had just the thing; a deceased Surgeon Rear Admiral's mess kit that actually fitted me. As Ikey said at the time, 'It's real doeskin; look at the reveres. You can't get that sort of material these days, my son. Trust me on that.' He promised to have it cleaned and pressed and to put my single stripe on the sleeves. I bought a double ended bow tie and a white shirt with a dickey front and a stiff wing collar from him at the same time; all for a fiver! Came the night, I took a good long time in my cabin just to dress carefully. Looking in the mirror, I thought I looked a million dollars. I swaggered down to the wardroom in my new finery, went straight up to the snooty commander, and asked him if I could buy him a drink. He looked me up and down, and began to show some faint traces of approval. Then he caught sight of my sleeves. I had my single stripe on all right, but you could still see where the old rear admiral's stripes had come off.

'You must have done something really, really bad in your time!' was all he said.

Over lunch Warwick asked for a run-down on the Huff-Duff.

"Basically it's just a little cathode ray screen. Admiral Karl Donitz, Hitler's U-boat chief, demands that all his U-boats surface and transmit a sighting report as soon as they see a convoy, in order that a wolf pack of U-boats can assemble, head toward it, and cause mayhem. As soon as they start transmitting, a beam comes up on the Huff-Duff screen on the relative bearing of the U-boat. Several escorts have this kit, and using very short wave radio called a VHF; they can transmit their various bearings to Captain D in the lead escort vessel. The various bearings can be plotted and the position of the surfaced U-boat that initiated the transmission can be ascertained within a few minutes. If there is any aircraft cover, a plane can be overhead dropping bombs and depth charges before the submarine has finished her radio message. Otherwise, a couple of escort destroyers can be there in a few minutes at full speed and they usually catch the U-boat on the surface. It's a magic bullet; the enemy apparently has no idea that the direction finding equipment is carried by the convoy escorts afloat nearby; they still seem to think the bearings are taken from shore bases thousands of miles away, and thus are only accurate to within thirty miles or so, which would merge their position with that of the actual convoy on any shore side plot if they are surfaced just out of sight of it. Our intelligence says that they are blaming our new centimetric radar for the increased detection of their U-boats and the much higher loss ratios that they are experiencing at present."

"Who have I got with me as my officers?"

"One for sure, your erstwhile third mate, young David MacDonald. His father is very insistent that he is kept under your wing. Says it's making a real seaman of him. He's due for promotion to lieutenant and will serve as your navigator. Otherwise, there's an RNR first lieutenant called Jock Liddle from Glasgow and two RNVR sub-lieutenants, one of whom has been serving as gunnery officer on a frigate for six months and the other is fresh from the King Alfred training establishment in Brighton. They were keen offshore yachtsmen before the war but have no real professional experience in big ships. There's a surgeon lieutenant-commander RNVR who's a recently retired Yorkshire GP, an RN lieutenant in charge of the mechanical side of things, a commissioned supply officer who will be your Pusser, and a mixed crew of petty officers and ratings, some RN, some RNR, and some RNVR. Many of them have served in one capacity or another in a deep sea ship before. Most of the POs are old Navy, long serving and highly experienced; retired in the thirties and recalled for the emergency in 1940. They will form the backbone of your crew if things get rough."

Sarah and his mother spent the week on the phone preparing for the wedding on Saturday. Warwick left it to them as women's work. He desperately needed to prepare for his new appointment. Command of a 14,500-ton escort carrier, even if only on ferry duties with a skeleton crew, was a huge step up from the old *SS Freshwater Bay*, especially as he would now fly the white ensign as a full-fledged, Royal Navy unit. He booked himself in for two days at *HMS Mercury* for a communications and coding course. It was a shore-based establishment nearby, up on the South Downs. He spent another day at *HMS Dryad*, located at Southwick House near Portsmouth, studying fleetwork and command strategy. He took copious notes, and signed out some instruction manuals of low classification for further study on the four-day sea voyage to Boston. One particularly useful one was *The Royal Navy Officers Pocket-Book 1941*. It had sections for a new captain, divisional officer, and doctor, as well as many helpful hints on courts martial, duties of the OOW in port and at sea, and a section on how to write standing orders.

They drove to Warwick's home on Friday afternoon. Edith and Sally had borrowed numerous camp beds and sleeping bags, and every upstairs room in the house was full of them. It was anticipated that most of the guests would stay over on Saturday night, especially Murdo and his wife, who would have to begin the long trek back to Stornaway on Sunday. The weather was warm, and the old barn had been decorated and prepared for the reception. At the last moment, Warwick had invited Robin King to attend with his wife, and to give Sarah away; he had accepted happily. In total they would be about twenty-four people there. An emergency marriage licence had been obtained, Frank Hursey had been granted special leave from his Army transport office in Londonderry and Sally had taken the week off from her studies.

The vicar had been a slight problem. Canon Felix Farson-Smythe DD (Oxon) had been the incumbent of Saint Margaret's Church, Warnham, for over twenty years. He was a tall, gaunt, lean man in late middle age who invariably dressed in a long black cassock with a much worn leather belt round it, summer and winter, when out and about on parish duties.

He was rather an austere, remote, forbidding figure and was complemented by a very dominant wife who nursed a not very secret grudge against the Church of England for leaving her husband to serve out his time in this rural backwater as opposed to being promoted to be a bishop at an early age. She complained long and loudly to anyone who would listen that this was his due. Neither she nor her husband were inclined to alter their long-standing social or parish arrangements to accommodate rushed weddings for a couple who did not reside in Warnham, had never come to a Sunday service, and who, it was rumoured, were already living together in sin in Hampshire. It took Sarah and the significant donation she made to the church roof fund to change their mind on that matter.

"After all," Canon Farson-Smythe confided to his wife later, "Saint Margaret's has been the beacon of hope and spirituality for this village for over eight hundred years, and it is not for us to let it deteriorate toward dereliction in our time over petty considerations of the temptations of the flesh. All life is transient, my dear, both good and evil, but God and the church are eternal!"

Edith had called Warwick lucky, and as if to prove the point, Saturday turned out to be a lovely English spring day, with the sun shining and hardly a breath of wind, and not a cloud in the sky. Warwick and most of the men were in uniform. Sarah had dug out an old white evening dress, and she and Edith had fashioned a headdress and veil out of some spare muslin they had found.

Clothes coupons were in short supply, but Warwick thought the result was stunning when he set eyes on her that day at the altar of the old church. With her brilliant red-auburn hair flowing free down her back and her gorgeous figure, she caused the smartly uniformed men in the pews to let out their breath with an admiring sigh as she walked past them down the aisle on Robin King's arm.

"Do you take this woman to be your lawful, wedded wife, to have and to hold, to love and to honour, until death do you part?" Felix asked Warwick.

"I do," said Warwick clearly.

"Do you take this man to be your lawful, wedded husband, to have and to hold, to love, honour and obey, until death do you part?"

"I do," said Sarah in a softer voice."

"If any of you here present know cause or just impediment why these two persons should not be joined together in holy matrimony, you are to declare it now or forever hold your peace," continued Felix, addressing the small congregation with those time-honoured words.

"She's an ungrateful bitch!" There was a high-pitched shout from the church door from fat, slatternly women in her late fifties who had just come in from outside. "I did everything for her, and in return she told vicious lies and upset my husband. She lived with that dirty old man, took all his money when he died, and here am I condemned to live in a hovel in my old age on my poor, pathetic pension. She hasn't spoken to me in ten years, the cow. Let me have a word with her bridegroom; I'll soon change his mind!"

"Oh shit!" whispered Sarah under her breath in Warwick's ear. "It's my bloody mother; how the hell did she get in here?"

The Reverend Felix Farson-Smythe drew himself up to his full six feet and six inches like a spring uncoiling. "Madam," he began in a sonorous and compelling voice, articulating every word carefully and slowly, "none of what you are saying is an impediment to these two people being joined in holy matrimony today. They are mature, intelligent, and they know their own minds. Now kindly behave yourself in this house of God, or leave its precincts forthwith!"

Sarah's mother subsided onto one of the unoccupied rows of pews at the rear of the church, muttering to herself. The service concluded with an air of some embarrassment. Warwick kissed his bride at Felix's bidding and they went to the vestry to sign the register. Meanwhile, Commander King, accompanied by Murdo and Major Frank Hursey, walked back to Sarah's mother and quietly persuaded her to move outside. What they said or did out there was never disclosed, but Sarah was certain it involved the exchange of some money. In any event, when she and Warwick came back into the church and walked down the aisle to Mendelssohn's *Wedding March* there was no sign of her. She must have returned to wherever she had come from and neither of them, nor any of the other guests, saw her again that day.

In spite of the interruption, the small reception back at his parents' home went well. Robin made an excellent speech as acting father of the bride. "I hope I am not intruding on the territory of our esteemed best man when I say that I have received a very important congratulatory telegram. I will read it out to you all." He paused, flourishing an official-looking piece of paper in front of him, then read, "Our most hearty congratulations to Lieutenant-Commander Hursey and Lady Sarah, from the Prince of Wales, the Duke of York," he paused for effect, and then finished hurriedly, "the Admiral Benbow, the Duck and Sextant, and all the other pubs along the Portsmouth waterfront."

Then it was Sam's turn to speak as best man. He retold some of their adventures and incidents of their time together on the *Freshwater Bay*, including a detailed description of Sarah and Warwick in the Newcastle nightclub on their first evening together. "Couldn't get a word in edgeways, me," he said. "Must have been love at first sight; he let her do all the talking!"

Warwick stood up and thanked Canon Farson-Smythe for sorting out the little embarrassment in the church so firmly and efficiently, and also his father, Murdo, and Robin for finally settling the matter outside and getting rid of the intruder. He thought it unnecessary to emphasise the fact that the intruder was actually Sarah's long estranged mother. He continued hastily by saying that he was the luckiest man in the world to be married to such a wonderful woman and that he had never been so happy in his life. He touched on his next task without being too specific, just that it was a much bigger ship and a major unit in the regular Navy that was his next command.

The wine flowed, and with it bonhomie and good will. Sarah's mother and her attempt to spoil her only daughter's big day passed into distant memory.

They left for West Lodge in the Packard at about eight p. m. with Robin and Betty King in the back, as they lived in the Meon Valley near Sarah's new house. Having dropped them at their home in Hambledon, they parked the Packard in the drive in front of West Lodge and went straight up to bed. After all, it was their wedding night!

The next day, Warwick packed his gear in the morning while Sarah packed a picnic hamper. At lunch time, they drove to the Forest of Bere nearby, laid out a blanket, and sat together on the grassy slope down to the river. It was another fine, sunny day.

They both knew it would be their last together for sometime, so they lazed in the sun under a big umbrella that must have dated from the turn of the century. Warwick had it found in the pile of old artefacts in one of the brick buildings adjoining the stable block and cleaned up, patched, and repaired. It was an idyllic spring afternoon, over all too soon, bringing them to the mutual realisation that the night to come was their last together for a month or so at least, and possibly forever, bearing in mind that Warwick would be crossing the Atlantic twice and braving the wolf packs of U-boats before he could hope to return to his new wife.

They had reached that stage in their relationship that takes years for some couples and is never actually achieved by others, in that they were not only lovers, sexually attracted to each other, but friends and companions, chatting about everything, finishing each other's sentences and happy at just being together.

Swearing had become a term of endearment between them. Sarah affectionately called Warwick "you clumsy old bugger" when he knocked over his glass of wine on the grass. When she nagged him about some triviality, he would come back with, "Don't be a pain in the arse all your life, woman!" with his feelings for her showing in every syllable. And so their remaining time together passed, happy with themselves, happy with each other, and very much in love.

They clung together a little desperately that night in bed, both afraid of the dawn and the inevitable parting it would bring. Dawn came too soon, as it always does, and Warwick loaded his gear in the Packard and drove with Sarah to Southampton Central Station. They had agreed not to prolong the parting, so they embraced, kissed, and waved goodbye as Warwick and a porter disappeared through the station entrance with his baggage. Sarah didn't cry at all until he was well out of sight.

CHAPTER FIFTEEN

The train was slow, dirty, and crowded with service personnel: Navy, Army, and the RAF. The corridors were thick with smoke and the floor with ash, crumpled packets, and stamped-on cigarette butts. Being a lieutenant-commander, Warwick was entitled to a first-class travel warrant. The first-class carriages, like the whole train, were made up of miscellaneous LMS and LNER obsolescent rolling stock, brought back out of peaceful retirement on remote sidings to fill in for the duration of the war. They were not much more luxurious than those of the third-class section, but less crowded and populated only by senior officers like himself and the odd civilian who had paid for a first-class fare. In his compartment was a squadron leader who flew a B29 Liberator bomber on anti-submarine patrols and was going on leave, a lieutenant-colonel in the Royal Engineers who had been posted to Liverpool to supervise the urgent reconstruction of some of the bomb-damaged docks, warehouses, and cranes, and Captain Bertram Franks, Royal Navy, who was also due to travel to Boston on the *Aquitania*, and thence to take command of *HMS Aurora*, a 6-inch cruiser which had been torpedoed on convoy escort duty off Nova Scotia, had managed to limp into Boston with the aid of a rescue tug from Halifax, and was currently completing her repairs in the River Charles Dockyard.

From Captain Franks, Warwick learned that the *Aquitania* would proceed unescorted, as her service speed of twenty-three knots made it almost impossible for a U-boat to torpedo her, especially if she was zigzagging. He also learned that the

U-boats were now mostly deployed in the Caribbean and along the Eastern Seaboard of the USA, where there were no convoys, ships still steamed with all their navigation lights on, and there were no escorts to protect them.

The USA had initially eschewed the well-tried and tested British convoy system. For the first few months after Germany had declared war on America, they preferred deploying small groups of warships sent out on patrols, randomly searching for U-boats to attack and sink; a method that the Admiralty had tried and discarded as ineffective two years before. In May 1942, rather than braving the violent storms and depth charges of the Atlantic, U-boat commanders were notching up large tonnages of sunken ships in the warm waters off Florida, the Bahamas, and Cuba. Tankers proceeding singly and unescorted from the Dutch oil islands of Aruba and Curacao were a special target, since their oil was eventually intended for England. Some of the submarine commanders even found deserted coves in the remoter Caribbean islands, and held rest, recreation, and bathing parties in the sun there between patrols. Less fortunate U-boat commanders were re-based in the Norwegian fiords to attack and sink the merchant ships in the Murmansk convoys supplying Russia with essential weapons and war materials from England. Meanwhile, the big convoys between New York, St Johns and Halifax, and the West Coast ports of the UK remained, for a short while at least, unmolested.

The squadron leader, Archie Fowler, told Warwick that Catalina flying boats together with American B29 Liberators, specially fitted with long range tanks, mines, and depth charges and flying from England, Nova Scotia, and Iceland, were gradually closing the Greenland air gap where there was currently no anti-submarine air cover in mid-Atlantic. The area was known to the seafarers as "The Black Pit."

All this gave Warwick some cheer and encouragement that he might well bring *HMS Striker* and her hugely important cargo of tanks, trucks, guns, and planes back to England safely.

Otherwise, cheer and encouragement were in short supply on that train, as it slowly proceeded on its interminable journey. The daylight began to fade before they got to Crewe. The weather deteriorated as they got further north-east, and it got colder in the unheated, draughty old carriages. There was no dining car or sign of any refreshments on the train. Warwick had brought some sandwiches and a small bottle of Tizer, a sort of flavoured lemonade. Captain Franks had a hip flask with a cup attached to its base, full of old brandy. By mixing the Tizer with the brandy in tin mugs borrowed from some of the troops standing in the third class passageway, they made themselves a tolerable drink. Warwick shared out his sandwiches, one round each, and Archie had some fruit cake, which was also shared out between the four of them. It could not have been said to be a fully satisfying meal, but it filled a hole and warmed them up and they all felt the better for it.

The train was delayed for an hour just outside Crewe, and started on the last leg of its journey to the Liverpool Dock Station at eight thirty p.m., just about twelve hours after departing from Southampton. It stopped again just outside the outskirts of Liverpool at a suburb called Garston, and all the lights went out, both inside and outside the train. There was a heavy bombing raid in progress on the docks and central part of the town; the flashes were clearly visible from the compartment window, and the sounds of the muffled explosions could be heard after each flash. After another hour or so, they moved off again and finally arrived at ten fifteen p.m., about six hours late.

A taxi was hailed with some difficulty to take Captain Franks and Warwick together with their trunks down to the *Aquitania* on the Cunard passenger landing stage on the River Mersey, where she dominated the skyline with her four funnels and hull all painted in naval grey. She had arrived a week back, inbound round the Cape from Perth, Western Australia with two thousand Australian and New Zealand troops aboard, plus their guns and equipment in the holds. She was due to sail within the next forty-eight hours. They skirted heaps of rubble, driving slowly with the regulation wartime-dimmed headlights.

When they arrived at the landing stage, their papers were cleared by the sentries at the gangway, and their baggage taken by hastily summoned stewards. They were finally shown into adjoining staterooms just under the bridge deck, in the first class passenger section. They went down to the deserted dining saloon, where the stewards were about to clear up for the night and managed to get a cold roast beef salad with mustard pickles and a pint of beer each. Feeling much refreshed, they went back to their respective beds and slept soundly until the following morning.

After a full, cooked breakfast Warwick began to round up his officers, who were berthed in the second-class passenger area. There he found Jock Liddle, his first lieutenant, David MacDonald, navigator, RNVR Sub-Lieutenants Wearn and Watson, Lieutenant Tony Mayley RN, Surgeon Lieutenant-Commander Frederick Woods RNVR, and Commissioned Supply Officer Peter Darley RN.

They all sat down together in the first-class lounge and discussed the forthcoming task of bringing *HMS Striker* back to England. Warwick asked them to take note of his list of petty officers and ratings in each of their departments and check that they were on board and fit for duty. As soon as everyone was present, he intended to muster them on the boat deck, introduce himself, and deliver a short speech on their task and what he expected of them. He then gave each officer a time to report to his stateroom so that he could get to know them and have a private chat.

Jock Liddle had been a second mate in the Anchor Line before the war, and had served for a year in a corvette escorting the North Atlantic convoys. He was an experienced seaman and well versed in the Navy and its requirements and customs. *Probably more so than I,* thought Warwick to himself. A lean and purposeful man of twenty-four years, he was just the kind of second-in-command that Warwick needed. He had been in the RNR for some years before the war as midshipman and sub-lieutenant.

Jock had already met Striker's CPO and Master at Arms, Fred Bates, and reported that he had served thirty-five years in the Royal Navy until he retired in 1932. He was now sixty-four but strong, experienced, and fit. He seemed just the sort of father figure to pull the crew together and nurse those new to the sea.

He then had a chat with David MacDonald. They knew each other well and Warwick had no worries about David's navigational abilities now. After all, he had taught him personally. Of the two RNVR sub-lieutenants, Robin Wearn had some sea time escorting convoys under his belt; he had been the gunnery officer on a frigate. Jack Watson was fresh from training school.

Doctor Woods had only recently retired from his country practice to volunteer for service in the hard school of the North Atlantic. So far he had been confined to supplementing the medical departments of shore establishments. Warwick wondered if he suffered from sea sickness; time would tell. A case of 'physician heal thyself,' if he did. Otherwise he was a calm, competent general practitioner in his mid-sixties, pipe-smoking, rotund, grey-haired, and with a wicked sense of humour. Warwick took to him straight away.

Lieutenant Tony Mayley RN had served as the chief engineer in a frigate after taking his BSc (Engineering) at the Navy's new engineering college at Manadon. He was obviously competent, although the big steam turbines of *HMS Stalker*, coupled with her sophisticated electrical and mechanical systems, would be a step up in complexity from anything he had been responsible for in the past.

Finally, there was the hugely experienced and time-served Peter Darley, Commissioned Supply Officer. He was another retiree who had been recalled for emergency war service, and was in his late fifties; small, spry, and nearly bald. He was a lifelong chain smoker with yellow/brown stained smoking fingers on his right hand and premature wrinkles on his tanned face. Warwick didn't like smoking; he had never smoked himself, which was unusual for those times. Darley's hands trembled slightly and Warwick wondered if he was a drinker, or, alternatively, was just nervous about meeting his new captain. Nonetheless, he summed up Peter as someone who could safely be left to get on with his job as Pusser with minimal interference from above.

The next day, *HMS Striker's* officers and crew were mustered on the boat deck. Warwick addressed them.

"My name is Warwick Hursey. It goes without saying that what I am about to tell you is confidential and not to be repeated. I am the designated commanding officer of the escort carrier *HMS Striker*, presently completing her refit in the Constitution Yard on the Charles River in Boston. She is a large, converted, ex-merchant ship, with a flight deck of five hundred and fifty feet. However, we are a skeleton crew; we have no active planes or pilots, and no trained flight handling crew. Our job is to commission the ship as a ferry for vital equipment provided to England by our allies in the United States. We will carry Grant and Sherman tanks inside the ship, together with ammunition, field guns, trucks, M3 half-tracks, and jeeps. There will also be crates of spare parts for American equipment already in the UK. On the flight deck, we will carry B25 Mitchell light bombers and P40 fighters, lashed down against bad weather."

"These Archer Class carriers have quite a heavy armament for air and surface defence. We have an experienced gunnery officer and time-served gunners on board. We can man and operate our guns and defend ourselves, even though we will be within a fast convoy with at least six escort vessels. In addition, we have several new bits of electronic kit which are presently causing Admiral Donitz's U-boat commanders a lot of headaches."

"This great ship sails at 1000 tomorrow. You are all granted one night's leave tonight. Do not drink too much and do not, in any event, repeat what I have told you. Shore leave ends at 0600 tomorrow morning. We shall be at sea for nearly four days; that will be time enough to get to know me, your officers and petty officers, and your shipmates. We will be carrying out instructional lectures and drills while we are on our way to Boston. It only remains for me to say what a pleasure it is to have you as my crew. I am sure that together we shall enjoy success in our mission."

He dismissed them and they broke away in little groups with their departmental officers and POs to plan their various separate arrangements. They seemed happy with their situation and with his little introductory speech. He had not thought it a good idea to tell them that his last ship, his first command, was now lying on the bottom of the River Itchen.

He had decided that Jack Watson would be the communications and anti-submarine officer and would work with David on the Huff-Duff and radar plotting. Robin Wearn would be guns. Jock, as First Lieutenant would be responsible for maintenance, discipline, and ship's organisation. He had three watchkeepers and Jack Watson, the new sub, under training to become one. Tony could be expected to sort out his personnel without further interference from him, as could Doc Woods and his medical team.

That night he went up to the *Aquitania's* officers' accommodation to speak to the ship's Master, who turned out to be Captain Francis William Bailey OBE, a large, grey-bearded man in his late fifties with an impressive stomach. He was a widower, gruff and a little aloof, but he made Warwick welcome with what he called, 'A mate's two-fingers of whisky.' This consisted of him placing his index and little fingers alongside the tumbler, top and bottom, with his middle two fingers curled up. Pouring to the level of the finger which was uppermost resulted in a virtually full tumbler of neat spirit. To Warwick, this seemed a friendly gesture from a lonely and rather shy man.

Captain Bailey had been in the Cunard Line for all his seagoing life, some forty years, man and boy. His previous command was a cargo ship that had carried only twelve passengers before the war. She had been torpedoed and sunk a year ago, and he had spent five days in winter in the North Atlantic in a lifeboat. Despite the foul and bitterly cold weather, he had managed to keep the boats together and delivered all his crew to a passing destroyer, intact and healthy. For this feat, he had been awarded his OBE.

He readily agreed to Warwick's suggestion that David, Robin, and Jack should keep the morning watch with the ship's regular watchkeepers and take star sights and work out their positions individually, and also that they should shadow the *Aquitania's* watchkeepers and learn as much as they could about the running of a big, old ocean liner. They agreed that Tony would be introduced to the Chief Engineer and have free run of the engine room. Doc Woods would liaise with the ship's doctors and become more familiar of sea-going medical practice. They would have plenty of time and opportunity to explore the ship, as there were only about three hundred and fifty passengers aboard, including the hundred and ninety-five of *HMS Striker's* ferry crew. The rest were US officers and men returning to America, and British officers travelling out to take up official posts in Washington and the ship building yards. The mix was leavened by a few civil servants and diplomatic staff of both nations in transit, and about twenty wives of service personnel.

Before he went to bed, he rang Sarah to make sure all was well. She had managed to buy a decent Belling electric cooker in the closing-down sale of a Southampton retailer, and also a Kelvinator refrigerator with a big cooling coil on top and a freezer compartment in which she could make ice. The local builder was taking out the cast iron range, making good the holes it left, and re-decorating its alcove. The local electrician had eventually found enough wire, a fuse box, and sundry other equipment in his stores to install the new units there safely. She promised he would enjoy her gourmet cooking, so far as their ration books allowed, when he returned.

The *Aquitania* sailed on time, with Warwick on the bridge to watch the procedure. They had four Liverpool harbour steam tugs to pull them off the landing stage, and they proceeded down the Mersey to the pilot vessel off the Fairway Buoy, where they dropped the pilot. Heading along the North Welsh coast past Lynas Point Lighthouse, Captain Bailey rang passage at 1100 and the ship settled down to her full cruising speed of twenty-three knots.

It was a cold, grey, overcast day in early April, with visibility of only a mile or so. There was a light northerly breeze and a big ground swell from the west that made the old ship pitch moderately as she ploughed into it.

The experimental radar set was in operation, and Warwick wasted no time in getting the third officer on watch to show him how it worked. It had only just been fitted and had a new nine-inch PPI display that showed the echoes at their correct relative bearings and distances. The earlier C-scan radars had to have their transmitters trained manually and relied on a blip appearing on a small oscilloscope screen when the beam intercepted a target. *HMS Striker* was to be fitted with a radar of American design with PPI presentation, and Warwick, the petty officer, and the leading seaman wireless telegraphists in his crew needed all the practice and information they could get from the advanced centimetric set on *Aquitania's* bridge.

The four-day passage passed quickly. They were all busy in the daytime. Lifeboat drills were held each morning, with Warwick's officers detailed to take charge of some of the boats. For the main meals, Warwick, Doc Woods, Tony Mayley, and Jock shared a table with the *Aquitania's* Chief Officer and Captain Franks. They docked in Boston on April 10 and disembarked.

CHAPTER SIXTEEN

HMS Striker was lying alongside the Constitution Dock at the mouth of the Charles River in Boston. Her crew were billeted in the adjacent US barrack blocks for the few days it took to store her and prepare her for her Atlantic crossing.

They were fed steaks and eggs in unlimited quantities. Food rationing did not seem to have hit the eastern seaboard of the States thus far in the war. Warwick and his officers were put up in the wardroom quarters. Warwick's spacious en-suite room overlooked the ship.

She looked huge when compared with the old *Freshwater Bay*. She had been the passenger ship *SS Maui* of the US Matson Line, built originally in 1917 and employed mainly on the West Coast Pacific run to Hawaii. In the late 1930s, she had been converted to be a cargo ship, with her passenger accommodation removed. The US Transport Board commandeered her in 1941 after she had been involved in a bad collision with another ship in fog, in San Francisco Harbour. They patched her up, brought her through the Panama Canal and up to Boston, and converted her to one of the first escort carriers of the Archer Class. With her long, low hull and big steam turbines, she was ideal for the job. She was officially a seventeen-knot ship, but in her passenger days she used to cruise at eighteen to nineteen knots, and could probably still make that speed in an emergency.

The crew began to sort out their departments and accommodation the day they had arrived. Tony had the biggest job in the engine room, and he and his team were working twelve-hour days. She was due to depart in five days' time, on April 16, and join the fast convoy then scheduled to assemble off Halifax, Nova Scotia. Meanwhile, tanks and half-tracks, as well as jeeps, cases of spare parts, and ammunition were being loaded on to the flight deck and taken down to the hangar space on the aircraft lift to be secured to adjacent lugs welded to the deck with one-inch wire rope and bottle screws.

Tony came to see Warwick after dinner in the evening of their second day in Boston. He was obviously very concerned and upset about something. "It's the wiring, skipper," said Tony. "The original installation that was on the old ship is pretty ancient, since most of it dates from 1917 when she was built, but it's heavy copper stuff and it's okay. The problem is that the new wiring they have fitted here is absolute crap. We fired up one of the generators yesterday and put power onto the gun mountings to test them, and the fuse box caught fire and the wiring all overheated and burned the paintwork. Some of it looks like poor quality domestic specification. I don't know if it's connected with the installation of a 240 volt AC ring main as opposed to the American 110 volts, but we've checked both the US and English marine wiring specs, and what we've been fitted with is nothing like that, and it's positively dangerous on load."

"How long would it take to correct, Tony?" asked Warwick.

"I'm no electrical contractor, but I don't think they could do a proper job, even working night shifts, in under a fortnight."

"My God," exclaimed Warwick. "That would be a disaster! We are due to run trials in three days and then I have to accept her on behalf of the British government. What we are carrying, which is being loaded now, is absolutely vital to the war effort. My naval career will be pretty short if I don't sign the acceptance form and we don't sail on time."

"Well, sir; I have to inform you officially that this vessel is not fit for sea in its present state by reason of its grossly substandard wiring, and that is my professional opinion in my capacity as her designated engineering officer."

"Let's have a drink and discuss this rationally," said Warwick gently. He poured them a scotch and soda and put a couple of ice cubes in each glass. They sat down.

"Who's your boss in Washington in the engineering department of the Royal Navy purchasing team there? You get on to him tonight, and also to the yard manager and the local Lloyds' Surveyor, if there is one; otherwise, get the ABS surveyor to inspect the installation. Arrange a meeting on site in the engine room tomorrow morning as a matter of urgency. I will be there to support you. I'll get onto the naval Attaché in our Washington Embassy tonight myself. This could easily turn into a diplomatic incident! We really need some high-level support here; otherwise we'll end up as the sacrificial goats."

Warwick rang the embassy and, after a five minute wait, was put through to the naval attaché, Captain David Shepherd. He told his story and asked for some assistance. At first Captain Shepherd tried to play down the problem, suggesting that his engineering officer was overreacting, but when he heard that putting power on to the gun turrets had caused a small fire and the wiring to them to burn out, he became more serious.

"I'll talk to Rear Admiral Wixon about this; he's head of the purchasing mission here and an engineer. I'll try to get him to come over to you tomorrow if I can. As you say, this is going to be a real problem. *The Striker* is a new type of ship and an important contribution to the lend-lease programme. We don't want it to look like we're biting the hand that feeds us!"

"My feeling sir is that there's been a very distinct lack of supervision concerning the recent electrical installation. There's nothing else we can see that isn't anything other than quality work. They've even provisioned the ship with steaks and eggs and put cartons of cigarettes in the cabins and on the mess decks. Anyway, I'm hoping to get the yard manager down for a meeting tomorrow on site, and my engineer is contacting the Lloyds' Classification Surveyor."

Warwick rang off satisfied that he had done all he could that night. He invited Tony ashore for a drink before they went to bed. They settled on a small Irish bar outside the barrack's gate, near the Charles River Bridge. The atmosphere was smoky, and a few tired-looking women were at the bar. A juke box in the corner was playing sentimental tunes. Two of the women made desultory attempts to interest the new arrivals, but drifted off after a while.

Tony and Warwick sipped their beers and talked over the problem. They decided that to save time they could prioritise the wiring. The bridge, communications, guns, and power lift from the hanger to the flight deck would be the essentials for re-wiring, and emergency lighting in the cabins and operational spaces would also have to be rigged up. The rest of the work could wait until the ship got to England.

Just then, they became aware of a couple of beefy, middle-aged civilians standing close alongside them. The larger one introduced himself. "My name is Hegarty, Joseph Hegarty," he said in a heavy Boston Irish accent. He wore a baggy suit that had seen better days, and a cloth cap. He breathed whisky and cigar smoke into Warwick's face. Warwick took an instant dislike to him; he was standing too close, as was his companion, and there was something in his big red face and blue-veined nose that made Warwick want to punch it.

"I'm the boss of Harvard Marine Electrics. We're the people that fitted out *HMS Striker's* electrics on exclusive contract to the yard. Now, a little bird just told me that you might just have a few small complaints about our work, although I find that hard to believe, Mister Hursey."

Warwick wondered in passing how Hegarty knew who he was. "The new electrical installation on *HMS Striker* is appalling," he began. "It is completely sub-standard and a big fire risk. At the moment, we can't get power to our guns, and I doubt we'll be able to get the hanger lift up to deck level again once the cargo is loaded. I'm afraid it will all have to be re-done.

I've got the surveyor coming down tomorrow morning to report officially, but I am in no doubt that his recommendation will be to tear it out and redo it properly, with standard specification for marine cabling and junction boxes. If your firm did the work, I'd sack the manager responsible, if I were you!"

"You're a young man," Hegarty said firmly, quietly, and with a hint of menace, moving even closer and covering Warwick and Tony with a fine spray of spit and scraps of cigar tobacco, "and you don't know much about Boston. This town is ruled by the displaced Irish who have no love or admiration for the glories of the British Empire. I'm one of them myself, and I can tell you that working on your ships is not too popular around here, buddy! All my guys are good tradesmen and union members, so I wouldn't be so free with talk about sacking people if I were you."

"I'm not going to get into all that," said Warwick. "My job is to get the ship and her crew and her cargo safely to England. You can tell all your brave Irish friends that if it's a choice between the Atlantic in winter with German U-boat packs to stop me getting bored, as opposed to a gang of boozy Irishmen hanging around bars and doing piss-poor work during the day, and then going home to a fat wife and a safe bed at night, I know where I stand, Paddy."

Hegarty took a quick breath and moved back sharply, as if gaining space to take a swing at Warwick. However, he took in Warwick's size and bulk and thought better of it. "Well, my brave young captain, you can talk a fine talk now, but if you'll take my advice, you'll watch yourself while you're in this town! If you go on complaining about the good work we've done on your ship, it may be that, despite our better principles, you might just meet with a bit of an accident on a dark night. Sad, that would be; you'd be better to think of your wife and kids at home before spouting off at me when I'm only trying to straighten out a little misunderstanding between us."

"Why don't you and your dumb friend here just piss off and creep back under your stones and leave us in peace? I don't know what contractual arrangements your company had with the yard, but the whole thing stinks. One thing you can take on board straight away is that we're not sailing until the wiring's safe, and if your lot have to re-do it all again at great cost to you, I won't lose any sleep over it, for sure."

Hegarty and his sidekick moved off, muttering.

"I think we'd better finish up our drinks and get back to the barracks," said Tony. "We don't want him summoning up a lynch mob, and this hole is supposed to be an Irish bar."

The next morning, they were both in the engine room early to go through the problem in more detail. They had the electrical system drawings spread out on the work surface in front of the control platform. The original wiring was marked in blue; the new in red. They were soon joined by the Lloyds' surveyor, Mr. Bristow. Later on, they were joined by Patrick Murphy, the yard manager, with his foreman, both of whom Warwick thought looked worried and furtive. Of Hegarty and any of his Harvard Marine team of the Boston Irish trade union electrical engineers, there was no sign. A little later on Rear Admiral David Wixon RN arrived, accompanied by a USN captain called Osmond from the American Bureau of Ships. There was no doubt from the look on their faces that the arrival of the latter two senior officers caused Mr. Murphy and his foreman some surprise and a good measure of alarm.

After an inspection of the burned out runs of wiring and the blistered paint around some other areas, Mr. Bristow gave his initial opinion. "I will produce a short report for you, Lieutenant-Commander Hursey, as your engineer Lieutenant Mayley requested, but there is little doubt in my mind that nearly all this wiring marked in red on the drawing here is sub-standard and will have to be replaced with new material of an acceptable specification. The same goes for the fuse, distribution, and junction boxes. I am fully in agreement with you that this ship cannot safely sail to England in its present condition."

"I am in entire agreement with you, Mr. Bristow," said Admiral Wixon. "I have seldom seen such shoddy and sub-standard work in thirty years in the Royal Navy. May I suggest that Captain Osmond here of the US Bureau of Ships sort out the logistics with Mr. Murphy of the yard? What's your opinion of the minimum that needs doing, Lieutenant Mayley?"

"Sir," said Tony, "I have discussed this with Lieutenant-Commander Hursey and we feel that if we can get the bridge, guns, aircraft hangar lift, and emergency lighting reliably wired up, we can go. It doesn't matter if the old wiring remains in place and the new wiring is just securely lashed to the old wiring runs. The fuse, junction, and control boxes will have to be supplied in a much higher capacity size, but they can easily be screwed to spare spaces on the bulkheads, especially if the current stuff is removed."

"There is one other thing that I ought to mention, sir," interjected Warwick. "Last night, Lieutenant Mayley and I were having a drink in a local bar, and a Mr. Hegarty, who passed himself off as the boss of the contractors who carried out the electrics on this ship, and a tough looking sidekick, came up and threatened us with physical harm if we persisted in this matter. I can tell you that we wasted no time in getting back to barracks as soon as they left us!"

A look of pure panic passed over Patrick Murphy's face as Warwick spoke.

"This isn't the first time we've had a problem with this yard." Captain John Osmond USN had been listening with growing irritation to the unfolding story. He was a tall, lean man around forty, with a well-educated, Ivy League American accent. He was obviously upset, although he controlled his irritation well and spoke in calm, even voice, "About eighteen months back, we sent five old four-stacker destroyers here for refit and re-commissioning. There were fifty of them altogether, built in 1919 and laid up in 1925. The Canadians took twelve of them and you guys the rest, as part of our support for England's convoys. We had the same problem then with Hegarty and his company;

inferior, non-spec materials and unsupervised workers. It's my belief that the Irish Mafia in this town colludes with the Charles River Yard and that money changes hands in exchange for zero supervision and inspection of the work that they do on the ships destined for the Royal Navy. They work on the 'out of sight, out of mind' principle."

"Oh no, sir; not at all, sir," said Patrick Murphy in a panic stricken voice. His foreman looked at his feet and said nothing. "I can assure you on my old mother's grave that we are very concerned and careful with all the ships we get, especially those that are going back to the old country. After all, there are many fine, upstanding Irishmen serving in the British Navy and we wouldn't want any harm to come to them, now would we?"

"These ships are refitted at cost to the British and you can be absolutely assured that this matter will be looked into in the greatest of detail," replied Captain Osmond. "Meanwhile, I'll make it my personal business to make sure that this is the last contract we give the yard, at least until I've got to the bottom of this matter."

For the next few days, the yard put on a night shift, with a mix of their personnel and the Harvard Marine electricians. With three shifts working and the new cables secured to the old on a temporary basis, the work proceeded at a cracking pace. Tony and his mechanicians supervised the work for the ship and Mr. Bristow paid daily inspection visits. Patrick Murphy came aboard several times to check on the work. He was obsequious to Warwick to a large degree.

Nonetheless, neither Warwick nor Tony thought it wise to go ashore again in the evening, and so their entire experience of Boston was condensed into that one visit to the Irish bar close to the bridge.

The ship was re-scheduled to sail a week late and join the same convoy as was originally intended, since, due to some problems with its escort ships, it had been held up and was departing late, too.

CHAPTER SEVENTEEN

HMS Striker, temporarily rewired, ran her acceptance trials off Boston, Massachusetts on May 1, 1942. She had checked her magnetic signature at zero on the degaussing range just outside Boston Harbour at the same time. Warwick signed the acceptance forms and documents on behalf of the British government, and they hoisted the white ensign and the commissioning pendant to the sound of a single bos'n's pipe. Warwick regretted not having a Marine band aboard to welcome properly the new Royal Navy escort carrier's entry into His Majesty's service, but after all, it was wartime. They were due to sail for a rendezvous point near Halifax to meet up with the convoy from Saint John the following day.

Neither he nor Tony Mayley had been ashore since the night in the Irish bar by the Charles River Bridge and they had neither seen nor heard from Joseph Hegarty since then. Warwick was sure that Captain Osmond USN would sort the matter out internally and that there would be no further problems of that nature for future ships built or refitted in Boston under the lend-lease programme for the Royal Navy.

He had had a couple of letters from Sarah and one from his parents, which he had answered during the long evenings kicking his heels in the barracks. Sarah's refurbishing of West Lodge was going well. She had completed the simple interim decoration of most of the rooms and passages; gloss white and magnolia wash, which made them light, clean, and airy. The local electrician had discovered more wiring and other materials from a bombed out electrical store in Southampton and had begun the first fixings for the kitchen and adjacent rooms. Warwick thought that some of the heap of useless wiring and the sub-standard fuse and junction boxes still in place on board might just come in handy for domestic purposes when it was stripped out in Portsmouth, and resolved to try and buy it for West Lodge if he could. Most of it was of good domestic quality, completely unable to cope with the load the turrets and aircraft lift would put on it, but quite adequate for the ring main of a large house.

There was one disquieting note in Sarah's most recent letter. She had received a barely legible letter from her mother forwarded from *HMS Victory*, and addressed to "Mrs. Lieutenant-Commander Hursey, Royal Navy Barracks, Portsmouth, Hants." Her mother had no money. She was living in a rented room in Bristol and in danger of being evicted. There were bombing raids on most nights on the town and the nearby docks at Avonmouth. She had barely enough to eat for much of the time; she found problems in sorting out her ration book and the little coupons it contained. She was convinced that the grocer and the butcher were cheating her. She had no heat, nor any means to pay for any. The power had been cut off twice through her non-payment of the bills and now they had fitted a pay-as-you-go meter, for which she never had any shillings or half-crowns available. She didn't want Sarah, her only daughter, to feel guilty if her old mother died alone through poverty and neglect. As Sarah remarked, the only thing she didn't say she was short of was booze and cigarettes. They were where Sarah suspected most of her meagre income was spent. For the first time in their relationship, Sarah, so self-sufficient normally, asked for Warwick's advice and help.

Warwick gave the matter some thought. The last thing she wanted was for her mother to join them in West Lodge. On the other hand, there was plenty of room and they could convert a little flat for her in the upper floor of one of the stable buildings, so that she could live an independent life. Neither of them would allow anyone to smoke in the main house. Sarah's mother didn't have a car; he didn't know if she could drive or not, but regardless of that, she wouldn't be allowed near the Packard. That would keep her out of the pubs, so they could control her drinking. If they didn't put on an extra phone line (almost impossible in wartime anyway, without some high priority reason) she couldn't ring a taxi without their approval, and in any case, taxies were few and far between in the deepest Hampshire countryside.

What were the alternatives? Leave her to die alone in Bristol? Try and find a house near to West Lodge where she would be clear of them, but unsupervised. That was unsatisfactory and would be much more expensive. Warwick remembered her performance at their wedding. There was no point in sending her money; she had already demonstrated that she was unable to handle it. He would have to make it quite clear to her that Sarah was in charge and that she was living grace and favour. He would have to insist that the choice was hers but the terms of her moving into a flat at West Lodge were non-negotiable.

He wrote back to Sarah outlining his thinking. He told her that he loved and missed her, and was hoping to be home in a fortnight or so. The thought of having Sarah's mother so near when he was on leave rather depressed him.

He had plenty more to think about as he stared out the bridge windows that day before they were due to put to sea. It was a cold, calm day with a sea mist creeping inland. *HMS Striker* was a far bigger ship than the old *Freshwater Bay*, with an offset bridge and a huge ops room below it full of new communication and other equipment. There was a big, American, ten-centimetre band radar with a large, wire-mesh, parabolic aerial towering over him and the famous Huff-Duff set in a little secluded anti-submarine warfare alcove off the ops room. There were two very short range radio sets (VHFs), allowing them to communicate with the escorts and convoy commodore directly, without danger of their being overheard by prowling U-boats. There was a large plotting table with a lighted pointer shining under the chart spread on its glass top, mechanically moving, being connected to the gyro compass and log to give the ship's position continuously once correctly set up to scale. The position of the escorts, convoy, and any reported submarines could be set up on templates on this plotting table, so that Warwick had the complete picture should any engagement with the enemy ensue. Warwick looked out on to the flight deck, all 556 feet of it, and covered in lashed-down aeroplanes, most with their wings folded for a tighter stow.

This is a big step up for me, even though it's only a ferry run, he thought to himself, feeling the weight of responsibility sitting heavily on his shoulders. *Just to think that only eight months ago I was an obscure second officer on a moderately sized passenger ship, with a captain and three senior officers above me to seek guidance from and report to.* His accommodation was palatial, with a day room, bedroom, bathroom, and study. When *HMS Striker* was fully operational as an aircraft carrier, she would be commanded by an RN commander or even a captain, if she was the senior escort ship. Meanwhile, he had to fulfil the role.

They had spent their days alongside in continuous drills: fire fighting, damage control, gunnery, anti-submarine, fog, pilotage, and abandon ship. The crew were not as worked up as they would have been had they spent a month at the RN training centre at Tobermory in the Hebrides, under the redoubtable Vice-Admiral Stephenson, but they knew the basics of where to go and what to do in most of the various emergency situations they might find themselves. They were a pretty competent bunch, with the old hands looking after the inexperienced. He got on well with his officers. Tony Mayley was an exceptionally competent engineer, Doc Woods was a father figure to Warwick and everyone else – someone you could confide in and not just about matters medical. Jock Liddle was a tower of strength. He seemed to be everywhere at once, cajoling and urging the crew. David MacDonald was an old shipmate. The two sub-lieutenants seemed promising, especially his gunnery officer, Rob Wearn, with his previous experience in the North Atlantic in a frigate. Cox'n Fred Bates was a CPO of the old school; another retiree called back into service and a real stalwart. There was a similar CPO Mechanician in the engine room and a time-served CPO Gunner. All in all, at the stage of the war, he had a very experienced crew, especially as most of them would be re-drafted when the ship reached Portsmouth.

He thought back over his past career which had brought him to this. Certainly when he had joined the training ship *HMS Worcester* on the River Thames at Greenhithe in 1928 at age thirteen, he'd had no inkling that he would command an aircraft carrier fourteen years later. His ambition then had been to pass all his professional certificates, one day to take his Extra Masters' ticket, and then gradually to work his way up to be a captain of a big passenger ship, the acme of the profession of a Merchant Navy officer at the time. When he joined, he had been a big lad for his age. It took him a couple more years to grow into his full strength. He had never left home before, and his homesickness as he lay in his narrow hammock at night conflicted with his enthusiasm for this nautical training, considered second to none in the world. It was a huge contrast to the stuffy collection of Victorian schoolmasters in the local grammar school he had recently left; unworldly, chalk-dusty men in their black gowns and mortarboards, steeped in Latin and Greek classics. He had not shone there; he never really saw the point of learning Latin, but given the chance of formal instruction in seamanship and nautical astronomy, ship stability and naval architecture, he had discovered his metier. This was his real world!

The captain superintendent of *HMS Worcester* at that time was an unmarried First World War hero, Commander Gordon Steele VC RNR. The ship was mainly run by its senior cadets. They were big lads of sixteen or seventeen, and were graded from badge cadet, which was an indication of seniority only, through senior badge cadet, cadet captain, to the four divisional senior cadet captains, and above all, the chief cadet captain. In Warwick's first term, this godlike office was held by one Redvers

Martin. Not that the new cadets had much contact with him in the bustle and rush of the ship's organisation. They were kept busy just surviving and learning all the arcane customs that had grown up over the seventy years of the *Worcester's* existence.

Everything was timed; two minutes to undress at night and to contend with stiff collars, collar studs, and cufflinks; all to be neatly stowed in your sea chest with your name in white thereon (this chest and all the kit in it supplied by S. W. Silver & Co. of Eastcheap, London, 'Tailors to the Gentry and the Merchant Navy'). Then a minute's prayers, when you could surreptitiously continue the undressing and stowage, kneeling devoutly while keeping a weather eye out for the duty cadet captain patrolling the decks. Then smartly into your hammock and a bos'n's pipe for lights out. Peace and security at last, unless some roaming group of toughs untied your head rope in the darkness, letting your hammock down with a shattering crash on the deck or sea chest below.

The ship was an old wooden battleship dating from 1845, and had three broad wooden decks with the sea chests arranged in lines and gun ports around the sides. The classrooms were in the bowels of the ship. Those on the starboard side had a view of the Thames, and the stern of the *Cutty Sark* to divert them from their studies. In the evenings, when the junior cadets had swept, cleaned, and polished everything that didn't move first, they walked arm in arm (known as 'slewing') around the upper deck, making friends and chatting, only to break off to look at an interesting ship going past. They had to request permission from the duty cadet captain by shouting "Ship please!" Warwick would always remember those warm, fine, early summer evenings slewing with his friends under the mainmast yards and rigging, and watching with fascination the deep sea traffic on the river, with the attendant gaggles of tugs, coasters, and barges.

Almost inevitably, first termers transgressed some rule or other. Justice was mostly summary. The duty senior badge cadet would order you to bend over, give you a couple of swipes across the backside with his twisted belt, and send you on your way. The brass belt buckles had a raised anchor pattern in the middle, surrounded by a circlet like a wreath. This left the mirror image in red and purple skin on the white background of the miscreant's bottom for a few days, and lent some interest to time spent in the communal showers.

There were, however, more serious offences which required the personal attention of the Chief Cadet Captain. Warwick could remember still the tingle of fear and anticipation at cocoa time in the big mess hall, when the cadets sat on the long tables in dressing gowns and pyjamas, listening to the tall duty cadet captain, his face set like an Easter Island statue, make the daily announcements. These always ended with the punishment list.

"The following cadets will fall in outside the cadet captains' cabin tonight," was the grim introduction to this announcement. If your name was on that list, there was a feeling of imminent doom as you made your way up through the gloomy decks to wait with other unfortunates in the dark alcove outside the 'cabin,' as it was familiarly known. In the gloom, waiting there, you could hear the three or six strokes the unfortunate cadet inside was receiving. Then it was your turn. Into the brightly lit cabin full of beefy, unfeeling cadet captains to face Redvers Martin, dressed in a white singlet, white duck trousers, and white plimsolls. He used to hold the three-foot bamboo cane clearly in your visibility while he gave you a lecture on your particular sins. He would often introduce a biblical quotation to reinforce the lecture, usually from Leviticus or Isaiah. 'The eyes of the blind shall be opened, and the ears of the deaf unstopped' was one of his favourites. He was of middle size and build, but an expert gymnast and very muscular. His biceps, triceps, and associated sinews rippled up and down his arms and shoulders as he flexed the cane he held horizontally on the level of his chest. His face was rather thin and sallow, with dark brown eyes.

Warwick soon forgot all that when he went to sea, but he would never forget his pitying smile with the corners of his mouth turned down, which made his expression appear unwontedly cruel and merciless. In actual fact, he was normally a good and considerate man, always ready to spend his time helping young cadets. He remembered glancing out of the cabin window while Martin was lecturing him, through the open port past his shoulder. The evening tide was rushing past and he could see the lights of ships and tugs passing downstream toward the sea. Warwick remembered so clearly those awful moments in the bright lights of the cabin and wishing fervently that he could be somewhere else – anywhere else – at sea and a respected member of a ship's crew, his pre-sea training over, and away from this horrible moment.

Well he'd certainly been granted his wish now, possibly squared or to some higher power. Warwick shook himself out of his reverie. That was all past; it was the present that concerned him. He had to get this ship and her crew across the pond in one piece. For the first time in his life, he experienced a flash of self-doubt. Was he really up to the job? One thing about the Merchant Navy in peacetime; promotion was slow and everyone in the hierarchy knew their own duties inside out. In the last few months, he had been promoted to command, missing out the intervening stage of chief officer. During the depression of the 1930s, there were men in their late fifties who were still chief officers and had been in that rank for twenty years and more, without much hope of further promotion to captain. Then he had been made acting lieutenant-commander RNR without the benefit of the extensive training with the Royal Navy that regular reserve officers received in peacetime. And now he was in command of an aircraft carrier with millions of pounds worth of vital supplies and armaments on board, and nearly two hundred men under him, trusting their lives to his experience and skill.

That night they all had dinner together in the spacious wardroom. Grilled fillet steak was on the menu, preceded by tomato soup, and the meal was rounded off by scoops of chocolate ice cream. There were two bottles of a Californian red wine on the table of a very acceptable quality. The Americans had stored the ship without regard to cost or rationing. Warwick felt a little guilty, thinking of the ration coupons, shortages, and the unappealing offal which was off ration at home. In the North African Desert, the British Eighth Army was struggling against heat, flies, sandstorms, and General Rommel. Somewhere out in the Atlantic, there were probably mountainous seas, thick, worrying fogs, and U-boats a-plenty, but here they were in a warm and fairly luxurious wardroom, thick blue carpet on the floor, and pleasant shaded lighting, being waited on by the wardroom steward and living like kings.

Toward the end of dinner, the talk around the table turned to a review of the intelligence reports they had received and a consequent appreciation of the task they were to face. Jack Watson had been appointed communications officer and he had a sheaf of intelligence intercepts in the radio office from which he quoted the favourable factors. Warwick thought that Jack had grown in stature during their voyage over and their time alongside. A small, unprepossessing man of twenty, fair haired and freckled, he had come straight from the King Alfred training school in Brighton to join the *Aquitania* in Liverpool. He seemed to have mastered his communications brief well. He outlined the strategic situation in the North Atlantic.

There were many favourable factors in mid-May 1942 for an Atlantic convoy bound from Nova Scotia to England. Hitler had decreed that a dozen or so U-boats be diverted to the Mediterranean to try to prevent the Royal Navy from destroying the ships taking supplies to Rommel's North African Army. This was in spite of Admiral Doenitz's protests that the decisive theatre of the war was in the Atlantic. Further, U-boats were taking part in the Battle of the Caribbean, sinking unescorted American ships by the dozen. There were, consequently, few U-boats left to molest the well escorted convoys crossing the North Atlantic that month. In addition, this was to be a fast convoy, with a sustained speed of seventeen knots. This was nearly as fast as a submarine could manage when surfaced and vulnerable to escorts, and far faster than her sustained underwater speed. Submerged, she might keep up eight knots for forty minutes or so with her batteries grouped up, before needing to recharge on the surface.

The area known as 'the Black Pit,' off Greenland, was shrinking as longer range Liberators flying from Nova Scotia, Iceland, and Northern Ireland extended the range of their anti-submarine patrols, aided by their new airborne radar. Lastly, because of the preponderance of fast and valuable ships it contained, their convoy had an unusually strong escort consisting of six destroyers, a cruiser, and the old WWI battleship *HMS Warspite*. The latter was deemed necessary in case the Scharnhorst or Gneisenau were to break out from their Baltic base after their dash up the English Channel from Breast three months before. There were none of the sturdy little Flower Class corvettes escorting them this trip; with their maximum sustained speed in calm weather of fifteen knots, they couldn't keep up with these fast convoys.

CHAPTER EIGHTEEN

It was a still morning and the mist had persisted from the day before. Two tugs pulled the ship steadily off the dock with a series of hoots and then abandoned her and steamed off up the river. Warwick had engaged a Boston pilot who turned out to be a bluff Irish American, open, friendly, and pleasant. *Such a contrast to the shifty Joseph Hegarty*, thought Warwick.

They dropped the pilot at the Bar Light Vessel and headed north-east to the rendezvous point off Halifax at an even eighteen knots. Visibility was poor, not more than half a mile, and the big radar scanner rotated above their heads on the bridge. All the watchkeeping officers were interested in the radar display. They could pick up the coast of Maine and its off-lying islands at twenty miles and more. They practiced using the relative bearing and distance combined with their true heading, to obtain radar fixes. Twice during the day, a big, anti-submarine Liberator plane swooped low to identify them. On the designated VHF channel, they could now speak to these patrol aircraft and, from the second plane, they learned that there was no enemy activity reported within the patrol area and that the convoy was currently forming up off Halifax some two hundred and seventy miles ahead of them. David reported that they should sight the convoy at first light the following day, and the aircraft noted this for onward transmission to the Rear Admiral flying his flag from *HMS Warspite*.

The evening proceeded without incident, and Warwick wrote his night orders and retired to bed early. Before he went to sleep, he looked around his night cabin at the steel furnishings, the carpeted floor, and the brass-capped voice pipes by his bedhead. There was only a slight sea, and the mist had dispersed. The steam turbines gave off a reassuring, steady and muted note while steaming at nearly full speed, quite unlike the steady beat of the old *Freshwater Bay's* lone triple expansion steam engine.

He was called by the watchkeeper at around five in the morning when the dawn had just broken. David had completed his star sights and had put the ship twenty miles from the rendezvous position. With his permission, the radar was warmed up and when fully operational revealed a cluster of echoes about nineteen miles on the port bow. Within half an hour the upper works of the old battleship *Warspite* rose above the horizon, and the signalmen got busy with the ten-inch signal lamp, flashing *HMS Striker's* coded recognition signal.

They were ordered to form column behind the battleship, course 069 degrees, true speed seventeen knots, with no zigzag pattern at this time. This was acknowledged and Warwick and David struggled with the Battenberg plotter to calculate the course which, allowing for the intervening movement of the *Warspite*, would place them straight into their assigned position, at the correct distance dead astern of her. Then it was a matter of using the little optical distance meter with the height of the battleship's main top set upon it to maintain that distance exactly. Warwick was determined that his ship would not let the Royal Navy down, knowing that every move was being carefully watched, not only by the *Warspite* and its rear admiral, but also by the cruiser, *HMS Sussex* and the six destroyer escorts. He was in command of the second largest naval vessel in that task unit, and it was the only Navy ship in that convoy with a reserve officer in command.

There was a slight sweat on his brow and his hands were clenching nervously as he gave the orders. "Increase to 120 revs, port ten, steer course zero-six-zero." He was working the angles and closing distances out in his head as he spoke; a nice problem in moving plane trigonometry.

"Revolutions 105; starboard twenty. Steady up on fleet course zero-seven-seven."

He had done his best to allow for the advance of the ship between his order and the resultant physical effect, and also the sideways transfer bodily as the ship turned. More by luck than good judgement (as he later admitted to himself), he managed to place his ship just in the right position behind the *Warspite*, steering the correct fleet course and making the correct speed. *HMS Sussex* went through a similar manoeuvre and lined up on *Striker's* stern, so that she was between the two principal Navy ships. The sixteen merchant ships and tankers forming the rest of the convoy were spread out on either side, with two destroyers patrolling ahead, two on the port and starboard beams, and two astern. Warwick realised that the reason his ship was in the middle of the entire convoy was that her cargo combined with her function as an escort carrier was so very valuable and needed to be the most protected.

The ship settled down to its routine for the next few days. The weather was fine and the wind never exceeded force four. The thin May sunshine was welcome and improved morale, although the nights were still cold. It would take seven days to reach the position thirty miles south of Cape Clear, the southern tip of Ireland, where *HMS Striker* was due to break away and proceed at full speed for Portsmouth, escorted by the destroyer, *HMS Vindex*. The rest of the convoy was due to proceed to Glasgow. There was no sign of U-boat activity; obviously the intelligence reports had been correct. They must have all been diverted to the Mediterranean or the Caribbean.

The only diversion was Warwick's first captain's defaulters. Two stokers had been caught fighting in a remote part of the aircraft hangar by Chief Petty Officer Bates acting as Master of Arms. Both were a sorry sight when they were marched up to the Captain's dayroom, accompanied by Lieutenant Liddle as the prosecuting officer and Engineer Lieutenant Mayley for the defence.

Leading Stoker Ashley Elliott was first to the table. "Left, right, left, right. Halt! Off Caps! Leading Stoker Elliot, sir."

Chief Bates was getting into the swing of the occasion. "Charged with conduct leading to the prejudice of good order and naval discipline, in contravention of Sections 18 and 43 of the Naval Discipline Act in that he did engage in a fight with another rating while at sea and on active duty in wartime," said the chief on one breath.

Elliott was a small, freckled Scotsman who appeared to still have a chip on his shoulder. His body language and general attitude breathed that of an aggrieved man who was wrongly being made to take blame. He had three good conduct stripes on his arm, and so obviously was a time-served regular. His arm was in a sling and his left eye was blackened, with a cut above it. He wore a wedding ring on his left hand.

"Stand at ease, Elliott. Lieutenant Liddle?" said Warwick.

Liddle came to the table and saluted. "Sir, Elliott and Hill were found by CPO Bates fighting this evening at the after port end of the aircraft hangar, behind some cargo crates. There were two other stokers with them, whom we believe were there to act as seconds. They have not been charged, being merely onlookers when CPO Bates came on the scene. They are, however, available to act as witnesses, although I understand that the fact that Hill and Elliott were fighting is not in dispute. The evidence of the results of that fight is plain to see."

"Leading Stoker Elliott," began Warwick, "you understand that you are not obliged to say anything unless you wish to do so, but whatever you do say may be taken down in writing and may be given in evidence at a later date. Do you understand?"

"Yes, sir. I'd like Lieutenant Mayley to speak for me, sir."

"Lieutenant Mayley," asked Warwick, "can you now outline Elliott's defence?"

Tony Mayley moved to the table front and saluted. "My understanding is that this fight was pre-arranged clandestinely to settle a major dispute. Elliott has been married for six years

133

and has a small child. They reside in the Plantation Dock area of Glasgow, as does Stoker Hill. Elliott's marriage has had its problems and he has confided in me of these, as I am his divisional officer. Matters came to a head when Elliott suspected that Hill had been having an affair with Mrs. Elliott. In the final UK mail delivery before we sailed was a letter from Mrs. Elliott, addressed to her husband, but containing a missive intended for Stoker Hill and couched in very affectionate terms, leaving little doubt in Leading Stoker Elliott's mind of the terms Stoker Hill and his wife were on. The fight was pre-arranged, with appointed seconds to ensure fair play, to settle the matter once and for all, sir."

"I see," said Warwick. "Leading Stoker Elliott, have you anything to add to the account of the matter advanced by your defending officer?"

"No, sir; only to say that if I won, Bill Hill agreed never to see my wife again, and if I lost, I was going to leave her, and Bill agreed he'd move in and look after her and our kid."

Warwick now realised why Elliott had seemed so aggrieved. What a mess! What a silly woman to mix up the envelopes to the two men in her life. "Thank you, Elliott. I will let you know of my decision after I have spoken to Stoker Hill."

"On caps, right turn, quick march, left, right, left right." The Chief marched Elliott out of the room.

Stoker William Hill was marched before the table. He was a taller man, and his face bore evidence of cuts, abrasions, and pink patches. He was somewhat sullen, obviously resenting the semi-public airing of his affair with his messmate's wife. Jock Liddle gave the same speech as the prosecuting officer, and Warwick cautioned Stoker Hill. Tony Mayley then outlined the same defence. Stoker Hill elected to remain silent and was marched out by CPO Bates. The officers stepped back.

"Gentlemen, this is mainly a matter for Tony as their divisional officer to sort out when we get to Portsmouth. There is a Royal Navy Family Welfare branch in Glasgow, and I suggest that you get in touch with them as soon as we dock to visit the wife and try to drum some sense into her. At the moment, I am going to give both men only minor punishments. This seems to me more an emotional than a disciplinary matter.

Elliott and Hill were marched in again by Chief Bates. "I find you both guilty as charged. Leading Stoker Elliott, I accept that you were very much emotionally provoked and more sinned against than sinning. On the other hand, you are an experienced leading rate with three good conduct badges to protect. There is always your divisional officer, Lieutenant Mayley, to confide in, and I have already asked him to contact the Family Welfare branch in Glasgow, so that they may visit your wife and try to straighten things out. At this stage there is little point in stopping your leave; in fact it may be that you should be granted compassionate leave in the circumstances, should you request it. I therefore sentence you to be admonished, such admonishment to remain on your papers for six months only."

"Stoker Hill, this affair is largely your fault, although I appreciate that you probably could not have foreseen this outcome, with Elliott receiving a letter intended for you from his wife. Nonetheless, your behaviour toward a messmate has been reprehensible and you are to blame for encouraging Elliott's wife to be unfaithful to her husband while he is absent and fighting for his country. I therefore sentence you to an admonishment to remain on your record for six months, plus seven days loss of leave.

"Now both of you, you are valuable and respected members of this ship's company, so I am relying on you to behave yourselves while on this ship, on active duty in future. Dismiss them both chief."

Warwick felt that he had dealt with the matter reasonably well. It was a difficult situation, which the family welfare people on site were far better qualified to sort out than he was. He was constitutionally unable to moralise and preach abstinence from sex and loose women. He had had several affairs in his twenty-seven years, and the thoughts of Esperanza in Gibraltar were still there under the surface. He had never really considered the chastity and silence required of a Trappist monk as a career choice.

CHAPTER NINETEEN

On May 10, they reached the break-away position south of Ireland, and left for Portsmouth, accompanied by the old WWI destroyer *HMS Vindex* as their escort. They headed for their landfall at the Wolf Rock Light off Land's End at eighteen knots. There were no U-boats reported in the vicinity and they were well covered by continuous Coastal Command air patrols. The weather continued fine and clear, with a light south-westerly breeze.

Warwick's spirits lifted as they neared their destination; he had experienced some doubts as to his competence to bring this new, US-built carrier home, but in fact it had turned into a pleasant voyage; almost a yachting trip. That morning, he settled down in his cabin to deal with the endless reports and returns that fell to his lot as commanding officer at the end of a voyage. The ship would be de-commissioned in Portsmouth to be unloaded, re-wired, re-equipped, and re-crewed as an operational aircraft carrier. She would then go to Tobermory to be worked up, and after a month or so would join the convoy escorts across the Atlantic or up to Murmansk. She would have a new, Royal Navy captain and Warwick would join *HMS Victory's* spare crew list again under Robin King. Meanwhile he, Jock Liddle, the doctor, and Tony had to get their respective paperwork up to date. He inspected his monthly books. There was the Wine Book, the Daily Record, the Minor Punishment Book, and the Ship's Log. The Engine Room Register, the Defect Book, the Night Rounds Book, the Signal and W/T Logs, the Provision Account, the

DAVID ARNOLD

Loan Clothing Account, the Store Accounts, the Navigational Data Book, the RDF Log, the Sick Book, and many more like them. Warwick wondered how the Navy had managed to acquire so many compulsory books and records in wartime. He had yet to go through all the non-public fund accounts. He needed a secretary, although Jack Watson was doing a sterling job as correspondence officer, which took some of the office work off him. It was a moment of peace, quiet serenity, and concentration, and Warwick would remember it as such for the rest of his life. The cooling breeze blew in through the large round scuttles with their polished brass surroundings. Snatches of song came from a party of seaman working on deck; they were a happy crew, with only thirty-six hours to go to their home port. The mess cooks rattled their cans as they converged on the galley to collect the lunches that had been cooking on the stove. Pleasant cooking smells arose and wafted through the open door from the galley below. As is usual in war and business, the most peaceful moments come just before Nemesis strikes.

There was a huge explosion. The ship shook with the concussion and continued steadily on her course without a shudder. The action alarm bells rang through the ship. Warwick dashed outside to the wing of his private bridge. No torpedo tracks were visible, nor any sign of an enemy aircraft diving on them. He looked ahead, out on the port bow. About half a mile ahead, *HMS Vindex* had been lifted up bodily amidships on a huge column of black smoke, flame, and water.

"I think she's hit a mine, sir," shouted David from the bridge above where he was the watchkeeping officer. "There's been no sign of any submarine or torpedoes or anything."

"It would be us that a U-boat would be after, not an old destroyer like the *Vindex*," muttered Warwick to himself. She was on their port bow, on the landward side. Warwick reached the bridge in about three giant bounds, just ahead of Jock.

The *Vindex* settled down in the water, her back broken. She came to a gradual stop, still turning in a slow circle to starboard.

138

Fire and smoke came from amidships as the water flooded into her turbine and boiler rooms. She was already beginning to sink lower. There were little figures struggling in the water and others letting go the Carley floats on deck.

"We're going alongside her, Jock," said Warwick, making a sudden decision. "Jack, make the cyphered report to COMCEN Portsmouth for our escort ship hitting a mine; it's all there in the Confidential AFOs."

"Aye aye, sir," said Jack, hurrying off to his communications room.

"Jock, get fend-offs and scrambling nets over the side and alert the damage control teams to get the hoses rigged port side to. She seems to be well on fire amidships. Alert the doctor to get his sick bay organised; there's over two hundred crew on those old V and W destroyers!"

Warwick slowed his ship as she approached the wreck. She had split into two halves just about held together by some steel side plating and port side stringers. He decided that he would come alongside her starboard side, which was clear of crumpled metal and steel projections with *Striker's*, port side to the wreck, in spite of the fierce fire on her deck and the danger of her magazines and boilers exploding. Her deck was much lower than the flight deck of the escort carrier, but there were several openings below it at the hanger deck level that men could scramble across on to, and the fit ones could make it to the flight deck up from the destroyer's bridge on the nets over the side.

Acrid black smoke blew across *Striker's* bridge and decks, making their eyes weep. There were a series of smaller explosions as the fire reached the on-deck magazines of the midship anti-aircraft guns. Small shells flew in all directions like a firework show, with a few ricocheting off *Striker's* steelwork. The party on her bridge ducked down behind the steelwork instinctively. It suddenly became very hot as they approached the burning ship downwind. The damage control team under Jock's direction were playing water hoses on the areas that were aflame as well as on the surrounding steelwork to cool it down. It was hard for Warwick to judge the distance between the two ships as *Striker's* bridge was offset to starboard, on the other side of the sinking ship. There was a violent thump as fourteen thousand tons of carrier landed against the two halves of the fifteen hundred-ton destroyer, and *HMS Striker* shuddered and heeled to starboard with the impact.

"Not my best come alongside," muttered Warwick to no one in particular, "but needs must and all that. Pity to bugger up our nice new grey paintwork." He wondered if he had crushed any men in the water when he came alongside so abruptly, but decided that it was a matter of rescuing the largest number of people in the shortest possible time.

Men were scrambling up on board now, some with bloody wounds and blackened faces. Doctor Woods was in evidence with his medical team, holding stretchers, blankets and drips on stands, and administering emergency first aid on the open deck. Jock and Robin Wearn were getting the fit and the walking wounded below to the spare mess rooms. CPO Bates was taking names and numbers and generally organising things. It was what he had been doing for the last twenty years.

The fires were dying down a little and the for'd end of *HMS Vindex* had listed over about twenty degrees and was beginning to sink. A party led by the Medical PO, assisted by some of the deck and sick berth crew, was on her tilting forward deck, finding and evacuating the wounded there.

Warwick noted their courage and commitment for later reference, but was forced to call them back after a few minutes; it was obvious that the front half of the destroyer was about to capsize. Time and the action all seemed to be played for him in slow motion. He stood on the carrier's bridge wing as the smoke billowed about him and the ships ground together with the sound of tearing, rending metal, while exploding ammunition fired off in all directions. The front end of *HMS Vindex* listed further to starboard and the forward four-inch turret came into contact with *Striker's* bow. There was a grinding noise, and *Striker* was forced bodily to starboard, temporarily separating the ships by a few yards, then the whole forepart of the destroyer capsized and only her upturned forefoot was visible. After five minutes or so that sunk, too, and the ships moved tight together again.

"Launch the starboard sea boat!" Warwick ordered. "There are still men in the water astern." Undoubtedly his coming alongside the stricken ship had allowed a very rapid crew transfer. He noticed that the after end of her, from the forward funnel to the stern, was still upright and afloat. Thank goodness the sea was relatively calm. The engine room bulkheads must be holding.

There was a brief flurry of activity with the guns as the lookout reported a plane approaching, but it turned out to be the duty patrol B19 from Coastal Command at Culdrose, which had been scrambled when *Striker's* initial signal had been received. A brief report of the situation was made to the circling aircraft over the VHF.

"The evacuation is just about complete," reported Warwick. "So far we have 176 persons on board, including the commanding officer, who is badly wounded. As far as we can ascertain twenty-eight of her crew are missing and eight bodies have been picked up, mainly engine room personnel. The after part of *HMS Vindex* appears to be salvable, and I intend to take it in tow for Portsmouth until a rescue tug can take over."

HMS Striker completed the evacuation of the casualties and detached from the remaining part of *HMS Vindex*, leaving a petty officer on board with a party of six able seamen to take the tow line. Warwick manoeuvred his ship so that the two sterns were in line and about twenty yards apart. The deck crew unreeled the heavy insurance wire that had been left on board from her merchant marine days, and using a heaving line and an intermediate rope, it was made fast to the bollards and capstans on *HMS Vindex's* after deck.

Warwick steamed very slowly ahead until there was three hundred yards between the aft end of the destroyer and *Striker's* stern. The stern bollards took the strain, and he brought his ship round 180 degrees to resume the original course for the Solent at a maximum of five knots. Any faster, they discovered, and the stern sheered about violently with the towing wire at the end of each swing at about 30 degrees to the tow and threatened to capsize it with the sideways pull.

Striker's sea boat had been left towing alongside the destroyer's stern in case the forward engine room bulkheads gave way. Her transverse engine room bulkhead had not been shored up and might fail at any time, in which case the remains of the destroyer would capsize and sink very quickly.

The seven men still on board soon returned to their ship in the sea boat, leaving the stern part of the old *Vindex* unmanned. It was too much of a risk to leave them on board the tow overnight.

As soon as things had settled down on the bridge, Warwick went down to the sick bay, leaving Jock in charge of the ship. There were seventeen injured there, eight of them seriously, with four of those badly burned by superheated steam from the Yarrow water tube boilers, which had taken the main brunt of the explosion, as it had occurred right under the forward boiler room. Doctor Woods and his medical orderlies had pumped large amounts of morphine into them. He did not expect them to live. Their skin was flayed off over large areas of their bodies and there was little he could do for them but make them comfortable for their last few hours.

Of the other four, two were very marginal, with major burns and bad fractures. The other two, including *HMS Vindex's* commanding officer, Lieutenant-Commander Samson RN, had reasonable hopes of recovery.

Warwick sat for a while by James Sampson's cot. He was semi-conscious. He had lost a leg below the knee, and his rib cage had been badly crushed. He held Warwick's hand for comfort. He was worried that his wife and children would think him lost. Warwick comforted him, saying that his survival had already been reported to Portsmouth. Warwick spent some time with the old doctor, doing the rounds of the more lightly injured. In this, he was joined by *HMS Vindex's* first lieutenant, who was unwounded.

CPO Bates had managed to accommodate the survivors; there were plenty of spare messes and cabins; the ship had been all kitted out for the full, operational carrier crew of nearly six hundred in Boston.

Eight bodies had been recovered; they had been identified and laid out in the brine room near the refrigeration plant where the temperature was below zero, ready for burial on arrival at Portsmouth.

When Warwick returned to the bridge, Jack Watson handed him an urgent signal marked CONFIDENTIAL, which had just been decoded. The rescue tug *HMS Shorefire* had been dispatched from Portland to take over the tow and would be with them in less than five hours. He was to transfer the tow to the tug and then proceed with all speed to Portsmouth. In the late afternoon, the tug was sighted and they exchanged recognition signals with the big signal lamp. The tug was not fitted with VHF, so the signallers got some useful Morse and semaphore practice while heaving lines and wires were exchanged and the tow of *HMS Vindex's* stern passed to the tug. Warwick then ran full ahead for Portsmouth and the old ship worked up to her full nineteen knots.

They arrived without further incident alongside "C" Jetty, Portsmouth, the following morning, under the big dockside cranes, just over the way from *HMS Victory* in her permanent dry dock. The four men who had been caught in the boiler explosion had died in the night, and the twelve bodies were carried off down the gangway by base medical staff, each covered by a white ensign. The wounded were taken care of and *HMS Vindex's* crew disembarked for temporary accommodation in the barracks.

There were a number of long articulated lorries on the dock with Royal Air Force roundels on them, and the unloading of the aircraft on deck began almost as soon as they had tied up.

Officers and men of various specialisations swarmed aboard to organise the unloading and size up the final refit work. There was a heap of correspondence and non-urgent signal traffic for Warwick and Jack to wade through and distribute.

A middle-aged SD lieutenant with a green insert between his stripes presented himself to Warwick, who had just finished a belated breakfast. "I'm Jones, sir, here to supervise the rewiring. Lieutenant Mayley sent me to see you about the disposal of the old stuff we've got to strip out."

"Thanks, Jones. I'm doing up our house, and we can't get wiring and junction boxes for love or money. Is it possible for me to buy the stuff you don't need from the Navy?"

"Well sir, the scrap comes under the heading of 'arisings' in Navy terms. Since it's not on anyone's books, there won't be any arisings, so no one will have to account for it. In any event, it's all American specification and no good to us except as scrap copper. I'll speak to my boss, but I'm sure he'd agree that if you contribute £10 to the Royal Navy Welfare Fund, he will issue a release and a dock pass for you to take it all out. You'll only have to arrange the transport.'

"Thank you so much, Jones. I'll bring the £10 round to your office today if you'll have the material release and the pass made out sometime. I imagine it will be a fortnight or so before it's all ready to collect." Warwick thought that his father might come in handy for arranging the transport; he had several friends in the Southern Transport Command.

His next visitor was none other than Commander Robin King, who came into the cabin with a big, welcoming smile on his face and was obviously very pleased to see Warwick and *HMS Striker* alongside safe and sound. "Welcome back, Warwick! I'm going to need you to come up to the base this morning at 1130. The admiral wants to see you."

"Oh Lord! What have I done now? I suppose he saw the dents, scrapes, and burnt areas in the port side paintwork when we came in."

"Not a bit of it. All in a very good cause. He didn't get to be a vice-admiral by worrying about minor damage and paint scrapes in the middle of a war. No, he wants to see you to tell you that he commends your actions. Really, he's overjoyed. The back bit of the old *Vindex* was towed in to Portland last night, where they'll shore up her bulkheads and then tow her here. A week ago, they towed in another V and W class destroyer, *HMS Victor*. She had her stern blown off by a torpedo off Ireland, including the propellers, rudders, and shafts. Her power plant and boilers are intact. It would take as much dockyard time to rebuild her stern as it would to build a Flower Class corvette from new. Hence the dilemma; what to do with her? She was built in 1917 and is now twenty-five years old and it really isn't worth rebuilding her stern, in spite of the shortage of escorts. You've gone and solved the problem. You've provided a complete back end to join to her. If they cut both ships off at their aft engine room bulkheads, they should manage to get themselves one operational destroyer out of two wrecks."

"Any idea what's in store for me, sir? I could do with a bit of leave and married life."

"I'm sure you'll get a fortnight's leave, and I've a very good idea what you'll be doing next, but the admiral is very keen to talk to you about that himself, so you'll have to wait in anticipation. Commander Perkins is due aboard this afternoon to relieve you. After you have handed over to him, you can go home. They are going to leave the ship in commission and supplement most of the crew with the flyboys and aircraft staff for operation as a proper carrier. I think she's due for Murmansk convoy work, so you're probably better off doing something else. Never could stand all those freezing fogs and darkness for twenty hours, and German battleships and prowling U-boats."

Warwick just had time to phone Sarah before he left with Robin King in his smartest uniform and the waiting staff car. He told her he might be home that night and that he had some electrical kit that would allow her local, tame electrician to complete the re-wiring of West Lodge.

Sarah was not quite so overjoyed to hear from him as he had hoped. The reason soon became apparent. He mother had arrived the previous night, moderately drunk, and things between them had started off badly and subsequently deteriorated.

They drove round to see Vice Admiral Christie. He was a large, bluff, affable man and welcomed them into his office with a smile. He had his flag lieutenant with him, in an immaculate uniform with aiguillettes attached to his shoulder.

"Well, young Hursey, you've been causing quite a bit of trouble and no mistake!"

"I am so sorry, sir; things just seem to keep happening and I try to deal with them as best I can in the circumstances."

"Don't worry, my lad. I can't tell you how pleased we were to sort out that business with the Charles River Shipyard. Yours wasn't the first ship fitted out there with wiring problems. Your American friend Captain Osmond has deducted $250,000 from their refit bill and credited our lend-lease account with it. He has also had Harvard Marine Electrics struck off the contractors list for the US Navy. They had a real racket going there, Hegarty and Murphy."

"I hope they don't take it out on me when I get back to Boston, sir." While we're on the subject, may I commend my engineer, Lieutenant Mayley, for being so insistent that the wiring work be redone?"

"All noted, young man. You won't be going back to Boston, or anywhere in the States for that matter, in the near future. We have other plans for you."

Warwick waited in anticipation. Not the States, nor the Russian convoys. At least he knew that.

"This afternoon, you will hand over *HMS Striker* to Commander Perkins. You can then go on leave for a fortnight. On June 8, you are to report to *HMS Dryad* at Southwick house for the Senior Officers' Command Course. You'll be one of the few of your rank there, and the only reserve officer; most of the course will consist of regular RN commanders and captains. It is a three-month course and you should be clear by the first week in September."

Warwick felt somewhat apprehensive; this course didn't seem like a soft billet at all.

"Now, Rear-Admiral Macdonald touched on Operation Gymnast when he spoke to you in Gibraltar earlier in the year, I believe," the admiral continued. "Well, they've now firmed up on it and re-named it Operation Torch. Basically, and this is Top Secret, it is a combined Allied landing on the Vichy French coast of North Africa sometime in the autumn. The idea is to land a couple of divisions and either persuade the local Vichy French forces to change sides or to suppress them by force. There's a new Eighth Army commander facing Rommel in Egypt, Lieutenant-General Bernard Law Montgomery. Mr. Churchill has great hopes that with Rommel's supply lines severely disrupted by our submarines and surface fleet in the Mediterranean, and Montgomery receiving tanks and fresh troops from round the Cape and Australasia, the tables may be yet again turned and Montgomery will prevail and drive the Germans west. If we can land an army behind his lines in Morocco and Tunisia, he will eventually have to capitulate. Well, that's the plan anyway."

Warwick said nothing, waiting to find out what his part was to be in Rommel's projected downfall.

"You have come a long way in the service over the past few months, Hursey. Napoleon said that he only liked lucky generals, and I like lucky officers. You have handled your commands and what the war has thrown at you very well. You have had more experience in the last few months than some officers get in ten years. You were instrumental in a U-boat sinking, have delivered three valuable cargoes successfully, and have managed to salvage half a destroyer and save most of her crew. However, your next job is a step up from all that. Obviously it concerns Operation Torch. More than that, I'm not prepared to disclose at the moment. Come back and see me after you have completed your course in early September."

Warwick thanked the admiral and left his office with Robin King in a slight daze.

"It's no good asking me," said Robin apropos of nothing, "I don't know what he has in store for you, but it has to be something big. There's a lot of competition to get on the Senior Officers' Command Course, and you will be a real first, being relatively junior, and an RNR officer to boot. Now let's have a pre-lunch drink in the wardroom. *HMS Striker* can look after herself for an hour or three."

CHAPTER TWENTY

Warwick completed his paperwork, mustered his confidential books, and handed the ship over to Commander Perkins during that afternoon. There were a few things to clear up and it was evening before he managed, with Robin King's authority, to commandeer a staff car. He called in at the base sick bay before heading for West Lodge.

James Sampson was awake and his wife was by his bedside. He was obviously much better, although still bound up where his ribs had been broken. A fine man in the prime of life, he was recovering quickly. He welcomed Warwick as his friend and rescuer, as did his wife. The fact that he had lost the lower part of his leg seemed to weigh lightly with both of them. Doc Woods had done a neat and sterile amputation, in spite of the fact that, in thirty years as a country GP, he had never done any surgery apart from lancing the odd boil.

He arrived at home in time for a late dinner. Sarah met him at the door. She hugged him, then clung to him desperately, then burst into tears.

"It's Mother," she sobbed. "She's only been here twenty-four hours and she's ruined everything!"

"Steady, darling, I'm back safe and the admiral is very pleased with me. I've got a fortnight's leave and then I'm on a three-month course just down the road. We'll be together until September. It's the longest we've ever been together. We deserve it, darling, both of us. Isn't that wonderful? We can soon sort out your wretched mother."

"Well, my dear," Sarah sobbed, becoming slightly more aggressive, "she's in the house now, smoking away and drinking gin and swearing at anyone who comes near. You can make a start at sorting her out right now!"

"What about dinner?" said Warwick.

"There isn't any bloody dinner; she got to the new stove and has managed to burn it out, as well as the dinner inside it. She's completely impossible. That was a really great idea of yours, suggesting she live here with us. Thanks very much for the suggestion, my love. If you get any more bright ideas like that, do have a long cold shower and stay under it until the thought goes away again."

Warwick felt somewhat unappreciated by his wife, whom he'd been so longing to see. He'd never been the brunt of Sarah's aggression before; previously he had only experienced her uncompromising love and admiration. After all, he reasoned to himself, in the last forty-eight hours, he had rescued nearly two hundred men, saved half a destroyer, and delivered his vital cargo from America. He had expected a big welcome from his lovely Sarah, and perhaps a word or two of admiration and praise for his achievements. All he was getting was the blame for the trouble her own mother was causing. She wasn't his mother; that was for sure; his mother had come up trumps when she first met Sarah, and later at the wedding. So far, he had received more appreciation from the admiral than from his wife.

However, duty called, so he squared his shoulders, said, "Leave this to me!" to Sarah, and headed off in the direction of the kitchen.

He paused at the kitchen door. All was chaos inside. Sarah's mother was a short, stubby woman with the remnants of a full and attractive figure like her daughter's. Now, in her late fifties, it was largely unsupported, and her bosom sagged down on her stomach in consequence. Her straggly greying hair still showed some streaks of Sarah's glorious auburn colour. Warwick thought that she must have been attractive and seductive once, but her broad face, red-veined and puffy, told of the many measures of spirits that had been bought for her over the years and that she had seldom refused.

She stood near the stove, a half bottle of Booth's Gin in one hand and a glass apparently full of it in the other. She had a wild and challenging look in her somewhat bloodshot eyes. She was wearing a sort of beige sack dress that looked as if it had been put on in the dark and not adjusted since, with a tight belt a little below the general area of her waist which only served to emphasise her stoutness. Warwick remembered his father's phrase from his teenage days. "Like a sack of shit tied up in the middle." She wore scuffed flat pumps and no stockings; on her white, slightly thickened legs, varicose veins stood out like strands of blue string.

Warwick took off his uniform jacket and rolled up his sleeves. He looked around the kitchen. There was a wisp of dark blue smoke curling up from the oven to the high ceiling and he could smell a trace of burned electric wiring. Behind her, the new stove looked blackened at the top and was covered in a burnt and gooey mess of what he supposed was originally intended to be his dinner.

The whole place had been rewired and redecorated. There was a clean, cream-coloured Kelvinator refrigerator in the corner, with a big, white cylindrical condenser coil on its top. There were new tables and chairs, and some new cupboards on the wall. The old worn and dirty lino had been taken up from the floor, and the original buff and white checkerboard of stone tiles had been cleaned and restored. The sink and taps had been replaced with more modern ones. On the other hand, there were heaps of dirty crockery, glasses, mugs, and cutlery everywhere, together with opened tins, bottles, spilled food, and overflowing ashtrays. No wonder Sarah, who was so house-proud, tidy, and the absolute champion of efficient household order, was upset.

"I know who you are, sailor," Sarah's mother hissed at him. "You think you're so fucking great, but you're just another of her stuck-up lovers. It don't cut no ice with me!" Her voice was husky and slightly slurred, but there was no mistaking the venom in it.

"Mrs. Walker," Warwick began in a calm steady voice, moving slowly toward her.

"My name isn't Walker," she shouted, her voice an octave higher. "It's Johnson, after my second husband, the one your precious Sarah upset by her fucking adolescent fancies; so much so that he upped and left me." She was swaying slightly and was obviously working herself up for some kind of offensive action.

Warwick sized her up. She was about five feet two, and eleven stones. She was certainly giving some height and weight away if she intended to attack him physically. He began to feel his own temper rising. He had been happier than he had ever been in his life with Sarah. They had a beautiful house, plenty of money, and he had a wife whom he loved and who loved him. He had achieved a lot in his short naval career and, in a way, he had performed all the better with Sarah in mind. He wanted her to admire him and appreciate what he was capable of. He wanted her to be glad she had married him and entrusted her future to him. He was conscious of his concern for Sarah's opinion of him when he told her about his exploits.

Yet here was this horrible woman who had spoiled Sarah's life. She had married the egregious Mr. Johnson, who had tried to rape the fourteen-year-old Sarah and had caused her to leave home when her mother disbelieved her story and punished her for her accusations. Johnson had long gone and good riddance, but her mother had aimlessly drunk her way through the next twenty years, then turned up uninvited, unwashed, and unwanted at their wedding, embarrassed everyone, and had to be paid to leave. Now, when offered her a home with some sanctuary and prospect of a better life with her daughter and her husband, she was intent in wrecking their lives together.

Sod it; he wasn't going to be controlled by this disreputable, rancorous, evil, vicious, drunken old crone in his own house! He moved toward her purposefully.

With a speed and force he had not thought her capable of, she hurled her glass at him. His old boxing training kicked in and he managed to duck. The glass shattered against the far wall, putting a dent in the new plaster. Gin spread over his white shirt. He had the momentary thought that it was a good job he'd taken his best uniform jacket off. He closed with her. She swung the bottle back with her left arm intending to hit him over his head.

"Never telegraph a punch, my dear," he said through clenched teeth. He grabbed her arm and shook it. The bottle fell to the ground and shattered on the stone floor. The smell of neat gin arose on the evening air to join that of sour, unwashed female, burned wiring, stale food, old cigarette ash, and sweat. She bent over to try to bite him. He raised the elbow of his right arm, which was still holding her wrist, to ward her off. His elbow caught her under her chin as she bent down with her mouth wide open. Her jaws shut with a clunk, causing her to bite deeply into her tongue. She made a gurgling noise and sat down on a kitchen stool sharply, while blood streamed from her mouth and trickled down her dress. Warwick let go of her arm and looked around guiltily.

Sarah was standing in the kitchen doorway watching with mouth pursed and silent.

"Ring the doctor, love, quick! Her tongue's badly bitten and I think she's got the DTs."

"I'll try," replied Sarah, "but I'm not sure he'll come. The sky to the south is alight and I can hear the anti-aircraft guns. They're bombing Southampton again and he may have been called in to help with casualties in the big general hospital there."

In spite of the bombing, the local general practitioner, old Doctor Williams, arrived at the front door within twenty minutes. He was an elderly man, past retirement age; all his young partners had been called up for service early in the war and he had been left to look after the general health of the area on his own. He had been trained at Guy's Hospital in London in the Victorian age over fifty years before, and was dressed in a morning coat and striped trousers, with a wing collar and black bow tie. He was a sprightly, cheerful, active man who lived with his wife of forty years in a big house in the village.

Sarah and Warwick explained the situation as they walked through the house. They had laid Mary Johnson on a blanket in the corner of the kitchen, pillowed her head, put a sterile pad in her mouth, and covered her in a blanket. She was in shock, pale, and reasonably calm, although she occasionally raised her voice in alarm when she imagined she saw a large spider or lizard advancing toward her on the ceiling. Sarah and Warwick had cleared up the debris in the kitchen. The ashtrays had been emptied, plates washed, floor swept and swabbed, and most of Warwick's dinner scraped off the top of the cooker into the bin.

"I'll sedate her for a start," said the doctor after he had carried out a cursory examination, without much opposition from his new patient. "I'll give her five mils of paraldehyde; that should calm her down for tonight. Her tongue has stopped bleeding. It's a little swollen, but it will heal itself in a few days. She's a bit pale and slightly jaundiced. She is in mild shock and may have some liver malfunction."

"What should we do when she wakes up?" Sarah sounded worried.

"She must be kept clear of alcohol, that's for sure. If you can't dry her out, she's got a short life expectancy. You were absolutely right; she's suffering from delirium tremens and she'll have withdrawal symptoms which will make her very difficult."

"Can't she go into hospital and get proper care?" Warwick was beginning to see his long anticipated leave time with Sarah, which he had so looked forward to, in a different light if Mary Johnson remained their responsibility at West Lodge.

"We don't really regard alcoholism as a disease as such these days. It's more an addiction for the sufferer to make up their mind to conquer. Mind you, she's in pretty poor shape and may have other problems as yet undiagnosed. If it were peace time, we would admit her for a week for tests and observation, but now most of the wards are filled with war and blitz casualties. I'll give Southampton General a ring tomorrow to see if they'll take her; otherwise, the only option is a private clinic. I'm pretty sure that the local cottage hospital wouldn't want her when she wakes up. She may well be difficult to control then, especially if she can't get a drink."

Doctor Williams left. It was nearly ten thirty in the evening and Warwick suddenly felt very tired and hungry.

"What are we going to do with your mother?" he asked Sarah.

"Leave her there for the night. The lavatory is just outside in the passage and she knows where it is if she needs it. I've hidden all the alcohol in the house and thrown away all her remaining cigarettes. We're going to sober her up and try to make some kind of a life for her."

Warwick was aware that she was putting a brave face on a continuing problem. Anyway, she'd stopped blaming him and started being her usual practical and constructive self. He'd never yet known anyone so far advanced in alcoholism to recover by their own will power (or for that matter to recover at all) but there was always a first time. Anyway, he'd been used to drunken seamen; Sarah's mother was in a different category.

"I suppose there's nothing to eat," he said with a note of pathos in his voice. "I haven't had anything since lunch and that wasn't much." It was only a little over twenty-four hours ago when he had been transferring the towline of the stern part of *HMS Vindex* to the tug from Portland.

"I can get you bread and cheese and some pickled onions," said Sarah. "There isn't any butter, I'm afraid. There's some stewed plums in the refrigerator if you feel like them. I could put some sugar on; they're a bit tart. I think they were picked too early. The beer is all locked away, but you can have a glass of lemonade cordial with it."

Warwick investigated the stove while Sarah prepared the food. The plug had burned out at the back and a 10-amp fuse had blown. He had some fuse wire and a spare plug in the workshop and he could fix it himself.

"If you can get the top cleaned off, I can fix the electrics to the cooker," he said. "There doesn't seem to be anything wrong with it other than the plug and fuse."

Sarah brightened. "I'll clean it up tomorrow. Let's eat now, darling. I'm dog tired."

They ate their meagre dinner together while Mary Johnson snored softly at their feet. Their eyes met and for the first time that day they were in harmony. Warwick's thoughts began to turn to the bedroom. He had been away a long time. In the subdued light of the kitchen, Sarah looked more beautiful than he remembered. He had two weeks before he had to report to *HMS Dryad* for the Commanding Officers' Course. The thought of that with all the commanders and captains who would be his course mates was frightening, but that was fourteen days away, and meanwhile, he had Sarah to himself. He reached across under the table and held her hand gently. She squeezed it and they began to clear up with some haste. Her mother gave a groan and rolled over. Warwick wished that dear old Doctor Williams had doubled the dose of paraldehyde; she could sleep for the whole fortnight as far as he was concerned.

He went upstairs, undressed, and showered. Feeling slightly shy, he put on his clean and ironed pyjamas in the bathroom and went into the big bedroom where Sarah was already lying back in bed, naked. She had left his light on and switched off her own.

"Take those bloody things off, for a start," she commanded. "Where do you think you are, back at prep school?"

He quickly took off his pyjamas and dropped them the floor, then climbed into his side of the bed. It was a warm night, and they only had a thin sheet to cover them. He turned off the bedside light and snuggled up to her. He felt strangely reticent. He had been away for months and without female company in his bed (or outside it, for that matter). Somehow he, like most married sailors, had developed an attitude that excluded females and their company while they were away from home. It actually amounted to a mild and temporary aversion to the other sex.

Sarah promptly took charge of the operation. She well understood the man she had married by now, and she certainly shared neither his shyness nor any trace of an aversion to him. He was kissed, caressed, fondled, and generally aroused until he entered into the spirit of the first night of his return from duty. They made love for a long time and very satisfactorily, and then lay back in each other's perspiration, content and happy. They were both tired, but still wanted to talk to each other. They were friends as well as lovers; the unvarying recipe for a successful marriage.

There was a gurgling noise from downstairs, and the sound of a cistern flushing.

"Damn it, that's mother being sick!" whispered Sarah.

"Do you think you ought to go down to her? She's only on a blanket on a hard, stone floor. There's a camp bed somewhere we could rig up for her."

Warwick switched on the bedside light, got out of their bed, put on his pyjamas again, together with a dressing gown, and went off to find the camp bed. Sarah went down to her mother, who was very subdued and sleepy and could hardly talk with her swollen and sore tongue. She was very hung-over from the effects of the gin and paraldehyde. Mercifully, she had managed to vomit into the lavatory basin. They erected the camp bed in the passage and made it up. Sarah took her mother upstairs, stripped her unresisting body naked and showered with her to prevent her collapsing in the shower cubicle. She dried her off and put one of her nightgowns on her. They tucked her in with a bucket by the head of the bed. Sarah dropped all her mother's clothes in the wicker ali-baba for the wash the following day.

"She's in a pretty bad way, love," said Warwick as they went back upstairs to bed.

"The doctor said that she wouldn't live long if she goes on like she has been. It's strange, I haven't seen her for twenty years and then she turns up at our wedding. How the hell did she find out about that? It was only decided a week or so before. Then she writes to me right out of the blue. I mean, she comes over as hostile and vicious, but maybe subconsciously she knows she's reached the end of the road, and she's crying for help, although she'd never admit it."

"We'll see how she is in the morning, but if Southampton General will take her for observation, I'm all for it. I'm already fed up with all the alcohol being locked up. I could have done with a stiff gin or three myself tonight!" He rolled over on his back. He was dog tired and it was nearly midnight. He needed sleep.

Just then, Sarah's questing hand made gentle contact with his lower stomach, and began to creep slowly but inexorably south.

CHAPTER TWENTY-ONE

The following morning they awoke early. Thumps and movements from downstairs together with the flushing of the cistern told them that Mary had woken up and gone to the lavatory. Warwick showered and dressed while Sarah went down to tend to her mother. After about a quarter of an hour, she came back to the bedroom.

"I've called Doctor Williams, darling. He'll be here in half an hour. She's really poorly; I think she's running a temperature. She's burning up and she's sweated right through two pillow covers and the under sheet into the mattress. And she's much more yellow this morning; the jaundice seems to have got worse."

"Where have you put her?" Warwick asked.

"She is in the drawing room in a chair with a blanket over her and the bucket at her side. As soon as I've dressed, I'll get her dressed. I've got some sweaters and old skirts in the big clothes press that will just about fit her. Her own clothes are really only for the bonfire, although in these days of clothes coupons and rationing, I suppose I'd better wash and iron them."

Doctor Williams arrived with the District Nurse just as Warwick was finishing repairing the cooker electrics. The two of them went into the drawing room and the doctor examined Mrs. Johnson with the nurse present. They came out of the lounge to talk to Sarah and Warwick, who were waiting in the study.

"It doesn't look good," was his initial verdict. "I'm not exactly sure about all of what's wrong with her, but the jaundice is much worse and the whites of her eyes are very yellow this morning.

Her stomach is much distended and she has a lot of little red raised spots with small red blood vessels radiating out from them; what we call spider naevi. She's covered in big bruises from last night's fracas, more so than one might normally expect. These are all well-known indicators and I'd guess her liver is packing up. I suspect she has developed cirrhosis of the liver caused by her years of excessive alcohol consumption. If I'm correct, then the condition is irreversible. I've rung Southampton General and they will take her in. They'll keep her under observation to confirm the diagnosis. My view is that she's pretty bad and won't live that long. With no more booze and palliative care, she might make a few more years; if she ever takes to the gin again, you can make that months, not years."

"How much of this does she realise?" asked Warwick.

"She probably knows she's very sick and maybe terminally so. I'm a country GP, not a psychologist, but if you want my opinion, that why she's made contact with her only daughter again after all this time. Her performance yesterday was more due to the alcohol and a bout of delirium tremens than any hostile feelings she has for you two. As I understand it, she has no other living relative; no one else in the world to turn to."

They packed a case of clothes, nightdresses, toiletries, and a couple of books for her and she went off in Doctor Williams' car with the District Nurse to the hospital. At that stage of the war, ambulances for civilians were seldom available.

Sarah promised her mother that she's look in the following evening. The two women hugged each other and parted tearfully. As the doctor's car disappeared down the drive, Warwick and Sarah embraced, kissed, and both of them brightened up at the prospect of being alone at last. Alone that is, apart from two painters, the jobbing gardener, and Sarah's captive electrical contractor, who was doggedly working his way around re-wiring the house, room by room.

"Alone at last! We've got thirteen days together, and then three months with me home here most nights. All we've got to do is drop in on your mother for an hour or so every couple of days."

"They may only keep her there for a week," said Sarah gloomily.

"They'll keep her in longer than that. She won't be fit to come home for a while yet."

The day passed happily. They started with a big cooked breakfast in the kitchen. Then Sarah showed him all she had had done to West Lodge while he had been away. They toured the stabling and outbuildings.

The upper spaces could easily be turned into a flat for Mary Johnson. It only needed decorating, wiring, and furnishing, and a few studwork partitions and doorways. There was a working gardeners' lavatory and washroom with hot and cold running water downstairs. It wouldn't be difficult to fit out a bathroom upstairs using the existing water supply and drains.

Warwick offered to drive into Portsmouth and get a simple bathroom suite in white while Sarah rang her builder to arrange for the conversion work to begin. Warwick rang Lieutenant Jones at the refit department of the dockyard and learned that there would be a big consignment of the torn out American wiring plus fuse and junction boxes available for him to collect the following Friday. He rang his father and asked if he could manage to get one of his friends in Southern Transport Command to commandeer a two-ton Army truck to drive to West Lodge, pick up the release papers and dock pass, drive to Portsmouth Naval Dockyard, see Lieutenant Jones, and collect the electrical arisings.

This his father promised to arrange, saying it would cost Warwick a fiver for the transport base sergeant and the driver, cash on delivery. They talked for a while about Warwick's exploits since the wedding. Warwick didn't mention the scene with Sarah's mother the previous night, but did say that she was sick and in hospital. His father told him that he was being transferred to Scotland to take charge of the Army transport there for a new and secret operation, details of which he could not disclose over the telephone. He was also to be promoted to his peacetime Territorial Army rank of acting-major. Warwick congratulated him, forbearing to mention that his father was now his equal in rank; lieutenant-commander being the naval equivalent of an army major.

He rang his mother and promised they would both visit her in a couple of days. Petrol coupons were not easy to get and he needed more. The big Packard might look like an American version of a Rolls-Royce, but its V12 engine just drank up petrol. And so the day passed. They went out to dinner at another pub in the vicinity, the Bold Forrester, where the conjunction of the shiny, big, black car and Sarah in her sheer white blouse and split pencil skirt with high heels caused the bar to fall silent as they came in. They soon made friends with the locals, however, and had game stew for dinner with a bottle of wine between them. They were safe in bed by eleven.

In the next few days, they drove over to see Warwick's mother, Edith, started the conversion work in the stable and had the wiring and boxes from the dockyard collected and delivered. Edith Hursey was pleased to see them both and made them very welcome. Warwick's feat in towing in the stern part of *HMS Vindex* had been featured in the *Daily Telegraph* and she told them of how proud it had made her to read it. She hadn't realised he was the captain of an aircraft carrier.

Warwick forbore to mention that it was a small escort carrier on a ferry trip, and not the *Ark Royal*. Sister Sally had taken her finals at the medical school and was awaiting results. She was thinking of joining the Royal Navy if she qualified, as a surgeon sub-lieutenant. They spent a very happy afternoon in Sussex, and Warwick even managed to scrounge some more petrol coupons. Edith didn't drive and Frank was only home to use the Rover at irregular intervals, so the coupons he was issued with as a serving officer tended to accumulate.

One evening, they drove to Southampton to see Mary Johnson in her ward in the General Hospital. This was a much less happy visit. Mary Johnson seemed to have shrivelled up in the few days she had been there. She was very yellow, and looked like an old Chinese peasant woman with her sallow, wrinkled skin, her bloodshot, yellowed eyes, and a blanket around her shoulders. The staff nurse told them that she hardly ate anything. She apparently had a real problem with digestion. Her tongue had healed up, though still slightly swollen, but the bruises on her body remained very evident. She was reticent and depressed.

They had bought her some plums and flowers from the garden and they did their best to cheer her up, to little effect. In contrast to her violent and strident activity on the night Warwick came home, she seemed wrapped in self-contemplation.

Afterward they spoke privately to the senior registrar of the female general ward. "Her liver is failing rapidly and there's little we can do about it. Doctor Williams was right; she is far gone in alcoholic cirrhosis of the liver and it has virtually ceased to function. If we could have got hold of her a couple of years back, there might just have been just enough unscarred liver tissue left to support life; that is if she took it easy and didn't touch any alcoholic drinks, but not now. The thing with cirrhosis is that the patient doesn't really notice much is wrong until it's too late. Mrs. Hursey, I am afraid you'll have to face up to the fact that your mother is dying."

"How long do you think she's got?" asked Sarah.

"I'd say between a fortnight and a month, although it's very difficult to predict these things accurately. Some pop off overnight, and some go into a sort of suspended animation for months, even a year or two."

They drove home that evening, both rather depressed.

"She said something about her old tin box," said Sarah. "She seemed most anxious that we find it and sort out its contents."

"What sort of contents would they be, do you think?"

"Oh, I suppose her old jewellery and souvenirs and the like. I don't think she's got anything of real value or she wouldn't be living like a pauper now."

When they got home, they opened Mary's other suitcase, and sure enough, there among the raggedy old clothes and shoes, was a stout, black, tin document box, somewhat larger than the average office petty cash container.

"Did she mention where the key was?" asked Warwick.

"Yes, she said to look in the pockets of her brown coat."

They pulled out the coat, felt in the pockets, and there was the key. It took only a moment to open the box. It was full of yellowing, old but important-looking legal papers. Warwick picked up the one on top and began to read it. It was brief and to the point.

This is the last will and testament of Mary Sara Johnson of 31 Claymore Street, Cheltenham, in the county of Gloucestershire.

Now this deed witnesseth that I, Mary Sara Johnson [formerly Walker, nee Harmon] do hereby bequest and bequeath all my worldly goods and possessions to my only daughter, Sarah Ann Walker.

In the event of the said Sarah Ann Walker predeceasing me, then to her issue living at the time of my death, in equal shares on trust. If she has no living issue at the time of my death, then to her legally married spouse.

In default of the possibility of performance of these bequests, I leave my entire residual fortune to the society or organisation known as Alcoholics Anonymous in the hope that they may continue and expand their good works

Signed: Mary Johnson, this day, the third of May 1940.

It was witnessed by two signatures and sealed. There was the name of a solicitor with an address in Cheltenham on the cover of the document.

"What the hell did she go to the expense of a solicitor to draw that up?" asked Sarah. "She's only got the clothes on her back to leave me, although it's a nice thought that she actually wanted to give me something to remember her by."

Warwick was looking through the rest of the yellowing documents.

"Wait a minute, look at this lot! Here, a certificate for three thousand one-pound ordinary shares in Williams and Glynn's Bank in her name. And here, four thousand, five hundred pounds of two percent British Government Stock to be redeemed in June 1953 at par. And this one; five thousand United States of America, five percent running redemption stock of par value of one US dollar; and there's more, much more. There's a bloody fortune in this box!"

"Holy shit! said Sarah, sitting down suddenly, her face going white. "Where on earth did she get all that stuff from? She rented a grotty little flat in the poor part of town, and spent what money she had on booze and cigarettes, so far as I knew. She looked like a tramp when she was here. I had to pay off the taxi from the station because she didn't have any money on her at all. I don't understand it."

Warwick was still going through the papers. He picked up the daily newspaper and turned to the City section. With a pencil and pad, he began to match the securities in the box with the current prices shown in the paper. He worked steadily and methodically in a large, neat hand; it was the way he worked when he calculated the position lines from his astronomical observations at sea. He carried on in silence, with Sarah looking on, incredulous, over his shoulder. The tabulation grew longer. Finally, he listed the last certificate, then placed them all carefully back in the box, locked it, and put the key in his pocket. Then he added up the values. The total came to forty-two thousand pounds. They both stared at his calculations in disbelief.

"I seem to have married an heiress," said Warwick, "I never expected that when I proposed to you, although I knew you were comfortably off. We're a bloody long way from the boarding house in Newcastle, fitting out the old *Freshwater Bay*, aren't we, darling?"

"Steady, my love; she isn't dead yet. She could still change her will. She's more or less of sound mind out there in the ward."

"She wouldn't have wanted us to see what's in her special box if she was going to leave it to someone else. Anyway, there isn't anyone else; you're all she's got."

"So what do we do now, my love?" asked Sarah.

"I'll ring her solicitor tomorrow to talk things over and put him in the picture. Then we'll go into the hospital and have a chat with her. At least we ought to show our gratitude and do everything we can for her while she's still alive. One way and another, she's had a crappy life; a lot of it was her own fault, but it's nearly over now and she can't re-live it. All we can do is make her last days as happy and comfortable as we can. I expect the hospital will eventually want to discharge her into our care. They need all the beds they've got in wartime and they can't do much more for her. We'll get her rooms prepared and do up a couple of extra bedrooms as well, out there over the workshop and stables. We'll employ two or three temporary, live-in nurses to look after her. It will be expensive, but it's the least we can do."

They went to bed, talked the matter over for an hour or so, made love, and then both of them fidgeted for another hour. They were much too excited to sleep. So they made love again, and finally, somewhere around two in the morning, they fell asleep in each other's arms. All was now peaceful in West Lodge. A hint of Chanel No. 5 mingling mingled with the cool night air that drifted into their bedroom through the open window.

Warwick rang Mary's Cheltenham solicitor the following morning while Sarah instructed the builders to leave the work on the main house for a while and concentrate on fitting out the upper rooms of the stable block and outbuildings. The solicitor was a little guarded but confirmed that he had drawn up Mary Johnson's will in 1940 and that its contents were as Warwick represented them to him. He also added that there was a deposit account in Mary's name with the local National Provincial Bank which had a considerable balance in it, being the automatic repository of all the interest and dividends from all the bonds and stock that she held. Apparently she seldom if ever drew on this account, having another with the same bank into which her pension and some other small income was paid, and on which she lived.

That evening, they visited Mary in the hospital. If anything, she had deteriorated in the intervening twenty-four hours, and looked very shrunken and shrivelled up.

"I'm afraid that her deterioration has been most marked," the staff nurse confided to them in the passage, out of earshot. "I can't see her lasting the week at this rate. She won't eat or drink much. She seems to have lost the power to digest anything."

They sat by her bedside. She was awake and alert, but at first rather uncommunicative. They talked about the box and its contents, and Sarah thanked her for bequeathing everything to her.

At this Mary began to open up. "You're wondering where it all came from. Well, it was always yours and not mine, and I've only drawn from it once or twice when I was really desperate, with the bloody bailiffs at the door and no food in the flat."

"Why was it always mine and where did it come from, Mother, please? We really need to know with you so ill."

"It was your father, Graham. He was a brilliant engineer and they made a real bloody cock-up when they sacked him. He kept that firm together and it went downhill as soon as he left. He used to have a little workshop down the bottom of the garden and go down there in the evening after he came home, working on his pet projects."

She slumped back on the pillow and shut her eyes as if to sleep.

"Go on, Mother," said Sarah, a little impatiently.

"I'm just too tired now; really, girl," she sighed, licked her lips with her purple tongue, wiped the crusty foam off her mouth with a cloth, and then continued in a low monotone. "Anyway, he had dozens of lenses and prisms, binoculars and contraptions on his work bench. I wondered if he went down there late to spy on the newly married couple next door, but he didn't. I tackled him about that and he showed me his prototype that he said would make us rich. He was right, although I didn't believe a word of it at the time. What a load of bullshit, I thought. It turned out to be a pair of ordinary binoculars with a magnetic compass on the top fixed so's their reading would show up in the eyepieces. He said all the armies and navies in the world would buy them in hundreds."

"You could identify a far off object like a lighthouse or an enemy gun emplacement and take a bearing of it at the same time," remarked Warwick. "That was a very valuable invention of your late husband's, Mrs. Johnson. I've been at sea all my working life and I'd really love to have a pair of those binoculars with a fitted compass on my bridge."

She lay back with her eyes shut. They waited patiently. After a few moments, she opened her eyes again and resumed her story. Her voice was quite weak now. "He spent most of our savings taking out patents in England and in the States. Then they made him redundant. He'd been there at that factory for thirty years and had come up from a young apprentice to be the production manager."

"I know all about that, mother. I was about twelve at the time; it must have been late in 1920."

"Yes, yes; don't interrupt me now I've started. It's not easy talking; my tongue's still all swollen up for a start, thanks to your husband. Well, he left everything to me; not that there was much to leave, just our little house and a mortgage, really. About two years later, I got a letter from a German firm. They wanted a licence to use his invention as an addition to their range of binoculars. It was before I'd met Fred Johnson; I was on my own and bloody hard up. I spoke to a Mr. Pearson who I found in the phone book. He was a solicitor in Cheltenham. He drew up a licensing agreement with the German optical company. They paid me about fifteen shillings for each one they sold. In the first year they sold seventeen hundred. I paid off the mortgage with their cheque, and Fred Johnson moved in and we got married a few months after."

"Surely we ought to have these things here in England now," said Warwick with some asperity. "I mean, there's your late husband's invention available to the enemy, and we can't get hold of them for our own Army and Navy."

Mary Johnson stopped talking, and coughed up some greenish phlegm into the cloth. She breathed heavily and wheezed as she did so, but she was determined to finish the story of her late husband's invention and her hidden riches. "Mr. Pearson's advised me to buy government stock and shares. I paid all the cash into a special bank account.

"That's absolutely amazing, mother," said Sarah, "but why do you keep saying it was always mine? You were married to my father, and he left everything he had to you. You could have had a comfortable life all these past years. You could have bought a decent house, travelled Europe, and stayed in smart continental hotels. You could have had a real life!"

"That was your dad, love; you were his only daughter. Before he died, he made me promise that all the money his invention made would go to you. I may have been mostly pissed and a bit out of it for twenty years, and I wasn't the best of mothers, but I promised, and I've kept my bloody promise since, whatever else, apart from that first payment. Shit, I feel awful; I'm so very tired."

"Just one more thing, Mum," said Sarah, "Where's the money coming from now? Surely not from a German company."

"No, that packed up in September 1939. They are paying my money into a Swiss bank account. Maybe you'll be able to access that when the war's over. I won't be there to see it, but Mr. Pearson has all the details."

She was obviously completely exhausted. Warwick and Sarah left her and discussed everything Mary had told them while they were on their way home in the car. They were both surprised at the change in her over the last three days. While her body had lost the drunken power it had shown when Warwick first returned and had shrunk back with the increasing onset of her liver degeneration, her brain, freed of the drug of alcohol for the first time in some years, had regained the intelligence of her earlier days. With the absence of her daily bottle of gin, her DTs no longer manifested and she slept soundly at night. Equally surprisingly, she did not seem to crave either alcohol or cigarettes nor did she try to get the staff to smuggle them in for her.

"They don't think she's got long to live," said Sarah. "It's a great shame; if she'd been like she is now we could have lived happily together at West Lodge for years, provided she lasted that long."

"We don't know that she'll die that quickly," said Warwick. "Even the doctor said that such things are notoriously unpredictable. I think we ought to continue fitting out her accommodation in the outbuildings. Even if she dies, they will be an asset. A house that size needs some provision for staff accommodation when the war is over."

Warwick's leave passed all too quickly. They spent a few days with Warwick's mother and Major Frank Hursey, who was home prior to his new appointment in Scotland. He confided in Warwick the secret information that he was in charge of organising the British end of the transport logistics for the forthcoming Operation Torch, the combined American and British invasion of North Africa.

"We might yet be together, dad," said Warwick. "Vice-Admiral Christie told me that I would be involved with Torch when we got into Portsmouth a week or so back, but he wouldn't tell me exactly what I was being lined up for. He's sending me on the Senior Officers' Command Course the week after next. Apart from me, there's no one on it under the rank of full commander, so he must have something pretty big in mind."

When they got back and went to the hospital, it was obvious that Mary Johnson was nearing the end of her life. The short period of intelligent animation she had shown when she spoke of her first husband's engineering genius and the huge amounts of money it had provided for his daughter had passed and she lay in her bed, shrivelled and mute, with her dull, yellow tinged eyes glazed and uninterested in her visitors. Sarah held her hand and talked to her for hours, telling her about her own life over the past twenty years and of Warwick's exploits during the war. She hardly responded, though she did appear to understand some of what Sarah was telling her.

Mary Johnson died peacefully in her hospital bed on May 21, 1942. Sarah arranged a quiet funeral in their village church a week later. It was a warm, sunny day, with the smells of the countryside blowing in from the south-west as the vicar read the service over the fresh grave. She was buried under the shade of the ancient churchyard trees. Sarah thought it was a peaceful place for her mother to end up after a life that had been anything but peaceful.

Sarah, Warwick, and Mr. Pearson, her solicitor who had driven up from Cheltenham were the only mourners. Sarah did wonder if the egregious Fred Johnson would show up, but there was no sign of him. He seemed to have completely disappeared, which was no loss to anyone, she thought. For that matter, he might well be dead.

After the funeral, they went back to West Lodge to discuss the will and the arrangements to be made. Sarah liked Mr. Pearson; he was a short, stout, cheerful, Dickensian character in the mould of Mr. Pickwick, and in his early 60s. He went through the arrangements for the disposal of the estate with Sarah.

"Mary Johnson named you and me as the executors of her considerable estate," he began when they were all sitting around the dining room table with cakes, sandwiches, and sherry. "I will, of course, deal with the legal and professional matters. I am happy to take the bond and stock certificates back to my office and put them together with Mrs. Johnson's other papers in the safe. I have prepared a schedule of her assets, which I will leave with you. Her stocks and bonds add up to around £42,560 currently. I will need instructions on what to do with them. There are two accounts with the National Provincial Bank in Cheltenham, one with a credit balance of £8,649 6s 10d and the other with £13 4s 6d in it. The latter one was the one she used to live on. She lived in a flat with a short lease in the outskirts of Cheltenham; the lease will determine with her death. I can arrange to have her effects cleared out and sent to you and the landlord handed the keys back. There may be some minor dilapidations to settle, which will be a prior charge on the estate, as will the hospital and funeral costs. Otherwise, there are no liabilities apart from death duties; she paid all her bills by return. There will be a liability to death duty of approximately £9,400 and we shall have to realise some of her securities to settle that before probate can be granted. One other thing, she still owned the freehold of the house you grew up in, Mrs. Hursey. It's on a long lease to a family tenant at £35 3s a quarter. That and a small pension was what she lived on. I am not a valuer by profession, but I suppose it is worth about £750. After all that is taken into account, I calculate that the whole estate amounts to approximately £41,200 net of liabilities and death duty. The grant of probate should not take long, as you are the sole and undisputed beneficiary"

"Thank you so much for all your help, Mr. Pearson." Sarah was busy scribbling down the details, "I'll leave you to deal with the investments and pay off the death duty for the time being. When you can, I'll ask you to have the Cheltenham bank close the accounts and transfer the balances to our usual bank account with the Southampton branch of Westminster Bank. I'd be obliged if you would ask the tenant in the house to pay his rent into that account on quarter days, too. I'll jot down the details for you before you leave"

"There are a few other matters." Mr. Pearson was shuffling through the papers in his files. "I have been in touch with my agent in Switzerland. There is a considerable balance building up the private account in Mary Johnson's name in the Raiffeisenbank, Zurich. I'll let them know that Mrs. Johnson has died and instruct them to change the beneficiary of the funds held to yours. You can't touch it at present, but it will be available to you after the war is over, whoever wins. Steiner Optika GMBH has continued to honour their licence commitments and the war has brought them considerably increased business from the German military establishment."

"We'll leave that in abeyance for the time being, depending on how things turn out; what are the other things, please, Mr. Pearson?"

"First, there's a new licence I've negotiated with Wray Binoculars Limited, a British company from Bromley in Kent. They are about to go into production and will pay you the same licence fees as did the German firm, less some development costs which they will amortise over their first five years of their production. We need to make arrangements with them to ensure that they know that you are now the party owning the patents and that their royalties will be paid into your account in future. I will take care of those matters, if you like. Then there is the rangefinder. Your father drew up some preliminary designs for binoculars with a rangefinder attachment. He reasoned that it would be extremely advantageous if one could obtain both a range and bearing of an object by looking at it with a pair of binoculars. I don't think any prototype exists; his workshop was cleared out and sold off many years ago, but I have his drawings in my safe and this element may be patentable, as well; especially if it is combined with the existing units with the compass fitted."

"That would be a wonderful instrument for us to have on the bridge," said Warwick. "And just imagine how useful it would be for the Eighth Army in the desert. It could be a real winner!"

CHAPTER TWENTY-TWO

Warwick put on his best uniform, packed a ruler, pens, and paper in his briefcase, and drove to Southwick House, just over two miles from West Lodge. He arrived at 0845 for a nine a. m. start. The huge, black and sparkling clean Packard was very conspicuous parked among the cluster of well-used Morris Eights, Austin Tens, Hilman Minxes, and the odd, grey, service Humber. The sun was shining, and there was a group of about twelve captains and commanders talking outside the front door, all with the straight, gold stripes on their sleeves indicating they were from the regular Royal Navy.

Warwick, with his intertwined lieutenant-commander's stripes of the Royal Naval Reserve, stood out amongst them, and he found himself reddening when everyone turned round to look at him and sum up his presence there as he got out of his car, collected his briefcase, put on his cap, and walked up the broad stone steps toward them.

A momentary silence fell, broken by a stout and friendly commander who introduced himself. "You must be Warwick Hursey; we've all heard a lot about you! My name is Ken Mills, and I'm a submariner for my pains. Welcome to *HMS Dryad*."

"Pleased to meet you, sir," said Warwick with real gratitude in his voice. "I've only been in the Navy for nine months, so I've a lot of experience and learning to make up."

"News of your exploits has preceded you, Hursey. The official view, as I understand it, is that while most of us were driving a desk in a shore base or the Admiralty in London and boning up on our manuals of seamanship in our spare time, you have been out there finding out by trial and error – and not too much error, either."

"You're very kind, sir; it's been a case of having to cope with things that turn up, rather than careful planning and execution." Warwick noted the several medal ribbons on Commander Mills' left breast, including a DSO. He obviously hadn't been driving a desk all the time.

"Well, you seem to be coping pretty well, one way and another." A tall man with captain's stripes had joined them and several others had moved round him in a loose circle. Warwick realised he was something out of the ordinary, very young, and a junior Reserve officer who had been in the local news recently; they were interested in him and what he had done. There wasn't anyone else in the group younger than thirty-five.

The course started with a series of refresher modules to bring them up to date with gunnery, communications, fleetwork, and damage control. The others had done all this sort of training before as sub-lieutenants. Most of it was new to Warwick, but he was a man who learned quickly as his exploits over the past few months proved. They spent time at Whale Island, the Navy's gunnery school in Portsmouth, at the gunnery range at Eastoke manning a quick-firing Mark XVI, 4-inch gun, at the Navy's communications centre at *HMS Mercury* in the Portsdown Hills, and at *HMS Phoenix*, the damage control centre.

Warwick was put in charge of one of the teams at the latter establishment and came out well in the wash-up. He re-lived his time on the old *Freshwater Bay* and the gun action with the U-boat. His classmates were friendly and helpful. There was no question of rank impeding the close cooperation required from the teams formed to compete with each other during the various exercises.

The next element of the course concerned the considerations and knowledge required to command a big warship in wartime. Lessons learned in the first three years of the war were a major part of the syllabus. Some of the course members had been in command of a corvette, frigate, or destroyer at sometime during their careers, but all of them had spent lengthy periods ashore in the recent past. Most were destined for promotion; this was a course designed to fit them for offensive action at sea as captain of a large RN ship such as a cruiser, or in respect of the most senior course members, a battleship or an aircraft carrier. Warwick parted from the other course members for a couple of weeks, being sent down to a secret establishment in Poole where they had various American built landing craft tied up alongside their dock. He was not surprised at this as he knew that he was to be involved in the planned landings in North Africa for Operation Torch.

Apart from the fact that his father would be in charge of the operation's transport in Scotland, that was more or less all he knew of his future. He was led through the various types of landing craft in use and instructed on their armament, range, and capabilities. He went to sea in the little American Higgins boat on a rough day and landed on the beach at Swanage Bay, getting thoroughly wet in the process. He tried to imagine the landing with thirty-six troops embarked and under fire from the shore. It wasn't a pleasant prospect. Next he went afloat in a Tank Landing Ship, which was 158 feet long and displaced three thousand tons and could carry four big tanks (or in its infantry variant, two hundred troops) from Britain to Africa. On board that day there were some lieutenants and sub-lieutenants RNVR who were training as commanders or officers of these large landing craft. There were also a group of petty officers, stokers with diesel qualifications, and leading seamen.

None of them seemed to know about Operation Torch or indeed why they were being assigned to landing craft. Warwick kept his minimal knowledge of the operation to himself, remembering that it was still classified as secret, as well as the "need to know" principle.

They practiced navigation and pinpointing their assigned landing areas from small-scale charts. Then they manoeuvred the clumsy craft in the prevailing poor weather. It was gusting force six on the beam, with a short, steep sea breaking white over the windward side as they approached the shallows. They had partially to turn into the wind on the approach to maintain their bearing on the flag-marked landing spot on the beach, and then straighten the ungainly vessel up at the last moment, rather like a cross-wind landing in an aeroplane. It was quite an art, as Warwick discovered when he was put in command. They took turns at running the craft up the beach at Sandbanks, remembering to drop the stern anchor at the right moment on the run in and winching the craft off the beach with it after delivering her imaginary cargo of tanks over the forward ramp. If the stern anchor were to be forgotten in the stress of judging the approach, the LCT might be stranded for several hours on a falling tide under enemy fire. The instructors were all old and experienced SD officers and had many hours operating these landing craft on this particular beach in all weathers.

Back at Southwick House, Warwick rejoined the main course. They had finished teaching command considerations and techniques for captains of battleships and fleet aircraft carriers. Warwick knew he was unlikely to be asked to do those sorts of jobs in the near future but, uniquely among the course members, he was able to say that he had already been captain of an aircraft carrier in the North Atlantic. The course continued with lectures on discipline, leadership, seagoing surgery and medical practice, and staff work and support (for those senior members who might soon be promoted to commodore or rear-admiral). There was a top secret week of instruction on the latest developments in codes and ciphers, including those used by the enemy. Another top secret session took a few days during which they were brought up to date by hands-on demonstrations of the most recent developments in radar, asdic, Huff-Duff, and other electronic weapons. They were lectured in the latest Tactical Anti-Submarine (TAS) methods.

They went to sea for a day in a frigate and a new anti-submarine weapon called the Hedgehog was demonstrated. This machine threw twenty-four small, two-pound bombs up to two hundred and fifty yards forward of the frigate. They exploded on contact with the dived submarine ahead, which was nearly always destroyed. The usual last minute avoidance manoeuvres by the submarine while the frigate passed over it and before she fired her depth charges astern were thus rendered completely ineffectual.

Warwick drove the two miles home to spend the evenings with his wife every night he was free. In later years, long after the war was over, he looked back on the summer of 1942 as one of the happiest times of his life. The refurbishment of West Lodge, the conversion of the accommodation over the stables, and the rewiring were all completed. They went out together at the weekends to sales of bomb-damaged drapers' stock to look for curtain material, sheets, counterpanes, blankets, and pillows. Purchasing damaged stock did not require clothing coupons. They found furniture for the empty rooms and second-hand carpets and rugs in antique shops and week-end auction sales. They bought a 1936, open topped, two-seater Alvis from a local accountant, both for driving through the country lanes together in the evening sunshine as well as to cut down on the frightening petrol consumption of the Packard.

Warwick completed his refurbishment of the sailing boat he had found in the outbuildings, cleaned up the trailer that was with it, and took it down for the two of them to sail on the lake in the Forest of Bere.

With their new-found wealth, they employed a middle-aged couple, Mr. and Mrs. Alfrey from the village, who agreed to move into the accommodation over the stables that had originally been prepared for Mary Johnson. Bert Alfrey was a competent gardener/handyman and his wife Ethel cleaned the house and acted as cook when they entertained. They were placid, local, God-fearing people and Bert had a driving licence and so could collect provisions from the village and act as their occasional chauffeur.

Two nights a week, Warwick made a point of dining at the officers' mess at Southwick house. He learned a lot about his course mates that way, as well as enjoying a good dinner accompanied by wine, an advantage in times of shortages and stringent food rationing. Some nights when he was home, they drove the Alvis down to the village pub, to sample Giles' cooking, which was usually rabbit stew with local vegetables, varied with roast pheasant that had been hung in the larder for ten days or so or jugged hare. On other nights, they ate a dinner cooked by Mrs. Alfrey. They pooled their rations between the four of them and supplemented their larder with fairly regular supplies of off-ration milk, butter, cheese, eggs, and game not declared to the area food inspector and sold to them for cash by the local farmers.

For their first formal dinner party, they invited Robin King and Ken Mills and their wives. It was a great success and went on late into the night. The guests were very admiring of the house. They said they hadn't realised that the Hurseys lived in such style and made jokes about how much liner officers in the Merchant Navy must be paid as compared with commanders in the Royal Navy.

West Lodge was the ideal house for entertaining and Warwick and Sarah agreed that they'd do a lot more of it in the future, especially when the war was over and food and wine could be easily obtained.

Most nights when he was home, they made love before they went to sleep.

CHAPTER TWENTY-THREE

It was mid-morning on September 4, 1942. Warwick gazed thoughtfully over his left shoulder out of the square cabin window of the rather battered, camouflaged DC3. They had just taken off from *HMS Raven* (Southampton Airport, in peacetime) en route to *HMS Quebec*, the huge Naval Base on the shores of Loch Fyne. It was the first time he had ever flown in an aeroplane, and he found the novel experience exhilarating. He leafed through the folder on his lap, its buff cover stamped *TOP SECRET* in red with *Personal to Commander W. M. G. Hursey RNR* in bold print underneath it. It contained his provisional, personal orders for Operation Torch. He had been handed them by Robin King as soon as he had reported back to *HMS Victory* for duty three days before. Robin told him that he must read them through and fully understand them so that he could discuss them with the admiral that afternoon.

At 1430, he had had a short interview with Vice Admiral Christie in the latter's office. He learned that he was being promoted forthwith to Temporary Acting Commander Royal Naval Reserve (to revert to his previous rank at the conclusion of the specified operational duty). It was explained to him that as this was a combined operation with the USN. Certain British officers had to have at least the equivalent rank to US Army and Navy personnel that might fall under their command. Admiral Christie had been relaxed and affable for a Monday morning, especially with a multiplicity of damage and accident reports on his desk to deal with, as well as a very serious court-martial to hear as a member of the adjudication board the next day.

"From all reports, you did very well on the Senior Officers' Command Course, Hursey, and now you're going to have to put what you learned into practice. You're bound for *HMS Quebec* at Loch Fyne, centred on the town of Inveraray. As you probably know, this is our major base for beach landing training. In addition, the base deals with signals and the latest navigational aids to enable you to land your troops and cargo in the right place. It also trains stevedore and beach officers on stowage and unloading priorities. As an experienced Merchant Navy officer, your expertise will be valuable in that latter respect. You will take over command of *HMS Bruiser* from Lieutenant-Commander Parker, who is going to join the American General Eisenhower and the Torch planning team in London. *Bruiser* is a new and very large landing ship. She displaces three thousand tons and is four hundred feet long."

"I am very grateful for my promotion, sir," said Warwick, "but surely I don't need to be a commander to command a landing craft. After all, I did bring a much bigger escort carrier back from Boston a few months ago."

"Yes, indeed you did. However, *Bruiser* is not the limit of your responsibilities in this exercise. The current thinking is for you to be in charge of another fourteen large tank and infantry landing ships in the main convoy. Five of them will be British, and nine American.

"Your task unit will comprise approximately thirty two hundred men, forty light and medium tanks, and around a hundred and fifty other vehicles, all loaded with stores and ammunition. That's apart from the landing craft crews. Two of the British ships will be equipped with rocket launching racks to discourage the local Vichy French service personnel, some of whom are likely to oppose the landings; some certainly will, some may not. Enthusiasm for the Axis cause is by no means universal among the Vichy forces there. You will fly up from Southampton this Thursday with other officers posted to Inveraray and report to Commodore Thomas Troubridge."

The next day, he went to Gieves & Co on The Hard at Portsmouth and had his uniform and epaulettes altered. He brought his brass hat with scrambled egg on its brim out of the cupboard where it had lain since he left M/V *Freshwater Bay* months back, and put his RN cap badge on it in place of his Merchant Navy standard badge. Mr. and Mrs. Alfrey had been most impressed. Sarah said she would love him forever; even if he was only an ordinary seaman, but there was no doubt the additional gold braid impressed her, however much she pretended otherwise. She had an adoring and admiring look in her eyes and she laid out his clothes, cleaned his black shoes, cooked and served him little delicacies; in fact she did everything a wife could do for a much admired husband, with the possible exception of standing behind his chair while he ate his meals. All this attention from his wife made Warwick feel about seven feet tall.

His orders indicated that he would be assigned to the central invasion force, which would land at Oran. The two other fleets would land at Casablanca to the west and Algiers to the east. They would probably stop, refuel, and regroup in Gibraltar before the final push. The senior officer appointed for the Central Group invasion force was US Major-General Lloyd Fredendall. Eventually he would command thirty nine thousand troops. Warwick had already made some enquiries and had discovered he was a small man, rapidly promoted in the twenty-one months since America declared war on Japan, and had the reputation of being somewhat of a martinet with a very short fuse, could be rough and abusive, and was reputed to jump to conclusions without sufficient investigation of the facts. He also found out that Fredendall's father had been the sheriff of Laramie in Wyoming at some time in the past.

He read the specification of his new command. As the admiral had told him, she was four hundred feet long and had a very prominent crane aft of the single funnel for unloading smaller landing craft intended to carry personnel and stores from the supply and converted passenger ships to the beach. She could carry thirteen Churchill tanks, twenty-seven jeeps and armoured cars, and a hundred and ninety three men. Because *HMS Bruiser* had a deeper draft than smaller, flat-bottomed landing craft, she couldn't get very close in to the beach and was fitted with a hundred and forty foot long disembarking ramp forward that retracted into the hull while at sea. Warwick thought she was a very strange sort of ship, purpose built, of course, but strange nonetheless.

She would be fitted with additional quarters and communications equipment, and he would be assigned three specialist officers for his staff, including a USN lieutenant-commander who would act as his deputy. She was capable of sixteen knots, was twin screw, powered by geared turbines, and her sole armament were six double mountings of 20mm Oerlikon anti-aircraft guns dispersed around her deck.

The plane passed through a blackish cloud and raindrops showed on the cabin window. It began to get quite turbulent. Warwick felt a growing feeling of anxiety, but as senior officer on board felt he must give an impression of experience and unconcern. He could see the two RAF flight lieutenant pilots forward through the open cockpit door. They seemed calm and unruffled from his view of their backs. They were looking at a paper map spread out over their laps.

He wondered if there was a lavatory on board; he felt a sudden need for one, but decided he had to hold on. The more he thought of it, the more he wanted to go. He broke out in a sweat. In any case, they were all strapped in and the plane was still bucketing violently at times. Just then, the cloud cleared to reveal rain-swept landscape of heather-clad hills and valleys with little white cottages scattered here and there. The plane banked to port in a descending turn and the undercarriage was lowered with a thump. Stunted trees appeared in the window at the same height as the aircraft. There was a slight bump, a squeak of tyres on tarmac, and the DC3 had landed at an RAF airstrip twenty miles to the north of Inveraray.

There was a dark blue Bedford bus waiting for them with "RN" in white prominently marked on its side. The rain came down in sheets and Warwick wished he had kept his greatcoat out of his suitcase. When they took off from Southampton, it had been bright, summer sunshine. He got in the bus first and sat next to the driver. Three despondent looking aircraftsmen loaded the suitcases and bags into the back of the bus.

"*HMS Quebec*, please, driver," said Warwick.

The driver was a tall, laconic, rather lanky man about fifty, with a prominent Adams apple, a weather-beaten face, and several teeth missing. The sodden remnant of a hand-rolled cigarette was stuck to his upper lip where it bobbed up and down as he spoke. His black tweed coat gave off the smell of old perspiration, stale tobacco and, less prominently, wet, hairy dog.

"Och, skipper, there's nae auther place tae go, y'ken!"

The bus ground off at a steady twenty miles an hour through the rain. After about an hour, they arrived at the Loch Fyne Beach Road, known as "The Caronage" (as Warwick later discovered). There was a long, somewhat rusty steel pier with a small landing craft alongside it.

Warwick turned round and addressed his fellow passengers. "Gentlemen, I think we'll just sit here until our boat arrives. Meanwhile, I suggest we get some heavy weather gear on."

They collected their suitcases and took them into the bus to unpack, helped by the driver, who turned out to be more willing that Warwick had at first thought. Warwick put his bridge coat on, with his new commander's epaulettes on the shoulder. He pulled the collar up around his chin and put his hat on. The rain had eased a little and he could see the far side of the loch. There seemed to be a lot of activity there, with landing craft running up the beach and soldiers disembarking and digging in.

It was an opposed landing by the look of it; there was fire from the high ground beyond the beach and a twin engine RAF Blenheim flew over the landing craft, dropping simulated bombs that sprayed out yellow liquid on the invaders nearby. Out in the bay was anchored a converted passenger liner painted grey, which Warwick identified as the afloat element of *HMS Quebec*, the rest of the base being a very large area of tin-roofed huts and low brick buildings. There were several transports and many LSTs and LSIs at anchor.

Beyond *HMS Quebec* was the unmistakable silhouette of *HMS Bruiser*; he recognised her by her flush deck and the huge crane behind her funnel. After ten minutes, a small landing craft with a canvas cover over the well deck and driven by three able seaman in oilskins came alongside the pier.

They walked down to meet it. Warwick, being the senior officer, got in last. It was the custom, although, as he thought to himself, it left him longer in the rain.

They went alongside the companionway of *HMS Quebec*. Warwick was first out of the boat. He arrived at the main deck, saluted the colours aft, and enquired of Commodore Troubridge from the duty officer on the gangway. A rating was detailed to show him up to the commodore's quarters. He knocked on the door marked by a shiny brass plate "Commodore T. H. Troubridge RN" and waited.

After a few seconds, a voice behind the door shouted, "Come in, for Christ's sake!"

Warwick opened the door and went in as bidden. Commodore Troubridge was a tall, rangy man in his early forties, with a heap of papers covering his desk.

"Commander Hursey," he said, rising to shake Warwick's hand, "we've been expecting you. We need to have a little chat and then you can join your ship. I've asked Parker to remain in command there for a few days to give you a proper hand-over. She's a new design and not like a normal ship. Normal ships don't have hundred and forty foot extending ramps and don't normally go aground in the middle of an action, or at least not on purpose. I'll send a signal to *Bruiser* to tell them you're here and to send a boat after lunch for you and your gear. "

"Thank you, sir; good to meet you," said Warwick. "I understand you are in charge of the convoy for the central invasion force of Operation Torch."

"Well, I'm certainly in charge of the marine side of it. General Fredendall of the US Army is in charge of our whole operation. From some of the signals I've received from him already, I suspect we're both going to be very relieved when we've successfully landed him and his troops. He boasts that he doesn't suffer fools gladly, but from my short experience of him, he doesn't seem to suffer anyone much, gladly or otherwise. Anyway, you'll spend the next month or so training in beach landings, first singly and later with your flock of landing craft, including the American ones. We have beaches suitable for landing craft and invasion training all around the loch. We train up the soldiers who land at the same time. Currently, we have a great number of American Rangers here, together with the Sherwood Foresters and the Duke of Wellington's Regiment. The later exercises in their training are carried out with live rounds. We do suffer the odd fatality in those, I'm sorry to say; they're hushed up, of course. 'Died in the service of his King and Country.' That's the standard story. The War Ministry feels that a few lives lost here will mean a lot less of them lost in the landings, and I agree. Mind you, it's easier to say that if it's not you that's being shot at."

They chatted about minor matters and then went down to the wardroom for a drink and lunch. Warwick felt he could get on with his new boss, who seemed capable and practical. Even at this early stage, it was obvious that the operation would benefit by close cooperation between them, plus a lot of mutual respect.

CHAPTER TWENTY-FOUR

That afternoon, Warwick embarked on *HMS Bruiser's* Cheverton motor launch that had come to collect him, and joined his new command. The rain had stopped, although it was still overcast. He was greeted at the head of the gangway by a swirl of bos'n's pipes and Lieutenant-Commander Parker, who made it clear how very pleased he was to see him.

"Good to have you aboard, sir. I'm Frank Parker. I've been in command of this great vessel since she was launched in Belfast six months ago. The crew are all fully trained and operational. We all did the regulation month's work-up at Tobermory. They don't have beaches there; it's all rocks, so our main operational training is concentrated here where the whole of this loch is surrounded by gently sloping sandy beaches. I'm here until the end of the week and we have three days of beach landing exercises scheduled before then. You'll soon get the feel of it. She doesn't handle like a normal landing craft; she's much more ponderous and she grounds a very long way from the beach. We have ten Higgins Boats on deck to be offloaded by the crane; in calm conditions, that is."

They walked up to the officers' quarters discussing the ship and the forthcoming week. Frank had cleared his kit out of the captain's cabin and moved into the spare cabin at the end of the passageway. He explained that there were four additional officer's cabins on this particular ship, as she had been built as a command ship with provision for additional staff aboard. Warwick unpacked while they chatted.

"You're off to serve under General Eisenhower, I hear," Warwick wanted to pick Frank's brains on what he might expect.

"Yes, I'm supposed to be the beach landing expert. I have to advise Admiral Ramsey on landing points and the methods to be adopted to get the landing craft to them with some accuracy, even in the event of rough weather."

"Do you have any inside info on the current thinking at Torch HQ?"

"Not a lot. There are two units of landing craft in the central group scheduled to take Oran, and you're in charge of one of them. The other is an all-American show, albeit with British liaison officers. You'll have a couple of American liaison officers on here, a lieutenant-commander to understudy you and an Army second lieutenant. They haven't been appointed yet, but you can expect them to join in a couple of weeks. The whole thing takes off at the end of October for an early November and the landing east and west of Oran shortly thereafter. They may land emissaries by submarine to negotiate with the Vichy French admiral before the main event. If they are successful, the landings may be unopposed, but don't build your hopes on it. It does depend to a certain extent on the attitude of the Foreign Legion; there is a big garrison of them in Oran and they're a pretty hard-bitten bunch.

"Your boss, Tommy Troubridge, will get his own command ship shortly. Apparently they have taken over an old French passenger liner that they captured and renamed it *HMS Largs*. That'll be his flagship for the entire maritime operation. There's another armed merchant cruiser, *HMS Bulolo* which will be the army and USAF headquarters ship with the US Generals Fredenhall and Doolittle on board. Bearing in mind that there are to be simultaneous landings at Casablanca and Algiers, they say that all of this will be the biggest amphibious landing in history."

"It looks to me that, if this operation is a success, it could be a turning point in the war. It's obviously vital that it all goes well," said Warwick, "There's a huge American input in men and material, but to my mind they are all untried troops and if they run up against Rommel's Africa Corps before they've had a chance to acclimatise themselves, Lord help them!"

"By the way, you've an old shipmate as your specialist navigator, young David MacDonald. He boasts that he was with you in *HMS Striker* and in that old merchant ship *Freshwater Bay*. He's really good; he's developed into an expert landing place navigator."

Warwick was cheered to hear this. "What about the first lieutenant?"

"That's Bill Browne. He's a special duties lieutenant, promoted up from the ranks during the Great War. He's sixty and would normally be long retired. He's a bit sluggish but he was attached to the base at Inveraray for eighteen months and knows everything there is to be known about landing troops and equipment and landing craft, big and small."

They agreed that Warwick would officially take over command at the end of the week when Frank Parker was due to leave the ship.

The next few days passed quickly for Warwick. They landed troops of the Duke of Wellington's Regiment and American Rangers on Rosebank and Saint Catherine beaches opposite *HMS Quebec*, with the Sherwood Foresters opposing the landing. They launched their Higgins boats with the big crane and loaded them with thirty-six troops each. They ran out their hundred and forty foot ramp through the open bow doors to the shore. They pulled themselves off the beach with their stern anchors. They conned the ship in to its flag-marked landing site using only radar and plotting on a paper chart taped to the top of the DR plotting machine without looking through the wheelhouse or chartroom windows. They landed Matilda tanks, armoured cars, two-ton Bedford trucks, and jeeps. Their Higgins boats, with the ship's crew members acting as their cox'ns, went alongside an adjacent transport and embarked troops from it, then landed them on the beach. A couple of Hurricanes flew over the landing beaches towing targets and the ship's gun crews had a chance to test their skill with the Oerlikon anti-aircraft guns.

Their target shooting was less than impressive. As one of the Hurricane pilots remarked in the RAF mess later, "They should have been told we were towing those targets, not pushing the bloody things ahead of us!"

Every day the rain came down in sheets. As he gazed out of his cabin windows, Warwick could see it blowing in from the sea over the dull brown hills around the loch, in cold, wet waves. Warwick wondered why anyone would want to live here; after all, it was only early September and Sarah had written him a happy letter saying that she was still sunbathing on the lawn down in Hampshire. He sympathised with the troops as they waded ashore with eighty pounds of kit on their backs, through wet, soggy sand and on up the beach to the tussocks of rye grass at its edge, throwing themselves flat on their faces as the simulated machine gun fire raked their vicinity and the odd thunder flash went off near them.

The only leave they were offered was in the town of Inveraray two miles to the east of *HMS Quebec* at weekends. Its population of five hundred were mostly members of the local Wee-Free Church which had strong views on the sanctity of the Sabbath, and from around nine thirty p. m. on Saturday night until six on Monday morning, there was neither a door open nor a person on the rain-swept, cobbled streets. There were Wrens quartered somewhere nearby, but they were a pretty tough lot, and even if any of the lads did manage to get a date with one of the younger ones who didn't look too much like an Easter Island statue, there was really nowhere for him to take her.

Warwick knew they were well out of range of German bombers, and therefore safe from the enemy, but felt, nonetheless that they paid a high price for their safety. He discussed the matter with David MacDonald and Bill Browne over a pink gin in his cabin one night after Frank Parker had departed and he had assumed command.

"The lads must be bored out of their minds," he began. "They work bloody hard all week, and there's absolutely nothing for them at the weekend to do ashore. What do you think we could do to give them a bit of entertainment?"

"There's a rich Danish couple with two beautiful, unmarried daughters in the big house overlooking Castle Beach," offered David. "They normally only invite officers to dinner but they have a huge ballroom there and we might persuade them to lay on an all-ranks party for us if we devote some of the accumulated mess entertainment funds to it. I'm sure that some of the less gruesome of the Wrens could be persuaded to attend if they thought there was some free food and drink on offer and if we provided transport."

"That's a fine idea, David," said Warwick enthusiastically. "Let's go for it. Bill can sort out the mess funding. I'll get the Pusser to arrange for drink and food. I'm afraid it will have to be soft drinks or beer only. I don't want our crew getting into the gin or whisky. If you can approach the Danish parents, I can lay on transport; my father's in charge of the Army Transport Corps here north of the border and he's sure to have a bus or three to spare on a Saturday night. Tell me more about this Danish family, David. It's the first I've heard of them."

"Well, sir, the father told me that they fled from their castle in Odense near the German border in late 1939. They could see what was coming, apparently. He was a banker and managed to transfer his considerable funds to London. They wanted to get away from the war, so they leased the big house overlooking the point here to sit out the hostilities. That's their story, anyway."

"How very prescient of them. What are their names?" asked Warwick.

"The parents are called Heimlich and Anne Zeigler. The daughters are both about twenty. Their names are Monika and Brigitte. They are very beautiful, as only Danish girls can be. They live in Morag House on the peninsula opposite the town."

"They sound a bit Prussian to me. How do you know all this, young man?"

"One evening I was having a quiet drink in the local pub on the Caronage; you know, the one that closes at 2130 on a Saturday night, and this lovely girl with long blonde hair right down the middle of her back came in. She was a real breath of fresh air amongst all the smoke, spilt beer, drunken fishermen, hard case Wrens in sensible shoes and woollen stockings, and disgruntled soldiers in there. She turned out to be the elder daughter, Monika. We got talking and she invited me back to her home. She had a little car outside; I think it was a fairly new Morris 8, and she drove me back to their enormous house. I don't know where she got the fuel for it, but a girl that looks like that would always manage somehow if she lived near a big naval base. She'd only have to bat her eyes at some jerk in the transport pool to get a couple of gallons on the side. When we got to her home, they all made a great big fuss of me, especially when I let on that my father was an admiral based in Gibraltar."

"Strange," said Warwick thoughtfully. "They are either very patriotic for the Allied cause, or people we ought to be suspicious of. I think we'll warn anyone who knows anything about Operation Torch to keep their knowledge to themselves if we go ahead with the big Zeigler social. The thing is that everyone within ten miles knows that we are preparing for a huge invasion here; the real secret is where we're going to land and when it's scheduled to come off and that mustn't get out or we'll have half the German and Italian armies on the beach at Oran to greet us. The general opinion around here is that we are getting ready to invade the continent to relieve the pressure on Russia. If civilians start spouting on about their pet theory that we're going to land in France and open the second front in the Calais area, don't deny it; just leave them with that thought in their heads."

David was detailed as emissary to the Zeigler family. He seemed very happy to organise this particular crew jolly and

Warwick suspected that a factor in his enthusiasm was the prospect of seeing the lovely Monika again while on semi-official business.

He came back brimming with success. The family would welcome Commander Hursey, his officers, petty officers, and selected members of his crew to an evening of dancing at Morag House. It was arranged that the evening would commence at 1930 next Saturday night and end at 0100 the following morning. The house was sufficiently remote from the town to avoid upsetting any pious members of the Wee Free who might otherwise object to drinking and dancing in the early hours of the Sabbath. There was to be a dance band, table, decorations, cutlery, crockery, and glasses provided by the Zeiglers, and food, drink, barmen and waiters provided by the mess funds. Warwick rang the Wren Chief Officer and arranged that she and thirty of her young ladies would be present. He rang his father in Glasgow and fixed up three busses and drivers, one for the Wrens and two for the crew on a shuttle service for the evening.

After another few days of varied exercises and hard work, they anchored for the weekend in their assigned spot and went to relaxed routine. The party was due the following night. There was an air of anticipation on board. Warwick was sitting in the wardroom with his officers over a gin before dinner.

The PO Steward knocked at the door. "An American officer to see you, sir," he said, addressing Warwick.

"Thank you, Morton. I'll come now."

In the wardroom flat, fingering his cap rather nervously was a very smart, very large black man in his early twenties, in the light khaki uniform of an American Army second lieutenant.

"Sir, I'm Josiah Crowthorne from Lafayette, Louisiana. I've been assigned as the US Army liaison officer to this great ship. Am I addressing Commander Hursey, sir?" He spoke in a pleasant southern American drawl.

"You are indeed, Josiah. Welcome aboard. Do come and have a drink. Have you had dinner? If not, I'll get PO Morton to lay an extra place. Is it all right if we call you Jo?" So saying, Warwick led Lieutenant Crowthorne into the wardroom and introduced him to the officers there.

Jo Crowthorne was a success from the start. Under a certain amount of interrogation from round the table, he told of his childhood in Lafayette and the strict segregation practiced there in the 1920s and 30s. He had graduated from an all-black high school *cum laude* and managed to gain entry into one of the lesser known military academies in the north. He had come top of his graduating class. The US Army had accepted him as an officer cadet on the basis that they always took the top five graduates from that particular academy. Life in the Army for a black officer had not been easy at times, but he had made firm friends with many of his white classmates. He was a natural athlete and had played football for the US Army team as well as being their reserve heavyweight boxer. The latter achievement meant that those who sought to denigrate him because of his colour tended to do so with some caution. He had just been appointed to be Warwick's US Army liaison officer, which was considered a critical and important posting.

He was a handsome man with light coffee-brown skin. Warwick realised that he must have shown exceptional ability to have got where he was in the face of ingrained racial prejudice. Most US wardrooms and officers' messes still had no black faces sitting round their dining tables and no white faces cooking and serving them.

"There's a big ship's party tomorrow night in a manor house ashore, Jo, said Warwick. "Are you up for it?

"Sure am, sir! Nothing like a party to get to know you English folks."

"Well we're actually in Scotland, and our host and hostess are Danish, but it's a good start for someone whose business is in the field of liaising. Now, I'll get PO Morton to show you your cabin."

CHAPTER TWENTY-FIVE

It was a magic evening at Morag House. Saturday had been free of rain and toward the evening there was even a glimpse of the sun between long, red clouds before it set. The ballroom was set with tables for six or eight, with white damask cloths and gleaming cutlery, glasses, and crockery. There was a long buffet table and another on the far side dispensing drinks. Streamers and paper chains had been affixed to the ceiling above, looking suspiciously like resurrected Christmas decorations. There were bowls of flowers and the local dance band was on a raised dais in the corner of the room, the musicians sweating in their slightly grubby white tuxedoes and black bow ties. The tall French doors were open on to the lawn beyond.

The officers and sailors from HMS Bruiser were all in immaculate uniforms. They had had a lecture from their divisional officers on correct behaviour and strict silence on any aspect of their programme, exercises, and Operation Torch.

Heimlich Zeigler, their host, was a short man in his mid-forties with greying hair and thick glasses. He was in full evening dress with white tie. His wife, Anne, was an elegant and beautiful woman, a little taller and a few years younger than her husband, resplendent in a royal blue, full length ball gown. They made everyone very welcome and obviously meant it. Monika and Brigitte were just as beautiful as David had described them and stole the show from the start.

Even the Wrens, in their civilian evening finery and having taken pains with their meagre and hard-to-get store of cosmetics, had morphed into the attractive and healthy young women they actually were.

Bill Browne remarked *sotto voce* when they entered the room in a body, "My Lord, the bloody Wrens have certainly scrubbed up well tonight!" He then made a beeline for the second officer Wren in charge of them.

Warwick thought they made an ideal couple, although, remembering his boxing days, he felt Bill was giving a bit of weight away in this particular contest. Anyway, Bill had been a widower for ten years, so he could probably appreciate a large, warm, bossy Wren officer to keep him company in the long winter nights.

David MacDonald had asked Monika for the first dance. Warwick watched the handsome young navigator in his immaculate mess dress and the tall and lovely girl with the long, golden hair with him. They danced very close together. At twenty-seven he began to feel like an old man as he watched them. The chemistry between them was obvious, as was their body language. He wondered if he owed any responsibility to Rear Admiral MacDonald for David's romances, and decided they were out of his sphere of duties.

Meanwhile, there seemed to be another, less predictable, romance brewing. Jo Crowthorne and Brigitte, the younger daughter, were dancing together a lot and spending their down time talking quietly outside in the garden alone.

Warwick knew his duty in these circumstances and this time, it was a very pleasant one. He walked to Anne Zeigler and asked her for a dance. She danced very well, as he might have expected of a rich, Danish society lady who used to live in a castle, and might well do so again when the Germans had been driven out of Denmark. He had spent most of his career on large P&O passenger ships and had been well schooled in dancing and the social graces since he had been an apprentice.

After a while she began to talk to him seriously. "Warwick," she began, as they had got to first name terms by now, "can you please speak to my husband in private? He's very worried and he thinks that you might be able to help."

"I'll do all I can, I promise. I'm eternally grateful to you and your husband for laying this wonderful evening on for my ship's company, and if I can do anything in return, you can rest assured that I will."

They left the dance floor and went into a smaller room, which Warwick guessed was Heimlich's study. Anne Zeigler left the two men alone after pouring them each a glass of brandy.

"Cigar, commander?" asked Heimlich.

"No thank you; I've never smoked."

"Then I hope that you don't mind if I have one. They're hard to get these days and I do enjoy smoking one with a fine brandy from time to time."

He took a cigar from a cedar wood box, cut the end off, lit it, and took a couple of puffs.

"The problem is the Directorate of Naval Security, the old DNSY. They want to round the family up, separate us, move us out of Morag House, and intern us in the Isle of Mann as enemy aliens. They don't like us here overlooking the base and all the naval operations going on. I've tried to explain to them that we took the lease on this house in 1939 before the Inveraray base was set up, and we would hardly have done that had we intended to spy on something."

"But you are refugees from a friendly country that has been invaded. I can't believe that DNSY would want to intern you and your family."

"We do have some problems which you don't know about. My late mother was born in Germany, although, being Jewish, it is unlikely that she would have supported the Nazis. That makes me half German, although I am a Danish citizen and carry a Danish passport."

"I've never had much connection with DNSY, but I can't think that they would want to intern the whole family for that."

197

"That's not the end of it, I'm afraid. Anne was born in Kiel, just over the border. Her family didn't move to Denmark until she was eleven. For some years, she held both a German and a Danish passport, although she didn't renew her German one when the old one expired four years ago."

"Well she's Danish now," said Warwick, "and you both fled the country because you didn't want to live under the Nazi yoke, leaving your castle and possessions, so I don't see what the fuss is about."

"I'm afraid that's still not all. My son Karl applied and obtained German citizenship in 1936 when he was aged twenty-two. He attended the Nazi Party Nurnberg Rally that year. There were lines of storm troopers all in identical uniform, Speer's temple of light around the rally created by searchlights elevated to ninety degrees, the forests of swastika banners, and above all, Herr Hitler, who spoke to the massed party members dramatically and at some length. Karl was completely won over. He joined the Waffen SS as a Storm Trooper. He's currently a Haupsturmfuher attached to General von Paulus's Sixth Army, which is about to capture Stalingrad and secure the German line on the banks of the River Volga."

"Damn it; that's not so good," said Warwick with a worried look. "Have you had any contact with him while you've been here?"

"We didn't hear from him from September 1939 when England declared war on Germany until he wrote a couple of weeks ago. He knew I had substantial interests in London and that Anne and I were both anglophiles. Then Anne got a letter from him addressed here. It had been opened and re-sealed in an official HMSO envelope, with a note from the censor. It told her what he was and where he was serving and said that the action was not going as fast as had been expected and that the Russians were putting up a suicidal resistance, but he expected Stalingrad to be in the Sixth Army's hands in a few weeks. He said that the Third Reich would conquer the world and that we were fools to look to England for sanctuary and protection. He said that England was finished. That letter started all this trouble with the DNSY."

"I'm not sure what I can do to help, but I'll try. I'll speak to the Inveraray Base Security Officer and to my boss, Commodore Troubridge, to seek some advice. I will also ask David MacDonald to talk to his father, Rear Admiral MacDonald, whom I understand is back in the UK at the moment. David seems to be very attracted to your daughter, Monika, so he'll be very keen to assist. Leave it to me, Heimlich; I'm sure I can get something going on this."

"Thank you so much, Commander Hursey; my wife and I are so grateful for your support."

Warwick went back to the ballroom where the party was in full swing. David and Monika seemed to have disappeared. Jo and Brigitte were sitting together holding hands. They made a pleasing contrast; the big, handsome black officer in his smart dress uniform, and the beautiful, slim blond girl in her satin evening dress. From the looks they were exchanging, the relationship had progressed somewhat.

"My God," said Warwick to himself. "I'm going to have two lovesick officers instead of one when we finally depart for Operation Torch."

The party ended about 0200 and the buses took the officers and crew back to the pier and the Wrens to the Wrennery. One of the Higgins boats *HMS Bruiser* carried had been launched and was running a shuttle service to and from the ship. Everyone had behaved well in Morag House; some of the sailors were pretty tipsy, but they had all managed to thank their host and hostess and get on to the bus without falling over. The Wrens had turned out to be good fun especially with their 2/O engaged in coping with Bill Browne. There had been some couples visiting the shrubbery and the little garden gazebo, but Warwick, again feeling like an elderly but indulgent parent, thought that boys would be boys and girls would be girls. Some relationships had been established, and everyone had had a fine time. They deserved it, when he thought about it, bearing in mind all the work they had put in so far as well as the action that was to follow. Almost certainly the young men would suffer casualties; some would not come back. He felt they deserved their fun that night.

The following morning, it being Sunday, Warwick and David went ashore to the Inveraray Base to attend divine service. After it was over, they called in on the base officers' mess and were directed to Captain Marc Andrew-Jones KC, RNR, the head of legal services and Judge Advocate for the No. 1 Combined Training Centre, Inveraray. They outlined the Zeigler family dilemma and asked him for his advice. He had been a well-known and wealthy commercial barrister before the war, as well as a reserve officer. He was in his early sixties and had the world-weary air of a man who had seen everything in his life, so that nothing more could surprise him.

"You're a young man, Commander Hursey, and fairly new to the area. Please don't think I haven't heard all about this matter already. The Zeiglers are in no danger of being deported or interned as enemy agents. They were visited about three weeks ago by some junior functionary from DNSY Glasgow when the letter from their SS son on the Eastern Front was received at the censor's office. He actually delivered it to them and was instructed to find out what it was all about. They weren't very forthcoming, so he wrote an adverse report and recommended further investigation. After all, it isn't every day that anyone from our local social circle gets an affectionate letter from a rabid Nazi SS captain currently engaged in besieging Stalingrad."

"Thank you, sir; I fancied as much," said Warwick respectfully. "What ought I to tell them at this stage? I did promise them last night that I would try and do something to help."

"By all means tell them that they can stay in Morag House until the lease runs out, so long as they keep paying the rent.

I have already told DNSY Glasgow that we will take care of it with our base security staff, and I'll send someone up to talk to them during the week. There is one thing we would like them to do, however, and you could ask them if they would, if you like."

"Anything I can do to help, sir," said Warwick.

"Well, could you ask them to write back to their son Karl. Just an anodyne letter saying that they are all well and have a lovely house in Scotland and the weather's awful, and that they don't agree with his views, and feel that the Allies have right on their side and will prevail in the end. That sort of stuff. Nothing about what's going on in the loch just below their front windows, of course. Tell them to address it to his SS unit in the Sixth Army, Stalingrad, but not to seal the envelope. We have ways of getting the letter to him via the Swedish Embassy."

"We'll go up to Morag House after lunch and sort this matter out once and for all, sir, and thank you so much for all the help and reassurance."

"Any time; you only have to ask. We're here to serve and all that," replied Captain Andrew-Jones, wearily handing his glass to a passing mess waiter in a white coat for a refill.

"May I come with you to help break the good news, sir?" said David when they were alone.

"Do not think for one instant that I don't know why you want to come with me to Morag House, young man," said Warwick with feeling.

He commandeered a staff car and a driver from the transport pool for the short drive. Anne Zeigler answered the door. Warwick assumed it was the maid's day off, unless they had a butler. The whole family assembled in the study. David slowly sidled close to Monika and held her hand surreptitiously. Warwick watched them out of the corner of his eye with a similar world-weary and knowing air to that of Captain Andrew-Jones.

"I've had a long chat with the Judge Advocate, Captain Andrew-Jones, who's an eminent Kings Council in civilian life. He assures me that there is no danger of your being deported or interned. He says that so far as the government is concerned, you can live here as long as you can pay the rent. He's sending someone up to see you one day next week to tell you all this officially, but he was happy that David and I come this afternoon to give you the good news."

Monika gazed up into David's eyes with a look of pure admiration. Obviously she thought that he had personally arranged the family's reprieve. Warwick sighed deeply; he supposed it was too much to hope that she might credit him with any input to the happy tidings.

"We couldn't be more relieved and grateful for your efforts on our behalf, commander," said Heimlich. "I can't thank you enough!" It was quite clear that the family had managed to convince themselves that they were in imminent danger of being separated and moved to huts inside a stockade on the Isle of Mann. "Will you have a celebratory drink with us? We have a jug of Pimms Gin Sling made up if you gentlemen would join us on the lawn."

The weather was quite pleasant for a change, with a light, warm breeze blowing off the loch and puffy little cumulous clouds which kept well clear of the sun. They sat under a big cedar tree on teak benches and chairs with the jug of Pimms on the table with six polished glasses. David kept close up to Monika. Brigitte sat on one side of him, Anne on the other. Warwick wished he had invited Jo Crowthorne to come with them, but it was too late now.

"You could do the Royal Navy some service; some service that is apart from hosting delightful parties for us, for which many thanks. I'll be writing officially to thank you on behalf of *HMS Bruiser's* ship's company, but it was a really lovely evening and we're all most grateful."

"What can we do?" asked Heimlich. "We would do anything to help win this war. Don't forget that we have a home and most of our treasured possessions in Odense. It is probably being used by the occupying force as a Gestapo headquarters by now."

"They want you to write back to your son Karl. Just talk about how good it is to be in Scotland. How bad the weather is, how you don't agree with him concerning Hitler and feel that the Allies will eventually prevail. How the girls are growing up and that you two are both keeping well and have settled in. Write nothing that would give any information to the enemy such as what goes on here with all the transports, soldiers, and landing craft out in the loch of course. Address the envelope to Waffen SS Haupsturmfuher Karl Zeigler, Reich Sixth Army, Stalingrad. Don't seal the envelope. The man from base security will collect your letter next week when he comes to see you. They have ways to get the letter to him through a neutral embassy."

"We'll write the letter tonight, but why would that help?"

"Well, when he gets your letter, he will know you received his and with luck he will write to you again. It is possible that he will tell you something that might constitute useful information which the censor will pick up. In his last letter, for instance, he told us that they were having a much tougher time taking Stalingrad than they thought they would and that the Russians were resisting in what he described as a suicidal matter. Nearly a month has gone by since then and the Germans have not yet taken the entire city. This is a vital battle; huge forces are involved. The outcome of the war might be materially changed if the Nazis are repulsed on the Volga."

They chatted on together happily and Warwick left in the staff car in an hour. David elected to remain behind. He said that Monika would drive him back that evening. Warwick turned his mind to the plans for more intensive training for the following week. They would have a fleet of LCTs and LCIs to control, as well as the ship.

CHAPTER TWENTY-SIX

When Warwick got back to the ship that evening, there was a letter from Sarah marked 'URGENT' awaiting him, having been delivered from the base that afternoon. He opened it and read it through quickly and then again much more carefully as he realised what he was reading.

My Darling,

'I hope that you will be as happy as I am when you hear that I am about seven or eight weeks pregnant. I saw Doctor Williams this morning and he confirmed it. He examined me a few days ago and now feels that all appears to be going well, although thirty-four is a little old to have a first baby. He called me an elderly prima gravida, which sounds like someone in an old peoples' home for the bewildered. I never thought that I would become pregnant. We've talked about this before; as you know I have some kind of growth or blockage in my fallopian tubes which I always understood would prevent pregnancy and until now it always has. The thought of becoming a mother is a new one for me, but I am so happy for both of us. We will be a real little family now. I will be able to tell him or her all about his famous father's brave seagoing exploits long after this wretched war is over.

Otherwise, things go on as usual here. The weather remains fine and I think we are going to have a real Indian summer. Bert and Edith Alfrey are real treasures and both of them come in to the kitchen to keep me company in the evenings. I have written to the Wray Optical Company and they are very interested in developing the binoculars with the compass and rangefinder attachment, which dad designed before he died. They have spoken to the Ministry of Defence who asked for samples as soon as they are available. They have placed a preliminary order for one thousand units of the compass binoculars which are just going into production. I have asked Mr. Pearson to draw up an agreement with Wray's for the rangefinder attachment. They will have to pay the development costs this time, so the new royalty will be a bit less as there isn't a prototype for them to work from.

I only have to say before I close that I love and miss you so much, my darling. Please write to me as soon as you receive this and tell me you are as happy as I am that we've got a baby on the way.

Your loving wife,
XXX Sarah
West Lodge, 14 September 1942'

Warwick put the letter down on the desk and sat back in his chair to think about it. He had never really considered himself as likely to be a father the foreseeable future, although, paradoxically he had always assumed that in the natural course of events, he probably would marry and have children at some time or other. He hadn't thought much beyond that. Merchant Navy officers tended to marry late in those days, being unable to afford a wife and family before they were promoted to master or at least were senior chief officers on the big passenger ships.

He pondered on this new and novel prospect. What sort of world were they bringing a little child into? Did he want a child to grow up under the Nazi heel? Hitler controlled the continent of Europe and most of the Mediterranean as well as large parts of Russia and the war in Asia was going from one brave retreat to another. Yet Hitler was at war on the most populous and powerful countries in the world, America, Russia, and the British Empire. In addition his occupying troops were suffering from extensive sabotage from partisans behind their extended lines of supply. Germany only had the remote assistance of Japan, and the rather dubious alliance with Italy, with reluctant troops from Hungary and Romania to guard the flanks. General Montgomery had just taken over the Eighth Army in North Africa, where his predecessor, General Auchinleck had held Rommel at el Alamein, seventy miles from Alexandria that summer. The Russians had managed to stop the German Sixth Army at Stalingrad in the middle of their summer offensive. The Americans were pouring men and material into England, and they were planning a huge invasion of enemy controlled territory. Surely the Allies must prevail eventually.

Well, it was settled now, regardless of the war situation and potential outcomes. Sarah was going to have a baby and was delighted by the thought. He supposed it was a feminine thing. She was fulfilling her natural instincts and functions as a woman, and was now busy gathering twigs to make up a nest. He knew his duty in spite of only being married for six months. He'd must write an affectionate letter back to her without delay and tell her that he was overjoyed and loved her even more. So he did, and marked the letter 'URGENT' and gave it to the quartermaster to send on the evening picket boat. Then he got back to his plans for his joint exercise with the American landing craft attached to his command.

The following morning, they ran the ship up the Cambrai Beach, near *HMS Quebec's* shore establishment, extended the ramp, and proceeded to embark several hundred US troops from the First Engineer Amphibious Brigade commanded by Colonel James Wolfe, together with ten additional landing craft all of which were American and crewed by USN personnel. They had arrived from Norfolk, Virginia, over the weekend.

While the troops, plus some light tanks and jeeps, were being loaded, Warwick held a meeting aboard *HMS Bruiser* with the ten USN lieutenants in command of the landing craft, Jo Crowthorne and a Major Brightman at the back of the room representing Colonel Wolfe. The US troops had undergone some training in amphibious landings in Chesapeake Bay before they had been shipped to Scotland and they knew the basic drill. The Navy had participated in these training exercises, and the landing craft commanders present had brought their vessels successfully across the Atlantic to Scotland, but Warwick doubted they had done many opposed actual landings of troops and equipment in adverse weather conditions, and using live ammunition.

He commenced his briefing. "Gentlemen, my name is Warwick Hursey and I am in overall command Task Unit One which will consist of this ship and fifteen landing craft and is assigned to General Fredendall. We are one of two such task units, which together with supply ships and escorts will comprise the invasion fleet for one of the three sites chosen for Operation Torch. Five more British landing craft will join us later in the week to make up the total of sixteen ships in this task unit. Now I'd like to introduce US Army Lieutenant Jo Crowthorne, my staff liaison officer."

There was a stir on the right of the group from a couple of the older USN lieutenants seated there. Warwick thought he heard a muttered, "Where's he from, the briar patch?" but decided to ignore it. He hoped Jo hadn't heard anything and felt somewhat embarrassed nonetheless. This wasn't going to be quite as easy as he'd hoped.

"Gentlemen," he persevered, "there's a list circulating. Please put your name and the name or number of the ship you command. Also the name of your first lieutenant, in case of casualties, please. Now I need to know how much training in opposed beach landing each of you has had."

"More than you have, I'll bet, buddy!" This time it was unmistakable and came from the beefy, red-faced American Navy lieutenant on the far right.

"Could you introduce yourself please, lieutenant?" Warwick felt his temper rising. Who on earth was this redneck? He coloured, but continued to speak in an even tone.

"I'm Jerry Collins from Memphis, Tennessee, and proud of it!"

"Very well, Lieutenant Collins. I'm going to adjourn this meeting for a few minutes. I'd like to talk to you and your friend next to you who seems to be of like mind, with Major Brightman in my cabin next door. I'll arrange for tea and coffee to be served early in the interim and apologise for the delay." So saying, he gathered up his papers, put on his cap, beckoned Jo to accompany him, and walked from the room. He was followed by a buzz of interested chatter.

He asked Major Brightman in first, leaving the two USN lieutenants waiting rather awkwardly outside. "This behaviour is going to be a big problem if it's going to continue, major. We have a USN lieutenant-commander joining my staff at the end of the week to act as my deputy, but at the moment I need help with Anglo-American relations. We seem to have a couple of reluctant allies here, who have brought their racial prejudices over the pond with them as well. The USA appointed Jo Crowthorne as my liaison officer with the US Army in their wisdom and he seems a thoroughly competent man. It's neither his fault nor mine that he's black. He's only been with us for a few days, but he's very popular aboard this ship, I can tell you. If I can accept him as a staff officer, surely those two outside can, too."

"I'd get them in here now, sir, if I was you," said Major Brightman, "and I'll back you up if necessary, although you don't look as if you need too much assistance. There's a USN Captain Osmond who's just arrived at the base. If you have much trouble, you can hand these guys over to him to sort out. General Eisenhower is very keen that we all get along well and the behaviour of those two is a disgrace, in my book. They're both reservists. Lord knows where the Navy found them; some local hick boat outfit probably."

"Not Captain John Osmond who used to be in Washington in the Engineering Contracts Department? I know him. He's a good man."

"The very one, sir; he's been sent over here to take charge of the logistics of the invasion fleet in cooperation with the local base staff."

Warwick invited the two lieutenants in. Collins made as if to sit down in Warwick's easy chair.

"Stand to attention, Lieutenant Collins!" shouted Warwick.

Collins and his partner jumped at his shout and came to attention instinctively. They both realised rather belatedly that Warwick was not only their senior officer, but big and angry and not to be messed about.

"That's better," said Warwick in an even tone with an edge to it. "Now I've a few things to make clear to you two, especially Collins, before we continue with the general briefing. First, you have been placed under my command by the US Navy. Second, my deputy, who is a US Navy lieutenant-commander, will be joining this week. Third, I have your fitness reports in front of me here. If there is any further disgraceful and insubordinate behaviour on your parts, I will ensure it is recorded in writing, and Captain John Osmond USN is informed. He is a personal friend of mine and is currently the senior American Naval officer at this base, having just been appointed here. He has the power to relieve you of your commands and send you both back to the States. Are these points quite clear to you?"

"Now look, Commander . . ." began Jerry Collins, his posture relaxing into a slouch. His companion remained mute and at attention. Warwick thought that he'd managed to get through to one of them, anyway. He also noticed a faint smell of spirits had crept into the room.

"You address me as 'Sir'," snapped Warwick, "and that is the last time I will overlook that particular infraction. And stand up straight to attention. Surely you can manage to stand up for five minutes, or do you have some medical problem?"

Collins snapped to attention.

"You can leave now, you two, but don't think for one moment I'm not going to be watching you during these exercises. Dismiss!"

The two of them left the room. Just as Collins was about to go out through the door, Warwick called after him. "And another thing, Lieutenant Collins!"

Collins half turned back and froze in that position.

"Don't even think of taking the mickey out Lieutenant Crowthorne behind his back just because he's one of the few black officers in the US Army. He had to travel a lot harder road than you did to get there, believe me."

The briefing resumed. Warwick formed the impression that the majority of the young lieutenants were fully in support of his stand, with two, possibly three still somewhat sullen. He noted their names and the numbers of their landing craft down on the pad in front of him. After a friendly if slightly hesitant discussion, they dismissed and returned to their ships, walking along the beach where they were lined up. Warwick formed the impression that the experience of most of these young men had been limited to induction courses as reserve midshipmen, a month or so at sea, and then beaching their craft in the relatively sheltered waters of Chesapeake Bay, one at a time. Collins and his friend were full lieutenants and in their early thirties. They must have had some seagoing experience before the war.

The rest were junior-grade lieutenants, the equivalent to a sub-lieutenant in the RN. Still, they had managed to get their ships across the Atlantic, although they had been convoyed and escorted, which would have taken care of any navigational uncertainties. Warwick wondered how they would fare landing real troops and equipment, especially when they had to do it in the open sea beyond the loch, and their assigned landing beaches were being strafed by aircraft and entrenched defenders.

CHAPTER TWENTY-SEVEN

The fleet came off the beach at 1400 and spent the rest of the afternoon practicing beaching and fleetwork signals, taking it in turns to land their troops, guns, jeeps, and tanks, then re-embark them and pull off the sand with the stern anchors. They secured at 1930 and proceeded back to their designated anchorages for the night. After they had secured, Warwick sat in the wardroom over a glass of pink gin with Bill Browne and told him of the morning's problems with Jerry Collins and his like-minded friend, whom he had subsequently discovered was called Lieutenant Alan Royle.

While they were talking, they were joined by Lieutenant-Commander Fredrick Harden USN, who had just boarded, having flown in from Boston Navy Yard via Gander and Shannon, and who was appointed to be Warwick's senior staff officer and deputy for the operation. Fred Harden was a shortish, heavily-built man with a perennial smile on his face. He was a couple of years older than Warwick. His service record had arrived aboard before he had, and it indicated that he had come in the top ten in his class in Annapolis and had previously been the chief navigating officer of the battleship *USS Tennessee*. He was obviously a high flyer and had been picked for this job. He accepted a gin and tonic, helped himself to a few more lumps of ice, and sat down to chat. Warwick described the morning's briefing and the problems he had had with the two senior American landing craft commanders over their acceptance of himself as their superior, and their attitude to Jo Crowthorne.

"I've had some time on the flight to look though the service records of the US personnel assigned to us," Frederick Harden started to explain, "and Collins and Royle stick out like a couple of sore thumbs. The rest of them are conscripted reservists, selected for officer training and put in command of LSTs a little too early. All the hot shots want appointments to destroyers, cruisers, or aircraft carriers. Before this huge operation, landing craft were not seen as very glamorous nor much of a career path. They had to take what they could get, experienced or not. The US Navy has expanded to about ten times its peacetime numbers in just a few months. Collins and Royal are different from the others. They were fishermen in the Gulf and old acquaintances. They joined the USNR in 1935 and did their annual compulsory training in the off season for shrimping. It paid them a retainer when they wouldn't have been earning anything, which was important in the thirties with houses to pay for and families to bring up and educate. They are fine seamen, but undisciplined and slovenly, and they have the usual southern prejudices about blacks. I don't suppose they realised there were any black officers in the US Navy before they saw Jo Crowthorne in a second lieutenant's uniform. Lord knows, they're rare enough in our service."

"The problem is, Fred that these youngsters are impressionable and I don't want those two rednecks influencing them too much. We have four British landing craft joining us tonight, including an old tanker, *HMS Mohican*, which has been fitted with a bow ramp and converted to carry vehicles and light tanks in her holds. The young RNR and RNVR sub-lieutenants aboard will be as inexperienced and as easily influenced as the American ones. Two rotten apples can spoil the whole barrel. One of them smelled of bourbon or something similar. It was only eleven in the morning. I didn't think you had liquor on USN vessels."

"Leave it to me, sir," said Fred Harden confidently. "I'll keep close up to those two characters. I might do a bit of an inspection on their vessels to give them something to worry about."

They had a day at anchor the following day. All landing craft personnel were required ashore in the *HMS Quebec* shore base for lectures on the various aspects of the operation, especially inter-service cooperation as well as a standard operating procedure for both navies to follow. The two of them took the opportunity to settle down with Bill Browne and David MacDonald and work out a training programme for the next month. They agreed that Fred would ride with one of the US landing craft for three days per week to observe their performance in the exercises and general smartness and discipline. At the same time, he could keep an eye on Collins and Royle. On the other two days, Warwick would leave Fred to run the exercise as overall commander while he did the same within each of the English vessels in the task unit. The actual training planned consisted of unopposed and opposed landings around the various beaches of the loch, fleetwork, blind pilotage exercises combined with shoreside lectures and paper exercises. Most of the time, the rain fell in sheets and the warm, wet wind blew from the south-west.

As the days passed, they all learned how to handle their ungainly craft and some of the tricks of this new trade, such as that it was advisable to ease the landing craft off the beach every few minutes by taking up on their stern anchors on a falling tide. There was a ten-foot range of tide at the mouth of the loch at springs and one or two landing craft spent an uncomfortable eight hours high and dry in consequence of neglecting to haul off in time, with their soldiers still embarked, cold, wet, and grumbling.

Jack Watson, who had been with Warwick in *HMS Striker* and now a lieutenant RNVR, joined them as watchkeeping and gunnery officer. *Quite like old times,* thought Warwick. *At least I've a team I can trust.*

In spite of the pressures of training and the fact that it was only a month before they sailed for the Mediterranean, Saturdays and Sundays were usually spent either at anchor or alongside the pier in company with several other LSTs of Warwick's little fleet. When he had spare time, Warwick would go up to Morag House for dinner on Saturday night, or for Sunday lunch and an afternoon with the Zeiglers. Sometimes he took Fred Harden with him, and once John Osmond came to dinner there. Not surprisingly, both David MacDonald and Jo Crowthorne were much more regular visitors. Their romances with the Zeigler daughters seemed to be progressing well so far as he could see.

I suppose they are only young once, thought Warwick, sounding to himself like a seventy-year-old. *Besides, they will be in a real action in a month or so and if our landing is opposed they may not ever come back.* He gave no thought to the prospect of his own safety; somehow he had always assumed he was indestructible, even though he realised that he was as vulnerable to enemy fire as anyone else.

Anne Ziegler took him aside one rainy Sunday afternoon in early October. "What do you know of young David MacDonald, Warwick?" she asked.

"Why, what's the matter? I hope there haven't been any problems. He's a very capable and kind young man and he comes from a good family."

"He proposed to Monika last night when they were out in the little car together. They had been to the local picture house, and the main feature finishes around nine-thirty. They went for a drive up in the hills to look over the lights of the town, and the ships at anchor in the loch. One thing apparently led to another, and now she wants to marry him. He asked Hiemlich for her hand. He promised an answer by tonight. They both seem so young."

"Well, David is twenty-three and Monika twenty-one so far as I know. People do get married young in wartime. I suppose they realise how transient life is nowadays. When you think of it, their lives are the most precious thing that they have. They make a lovely couple and I'm all for it. I'll give you David's mother's phone number in case you want to talk to her; his father is still in Gibraltar and may be hard to reach."

"You're a great comfort, Warwick, "and a great friend of this family. I think we ought to welcome David into it without further delay. He does know about Karl being in the SS, doesn't he?"

"Yes, remember, he was with me when I spoke to the chief legal eagle at the base. Have you heard anything further from him after you wrote back?"

"That's still a constant nightmare for us. We think of him all the time. I sit in the bedroom looking at the photographs of him when he was a baby and then a little boy in his school uniform. He was a beautiful child; golden curls and very intelligent. He did so well at his school work. I know that we are on different sides in this war, but he's still our son. We wrote back as the naval security people asked us to and a few days ago we got a reply. He's still attached to General Paulus's staff in Stalingrad. He sounded a lot less confident than he had been. He said that the town had been reduced to rubble by bombing, but they were bogged down and not making much progress in finishing off the job. He said that the losses in German troops were horrendous. They are all worried at headquarters that their flanks are exposed to a counter-attack and that they might be cut off. The Russians are holed up in every ruined building and every cellar. They are being reinforced by boat across the Volga each night. He doesn't feel that Berlin fully realises what is going on. With the autumn rains and the mud, they are getting short of supplies. We're both worried about him; it's such a long way away, especially with the Russian winter coming on."

"I know how worried you must be, but I don't have an answer to this one, Anne. The only comfort I can give you is that the information in Karl's letter is likely to have been most valuable to our security and intelligence services. I'm sure it's very hard to get reliable, first-hand information from the German perspective out of the Eastern Front. How did the letter get to you from there, anyway?"

"They told us to tell him to write to us care of the Swedish Embassy. Apparently a lot of the Red Cross mail goes through neutral embassies. At the moment, I don't suppose they're too fussy about censoring mail from Stalingrad. The security people have asked us to write back, so they must think it's useful. I just wish we could get him out of there."

"Let's just be happy that your daughter has found herself a fine young man, Anne. Now I want to ask you and Heimlich a very special favour."

"You know we'd be only too glad to do anything for you, Warwick; what is it you want, please?"

"I want to get my wife Sarah up here for ten days or so. We've only been married for a few months and she's just written to say that she's pregnant with our first child. At the moment, she's stuck in a great big house in a lonely part of Hampshire. It'll be the last chance we have to be together before we take off. I wondered if she could stay here for a few days. We've got plenty of money; her mother left her a fortune recently. She can easily pay her way and she'll bring some spare food and her ration book. We might be able to lay our hands on some spare petrol coupons, as well."

"Warwick, you know we'd love to have Sarah to stay with us. Ration and petrol coupons are always very welcome; we might even be able to get the big car out again on a Sunday, but we don't need any money. You've done so much for us."

They went out into the big drawing room to chat with Heimlich about Monika and David, as well as Sarah's impending visit. The young couple were out again in the little black Morris for the afternoon.

Warwick explained that David's father, Admiral MacDonald, had virtually handed over his son to him to train and look after, to almost act as a surrogate father, and as a result, Warwick had developed a deep affection for David and was always solicitous of his welfare. The MacDonalds were not wealthy people, but they had brought up their two sons carefully and educated them well. David was an excellent officer and a highly skilled navigator. He had a brilliant career ahead of him in the Navy if he survived the war. When Warwick mentioned survival, they all fell a little silent, each with their own thoughts about the prospect of David and other fine young men from both sides dying or being seriously injured before the war was eventually over. Warwick remembered John Evered, another young man of much the same age as David who hadn't made it and whose remains now rested under the shade of the mountain pines overlooking the Straits in the cemetery in Gibraltar.

Monika and David came back at around six that Sunday evening. They left the little car at the bottom of the stone steps that led up to the front door of Morag House. They were both somewhat apprehensive as they saw their welcoming party of Anne, Heimlich, and Warwick awaiting them at the top of the broad flight of steps. They climbed up the steps, full of anxious anticipation. The tension was soon broken, however.

"David," started Anne, "we've been talking about you two with Commander Hursey and we agree that you two should get engaged. Your boss said some very nice things about you!"

"Thank you, sir; thank you, Anne; thank you, Heimlich," David gasped out all in a rush. "I can't tell you how happy that makes us both. I know we're pretty young by your standards, but we're very much in love!"

Monika burst into tears and buried her head in David's chest with her beautiful, long, blond hair hanging straight down her back. Her shoulders heaved and David put a protective arm around her. Warwick, all of twenty-seven and a half, felt like a satisfied father watching the two of them; they were so obviously happy that they radiated joy to the elders standing around them. He felt a warm glow throughout his body and even a slight prickling in his eyes.

Dammit! he thought to himself, *the last time I cried, I was a new cadet on the Worcester when I was thirteen, and that was when I was alone, in my hammock, in the dark.* He drew himself to his full six foot and three inches and cleared his throat noisily.

David and Warwick stayed on for an impromptu celebratory dinner that night and shared a glass or three of twenty-year-old champagne that Heimlich had managed to store away in his cellar. Monika drove them back to the shore base where, after a seemingly interminable period trying to get the local Sunday night operator to put him through long distance to Hampshire. He was finally connected to Sarah at West Lodge. He told her to pack and take a train up to Glasgow as soon as she could get away. If she telegraphed the details of the London to Glasgow express she was catching, he'd have her met by a staff car and pick her up off the pier at Inveraray.

Sarah thought that she could make a start the next day. He finished the phone call having told Sarah that he was overjoyed he was going to see her before they left for the big operation and that he had missed her very much. She was happy and excited at the prospect. He had the feeling that life was good at the moment; David and Monika engaged, and Sarah coming up to stay for a couple of weeks. A good ship and good officers and crew, and his little unit was beginning to perform much better. He could go on board and sleep soundly tonight. He walked back out into the main hall where David was waiting for him.

He was met there by a large, red-faced regulating chief petty officer. "Are you Commander Hursey, sir?" he began.

Warwick said that he was.

"There's been a most unfortunate incident with one of the American crews under your command, sir. Apparently you have a black US Army officer on your staff. He was in a cafe with a local girl who he's been going out with. She comes from the big house on the peninsula, I understand. Some American sailors took exception to him being there with his blonde girlfriend and allegedly tried to manhandle him out of the premises."

"Oh lord, that's all I need!" Warwick exclaimed with rising anger. "Do you know what ship the Americans were off, chief?"

It was LST167, sir," said the chief.

"That's Lieutenant Collins's landing craft, sir," interjected David who had been standing nearby listening.

"That's not the end of it, sir," continued the chief. "There was a bunch of trawlermen in there at the time, and they took offence to what the American sailors were trying to do. There're hard men, sir; older and tougher than the Yanks, man for man. There was quite a fight until my regulating staff and the local police broke it up."

"What's the current situation chief?" asked Warwick, his feelings of contentment and bonhomie evaporating rapidly.

"We've got three US sailors in hospital under guard with cuts, abrasions, cracked ribs, and one with a fractured femur, sir. There are two Americans and two fishermen in the local gaol. The black lieutenant had some stitches in his forehead but was discharged to his ship about an hour ago. The young lady suffered a crushed hand when someone trod on it. They've x-rayed it and plastered it up. She'll be kept in hospital overnight. We've got an American Lieutenant-Commander Harden off your ship in charge of the situation at the moment, together with a Lieutenant Collins, who is the captain of LST167 as I understand it, sir."

"Thanks chief," said Warwick, "I'll just scribble a note to Lieutenant-Commander Harden, who's on my staff. Would you please be so kind as to see he gets it? Then I'm going back to my ship to check on Lieutenant Crowthorne, who's the black officer. David, can you get a lift out to the hospital and see how Brigitte is? You can ring her parents and tell them the story if she hasn't done so already."

"What a rotten thing to happen on our engagement night," remarked David mournfully.

"It's a rotten thing to happen on any night, David." said Warwick with feeling.

He went straight to Jo Crowthorne's cabin when he got aboard. Jo was sitting up in bed. He had a big, grey bruise on his right cheek and a plaster over his discoloured and puffy left eye. He was reading a detective story in a Penguin paperback.

"What a heap of absolute shit, Jo; I've just come from speaking to the Master at Arms at the shore base. David's gone out there to look after Brigitte, and Fred Harden has arrived to take charge of the US navy element of the problem now. He's been joined by that little prejudiced arsehole Jerry Collins, whose crew caused all the trouble in the first place."

"They're from the deep South on that ship, sir. They're all a bit like that down there. It's the home of the Ku Klux Klan. There's quite a few of them around. I wouldn't be allowed to sit at the counter of a milk bar next to them where they come from, even if I was in my officers' uniform and just back from combat." He talked with a slightly muffled voice as if he had a small ball tucked in the side of his mouth. Warwick realised that his jaw was swollen and probably painful.

"Jo, I am so sorry. I really am. I wouldn't have had this happen to you for the world. I'll speak to Fred when he comes back. I don't think we can court martial them for striking a superior officer here, because both you and they are Americans and I don't think we have the legal right to weigh them off. I'll speak to Captain Andrew-Jones, who's the Naval Judge Advocate for the area to get the legal situation clarified, but I anticipate that we can return the miscreants to the States to be dishonourably discharged, or whatever they want to do with them there."

"I don't really bear a grudge, sir," said Jo quietly. "It's just that it makes my job as liaison officer that much more difficult. Then there's Brigitte; I felt that I was there to protect her and I failed and now she's in hospital."

"Not many men would take you on, Jo, man to man. I'd trust you to look after my daughter if I had one. You're big and strong, but even you can't defend your young lady against a whole crew. Anyway, according to what the chief told me, the local fishermen gave them a jolly good hiding!" Warwick thought to lighten the atmosphere. "By the way, the good news is that not only is my wife coming up to stay with Heimlich and Anne and the girls, but also David and Monika got officially engaged tonight."

Jo put down his book and turned toward Warwick who was sitting in the tubular metal chair by his bunk. He looked sad and upset with his lopsided, bruised face. "Brigitte and I have discussed getting married, too, sir. We are as in love and as close as David and Monika are. But we decided that it would be impossible. I could never go home after the war, married to a blonde white girl. The Klan spirit is alive and well down there, and I'd probably get lynched or something."

"Well, you could live together here, or even in Denmark when the Huns have finally been cleared out of Odense."

"I might be able to, but what would I do? All my life I've struggled and lived with abuse and insults just to get to be a regular commissioned officer in the US Army. I've set my heart on being a senior officer. I'm not going to achieve that if I settle here or in Denmark. All I ever dreamed of was a good career, some respect from being a combat officer in this war and not stuck back in an office in the States. I thought I'd marry a pretty black girl who'd had a university education and who was a lawyer or something. I hoped I'd retire as a major or perhaps a lieutenant-colonel in New England where they don't worry so much about colour anyway."

"Don't give up too soon, Jo. Attitudes change over time; otherwise you'd be working on a plantation instead of being an officer and gentleman in the biggest army in the free world. Brigitte's a lovely girl and the Zieglers are a fine family to marry into. They like you and they've got money and position. Maybe you could end up as a general in the Danish Army, you never know."

"You're kidding me, sir," said Jo, looking a bit more cheerful nonetheless.

"Yes and no. I think that you and Brigitte should stick together and see what transpires. You're both young and the future is all yours. 'Don't give up the ship!' as one of your more famous sailor forebears once said."

CHAPTER TWENTY-EIGHT

The following day was a shoreside lecture and training day with the fleet remaining at anchor. Warwick made an appointment with Captain Andrew-Jones QC and he and Fred Harden were ushered into his office.

"A bad business last night, gentlemen." Captain Andrew-Jones was obviously not pleased. "We've had General Eisenhower's HQ in London in touch already this morning."

"What is our best course of action, sir?" asked Warwick.

"Because of the security aspect, we can't send the miscreants back to the States before the operation is complete. We are assembling a court of some senior American Navy officers with an American counterpart of me, a USNR captain who was an attorney in civilian life, based in London, as president. He is currently seconded to the British USN Legal Section. They'll weigh off these wretched sailors and tuck them away in our cells until the end of Operation Torch, then ship them back to Alabama or wherever they're from. I've arranged for their commanding officer, Lieutenant Jerry Collins, to act as their defending officer, and you, Lieutenant-Commander Harden, will be the prosecutor."

"Gee, thank you, sir," said Fred without much enthusiasm.

Their next appointment was with Commodore Troubridge, who had invited them to attend his office at 1130 sharp. He was not in the best of moods.

"The events of last night were just what we have been trying to prevent. If this Anglo-American operation is to be a success, we must avoid this sort of partisan brawl. It's not just me saying that, it's our overall commander, General Eisenhower's firm view."

"In fairness, sir, it was an all-American fight. Our British sailors were in no way involved." Warwick thought he was being rather unfairly stigmatised for the historic segregation problems of the southern states of America.

"So it was, Commander Hursey, until the local fishermen weighed in. Regardless of whose fault it was, we have to deal with it. We must stamp out any suggestion of 'them and us'. I have some organisational suggestions to that end."

Warwick's heart sank. The commodore was going to reorganise his little fleet.

"Of course you could turn down my suggestions." Commodore Troubridge was obviously reading his mind. "I hope you won't, but if you do and there is further trouble of this nature, on your own head be it. I'll know where to lay the blame."

"Yes, sir," said Warwick with resignation. "What had you in mind?"

"It seems to be LST167 that's the trouble. I intend to have her commander, Lieutenant Collins USNR, transferred to your ship as your staff officer. That way, you can keep an eye on him from close quarters."

"Where does that leave me, sir?" Fred sounded somewhat alarmed.

"Ah, yes; Lieutenant-Commander Harden. I hadn't forgotten you. You will take command of LST167. You'll soon square up the rest of her crew. You will remain as Commander Hursey's deputy, of course. We will send you an American Lieutenant as your staff officer and put some more sophisticated communications equipment on board, as well as fitting a radar set. It makes sense to split up the commander of the task unit and his deputy, when you think of it. Don't want to lose the whole command staff if *HMS Bruiser* happens to be sunk, do we?"

They walked back to the jetty both feeling slightly stunned. Warwick wondered how Collins would fit in with Bill Browne, Jo Crowthorne, and the rest of his officers. Fred faced the task of bringing a hostile and delinquent crew into some kind of order fairly rapidly. Neither felt their prospects attractive, but both rather grudgingly admitted to themselves that it made sense in the circumstances.

Warwick stood on the bridge of *HMS Bruiser* as they steamed down the loch toward the sea with their attendant fleet of landing craft, some ten days later. It was early October and a fine, crisp, autumn morning with a clear blue sky and a gentle breeze ruffling the water. There was a smell of damp peat and heather from the dark green and brown hills on either side of them. Little white cottages dotted the hillsides. It was a good morning to be alive. The landing craft were in three columns, with his ship leading the middle one as the guide. Out to port was the old converted tanker *HMS Mohican* and three British landing craft astern of her. To starboard was Fred Harden leading his column in LST167 with four American LSTs behind him. The remaining five US ships were following Warwick in the centre. They were on their way to a major rehearsal for Operation Torch and had over three thousand troops embarked, plus numerous tanks and armoured vehicles, with small infantry landing craft on deck cradles. The exercise was to take place on the Inverchasolin Peninsula, near Dunoon and would be opposed using live ammunition. The US First Engineer Amphibious Brigade under Colonel Wolfe comprised the bulk of the invading force, and their landing would be opposed by British troops of Royal West Kent Regiment. One large commandeered ex-passenger ship was following the fleet with more troops to be landed in the second wave on board. Warwick leafed through the complex exercise briefing papers yet again, to ensure he had all the times and signals committed to memory.

Things had finally settled down aboard. At first, Jerry Collins had refused to have anything to do socially with Jo Crowthorne, and their necessary working contacts had been very formal.

A typical exchange between them would be along the following lines:

"Second Lieutenant Crowthorne, I think you need to see this signal which is about the embarkation of the US troops tomorrow."

"Thank you, Lieutenant Collins. I am very much obliged."

That was the sort of thing that went on for the first ten days or so that Jerry Collins was on board. It made the usual banter of the wardroom stilted and awkward due to the obvious underlying tension between them and, in consequence, it was not the comradely, friendly place it should have been. However, a few nights ago at pre-dinner drinks, the relationship between the two of them began to thaw a little. Jo asked Jerry Collins to pour him a gin and tonic, and Jerry did so, not forgetting the ice and slice of lemon, for which service he received polite thanks with a hint of sincere warmth. They began to talk together in a group of officers that included Bill Browne and David MacDonald and the young surgeon-lieutenant, Doctor Ian Mitchell (known to the others at Mitch) who had recently been appointed to the ship. Being the only two Americans in the group and both being away from their home country for the first time, they gradually split from the others and started talking to each other directly. When the dinner gong sounded, for the first time, they sat down together.

Warwick observed all this with some satisfaction from his seat at the head of the table. Previously, Jerry had watched Jo take his seat at the big wardroom table, and then had deliberately chosen a seat as far away from him as possible. Warwick doubted they would become close friends any time soon, but they needed to have an element of mutual respect in order that the ship and the task unit function effectively.

With Sarah, now resident in Morag House for the past week, to act as hostess, he determined to arrange a wardroom party for all their friends ashore. The ship would entertain the Zeigler family, Captain Osmond, Captain Andrew-Jones, Commodore

Troubridge, Fred Harden, and the commanders of all the LSTs in his unit, plus their ladies, if any. Certainly they would have Anne, Brigitte and Monika Zeigler, Sarah, Bill Browne's 2/O Wren, and Mrs. Andrew-Jones to form the backbone of the female company. Jack Watson had found a local girl, a fisherman's pretty daughter, with whom he was going out to the pictures or the pub fairly regularly. He would certainly want to bring her.

They came back to their anchorage some twenty-four hours later, somewhat chastened, wiser and very tired. The initial landings had gone well, and the embarked troops had come ashore followed by their tanks, armoured cars towing anti-tank guns, trucks full of supplies, and jeeps. There had been quite a sea running and the landing craft had bumped hard on the sandy beach. There were deep holes in the sand, and a few of the troops had had to be rescued from a watery grave, loaded as they were with entrenching tools and eighty pound packs. The two-ton Bedford trucks turned out to be wrongly stowed, with the much-needed radios at the bottom and tents and messing equipment on top. The surplus equipment collected in large piles on the beach, where it was promptly scattered by live rounds from the defenders' two-pounder field guns.

Communications broke down due to malfunctioning radios. Two of the landing craft had set their stern anchors too late and were unable to pull themselves off the beach. They were judged as destroyed by the umpires observing the performance. The launching of the small infantry landing craft did not go entirely to plan. Two were smashed against the ship's side in the chop as they were being lowered. They soon learned to swing the crane out and use check lines for'd and aft. Some of the troops had problems with the scramble nets deployed down the side of the old passenger ship, and some were very seasick.

There were some good points, however. All his ships managed to find the right part of the beaches and land their troops in the right order. The bulk of the invading force was landed quickly and soon took the first line of sand ridges manned by the defending troops. The beach signals system to the oncoming landing craft worked well. The Hurricanes that flew over simulating beach strafing and towing targets ended their day with their targets well perforated by the ships' anti-aircraft fire. Fortunately none had perforations in their fuselages. It was generally agreed that the landing would have succeeded in establishing a bridgehead although there were weak points in the operation that needed attention before they left for North Africa.

Several signals were awaiting Warwick when they anchored back in the loch off *HMS Quebec* the following day. The first summoned him to a wash-up with Commodore Troubridge presiding. The second instructed him, accompanied by Lieutenant-Commander Harden USN and Lieutenant MacDonald RN, to attend the final Operation Torch planning meeting at the Operational Headquarters in London the following Monday in the presence of General Eisenhower, the overall commander, who would be leaving for Gibraltar at the end of the week.

The wash-up took up most of the following day and was attended by most of the officers and troop commanders who took part in the rehearsal practice exercise. Commodore Troubridge was backed up by Rear Admiral Sir Harold Burrough, Royal Navy, who was in overall charge of the entire Oran landing fleet.

Thomas Troubridge was in a dour and sarcastic mood. He first dealt with the each individual supply ship and its problems. He was mainly concerned with the slow progress of troop disembarkation, some confusion which had manifested over their designated positions and anchorages and the illogical choice of supplies that they had prioritised for the initial landings on the beaches. As he pointed out coldly, mess cutlery, spare boots, and cases of corned beef, while useful for an established bridgehead, were not urgently required for the first phase of the invasion; whereas radios, medical stores, ammunition, and mortars were. Then he moved on to the fifteen American LSTs in the second LC Task Unit. They had had real navigational troubles and at least half of them had beached and landed their troops in the wrong place. Two had grounded on rocks, perforated their flat bottoms and become semi-submerged, with the tanks, Bren gun carriers, and supplies all awash and the troops needing to be rescued by small wooden landing craft and Higgins boats, which had to be ordered alongside, and thus diverted from the landing of much needed soldiers and marines. Their disembarkation of troops and equipment had been too slow, and there was confusion on the beach as they sorted out supplies and stores. It was quite obvious to Warwick that the commodore was determined to exhibit all the faults inherent in the rehearsal landings and ignore all the things that went reasonably well.

"My turn next," he thought to himself grimly.

"I now bring myself to the landings by the British-led task unit with Temporary Acting Commander Hursey, Royal Naval Reserve in overall command, and Lieutenant-Commander Harden, United States Navy as his deputy."

"He would stress the 'Temporary Acting'" bit, wouldn't he?" muttered Warwick to Fred Harden, who was sitting next to him in the front row. "I'm afraid this is not going to be our finest hour."

"The navigation of this unit was satisfactory, as was the anti-aircraft defence from the beached landing craft. The beach and inter-ship signalling went reasonably well, although some radios turned out to be defective. The troops were landed with reasonable expediency and were judged to have taken their initial objectives after overcoming the defenders on the beaches. However, there were some significant problems and lapses which I will outline in more detail for the benefit of all, and especially the two officers in command whom I mentioned.

"We must pay attention to the stowage of the Bedford lorries. Commander Hursey, as a trained Merchant Navy officer, I charge you with that duty. You ought to be able to tell us all about cargo stowage. The kit contained in these is absolutely vital to the operation's success in its initial phase. Considerable quantities of stores were deemed destroyed because they piled up, being not immediately required, instead of being urgently needed and thus rapidly deployed. We have to consider the terrain. Soldiers must expect to be able to wade ashore; some of yours were nearly drowned. Sounding poles off the ramp must be provided in future. These difficulties and dangers must be foreseen, not discovered in the face of a determined enemy. Your radios must be checked and tested prior to the actual landing. We can't afford to lose contact between ship and shore at any time. I was particularly distressed to note that after all these weeks of practice, some of the large landing craft failed to deploy their stern anchors effectively. Commander Hursey, I would request that you deal firmly with the commanders of those particular vessels in addition to reporting their names to me. It is your responsibility to ensure that your commanding officers are competent and skilled at beaching and hauling off their craft. We had to call a civilian tug out from the Clyde at some expense to pull one of them off, it was stuck so firmly aground. There won't be any obliging civilian tugs available for you in North Africa!"

Warwick began to feel a helpless, despairing depression creep up from his stomach, which was tightly clenched. He suddenly needed the lavatory badly, yet didn't want to have to push past the others and walk out in the middle of the debriefing. *Fuck it*, he thought to himself. *The landing went pretty well. The umpires judged that a beachhead had been established. Nothing goes exactly to plan in wartime when the action has commenced; Clausewitz pointed that out a hundred and twenty years ago.*

"I take note of your criticisms, sir," he started to speak in reply. He felt his task unit had done better than the American one and that his team were being unfairly pilloried. He could hear the stiffness and dull unhappiness in his voice as he spoke.

"Well, you'd best sit back commander, because I have some more. I would have thought that your crew would have learned to launch your LCUs from the deck by using the big crane, yet two were smashed. You then discovered that it works better if the crane boom is extended and the craft launched well clear of *HMS Bruiser's* side. As a trained Merchant Navy officer, this should have been well within your and your crew's capabilities."

"Sir, we were on the limit of our ability to launch; the wind was force six on the beam and we had breaking waves inshore, some of which were eight feet from trough to crest by my judgement. In that situation, I felt I would have been justified in cancelling the launching altogether, as the conditions were far beyond anything we'd trained in previously."

"That's the point, Hursey. You've been in the loch in sheltered waters for weeks, just concentrating on getting your LCTs in the right place and the troops and equipment landed. This practice was to simulate landing on an open beach in adverse weather, which is just what you may have to do in North Africa soon. Once this huge fleet passes through the Straits of Gibraltar, there's no turning back and nowhere for it to go but the Oran beaches, bad weather or no."

After Colonel Wolfe had gone through the soldiers' and marines' performance and drawn some equally harsh conclusions, they dispersed to the wardroom bar.

Fred Harden offered his sympathies. "Don't take it too hard, Warwick; you did pretty well in the prevailing conditions and so did the rest of us. This Number 1 Combined Training Centre at Inveraray was set up when knowledge of invasion by beach landings from the sea hadn't advanced much since the Norman Conquest. Most of what they teach here is experimental, and this is their big chance to show what they've learned in the two years they've been doing it. Operation Torch is the biggest seaborne invasion in history, and it's also the commodore's one big chance to shine. He's not going to spare your feelings with all the personal honour and glory he'll get if this operation is successful, now is he? Besides, if we take North Africa from the Germans, it will be a very big step toward victory. Anyone can see how vulnerable that would make Italy. Old Mussolini will be shitting his pants if we succeed."

Later that day, Warwick went to see Commodore Troubridge in his cabin on a very different matter. "Sir, my wife has come up from Hampshire and is staying with the Zeiglers in Morag House. Is it okay with you if I spend a couple of nights ashore and off my ship? I can keep in constant contact; the house is on the telephone and it's only a few minutes' drive to the jetty. We've a farewell party arranged for the wardroom officers and their ladies, together with some guests from the base tomorrow night."

"Warwick, in normal times I would be only too glad to say yes without hesitation, but these aren't normal times. After that rehearsal, you've a bit more thinking and arranging to do and I feel it would be better if you slept on board. It's an unfortunate fact that wives and war and duty are uneasy bedfellows. By all means have your party tomorrow night, but don't stay ashore this close to the big event. I'll look forward to receiving my invitation!"

As he left the cabin, Warwick felt like a schoolboy who had been kept in after class to do his lines. Sarah would be unhappy if he had to go back on board every night she was up in Scotland. He had originally intended to invite Commodore Troubridge, but had yet to do so. When he got back to his own ship, he hand-wrote an invitation to Commodore Troubridge Royal Navy in his neat script and sent it off with the messenger. He thought the tall and dour commodore would probably be as cheerful and festive as Banquo's ghost, but there was really no alternative.

He rang Sarah and told her of the wash-up, what had been said, and that he had been ordered to spend their last few nights apart. He told her what Commodore Troubridge had said and how he had harped on the fact that his rank was 'Temporary and Acting' and that he was a Merchant Navy officer and, by implication, not regular Royal Navy.

"I don't think he likes us reservists, darling, even though two-thirds of our officers are not regular RN any more. Most of the fleet is made up of people like me, ex-MN RNR officers, together with an awful lot of RNVR ex-yachtsmen. Whatever he thinks, the Navy couldn't do without us now. I'm bloody well doing my best; he ought to appreciate that. I'll tell you, my love, just between us, after listening to Troubridge spout on, for the first time I'm wondering if I'm the man for the job. I always wanted promotion and responsibility; I always thought I could do my boss's job better than he was doing it. Now I wonder if I've gone too far, too fast. I've sort of lost confidence in myself. I'm wondering if the whole thing isn't too much for my little bit of experience. I lay awake at night worrying and sometimes I wish I was back skippering dear old clapped out *Freshwater Bay* again. I was good at that and everyone appreciated what I achieved with her."

"Don't worry about it one bit, my love;" said Sarah soothingly. "We can book into a hotel for a night when you have your big, final meeting in London with General Eisenhower next Monday. Then I'll go back to Hampshire when you come back up here. And don't ever worry about not being up to it. You're the best man they've got. That's why they put you where you are, and that's why I love you so much. Half those chinless wonders that hang around the base wardroom have never even seen a submarine, let alone defeated a U-boat in action."

Not for the first time Warwick found his wife's words very comforting, but he was still unhappy and upset.

CHAPTER TWENTY-NINE

The deck crew put the awnings up on the after deck; as Bill Browne said at the time, "More to keep the rain off the canapés than to shade the guests from the sun!" Coloured code and naval numeral flags and pennants were hung around and the electrical petty officer did wonders with strings of coloured lights. Green coir matting was laid down on the steel upper deck. Floodlights were affixed to the crane. Long tables with drinks and a running buffet were covered in crisp, white linen. The ship was moved alongside the jetty and the gangway was varnished and scrubbed within an inch of its life and illuminated with coloured bulbs. The gangway lifebuoy with the ship's name and crest in gold leaf was placed adjacent to it on its varnished stand. The base's Marine band, suitably rewarded out of Warwick's own pocket and fortified with a special tot of Navy rum (neat) arrived in their beautiful red and gold uniforms, white pith helmets, and shining brass instruments. They were ready for their last party before the big event.

As his mother had remarked when she first met Sarah a few months back (it seemed much longer), Warwick was a lucky man and always had been. The rain stopped for the first time in days, the clouds parted, and a watery autumn sun shone on Inveraray. There was a warm, light southerly breeze. It was the perfect evening and sharp on 1830 the guest started to arrive at the foot of the gangway, to be greeted by Midshipman Rodwick in his best uniform, cap, and leather gloves. They were shown to the wardroom, doubling as a cloakroom, by the immaculate quartermaster, and thence to the upper deck, where the band had begun with the overture to *Iolanthe*. Welcome drinks were handed to the guests by the white-coated steward as they began to mingle with the officers and other guests.

Rather in the spirit of Abu-ben-Adhem, Commodore Troubridge led all the rest, being the very first to arrive. Warwick hoped inwardly that he had also awoken, like Abu-ben-Adhem, from a deep dream of peace and was not going to use the evening further to explore Warwick's faults as a commander of a task unit.

Rather to Warwick's surprise, after his remarks about war and wives not mixing, he was accompanied by the somewhat younger and very attractive Mrs. Commodore Troubridge. Warwick quickly introduced her to Sarah, who was looking particularly beautiful with her long red hair in the autumn sunshine. The commodore's eyes flashed down quickly to her dress, which showed an inch or so of creamy white cleavage and from there further down to her now discernible bump underneath. Warwick hoped that meeting her would soften his boss's attitude toward him a little; Sarah usually had that effect on people, especially men.

They were soon joined by the Zeiglers, Captains Osmond and Andrew-Jones, the latter with his wife, Bill Browne's 2/O Wren, who seemed to have shed a couple of stones since Warwick saw her last, Jack Watson's girlfriend, and several others, including a local girl who turned out to be the barmaid in the pub on the High Street. The latter had been invited by Jerry Collins. Warwick noted a little nervously that Jerry seemed to have started on the drinks earlier than the rest of those present, but he was full of bonhomie, his big round face red and perspiring and split with a huge, good natured grin. Somewhat to Warwick's relief he gave Jo Crowthorne's shoulder a squeeze as he passed him, saying happily "Hi-ya, buddy!"

Warwick and Sarah circulated round the deck, briefly speaking to each of the guests, doing their bit as the host and hostess, and eventually fetched up against Commodore Troubridge.

"I hope you didn't think I was being a bit too harsh on you and your team the other day, Warwick. You can be frank with me."

"Well, sir, I must say I thought that all in all we didn't do too badly. After all, the soldiers we managed to land would have taken the beach and advanced on to Oran if it had been the real thing."

"We need this to be perfect, Warwick. There's no room for error. Failure would set us back in this war at least two years. I have to bear down on all my commanders, but don't think I don't get it in the neck sometimes, too, mainly from Sir Harold, but occasionally all the way up to General Eisenhower himself. I don't think I would be compromising security if I were to tell you that this operation has been timed to coincide with General Montgomery's offensive against Rommel at el Alemein. The hope is that Monty will push the Germans to the west, and we will capture Algeria and Tunisia from the Vichy French and establish a bridgehead behind the German lines. It really is an unprecedentedly vast coordinated operation between America and us.

"I didn't know all that, sir. What did Sir Harold think of the rehearsal?"

"The admiral was quite pleased with what you did, subject to a few minor points, of course. Just to come back to the grand plan, the final piece in the jigsaw concerns Rommel's supply lines. We are losing one submarine in every four that we are sending on patrol, but we are sinking one supply ship in two sent from Italy to replenish Rommel's fuel and ammunition. Particularly the tankers. We know that the Africa Korps are very short of fuel at present, which much restricts Rommel's ability to deploy in either attack or defence. You just don't know what a huge and war-changing event you have a very significant part in."

"Well, thank you for telling me that, sir. After the debrief, I admit I was worried. I thought you felt that my job wasn't one for a reserve officer."

"Not a bit of it, Warwick. Please believe me when I tell you that I only ever bother with those people whom I feel are worth it and can do better with my advice and encouragement. The useless ones I ignore and try to transfer to some other unfortunate command. They usually fetch up driving a desk in the Admiralty."

"That explains a lot, especially about some of the idiotic signals we are getting from London lately; priority and urgent signals about obscure corrections to obscure official manuals and the like."

"Yes, some of the people in the Admiralty and Combined Ops are brilliant, but many of them certainly ought to be weeded out. It's a safe and comfortable billet for them, but I suspect somewhat unsatisfying. When their kids grow up and ask their dad what they did in the war, they'll be hard put to it to give them an answer. Anyway, you'll get a thorough briefing on the situation Monday, when we meet the overall commander in London."

Warwick circulated round the deck again until he reached the girl Jerry Collins had brought aboard; the local girl who worked behind the bar in the pub in the High Street. She was on her own and looking rather lost. She was pretty and petite and had a plain, almost severe long dark dress on with little blue spots. Warwick wondered if she had borrowed it from her grandmother. *Nice legs,* Warwick thought, *but the woollen stockings don't do much for them, especially as they are too big for her and a little wrinkled in consequence. No make-up, not really what you'd expect for a barmaid, but then the church has a lot of influence on the youngsters around here, I suppose.*

"Welcome aboard young lady; tell me, where's Jerry got to?"

"He's had a little too much to drink, and I think he's feeling a bit sick, sir." She had the soft burr of the Western Isles, and looked up into Warwick's face without shyness or reserve. Warwick warmed to her immediately.

"I'm sorry to hear that. What's your name? Mine's Warwick Hursey, and I am the commander of this great task unit. Jerry's my staff lieutenant."

I know that, sir. I'm Jeanie Cameron. My father is the landlord of the Prince Charles in the High Street, and I work behind the bar there to help out in my spare time."

"Don't call me sir; call me Warwick, please. You're my guest tonight. I am so sorry Jerry isn't well. I'll get one of the other officers to escort you back home when you're ready to go."

"Jerry's a sweet man. He knew he had had too much before the party started. He was worried you'd notice. He regards me as a good influence but I didn't do much good for him tonight. He didn't want to let you down. He thinks the world of you."

The thought that Jerry Collins regarded him with anything but barely concealed hostility was a novel one for Warwick. He began to appreciate the frustrated confusion of an ex-shrimp fisherman from the Mississippi coast of the Gulf of Mexico with ingrained generations of racial prejudice and undisciplined Confederate pride being put in a situation where he had to deal with black officers and a British boss in deepest Scotland, cold and wet as it was.

He found the slight girl in her old-fashioned frock with the suggestion of her firm little breasts under it, strangely attractive. She appeared so honest and self-assured. He was quite sure she was a virgin. Not really the sort of girl he thought Jerry would be attracted to at all.

"What do you do when you're not helping out in your father's bar, Jeanie?"

"I'm taking a three-year correspondence course from St. Andrews University in accountancy. I hope to be a qualified Cost and Works Accountant in another year or so. I'm getting good marks. I want to get a management position in industry down south. This is no place for young people, especially when the war ends and all this base gets run down. There are 15,000 extra service people here now; when they leave it'll be just a bunch of old crofters on a Saturday night."

At that moment, Sarah appeared at his side. She was not a woman to let her husband chat long with a lonely but attractive girl at a party, especially when the girl in question was about fourteen years younger than she was. Warwick introduced them to each other, explained about Jerry, the pub, and the accountancy course, and left them to talk women's talk while he circulated further afield.

Warwick came up to Heimlich and Anne Zeigler. They were chatting worriedly together. He wondered if he ought to break in on their conversation and decided that few of the Zeigler family secrets were barred to him and it was his ship's party anyway, so he did. "Hello you two, welcome to the dear old *HMS Bruiser*," he started in a cheerful, breezy tone. "How's things in the Zeigler household?"

"Warwick, we're so worried. Karl has been wounded and refuses to let them fly him out of Stalingrad for proper surgery. He says he will be treated like the rest of the German soldiers in the temporary field hospital the Sixth Army have set up."

"What sort of wound?" asked Warwick, wondering how long they would be allowed to continue to send and receive mail to a son in the SS located on the Volga. He was amazed that their letters kept on flowing in spite of the war.

"He was hit in the upper left thigh by a Russian sniper," Heimlich answered his question. It has shattered his femur but fortunately left his femoral artery intact. If he does not get proper attention from an osteopathic surgeon in one of the big Berlin hospitals, he may never walk without a cane again."

"I am so sorry," said Warwick. "It must be a great worry for you to have your son so far away. Did he say anything else about how things are going there?"

"Yes; it's not good news, at least from the German point of view. Things were going so well at first that they diverted some divisions north to the Moscow front on Hitler's direct order. Now the Russians have dug in and conscripted workers. They are in every cellar and ruined building, and come across from the east bank of the Volga every night. He's so sad that so many fine, young Sixth Army soldiers are dying in the rubble of Stalingrad from stray snipers' bullets. They're all worried about what winter will bring. Already the temperature has dropped to minus ten degrees at night and there are flurries of snow most days and some light ice coming down the river. The wind always seems to blow from the north-east, right from Siberia, and there's nothing more depressing than the sound of it at night; a sort of eerie howl as it hits the ruined city from those huge barren plains."

Warwick moved on. Everyone seemed happy and relaxed. He wondered if he should have asked the admiral. Too late now.

He felt slightly guilty watching everyone chatting under the bright lights with glasses in their hands, while in North Africa and Stalingrad, men were dying alone and unrecorded in sandstorms and frozen tundra. He wondered if the war was at a turning point at last. He began to think ahead. They were entitled to party now; within a couple of weeks they would be in action themselves. He remembered from his history lessons that there had been a huge ball in Brussels on the night before the Battle of Waterloo, so at least there was some official precedent for partying before action. What was good enough for the Iron Duke was good enough for him.

He felt a gnawing feeling in the pit of his stomach at the thought of imminent action. He tried to put it aside. Best to concentrate on one task at a time, and the next thing was the London briefing meeting, in the presence of General Eisenhower. Lord knew what he was thinking when he considered the price of failure. He must have all Warwick's doubts and fears and anxieties squared or cubed or to some higher power.

At that stage, Sarah appeared at his side again and they began to bid goodbye to the early leavers. Warwick remembered to get Midshipman Rodwick to escort Jeanie home.

CHAPTER THIRTY

Late on Sunday night, Warwick and Sarah checked in to Claridges Hotel, Mayfair, and settled down in their smart, art deco suite on the third floor. They had flown down earlier in the day in an American Army DC3, from Inveraray to Northolt airfield in North West London. Their hotel was convenient for General Eisenhower's HQ, then situated at 20 Grosvenor Square, nearly next to the American Embassy. The initial meeting for Operation Torch was scheduled to start at 0900 the following morning, when the commanders of the various task units would receive their top secret order packs and general and personal briefings for the big operation.

They found Claridges was expensive and very luxurious, with a huge choice of wines and dishes on offer. Most of the items on the dinner menu had not been seen in the shops since before the war and even then not that frequently, if at all. Rationing didn't seem to be a word that applied in the hotel but as Sarah pointed out, they had plenty of money and might as well live up to it while they had the chance.

"Besides, dear, we can entertain some of the other officers. It won't do your career any harm to bring them here and wine and dine them a bit."

Nor for the first time Warwick felt a big surge of gratitude to his wife. Who would have imagined that his randomly chosen digs in Newcastle a year ago would have resulted in him marrying his landlady, and that she would have been so beautiful and loving, and turned out to be a rich woman who would willingly spend her money to advance his career?

"Thank you so much, Sarah. I don't know what I'd do without you."

"Don't even think about trying!" said Sarah with some firmness. Warwick wondered if she was still thinking about his *tete a tete* with young Jeanie Cameron at the party the previous night.

They were both tired. Warwick had had a long and difficult week, and the effects of the rum punches and horses' necks he had drunk at the party a few hours ago were beginning to make themselves felt. Sarah had not drunk very much, but she was pregnant for the first time, and in consequence she was feeling tired too. They contented themselves by undressing, turning off the bedside lights, and cuddling up naked together in each other's arms. For the first time since they had met, neither of them felt any compulsion to make love before they went to sleep. Warwick, drowsily considering this unusual non-happening, thought they must be beginning to turn into an old married couple at last.

The next morning they both woke early. To Warwick, peering out the window before he showered and shaved, the reluctant dawn revealed a typical, cold, grey London day in late October. It didn't look very inviting, and he wished he could dive back to bed and snuggle up to his naked wife.

"Where I really want to be is what we used to call 'in the lee of bum island' when I was an apprentice, and not staggering off in the cold and wet to some complicated briefing where I'm not even allowed to take notes," he muttered to himself as he washed.

He felt much better after a full English breakfast with racks of heavily buttered toast, freshly squeezed orange juice, and real coffee. It was served in their room by a smartly uniformed waiter with a Ronald Coleman, pencil-thin moustache, a dainty manner, and a French accent which occasionally slipped into inadvertent estuarial glottal stops. Warwick gave him a ten shilling note as a tip before he left the room, and felt rather reckless especially when he was thanked profusely for it. After they had finished and he had kissed Sarah goodbye, he walked the short distance to the European Theatre of Operations HQ at 20 Grosvenor Square in full uniform. There were some signs of bomb damage, but this area of Mayfair had been left relatively unscathed by the blitz. A few miserable looking civilians in overcoats, scarves, or cloth caps were walking to work, looking downward onto the grimy pavements. A cold north wind blew scraps of paper, dust, and debris along the street. The contrast to the warm, comfortable hotel couldn't have been more marked. Not for the first time, Warwick was glad he had been brought up in the Sussex countryside. He didn't like London very much, especially on cold, damp, windy mornings.

He passed the American Embassy, which had armed guards and blast-preventing mounds of stacked sandbags outside it. A little further on was General Eisenhower's headquarters, which was similarly guarded and protected. A couple of large and very smart American Military Police sergeants in white steel helmets stopped him at the entrance to the HQ. He fished out his ID papers, and, after a brief comparison of him with his photographs on them, they let him pass. The process was repeated in the entrance hall, where more armed military police were on duty. He was then accompanied to the lecture room on the first floor.

There were about thirty seats in the small auditorium, with a raised stage at the end with five seats, a long table full of papers, and a microphone in the middle. There was a screen behind the dais and a projector in a cubicle behind the chairs. Each chair had a small shelf attached to its back to serve as a desk for the person seated behind it. There were impressive looking red, green, or blue folders on each of these little desks marked OPERATION TORCH – FINAL DRAFT – TOP SECRET, together with a foolscap notepad and a pencil with a rubber eraser on its end. The desks had the attendees' names attached to them and there was a seating plan on a board under the raised dais. The whole room was curtained from ceiling to floor and staffed by half a dozen MPs with white armbands, white helmets, side-arms, and heavy boots. A dozen other officers were there already, talking to each other in little groups with mugs of black coffee. A steward in a white coat offered Warwick a coffee on a silver tray, which he took with some gratitude. At least it was warm in here!

Warwick wandered over to the nearest group, which consisted of some familiar faces such as Commodore Troubridge, Fred Harden, Colonel Wolfe, and Rear Admiral Sir Harold Burrough, together with a USN Commander named James C Williamson III, who was in overall command of the other task unit of landing craft and supply vessels due to land at Oran. The officers arriving tended to split into their own landing area groups, Casablanca, Oran, and Algiers. Warwick assumed that the different coloured folders probably covered each of the three invasion fleets and contained specific orders for each separate landing.

"Morning, young Hursey," boomed Admiral Burrough. "How's that lovely wife of yours?"

Warwick was not aware that the admiral knew Sarah. They must have met while he was at sea and Sarah was at the base for some reason.

He quickly thought on his feet. "She was rather hoping, sir, that you and all the officers here that are commanding our landing would dine with us at Claridges tonight. Do you think you could make it 1930 for 2000?"

The admiral visibly brightened at the invitation. Claridges was one of the smartest and most expensive hotels in London and was well known for its excellent cuisine and fine wines. "What a pleasant and welcome thought, my boy! I'd be delighted, as will be my wife."

"Of course, all your wives would be most welcome," said Warwick, still thinking quickly." Just let me know if you can make it by lunch time and I'll ring Sarah and set it up with the hotel staff." He wondered how much a slap-up dinner for twelve would cost, but decided that it was worth it. Money was the least of their problems at the time.

A huge and immaculate, black American master sergeant with a stentorian voice and a southern drawl called the attendant officers to order. They all gradually shuffled to their allotted places and sat down. The lights in the body of the hall were dimmed, while the platform remained lighted. After a few moments, they were joined by the overall commanders and planners of the operation. First to take their seats on the dais were Lieutenant General Eisenhower as the Supreme Commander and Vice-Admiral Sir Bertram Ramsey RN, the Deputy Commander of the Expeditionary Force who had done the bulk of Operation Torch's seaborne planning. They were followed by the three Army commanders or their deputies, Major-General James Dolittle, deputising for Major-General George Patton for the western landing at Casablanca (which was departing directly from the USA), Major-General Lloyd Fredendall, commander of the central, Oran landing, and the British Lieutenant-General Kenneth Anderson, the overall operational Army commander and scheduled to command the forces landing at Algiers to the east. Last, the two operational naval commanders, Vice-Admiral Sir Harold Burrough RN and Rear-Admiral Ken Hewett USN, took their places. General Eisenhower stood up and took the microphone.

"Gentlemen, you are privileged to be taking a vital and important part in the greatest seaborne landing in history. There are events afoot which will change the course of this war. On the Volga, our Russian comrades are gathering their strength to throw back the 250,000-strong German Sixth Army, presently bleeding to death in the ruins of Stalingrad. In Egypt, as I speak, the British Eighth Army is preparing to drive Field Marshal Rommel back to the west. The British Navy, especially their submarine service, is starving his Italian troops and the Africa Korps of fuel, ammunition and supplies for which he is so desperate. Our task is to land in Algeria, Tunisia, and Morocco to block off Rommel's escape route and seal him and his 250,000 troops up, so that they may pass into captivity and the whole of

North Africa may be free of Hitler's forces. If these three, vast, global offences are successful, the Axis will lose half a million veteran troops, plus countless tons of ships, vital equipment, and stores. Hitler will also be denied access to raw materials and vital strategic territories. Thus, gentlemen, we will all be instrumental in changing the outcome of the war in Europe. With a successful invasion fleet available to us and North Africa as our base, the whole of Italy and the French Mediterranean coast will be ours for the taking. Meanwhile, if Marshal Stalin enjoys success on the Volga, the Germans will be reeling back from whence they came, unasked and uninvited, having invaded, without provocation or warning, their erstwhile ally, Mother Russia. We have a great and unprecedented task ahead, make no mistake about that. I will be moving my headquarters to Gibraltar in a few days; from there I will direct the operation, supported by Admiral Cunningham, Vice-Admiral Ramsey, and Air Marshal Sir William Welsh. Now I will hand you over to Vice-Admiral Ramsey."

The audience stood up and applauded General Eisenhower. Warwick felt that even Winston himself would have been proud of that speech. He noticed an attractive woman with long dark hair standing at the side of the platform, in the uniform of a US captain. She was applauding the general as hard as she could, while looking up at him most admiringly.

"What's she doing here?" he asked Fred Harden who was sitting next to him. "She's a bit junior to be in this lot, isn't she?"

"That's Eisenhower's driver, Kay Summersby," replied Fred. "She's an Irish divorcee, although she may be an American citizen by now, for all I know. She's certainly in US uniform today. She stays with him and his staff officer Commander Butcher, in the house you Brits have provided him with; Telegraph Cottage. Some say she is a bit more than a driver and that she provides him with a few special home comforts as well; him being so far from his base and his wife and all that."

"Good lord!" whispered Warwick. "You'd think he'd have enough on his plate at the moment. A year ago he was only a lieutenant-colonel, now he's a lieutenant-general and going rapidly onwards and upward."

Admiral Ramsey spread out a multitude of paperwork in front of him and took the microphone. "I won't keep you long. In your folders, you have the complete paperwork that you need for the operation ahead of us. The operational orders are split into eight sections, called 'Tons' for some reason. You each have in front of you all you need to know to carry out your part of the operation. You now have the rest of the day to read through the orders and make notes. You will not be allowed to take either the orders or the notes you make out of this room. They will be sealed up and delivered to your respective ships or offices by the time you return to them. We will remain in the vicinity to deal with any queries you may have on any aspect of Operation Torch. A buffet lunch and drinks will be served in the anteroom at 1245. Thank you."

Warwick busied himself with his orders, working together with Fred Harden. There was a plan of the three proposed landing beaches at Oran, X, Y, and the main landing to the east of the town at Beach Z was where his force would go ashore, just to the east of the lighthouse on Cap Carbon, which would be their starboard hand mark for the approach. Naval parties would land with the first wave of soldiers to ensure the smooth flow of equipment, vehicles, and stores. Most of the orders followed the exercises they had already practiced several times. By lunch time, he was satisfied that he and Fred were conversant with what they had to do when they arrived off the coast. The section headed up Ton 2 dealt with the sailing and routing, as well as the convoy orders afloat. Tons 5 through 8 were concerned with the arrangements for supplying the bridgehead after a successful landing and the deployment of the landing craft and supply and troop ships at that stage. They were to sail from the Clyde on 22 October, in six days' time.

He rang Sarah and told her about the dinner party that night when they broke for lunch. She took it in her stride. "Leave it all to me, my darling; your guests won't be disappointed."

Not for the first time he thought what a capable woman he had married.

They spent the afternoon memorising the fleet orders and routing down to the Straits of Gibraltar, and the deployments prior to landing and afterward, when the soldiers were all ashore. Warwick spoke briefly to Major-General Fredendall, the US Army Commander at Oran. He was a brusque, peppery little man who barked at rather than conversed with his staff, sending a small cloud of spittle ahead of him when he did so.

"Sir, do we have any knowledge of the opposition we're likely to face? I've read through my orders and they seem rather vague on that point. It is important for my deployment of my ships. I do need to know exactly what we might expect on our initial run in to the shore."

"Son, we'd all like to know that, I can tell you. A US diplomat called Morgan together with one of our major-generals, Mark Clark, landed from one of your submarines a week or so back to try and persuade the Vichy French to change sides. That didn't succeed, even though we had the French Admiral Darlan in reserve to act as their commander. They have a fleet, including a battleship in Toulon, and then there's the Italian fleet, although it tends to stay in port a lot these days. The Vichy forces have a hundred and twenty thousand troops and a load of old equipment. Some of them are raring to fight us; others just want to put up a show and then capitulate. They feel the dishonour of France's collapse in 1940 very badly, and need to prove themselves. I can't say much more really. You'll just have to play it by ear like the rest of us."

"Thank you so much for that, sir," said Warwick. "That helps me a lot. You know we'll do our absolute best for you whatever; that goes without saying."

"Thank you, son, I know you will." His voice had taken on a softer tone.

Warwick's opinion of the rough-speaking, peppery little general had changed for the better. It was a very fair answer from someone who carried so much more responsibility than he did, yet didn't really know what his troops were going to be up against either.

It was evening when he handed in his papers, sealed up in the big labelled envelope provided, and went outside into the cold October mist. The blackout made the streets very dark and gloomy, and he had to pick his way carefully over the uneven paving stones. Most of the attendees had staff cars with drivers waiting for them, but it was only a ten minute walk to Claridges so he stepped out firmly as the autumn chill began to seep through his bridge coat and uniform jacket.

"Want to have a good time captain? You'll not regret going with me. Ten bob for an hour in a proper bed, darling. Only just around the corner."

A slight figure had come out of a side alley and pulled at his sleeve. He looked down at her. She was about five feet tall, shabbily dressed, overly made up, and looked about fourteen years old. She had wrinkled woollen stockings and a ragged coat with some kind of scraggy animal fur around its collar. As the coat fell open a little, he caught sight of a low-cut woollen dress, well past its best, and the bulge of her slight, white breasts. She reminded him of Jeanie Cameron made up for the Christmas Pantomime (always assuming the Church of Scotland allowed such frivolities in Inveraray). She was pale under her makeup and he realised that she was shivering and probably half-starved.

"Not for me, dear," he started. "I've a wife and a warm hotel to go back to."

"Please, please, sir. I ain't turned a trick for three days and I'll be thrown out of my room if I can't pay the rent on Friday. None of them don't fancy me; I'm too small and got no tits. I ain't got nowhere to go, sir, and that's the God's honest truth."

Tears began to run down her face. Warwick was sure she wasn't acting. He felt a surge of pity for her, thinking of his warm and luxurious suite and loving, rich wife waiting for him in the hotel with a gourmet dinner in good company to follow.

He wanted to help her. He remembered that old Prime Minister in Victorian times, Lord Gladstone, who had tried to reclaim prostitutes to a Christian and moral life by taking them home to his wife for tea. Warwick was fairly certain that if he were to be similarly moved to take this girl back with him, Sarah would be unimpressed, to say the least. He felt in his pocket and pulled out three £1 notes.

"Here, take these and get some food in you, love. Dry your eyes. You're not really cut out for this sort of thing."

He hurried on, brushing her and her thanks aside. He felt disturbed and upset. What a rotten crappy hand that girl had been dealt! He wondered how long his £3 would last. It wasn't as solution really, just a palliative; treating the symptoms of her problem and not its cause. Goodness knows, he'd seen enough whores in his time at sea; they were in every port in the world hanging around sailors. Why did this one's plight upset him now, he wondered?

The dinner was a great success, helped by Sarah's carefully chosen menu and the wines she had ordered to go with it. Warwick had not realised she was so proficient and knowledgeable in these matters; he supposed she must have studied haute cuisine when she was running the boarding house in Newcastle. Perhaps the old man she lived with for years had been interested in good food and wine and had been willing to pay for it. He resolved to ask her some time.

She had arranged a wood-panelled, private dining room for the twelve of them. The guests were welcomed with a glass of fine, pale, dry sherry, with the alternative of a horse's neck or gin and tonic. After about half an hour, they moved into their dining room, to a table set out as only Claridges knew how, with a multitude of silver cutlery, gleaming crystal, and blindingly white napery.

"By god, this reminds me of how life used to be before the war!" exclaimed Sir Harold. "I don't know what they pay you RNR boys, but you've certainly put on a grand show for us tonight."

To start the meal, there was mock turtle soup, delicate and translucent and served alongside a large glass of sherry. Next there was an appetiser of cod roes on fingers of lightly buttered toast. The fish course came promptly after that; poached turbot in white parsley sauce with a fine, lightly chilled Chablis to accompany it. The main course was roast guinea fowl with roast potatoes, green beans, and mushrooms, and was taken with half a dozen bottles of a deep red, full-bodied burgundy.

Finally the sweet came; an Australian pavlova meringue cake with cream and fresh strawberries. Warwick wondered how the hotel had managed to get hold of strawberries in the middle of October in wartime at short notice (or clotted cream for that matter), but thought it politic not to ask. A sweet, heavy, white pudding wine accompanied the pavlova, served in small, fluted, green-tinted glasses.

Then the ladies retired to the anti-room and the men were offered cigars from a large cedar box. A decanter of vintage port made its appearance, and was briskly passed round to the left, in accordance with immemorial tradition, by the admiral acting as ever as the President of the Mess. They were all in a very convivial mood by this time; most mellow and appreciative.

Warwick didn't like to think what all this was costing; probably more than his Navy messing allowance for the duration of the whole war. He marvelled that Sarah had managed to arrange all this with about six hours' notice. He didn't know she had been worrying the life out of the Maître de Hotel, the sommelier and the head chef in the kitchens all afternoon, striving to get everything perfect for her husband and his senior officers.

Around eleven thirty, they saw the last of their guests off from the pavement outside the front door of the hotel. It had grown colder and there was a slight but persistent drizzle. A nasty, cold wet night was in store. Warwick was more than glad he had a warm bedroom and an even warmer wife to go to. A series of staff cars had been called up by the hotel doorman, a huge, moustachioed, ex-Army sergeant-major who had served in the Great War, resplendent in a long green greatcoat with four gold stripes on his arms and a green-topped cap with a copious amount of scrambled egg in gold on its peak.

"Really," whispered Warwick to Sarah, "if his coat was dark blue instead of green, I'd take him for a Navy captain. He could pass himself off as a Peruvian general at the Officers' Club with that outfit, for sure!"

Just as the last car drove off into the night with its happy and slightly befuddled occupant, Warwick felt a tug at his sleeve as he was turning to go back into the hotel with Sarah.

"You were so kind to me, sir, and I never got the chance to thank you. I just waited here to tell you that. I don't get much kindness in my trade. I've paid me rent for two weeks and had a feed at the little Italian café, like you said."

It was the little prostitute, looking even more down at heel and bedraggled in the cold, damp night air.

"Who exactly is this person, Warwick?" Sarah began, sounding like Lady Bracknell discussing a handbag as she took stock of the new arrival.

Warwick's heart sank. "No good deed goes bloody unpunished," he muttered to himself, and then to Sarah in a louder voice, "Erm, well, you see darling, I met this young lady on my walk back here and . . ."

"Don't you darling me, Warwick! In case you didn't know, I've been working myself into an early grave to make your dinner with the admiral a success, and what have you been doing, meanwhile? You've been chatting up this little whore, that's what! And how did you manage to pay her rent and feed her? Perhaps you'd like to let me know what you got in return, Warwick. Payment in kind, was it? You seem to have taken quite a fancy to these young, thin birds, lately."

"It's not like that at all, Sarah," protested Warwick weakly. "She was cold and hungry and likely to be put out on the street. I gave her a couple of pounds to tide her over."

"That's right, missus; that's how it was. Just like he said. You've got a good, kind man there. He wouldn't even wait for me to say thanks" The little prostitute flew to Warwick's defence, "You're so lucky, you are; I wish I had a big, handsome man like that to look after me. I do, really."

"Well, you haven't, so will you now please piss off and leave him to me." Sarah was cross. "You've done enough damage already. You ought to be in school or home in bed with a cup of Ovaltine and not out on the streets at your age."

Warwick sensed he was in for a stormy night. Sarah turned her back to him and marched back into the hotel. He followed her at a safe distance. She got into the lift and pressed the up button without waiting for him. He arrived in time to take the next lift, which had just disgorged its passengers from the floors above. When he got to their suite, the door was firmly shut.

Fortunately, he had a key in his pocket, so he opened it and stepped into the room to face a furious Sarah, hands on hips. They had been married for nearly four months now and had never really had a one-to-one row before. The scene when Sarah's late mother had caused mayhem in West Lodge didn't really count. He realised that Sarah was a force to be reckoned with when she was this angry.

"You bastard!" she started. "You real bastard!" It was not a promising beginning. "I do everything for you, give you all my money and my dear old dad's royalties, give you my love, work for your career, have your wretched baby, and there's you out there while I'm doing it all, chatting up some scraggy little toxic cow off the streets."

"Now listen, Sarah, please don't let your blind prejudice get in the way of the facts of the matter. I was walking peacefully back to the hotel, looking forward to seeing you after a difficult day . . ."

"Difficult day? Difficult day did you say?" Sarah's voice rose a couple of octaves and increased in volume. "What do you think my day's been like then, fixing up that evening for all your upper class officer friends? Have you any idea how difficult it is dealing with all those fucking prima donnas in the kitchen here? They think that no one can tell them anything."

Warwick decided not to point out that there had to be someone to tell anybody something. He didn't think Sarah was quite in the mood for minor grammatical corrections.

"Sarah, let me talk to you. The girl tugged at my sleeve as I was walking back here. She wanted ten bob for a short time. She looked about fourteen and half-starved. She said she was going to be thrown out on the street if she didn't find the rent money by Friday. I took pity on her and gave her three quid. That's all there was to it."

"Three quid?" shouted Sarah unappeased. "And who's bloody three quid do you think it was?" You can't afford three quid on what they pay you, commander or not. That money came from me, mister, and I don't want it spent on underage London streetwalkers. And don't think I didn't notice that she was very young and very slim like that pub landlord's little barmaid daughter back there in Scotland. The one you seemed so fond of on Saturday night on the ship."

In spite of Sarah's continued high-grade verbal hostility, Warwick sensed that she was mellowing just a little bit. He remembered Clausewitz's dictum that war is diplomacy by another means and decided to take physical action. He moved forward and grabbed her firmly by the shoulders.

"Get your filthy hands off me, bugger you!" Sarah tried to wriggle free, and then, being unsuccessful, flailed at him with her open fists.

Warwick was a very big and very powerful man, and an ex-amateur boxer, too. He easily avoided her haymakers, and eventually pinioned her arms behind her back with his left hand, while holding her to him by encircling her waist with his right arm and clamping his right hand firmly on her buttock.

"Just for the record, my little nest of vipers, never telegraph your punches. I could see yours coming at me for about a week before they actually arrived. One day, when you calm down a bit, I'll teach you how to punch properly."

"Let me fucking GO!" muttered Sarah through clenched teeth, wriggling in his grip. But her struggles were not as violent as before.

"I love you, Sarah, and this is our last night for a month, possibly forever. I have to fly back tomorrow lunchtime and then sail for the Clyde to assemble the fleet and take on equipment and troops for the real thing. No one really knows what sort of reception we'll get from the Vichy French there – I have that direct from General Fredendall, himself."

He was giving away a few secrets and hoped the Admiralty would forgive him, bearing in mind the emergency situation he found himself in at the moment. He let go of his wife's hands, put both arms round her, and kissed her on the lips.

After a brief and wholly token struggle, she kissed him back hard.

"My god, your bump's grown a bit," said Warwick as their bodies pressed together.

"You didn't really mean that bit about our last night forever did you, darling?" Sarah was anxious.

Warwick marvelled about how a woman could change from screaming hostility to anxious love between two sentences. Never mind; he'd obviously pushed the right button with his little homily. He hadn't been married long, but he was learning.

"Of course not, my love. I'm the one who's indestructible, you know!" With that he picked her up in his arms and walked into the bedroom, throwing her gently on the bed.

"Mind my best dress," warned Sarah as he gathered a handful of it and bunched it up around her thighs.

Warwick was not in the mood to mind any best dress or best knickers either, as they were discarded in their turn and thrown far into the corner of the room. He stared at his wife, naked from the waist down, lying back on the bed with her legs dangling over its foot as he divested himself of jacket, trousers, and underpants, all falling into an untidy and untended heap at his feet.

"What are you looking at now?" asked Sarah softly. "Did you think my red hair came out of a bottle?"

CHAPTER THIRTY-ONE

Warwick flew back to Scotland the next morning, while Sarah took a train to Portsmouth where she'd left the Alvis in a friend's drive. They'd had a wonderful last night together, as a result of which, plus the lack of sleep and the accumulated alcohol in his system, he was feeling somewhat jaded. In his thoughts, he carefully avoided the words 'hung over,' but it amounted to much the same thing; a slight headache, a sense that he was a bit behind the aeroplane, and a compelling desire for a catnap.

There was little enough chance of that. The superannuated DC3 was not a comfortable plane at the best of times, with its tubular steel and canvas seats, and there was a moderate storm over the Midlands and North of England, with several masses of black cumulo-nimbus cloud towering up to forty thousand feet which the plane, flying at five thousand feet, had to make its way around. They bucked and rolled in the cross winds and rain, and occasionally hail rattled on the aluminium fuselage. The passengers could see lightning flashes outside the big, square windows.

Warwick, whose third flight this was, assumed this was fairly typical of an aeroplane in a storm and remained calm and unworried. Even with what he had recently eaten and drunk, his cast-iron stomach didn't let him down, although he noted quite a few senior officers on the flight were a little pale and one or two of them made surreptitious trips to the little compartment with the zipped canvass door which hid the Elsan chemical lavatory.

I sure hope we don't have to do a loop the loop, he thought to himself.

His thoughts then turned to Sarah. She had shown a side of her personality that he hadn't seen before last night. He had discovered that she had a fiery temper to match her red hair, and a strong streak of jealousy to match. He supposed it was only natural for a woman older than her husband to be jealous. He didn't regret it, though; it showed she loved him. He marvelled. She'd be thirty-five in December, he remembered.

How could she have been so unreasonable as to think he would have had any interest in that little street walker? His intentions had been entirely altruistic, charitable, and honourable, hadn't they? Well, hadn't they? Deep down, he knew she had a point, well hidden though it was. He had fancied her a bit; it wasn't just charity, and for the same reason he had felt just a little stirring deep down when he was talking to Jerry Collins's little girlfriend at the ship's party – the barmaid, Jeanie, he remembered. They were small, petite, and pale, and somehow vulnerable. He would have liked to undress them both, just to see what was underneath the unprepossessing clothes they were wearing.

"My god," he muttered under his breath, "don't say I've developed a fetish about little, pale, vulnerable girls. I mean, I'm happily married to Sarah; I love her and she's not like that at all."

It was true. Sarah with her full, voluptuous figure and strong and decisive nature was anything but a pale and dependent girl. He realised there was such a thing as womanly intuition. She had known him better than he had known himself. She had sensed that, however unfulfilled and harmless, he had been drawn and attracted to both those girls and she had fought against that trait of his with all the invective and physical strength she could muster.

"Anyway, she loved being overcome by brute strength and thrown on the bed and stripped," he mused to himself. "It had spiced up our lovemaking no end." No wonder he felt so clapped out. "Nothing like a bit of the old caveman stuff!"

He warmed to the memory of a few hours before. Just then, the plane dropped about ten feet vertically with a bump that shook him out of his reverie. He clutched the metal sides of his seat and looked around. The rest of the passengers weren't enjoying the ride at all, and Warwick hoped they were nearly there. It was all very well, but even the helter-skelter rides at the fairground ended fairly quickly.

After another hour of buffeting, the plane descended under the cloud base and made a bumpy three-point landing in heavy rain on the little aerodrome that served Inveraray. Warwick, along with the rest of the passengers and probably the pilots too, was relieved to stagger out down the metal steps and into the small, green painted, corrugated iron Nissan hut that served as the passenger terminal.

Back on the ship, he found several signals and his operational order pack with his sheets of notes awaiting him, the latter having been signed for as a secret document by Bill Browne as First Lieutenant in temporary command, and stored in the ship's safe for confidential books and papers. He called in David MacDonald and Bill, and outlined the content of the orders. They would need a thorough knowledge of them before the landing took place. He understood that smaller, less detailed operation packs would be issued to the individual commanders of the landing craft and supply ships in due course. His signalled orders required them to sail in convoy for the Clyde Estuary that Friday, with all equipment and stores on board. There they would anchor while the rest of the fleet assembled and the troops were embarked. All but the first wave of troops would be housed on the large commandeered liners that were to accompany them as troop ships. The American Rangers, together with some British Marine Commandos, would bed down on the landing craft, the majority of them on *HMS Bruiser*, which had a lot of accommodation below decks. There were trained Navy personnel on each ship who would go ashore with the first wave to organise and assist in the landing and distribution of stores.

There was a knock on his door. It was ship's Cox'n CPO Blessed, the senior non-commissioned officer aboard.

"Excuse me asking, sir," he began, "but I wondered if you could tell me what we're up to, and how much I can tell the lads. They've got wives and sweethearts who are worried about what their men are in for."

"It's still very hush-hush chief I'm afraid. But I can give you the outline of what we're about to embark on. Take a seat and rest your bones for a moment. Can I offer you a wee dram while we're at it?"

The chief had been thirty-five years in the Navy before retirement and had been recalled at the age of sixty, as his papers stated, 'For Hostilities Only.' Warwick did not consider him any kind of security risk; his service in the Royal Navy had been his whole life. When the chief was comfortably seated with a shot glass in his hand and a bottle of Haig whisky and a pitcher of water at his side, Warwick explained what their mission was to be. He outlined the nature of the strategic plan and brought in what was happening in Stalingrad and El Alamein to give the global picture.

"You see chief, we don't know how hard the local Vichy French troops will resist us on the beaches. They have over a hundred thousand service men in North Africa, some supporters of Hitler, some bitter about France's capitulation, some loyal to Marshal Petain, some keen to join the Free French forces on our side. We just don't know how this will play out when we actually land. One thing we do know for sure, though – if the Axis forces get wind of what we're doing, there'll be a strong German and Italian force to oppose us, plus the Luftwaffe and a selection of very enthusiastic U-boats."

"Thank you, sir; thanks for telling me all that. How much of it can I tell the lads, though?"

"Well, chief, it's obvious to everyone that we are planning huge amphibious landings somewhere in the near future, and that secret hasn't got out, as far as we can tell. The Germans must know what's going on here at Inveraray, but they probably think it's training for the eventual opening of the second front by landing on the French coast to liberate Europe. It's the location of our landing that's the real secret, and I'm afraid that must remain so until we sail. You can hint at Corsica or the Bay of Biscay if you like, without commitment, but do tell them that we're due to sail for the Clyde on Friday, where the whole invasion fleet will assemble. As soon as we've left you can tell them we're bound for North Africa. In any event I'll get them all up on deck and tell them all I can about where we're going and what's in store for them after we sail. On another tack, tell me chief, how's the general morale on the lower deck? Have we a happy crew?"

"Yes sir; they're pretty well all excited about the vast size of the fleet, and most of them are happy to be part of it. The food's good and they've been having plenty of shore time. Otherwise they've been pretty busy doing new things and a busy sailor is usually a happy sailor. There's been a bit of friction between them and soldiers, and just a little between the Yanks and our lot, but not much. Some have girlfriends in town here, but most of them will be glad to get away and out of the cold and rain and well clear of the Scottish winter."

After the chief left, Warwick busied himself writing letters and drafting non-urgent signals for transmission the next day. He was relaxed as he sat at his desk in his warm cabin in his shirt sleeves and without a tie. It was 2340 when he finished, and put his completed work in the out tray on his desk to be dealt with the next morning by Midshipman Rodwell, who acted as the captain's secretary. He sat back and thought to himself that it might be pleasant to take a walk round the deck of his ship before he turned in.

It was a clear, cool, moonlit night with no wind at all. There was a bright full moon and a silvery path on the still waters lighting up the huge fleet at anchor in the loch in its soft glow. He could smell the heather and the pine trees in the gullies between the hills. Warwick thought about the spring tides that came with a full moon and hoped Bill Browne had checked out some anchor cable to allow for the higher water levels that went with them. On the officers' deck, only one scuttle was still showing a light. The occupant had obviously forgotten to draw his blackout curtains. Warwick peered in out of curiosity, wondering who was up so late.

It was Jerry Collins's cabin. He was face downward on his bunk, his back and buttocks bare. He was moving purposefully up and down and appeared to be naked apart from his socks. He had a pair of brown, woollen-stockinged legs opened wide under him, one on each side of his rather spotty rump. His head was on the girl's right shoulder and she was lying back on the pillow with her left shoulder and small, white, left breast exposed with its little pink nipple. He recognised Jeanie Cameron's face. He pulled his head away quickly, but not before Jeanie had glanced up in alarm and, with a spreading look of horror, had realised whose face was at the porthole.

Warwick stepped back hastily; clear of Jeanie's line of sight. A raft of mixed and unrelated thoughts passed rapidly through his brain as he made his way back to the main deck. He would have to do something about this. Since the ship's party and for reasons of security, no women or unauthorised civilians had been allowed aboard. Jerry and Jeanie were clearly in breach of the ship's standing orders as he had amended them recently.

Dammit, he thought. He didn't want to get the reputation of a voyeur who prowled the decks of his ship at night, peering into open scuttles, hoping for some kind of cheap thrill at what might be on display within. What if Sarah were to find out? She already suspected that he was generally fascinated by slight young women with small white breasts and, in particular, with Jeanie Cameron. Anyway, Jerry was an American; surely he could have provided his girlfriend with a pair of nylons and not left her wearing those awful rumpled woollen things. Most of the US personnel had access to nylon stockings. Why let her look like a charlady if he was that fond of her? He approached the quartermaster on the gangway.

"Good evening, Robbins. Have you by chance allowed any women on board tonight?"

"No, sir, I only came on duty at 2200 and there's been no one coming aboard since then."

"The first lieutenant hasn't issued any special passes in my absence for visitors, has he?"

"There's none in the quartermasters' deck book, sir; hasn't been since the big party."

"Thank you for that. Would you be kind enough to go along to Lieutenant Collins's cabin in a few minutes? Knock on his door and wait outside for him to open it. Present my compliments to the lieutenant and ask him to see me in my cabin at his earliest convenience."

"Aye aye, sir!" replied the quartermaster.

Warwick went up to his cabin, put on his uniform jacket and tie, spread out some papers on his desk, took down a large volume of the *King's Regulations and Admiralty Instructions* and opened it at the chapter concerning ship's discipline. He took out a notepad and began making notes from the book on the misbehaviour of officers and the list of his available penalties and punishments. After about ten minutes, there was a rather tentative knock at the door.

"Come in!" shouted Warwick in his best deep, grim, stentorian voice.

Jerry Collins appeared in full uniform. He had taken some care with his appearance, as much as time had allowed at least. He had obviously been drinking during the evening, but was not drunk. His big, red face was beaded with anxious sweat.

"You asked to see me, sir?" he said in his soft, southern American accent.

"Where's Jeanie at the moment, Collins?" asked Warwick, getting rapidly to the point.

"I just asked Midshipman Rodwell to escort her ashore, sir. She's got her little Ford on the foreshore and can drive home herself, sir."

"There are two things here, Lieutenant Collins. One is your flagrant disregard of my ship's orders, and the other is that Jeanie is a nice respectable girl who has her good reputation to keep up in this little town, which is dominated by the Church of Scotland or the Wee Free or whatever. She's trying to study to better herself and build a career and she doesn't need seducing by the likes of you, here one day and gone the next. She deserves better. You ought to be ashamed of yourself; you're not some callow, lovelorn youth. You're well into your thirties. Then there's the security aspect. I have informed CPO Blessed of our mission and asked him to give a limited amount of information to the crew. We can't allow any more contact with civilians now; the importance of keeping our destination secret is too great. Any leak which the enemy got hold of would imperil the entire mission and thousands of lives, many of them American."

Jerry Collins stood before him shaking and white. He looked as if he might burst into tears at any moment. "Sir, Jeanie wouldn't do that; she wouldn't say a word to anyone. She's a wonderful girl; one in a million and we intend to get married if I get out of this war alive. She's willing to come home with me to Louisiana after we're married. I make a good living fishing shrimps. Sir, I love her and where I come from, we're God-fearing folk; all my family are regular church goers."

"Well, it's good that your intentions are honourable and I appreciate that. By the way, have you told her parents of your plans for their only daughter?"

"Er…. no not yet sir; Jeanie thinks it would be better if she broke the news after I'd left for Operation Torch. At least I'd be on active service, which would count well with her father."

"The fact remains that you flagrantly disobeyed ship's orders. Now get back to your cabin. I intend to deal with you tomorrow."

Breakfast in the wardroom the following morning was a subdued affair as the news spread of the happenings of the previous night. There was a distinct halt in the buzz of conversation when Warwick entered the room.

After breakfast, he sent for his deputy, Lieutenant-Commander Fred Harden USN, and summoned Bill Browne to his cabin. The three of them met there and he described what had happened and asked their advice and views on what to do about Jerry Collins.

"The problem is," began Fred Harden, "these guys are going into action for the first time shortly and there's no certainty that their girlfriends and fiancées will ever see them again. They've been training here for a long time and have formed very strong attachments to the local girls. They're only young, and it's the way things are."

"Yes, Fred, I quite understand; I'm only twenty-seven myself." But orders are orders, and this ship's discipline will disintegrate if the officers are allowed to pick and choose which ones they feel like obeying."

Bill Browne chipped in. "If you're going to punish Jerry Collins, then you'll have to consider punishing Jo Crowthorne and David MacDonald, too. They were entertaining Monika and Brigitte on board on Monday night while you were down in London."

"Bill, you should have told me. What did you do about it?"

"Not a lot, sir. The order banning visitors had only been issued that day. The Ziegler girls were very upset about their brother. They've just received another letter from him. Apparently he's developed gangrene in the broken leg that was hit by the Russian sniper. He may have to have it amputated in a very basic Stalingrad field hospital. They are short of any medical supplies, including anaesthetics and drugs there. In view of the circumstances I just reminded them of the order and they took the girls ashore and back home to Morag House."

"I'm sure you did right, Bill," said Warwick, remembering that Bill Browne at sixty had had a lifetime's experience of this sort of thing in the Navy. "I think the best thing is to put Collins on First Lieutenant's report, and let you deal with the matter. If we do it that way, I don't get involved as the unwitting peeping tom who discovered the girl was on board and what they were up to at the time." Warwick thought of Sarah again, and what she would think about him spying on Jeanie Cameron making love. He had no idea how she might hear of the incident, but had an uncomfortable suspicion that she would somehow if it were not rapidly suppressed.

"Sort of hush it up, sir?" enquired Bill. "Is that what you want?"

"I think that would be best, Bill. I'd think the best thing is to confine him to ship for a couple of weeks. We sail the day after tomorrow, so it really won't make much difference, because he won't be able to go ashore after that anyway. There's the ship's relationship with the Inveraray townsfolk to think of, too. If Jeanie's father gets to hear of what Jerry was doing here with his daughter, the whole ship's reputation and regard will suffer. I really wouldn't like to upset the locals who have been so friendly and supportive of us. Just think about it; second only to the Minister, the local publican is just about the most influential person in the community, not to mention his wife. We really don't want to bring shame on the family anyway."

"Jerry's a fine seaman," remarked Fred Harden. "He's trying hard to adjust to Navy discipline. He uses me as a bit of a father-confessor, and he's confided in me that he's fallen deeply in love, rather unexpectedly at his age. He's been to see me a couple of times for advice and encouragement. He's cut down on his drinking and also on his association with his erstwhile mate, Alan Royle, who tended to lead him astray when they were together. He gets on well with Josh Crowthorne now, and that's really something for someone who was brought up poor and white in the deep South. If you'll take my advice as a friend, Warwick, I'd treat him a bit more like a valued member of your staff, and not so much like an embarrassing and rebellious youngster. Believe it or not, he admires you and he'll appreciate your support and consideration a lot"

DAVID ARNOLD

It was the second time Warwick had heard that Jerry Collins admired him, the first being from Jeanie Cameron at the ship's party. He still found it hard to believe, but was prepared to believe that they had just got off to a bad start. In any case, they had to work together now the big event was imminent.

"Okay Fred, point taken. I wish he'd express his admiration for me by obeying my written orders, but no matter. Bill, you sort him out this morning, and I promise I'll be all sweetness and light when we next get together."

CHAPTER THIRTY-TWO

On Friday 22 October 1942, the whole fleet sailed for the Clyde Estuary, weighing anchor at 0500 to assemble there and take on troops and stores. There were the two units of landing craft, store ships, troop ships, and the headquarter ships, *HMS Bulolo* and *HMS Largs*. The assembled fleets were destined for Oran and Algiers. The Western force was entirely American and comprised ninety-one ships with US personnel. Major-General George Patton was in overall command. It was due to land near Casablanca and French Morocco, having sailed directly from the US East Coast. In all, 341 ships were involved in the three landings, East, West and Central. The Central (Oran) and Eastern (Algiers) task forces were escorted by no less than four aircraft carriers, five cruisers, five anti-aircraft ships, twenty-six destroyers, eleven corvettes, three submarines, fifteen minesweepers, a monitor, and various ancillary craft, as well as the actual fleet of landing craft, split more or less equally between them. It was to be the largest operation in history time and most of the available ships of the USA and Britain stationed in the Atlantic were involved, as well as several Free French cruisers and destroyers.

Warwick arrived on the bridge at 0430 to be greeted by Petty Officer Norton with a steaming cup of cocoa (known throughout the RN as kye) with a foamy top and so thick with cream and sugar that a spoon would almost stand up in it. It reminded him of a story about kye that had been told him by a lieutenant-commander who had been captain of an S-Class submarine.

A grizzled submarine cox'n was finishing his last five-year service period; his fifth five. They were homeward bound and he was on his last patrol. He brought a steaming and foamy cup of kye up on the bridge for the captain of the boat during a particularly dark, wet, and windy night.

"How is it that you are the only one who manages to get me a good cup of kye up here in bad weather, cox'n?' asked the captain. "All the others bring half empty cups mixed with the dollops of spray and seawater as they come up through the open area of the conning tower from the control room."

"Well sir, it's like this, sir. At the bottom of the ladder, I sucks most of it in me mouth, and when I get up here where it's not so wet, I blow it back out again into the mug. Foams up a treat, it does!"

He sipped his kye, trusting that it had been poured direct from the kettle this time, as he watched Jack Watson and the Navigator's Yeoman preparing the bridge in the gloom, only relieved by a few red lights for illumination. The quartermaster came to the wheel and David MacDonald got out his charts and orders with the fleet disposition, up-anchor timing, and Clyde anchorage positions marked out on them. There was a hum of generators and ventilation fans. Warwick walked outside to the wing of the bridge. It was a cold, clear morning with the temperature near freezing. There was a north-easterly wind that felt as if it had come directly off Bear Island. The gyro repeater dial glowed green as its helmet was taken off by the yeoman, who then put its azimuth ring in place. He looked over the front of the bridge toward the foc'sle where Bill Browne and his foredeck party were clearing away the capstans and the anchor chain preparatory to weighing anchor.

Warwick gave the orders to weigh and proceed. The anchor came up with a series of clanks and Bill gave the up and down signal to show the bridge that it was off the bottom.

"Slow ahead both," said Warwick softly, and the twin geared steam turbines came to life. They moved out of the loch at half speed, with their attendant landing craft forming columns behind and on either side of them. Warwick took station behind *HMS Largs*, flying the flag of Commodore Troubridge.

They anchored after dawn off Greenock. The whole of the estuary was covered by the vast armada of ships. Small LCIs ferried troops and supplies out, and fuel barges went from ship to ship topping up their tanks. With other senior commanders and their staff navigators, Warwick and David were ferried ashore by the duty Motor Fishing Vessel to take part in a last minute briefing held at the Victorian clubhouse of the Royal Northern and Clyde Yacht Club near Rhu, at the bottom of the Gareloch. It was a tall, gloomy building with dark wood panelling in every room, and reminded Warwick of a convent boarding school. It smelt musty, damp, cold, and unused. In the main hall, there were numerous aerial and ground level photographs of the various landing areas, plus a series of models of the Algiers and Oran landing beaches in sandboxes on trestle tables.

A very smart CPO approached them. "Commander Hursey, sir?"

"That's me," said Warwick.

"There's been a phone call from your wife, sir. She says could you please give her a call when you have a moment."

"How the hell did she know I was here and what this number was?" mused Warwick.

"She rang me back when we were in Inveraray, sir, said David. "She wanted to have a last word or two with you before we set sail, so I found out the number and timing for her."

"Well done, David, although you shouldn't really have told anyone where we were at this stage. The walls have ears and all that."

"I just gave her the base wardroom number and a time to ring to leave a message. That number's pretty common knowledge around Rhu and anyone looking out of their window can see the fleet's in."

At lunch, Warwick rang Sarah.

"It's me!" she answered in that sweet, feminine voice she always used. She always said that when she rang him or he rang her. "I wanted to say how sorry I was about starting a row in London, and that I love you very much. Don't get hit, darling; come back to me, please. You're my whole life now. Remember, you've a little one on the way now to call you daddy."

Warwick went back to study the photos and sandboxes with a huge, warm feeling welling up within him. Of course he'd come back to her. Wasn't he indestructible, after all?

He looked again at Beach Zulu; the main designated landing point for the Oran invasion. There were two forts marked on the point north of the village of Arzew to the starboard side as viewed from seaward. They were named Fort du Nord and Fort de la Pointe. They had some old 170mm guns and some smaller artillery in place but intelligence indicated that they were now dilapidated and not maintained in operational condition. His invasion area was centred on the small beach settlement of Damsesme with the village of St. Leu a little further to the east. The two groups of houses should be easy enough for the small LCIs to pick out and aim for. The beach was sandy and sloping and so far as recent, submarine-based intelligence could say, free of mines and obstacles. There was a single track railway behind the beach, and a valley which ran parallel to the main Oran Town highway. He would have to try to keep his lightly plated landing craft clear of the most prominent land feature, Cape Carbon, just north west of the two forts, and come in from the east.

Before returning to the ship Warwick was given his sailing orders. They were to depart for North Africa at 0400 the following morning, October 25.

CHAPTER THIRTY-THREE

It was a grey, blustery, late October Sunday at sea, with the strong south-westerly wind on the starboard bow. Feathers of spray whipped across the somewhat rusty foredeck of *HMS Bruiser*. At least it was a warm wind, and it was forecast to decrease from its present thirty knots or so in the next twelve hours. The ship was rolling and pitching moderately. Warwick hoped the troops on board were not feeling too sick and comforted himself with the thought that they'd certainly have their sea legs before they got to the landing site on November 8. He looked out through the rotating Kent Screen set in the bridge window. The big cargo and passenger ships accompanying them were making light work of the seas, but the LCTs were labouring somewhat and their speed was down to eight knots. There were ships as far as the eye could see spread across ten square miles or so of the approaches to the English Channel. Busy destroyers, frigates, and corvettes were engaged in anti-submarine patrols at the edge of the fleet. To port was the flotilla of Algerine Class minesweepers. Over thirty thousand men were afloat in the Oran convoy of which eighteen thousand would land in the first wave, 10,472 of them on his Beach Zulu in three groups, Green, White, and Red. He wondered how it was possible that the German High Command could remain in ignorance of the vast fleet approaching the Straits of Gibraltar, but they had so far been untroubled by either U-boats or the long-range Condor aircraft that guided them to Allied convoys. He knew there was a second fleet crossing the Atlantic from

America to land in Casablanca, and hoped that they were having an equally trouble-free passage.

Later, he did his Sunday rounds of the ship. Bill Browne had everything spick and span on deck and below, and the hands were smart and cheerful. The soldiers were comfortable enough in their billets, heated and cosy, with plenty of clean buckets provided for those of a weak disposition. The soldiers' mess deck was scrupulously tidy; he could rely on Jo Crowthorne to ensure that, although the US and British officers in charge were strict and efficient and, more to the point, few were suffering from seasickness. He moved down into the engine room, where the huge steam turbines were running at reduced revolutions to maintain the convoy speed of eight knots. It was hot down there, and the engineer, Lieutenant Eddie Freeland RNR, was awaiting his arrival in an immaculate white boiler suit and his regulation cap.

The inspection finished with a visit to the sick bay and a chat with Doc Mitchell and his assembled sick berth team. Extra beds and medical supplies had been shipped on board, and Mitch had a qualified assistant, Surgeon Sub-Lieutenant Agnew (known on board as Baby Doc) straight out of medical school. After that, Warwick joined his officers who were off duty in the ward room for pre-lunch drinks. There was an air of muted excitement and anticipation in the buzz of conversation. Major Bob Brightman of the First US Ranger Battalion and Lieutenant-Colonel Tim Street of the British First Armoured Division were arguing about the logistics of handling the rapid disembarkation and deployment of stores during the initial landing phase.

Warwick was pleased to see they had included Jo Crowthorne in their deliberations. He felt a fatherly duty of care for the smart, honest, and efficient young black officer. Deep down he hoped that Jo would survive to marry his lovely Brigitte and live somewhere in happiness and prosperity. He realised, as Jo had realised before him, that there were considerable obstacles to this fancy, but in his heightened mood, fuelled by the prospect of imminent action, he saw all the hurdles overcome and difficulties conquered as soon as the war was over. He walked across to Jerry Collins, who was standing on his own, sipping a lime juice without much enthusiasm.

"Off the hooch, are we?" He opened the conversation, remembering what Fred Harden had advised after his last run-in with Jerry over Jeanie Cameron. "This isn't an American Navy ship, you know; you're allowed the odd sherry before dinner." Too late he realised that an ex-Louisiana shrimp fisherman was hardly likely to take a glass of pale Amontillado before lunching, on or off a navy vessel.

"Trying to give it up, sir." Jerry's red, rather moon-shaped face turned toward him. "If I'm ever going to make it in this man's Navy, I'll have to cut it back some. I know that."

"Well done. I am so glad you're thinking that way. We're going into a big show in a few days and, for that matter, might be in action at any time now if a U-boat spots the convoy. Men perform better for sober officers, and too much drinking doesn't really improve the thought process when a lot of things start happening fast."

"It's not just that, sir. Jeanie made me promise to stay on the wagon until we see each other again, and I promised."

"Oh, dear!" exclaimed Warwick. "I hope she doesn't say that to all her dad's customers, or it would be a poor look out for their pub's cash flow."

"She thinks a lot of me, sir, and I miss her. We got very close in those last few days before we sailed. As soon as we are back in England, I'm going up to Scotland to spend my leave with her and the family."

Warwick thought he could personally vouch for their closeness on one of their last nights at least, but he only signified his approval to Jerry. "She's a fine girl with ambition, Jerry. She'll drive you to great things. You'll probably end up an admiral in the USN or something."

Warwick moved on, thinking while he circulated among the other officers that he had at least patched things up.

Looking back, he saw Jerry had moved over to talk to David MacDonald. He was animated and smiling and radiating contentment. Warwick realised that this change in his mood was due to their recent conversation, and felt a little guilty. He had engineered their talk in the spirit of Fred Harden's advice. It hadn't meant much to him; just a few passing words and witticisms to be friendly and show that he harboured no hard feelings. It dawned on Warwick that it had meant a great deal more than that to Jerry. It had made all the difference between his previous lonely depression on leaving his sweetheart and going to sea under a cloud of disapproval from his captain, and his newly found pride in his position and confidence in his duty for the task that lay ahead. After their chat, Jerry's morale seemed to have improved one hundred percent.

There were a couple of false alarms that night as twitchy lookouts thought they saw torpedo tracks or periscopes, but the convoy passed three hundred miles west of Ushant later the next day without incident. The wind dropped away and the sea flattened. The cloud base lifted and there were patches of blue sky and even sun, surprisingly warm for October in the Bay of Biscay. Out in the Atlantic far to the northwest, wolf packs of twenty or even thirty U-boats battled with convoy escorts and the increasing number of long-range patrol aircraft from their bases in Northern Ireland and Nova Scotia, but there was little enemy activity away from the regular convoy routes.

Unknown to any of them, they had actually been sighted by U-234 but her report had been delayed by overflying aircraft that had forced her to crash dive and the message eventually arrived in the German High Command HQ in a garbled form. There it was decided that the heavily escorted convoy was probably intended to re-supply Malta, and Hitler and Admiral Doenitz had agreed that it could be safely left to the twenty-five U-boats stationed in the Mediterranean, plus the Luftwaffe squadrons based in Sicily and Southern Italy. Consequently there was no need to divert any U-boats from their primary task of attacking the Allied convoys bound for Britain from the USA. And so the voyage went on, uninterrupted by the enemy or the weather.

They were due to pass through the Straits of Gibraltar on the night of November 6. This would be a time of maximum danger, as the huge fleet would be clearly visible from the Spanish coast, where there were many German observers and agents stationed.

Warwick ordered his fleet to double up on lookouts and watchkeepers for the passage and assume the amber readiness state – one below Condition Red (which meant that the crew remained at action stations). He lay down on his bunk in his shirt and old uniform trousers and switched off the bunk light to try to get some sleep, but his mind was too active and he tossed and turned restlessly. He thought of the forthcoming action, and worried that he was apprehensive and (he admitted this only to himself) just a little afraid. He had only been in action once before – in the old *SS Freshwater Bay* in these same waters nearly a year ago and that had been sudden and unanticipated.

Come to think of it, he hadn't reacted too well then, either, especially when he saw what the shell from the U-boat's forward gun had done to young John Evered and his damage control team. No one knew how sick and helpless he had felt then except his old and understanding first mate, Cyril Naismith. He had got away with it that time and received a lot of praise for a moderately successful action which had resulted in the eventual destruction of the U-168. How would he cope when the time to land on a hostile beach came? He had to keep command of his emotions and fears; the men all relied on him. He had been promoted beyond his years because of that. He must justify his promotion and the faith his superior officers had had in him.

He tore himself away from that unsettling train of thought. He would concentrate on planning for his future with Sarah and imagine what his life would be like when his child was born in a few months, with a comfortable house in the country and plenty of money coming in. When this war was over, he could leave the service with a good war record as a senior reserve officer and find a well-paid job in some shipping office in the City.

On the other hand, they might even buy a wooden forty-or even fifty-foot sailing yacht and then the three of them could go on long sailing voyages together. He imagined finding such a vessel in a neglected state in a remote boatyard, it having been stored in a tin shed for the duration of the war. He pictured the boat and what he would have to do to refit it. Scraping and varnishing; stripping back the hull with a blowlamp and scraper. Then there would be the task of removing the engine with a block and tackle and a tripod to support the lift. He knew how to rig that sort of gear; he had been well trained as a cadet. He went through the rope work, with its knots and splices in his head. He imagined having the engine reconditioned and cleaned, sprayed and replaced. He would have to reconnect the electrics, throttle, and gears. All the wiring would need to be secured and he would clean and paint out the engine compartment while it was empty. Then there were a couple of banks of batteries and a big, belt-driven magneto to fit to charge them up. The shaft would have to be realigned when the engine was put back in place by adjusting the shims under the bosses that rested on the wooden engine bearers.

Then he would need to build in a proper chart table. He could do that himself; he had always been adept at woodwork. There would have to be a place for his sextant and a chronometer. She would need her masts and spars scraped and several coats of varnish. He'd rub them down with wet and dry emery paper of increasing fineness between each coat. The boat would need a new suit of sails.

He thought through the process of swinging his yacht and adjusting her compass. They could sail to the Caribbean or perhaps the Mediterranean. He tried to remember the calculations for the changes in magnetic effect when the boat's latitude changed. Come to think of it, he really didn't have to work at all; they had all the capital and income they would need to live that sort of life. In his thoughts of peacetime, the sun was always shining.

Then he began to think of Sarah and how much he loved her and missed her. Now he really wished he had told her again how he felt about her in the hurried phone call he had made in the passageway of the Royal Northern and Clyde Yacht Club at the mouth of the Gareloch before they sailed. How she had changed his life and become the central part of it. Just over a year ago, he had been an obscure, impoverished, single, junior officer on a passenger ship, and now he was a commander with a fleet of sixteen ships and a small staff of his own. He had a big house and a beautiful and rich wife.

His mind wandered back to the current problems. He had to finish this war in one piece before his dreams could be realised. He went over his orders for the umpteenth time, making sure he had every detail of the planned operation firmly in his brain.

He was awakened by a gentle shake and the smell of a mug of hot kye.

"You put down for a call at 0730, sir." It was Petty Officer Steward Morton. "Lieutenant MacDonald asked me to tell you that Cape de San Vincente is in sight on the port bow, about twelve miles distant."

"Thank you, Morton; tell the officer of the watch I'll be up on the bridge in a few minutes, please."

He sipped his kye between showering, shaving, and dressing. He had managed to sleep for about six hours and felt much better. He was comforted by the fact that Morton had had to shake him awake. He knew most of the soldiers and many of the crew had taken to sleeping on deck fully clad, with their lifejackets on, in case of a sudden torpedo attack.

Morton would tell the mess deck that the skipper was sleeping like a baby and was obviously unworried by torpedoes and any resistance from the Vichy French forces in Oran when they arrived. Morton was an inveterate gossip and thus represented a subtle way to keep the mess decks informed of things Warwick wanted them to know about but couldn't broadcast overtly.

There were 155 miles to go to the entrance to the Straits of Gibraltar; about fifteen and a half hours at the current convoy speed of ten knots. They would be there at 2300 for a night passage, passing about five miles off the Rock where General Eisenhower had established the Operation Torch headquarters.

CHAPTER THIRTY-FOUR

The passage through the Straits that night was uneventful. There was a moderate southerly breeze and a slight sea and swell on the starboard beam. The ship was rolling gently. Up on the darkened bridge, the lights of Gibraltar and Tangier and Ceuta were clearly visible to port and starboard. Warwick could smell the pines and spices of North Africa coming off the land. The PPI display of the new radar set threw a greenish light over the face of its operator. It showed the attendant LCTs in their correct formation in three columns, with *HMS Bruiser* as the central guide ship with the converted tanker, *HMS Mohican* just astern of her.

Warwick was on the bridge with the watchkeepers, Bill Browne and Midshipman Rodwick. The supply ships were a mile or so behind them, guarded by aircraft carriers, cruisers, and battleships. The screen of destroyers, frigates, and corvettes was ahead, leading the entire convoy, all of which proceeded at ten knots toward the Golfe d'Arzew, just to the east of the city of Oran, and where Z Beach was located, some 252 miles away.

"*Bulolo* signalling, sir," Midshipman Rodwell reported as the flagship's 10-inch signal lamp began to flash at them from astern.

"It's from the admiral, sir," the midshipman reported after a while. In due course, the Yeoman of Signals pressed a signal paper into Warwick's hand. They were ordered to commence zigzagging to pattern three commencing at 2300, keep strict radio silence, and close up for action stations.

"Yeoman; make to our fleet; 'Execute to follow, zigzag pattern three. Close up for action stations and observe strict radio silence immediately on receipt. Acknowledge.' You'll need a signalman on the other bridge wing for column three and one behind the chart room for our column when we signal to execute at 2300." Warwick continued "Rodwell, you must call the time down to the signalmen for the execute signal."

Warwick went to the chart table with Bill Browne to have a look at the zigzag pattern. Their forward progress toward the landing beach would be reduced to eight knots. It would take thirty one and a half hours, which would bring them off the beach at around 0630 local time on November 8. Warwick realised that Admiral Burrough must have made the same calculation before sending the signal.

He remained on the bridge until 2315 to make sure all the landing craft maintained their stations and that they were all quite clear on the timing of each course change. Everyone was now in their white anti-flash gear, with their kapok lifejackets and tin helmets on. The 20mm gun crews were closed up on either side of the bridge. Warwick wished they had some heavier armament to deal with the forts on the run in; these twin 20mm guns were really only effective against aircraft and any Vichy infantry who might be opposing the landing from the ground behind the beaches.

He walked into the chart room and sat down. He felt the familiar butterflies in his stomach at the prospect of imminent action. He hoped the admiral would relax the Action Stations order at daybreak; everyone would be exhausted if they were kept closed up for thirty hours. There was little chance of a German U-boat or Luftwaffe bomber attacking them here; all the available German forces were engaged in trying to deter the Royal Navy sinking the Italian supply ships and tankers whose cargoes were so desperately needed for Rommel's Africa Korps, now being pushed inexorably westward from el Alamein by the British Eighth Army under their new and energetic commander, General Bernard Law Montgomery.

Warwick looked out of the scuttle to the receding lights of Gibraltar, now on the port quarter. He suddenly thought of Esperanza and then wished he hadn't. He wondered if she was still working at the Red Shoes Bar. She was only about ten miles away as the crow flew, if she was. Maybe she was in bed, making love to some hairy sailor at this very minute. He found the thought and the picture it conjured up in his mind strangely disturbing. He sat down on the chartroom settee, took off his helmet, and rested his head on the corner, padded by his lifejacket. He closed his eyes for an instant and nodded off.

Jack Watson gave him a gentle shake at 0540. "It's dawn now, sir. Sunrise is in about twenty minutes. You can see the convoy now quite clearly. I thought you'd like to be called when it got light."

Warwick awoke with a start. He hadn't written any night orders nor had he left any instructions as to when to call him and he felt somewhat remiss in consequence. At the same time, he was glad for the five hours or so of sleep he'd had, glad he was able to sleep so soundly in the face of impending action and glad that everyone would probably have subconsciously noted that fact. The admiral had stood down the fleet from action stations at dawn, so Warwick took time to shower and shave before coming back up on to the bridge.

It was a muggy day with no wind and eight-eighths, low, dark stratus cloud. Visibility was limited to around a mile and a half and radar transmissions had been ordered restricted to avoid nearby submarines picking them up. There would be no danger of an air attack unless the cloud base lifted. They were still zigzagging and Warwick doubted there was much danger from U-boats in the persistent poor visibility.

He left the ship in the capable hands of Bill Browne and climbed down the steel ladders to the troop decks. Here it was warm with a buzz of activity, with mechanics preparing the tanks and armoured cars for action, the gunners cleaning and oiling their guns, and little knots of American Rangers and the

British First Armoured Division cleaning their carbines or rifles, cat-napping, chatting, or playing cards.

He spoke to Major Brightman of the US Rangers who was also doing his rounds. "How's it going, Bob? All ready for the big one?"

"The US Rangers are always ready, sir. We've checked and re-checked everything. It's the waiting that gets them all; they just want to get to the beach and do their stuff. Do you have anything more about the likely level of opposition, sir?"

"Nothing new Bob that I haven't already told you. News came through this morning that Monty had broken out from el Alamein and Rommel is in full retreat, with the German and Italian troops fleeing to the west and huge numbers of prisoners of war captured; mainly Italians. They've also captured vast numbers of guns, lorries, and tanks, all completely empty of fuel and abandoned where they came to a halt."

"That's good stuff, sir," said Bob with a wide grin. "When our French friends in Oran hear that they might think twice about which side they ought to be supporting. It might discourage some of them from trying to shoot up our men and the landing craft."

"Let's hope so. There'll always be a few fanatics who want to die for Hitler or Marshall Petain or someone or other. Maybe some of the more sensible ones will shoot at them instead of us."

Warwick continued around the troop decks, stopping to pass a few words with the officers and men. He judged morale was high and everyone anxious to get to grips with the opposition and get the job done, for which they had trained so long and hard.

The day passed slowly with numerous signals flashed from the flagship dealing with minor details for the landing the next morning. The troopships were to anchor three miles off Beach Z and lower their Higgins Boats and LCUs, then embark the troops via scramble nets. At the same time *HMS Bruiser* would lower her boats with the big crane and man them with

US Rangers. Then the small landing craft would follow *HMS Bruiser*, *HMS Mohican*, and the fifteen big LCTs onto the beach so that the disembarkation of the maximum numbers of men and equipment could be as near simultaneous as possible and ensure the beach and its immediate hinterland could be secured as an initial bridgehead.

There was not expected to be any seaborne opposition from the Vichy French Navy but if there were, there were plenty of screening battleships, cruisers, and destroyers lying three or four miles offshore to deal with it. Warwick thought it all sounded very neat, cut and dried. He recalled Clausewitz's sobering dictum, 'War is the province of chance.' Clausewitz had believed that that the most detailed battle plans tend to go to pieces as soon as the battle is actually joined.

Action stations were ordered for the fleet at midnight and the flagship took up the guide position. Cape Ferrat showed up on the radar at 0010 on that cloudy, calm night of November 8, distant thirty-five miles on the starboard bow. More land appeared as they closed the beach. They could pick out Cape Carbon and the shoreline of the Golfe d'Arzew with bright patches on the PPI representing the buildings of the hamlets of Damesme and St. Leu which threw back stronger echoes than the sloping sand beach.

Warwick planned to make his approach at 90 degrees from seaward, with *HMS Bruiser* in the middle, just opposite St. Leu and one column of landing craft spread out on each side. A large, modern screening destroyer, *USS Hughes*, had been detailed to deal with the two forts near the point to the south east of Cape Carbon should they open fire on the beachhead.

They anchored just after 0500 and started offloading the small landing craft. The troop and supply ships anchored just astern of them while the warships detailed to Z Beach remained patrolling to screen the operation. That part of the exercise went without problems, in spite of the very subdued lighting that was all that was permitted in order to maintain the secrecy of the operation for as long as possible. It seemed to be working, as there was no observable activity or moving lights from the shore. By 0610, the unloading was completed and they raised anchor and headed for the shore with the large LCTs fanned out on either side of them.

CHAPTER THIRTY-FIVE

Twenty-five miles to the west off the old city of Oran, things were moving at a much faster pace. An inbound Vichy convoy escorted by four French destroyers had sighted the invasion fleet and broadcast a warning to the forces ashore. The landing at Oran had lost its element of surprise and ran into heavy opposition. Two US Coastguard cutters *USS Walney* and *USS Hartford*, each with three hundred troops aboard, found their approach to the harbour blocked by two big Vichy French destroyers from the convoy escort as well as coming under fire from heavy artillery from forts and gun emplacements that were defending the town. The *Walney* was set on fire, then capsized and sank. The *Hartford* was hit in the engine room and forward gun turret and her captain, severely injured, was forced to order abandon ship as all power was lost and she was helplessly drifting about in Oran Harbour; a sitting duck for the guns on shore. The two Vichy destroyers made their escape to the east at high speed on a course that would take them past Z Beach.

The invasion fleet at Z Beach knew nothing of this drama unfolding twenty-five miles away. As *HMS Bruiser* headed for shore with the large LCTs on either side and the little Higgins boats full of troops following, Fort de la Point near Cape Carbon to starboard opened fire on the beach with a single, 120mm gun. Another gun from the forts started firing on the *USS Hughes*, which swiftly responded with her five-inch guns. The shells aimed at the invasion fleet were not very accurate; the first two shells passing overhead with a "wirra-wirra" noise and landing far up the beach to port, almost up to the small town of La Macta. The rate of fire was very slow – around one shell every two minutes. The forts were over two miles away, and Warwick decided against responding with his 20mm anti-aircraft guns. They would be of very limited deterrent effect against fixed shore emplacements. After six or so shells had been fired to no affect, *USS Hughes* found her range and the forts were silenced.

There were some moving lights on the shore to port near the settlement of Port aux Poules, a mile or so past La Macta. Small arms fire and a few bursts from a heavy machine gun greeted them as the ship grounded with a shudder. Bill Browne, forward, began extending the hundred and forty-foot ramp. The LCTs with their shallower draft began to pass *HMS Bruiser* and take the ground further inshore. *HMS Mohican* grounded alongside and ahead and began extending her ramps from either side of her bows. When the landing craft ramps had been lowered, the troops, jeeps, and small armoured cars streamed ashore from them and crossed the pebbly beach, taking cover under the scrub at the top of the rise. The fire from the shore intensified. Warwick ordered the port side 20mm guns to sweep the beach where the scattered lights were moving nearer.

Dawn was breaking but some misty patches persisted. It promised to be a warm, calm day. The sound of many large aeroplanes could be heard overhead. Warwick knew there was a parachute brigade due to land behind the town of Oran, having flown in directly from Cornwall. He had a passing thought that they must be somewhat off course to be flying over Z beach, twenty-five miles or so to the east of the town, but other things were demanding his attention.

Now *HMS Bruiser's* big ramp was down and the first of the Matilda and Sherman tanks was charging up the beach. They were accompanied by the First Infantry Combat troops and elements of the First US Ranger Battalion. Bill Browne was designated as Beachmaster, organising the landing and the arrangement of landed stores and equipment, assisted by

Jo Crowthorne, who was liaising with the US Army. Two-ton Bedford trucks loaded with ammunition and stores followed the tanks and jeeps and began to unload in the designated areas on the beach. Smaller vehicles from the LSTs converged on the ammunition and stores dumps. More troops were coming ashore from the Higgins boats. The front rank of the invading army was over the crest of the low, scrub-covered dunes behind the beach and had reached the single railway line. There were some small field pieces firing from both the port and starboard sides now, but they were aimed at the troops on the beach and not the landing craft, which were mostly empty and beginning to wind themselves off by their stern anchors. General Fredendall and his staff were landed in the second wave, the beachhead having by then been firmly established to a depth of two miles or so.

At this stage of the landing, the LSTs were scheduled to steam out to the supply ships and take on additional tanks, armoured vehicles, and field guns as well as the heavier crates of stores if the sea remained calm, transporting them to shore to augment the landing. The Higgins boats would continue landing troops from the troop ships throughout the day. *HMS Bruiser*, her main work done, would go out to anchor just off the beach from whence she could control and organise the landings and prioritise the supplies, together with Bill and Jo on shore via the short range, line of sight VHF radios.

HMS Bruiser came astern off the pebbles easily. The small Mediterranean tide was flooding and although its total range was only about three feet, it had come up about nine inches in the hour they had been grounded, which was enough to make the refloating easy. Jack Watson was aft, attending to the party weighing the stern anchor. Jerry Collins was monitoring the VHF and operational radio net broadcasts from the port side of the bridge. Midshipman Rodwell was keeping the log and passing on the helm and engine orders, and David, as Navigator, was on the plot with his PO Navigator's Yeoman.

Warwick was just beginning to think how trouble-free it had all been after all their arduous months of training. Really, it had been a walk-over. A few ill-armed defenders, the odd ancient and badly aimed heavy gun to oppose them, and the troops landed with tanks, guns, and supplies and the beach head secured with very little fuss or confusion. It had been a text book operation.

There was a sudden shout from the VHF set. It was from *USS Hughes*.

"All ships, all ships; two in number, hostile destroyers bearing 302 degrees, distant three miles course 120 degrees, speed up to thirty knots!" It was the escaping Vichy destroyers, having made the twenty-five miles from Oran in less than an hour.

USS Hughes made a wide turn to port and engaged the leading enemy destroyer with her two forward five-inch guns. It was a well-executed manoeuvre from an experienced commander and crew. She registered a hit on the leading enemy destroyer with her second salvo. Meanwhile, the second destroyer, later identified as the *VFS Vauban*, was behind and about six cables to starboard of the ship engaging *USS Hughes* and was thus shielded from the latter ship's hostile fire. She altered course to starboard toward the beach.

"Port 30, emergency full speed ahead!" Without really thinking what he was doing, Warwick turned *HMS Bruiser* through 120 degrees to intercept the *Vauban*, acting on his subconscious instinct to protect his fleet.

"Give me a course to intercept her, David, assume her speed to be thirty knots at course 135 degrees and ours to be eighteen knots!"

"Steer 354 degrees, sir," replied David after a few moments work calculating with the help of the ship's Battenberg interception plotter.

The ship shook as the turbines worked up to their maximum revolutions. There was an urgent call from the engine room, which was taken by Jerry. It was Eddie Freeland, the engineer, advising that they had only about ten minutes at this speed before the turbine bearings overheated and seized up.

"Let him know that three minutes is all I need," snapped Warwick, "and make a broadcast for me. Tell the crew to hold on and keep their heads down. We're going to ram that bloody frog destroyer!"

Warwick watched as the destroyer's for'd gun turrets swung toward them. There was less than a mile between them now. Their closing speed was around forty-two knots – under ninety seconds to go. With the prospect of imminent action he was excited and fearless with the adrenalin pumping through his veins.

"Tell Lieutenant Watson to open fire on her bridge!" he shouted. "It's an open bridge and it will make them keep their damn heads down, if nothing else."

The light, 20mm anti-aircraft guns opened with rapid fire on the approaching *Vauban* and little flashes and dots of light showed where their shells were taking effect. Then the two 5. 5 inch forward guns of the French destroyer fired. The shells went high, as the range was very rapidly decreasing and her fire control system proved too slow to cope. One shell passed harmlessly overhead; the other hit the latticework of the big crane aft of the bridge, which folded up and collapsed on the after deck in a clattering shower of sparks. Twenty seconds or so went by and then the *Vauban's* forward guns fired again. One of the shells passed clear to port, the other hit *Bruiser's* bridge square on.

Warwick found himself on his back, looking up at the grey sky through the jagged edges of the shattered deckhead. The port side of the bridge was open to the elements now and smoke and debris rained around him. His tin helmet bowled away across the deck. He rolled over to look for it and saw Jerry Collins lying on his side about ten feet away. He noticed, as if in a dream, that Jerry had no head. He struggled to his feet. His scalp was bleeding into his left eye. He wiped the blood away hastily with his sleeve. Shrapnel had hit his left shoulder and his left arm was hanging loose. There was blood on his blue uniform trousers below his left knee.

David shouted, "Starboard twenty!" Warwick looked out forward. The *Vauban* was now very close; only a couple of cables away. Too late, the French captain had realised his danger and made an emergency turn to port to get out of *Bruiser's* way. The *Vauban* was doing nearly forty knots and made a magnificent sight as she heeled inward while she turned and presented her starboard side to the onrushing *HMS Bruiser*. David had anticipated the manoeuvre and had turned the ship to starboard to intercept her. *Vauban's* forward guns fired again at point blank range. There was a violent explosion on the after deck as one of the shells struck it, followed by a gout of smoke and flame.

That last turn away by the *Vauban* had sealed her fate. Bow to bow, she might have stood a chance against the much larger ship, especially if she had stopped her engines to lessen the impact, but there was no hope for her now as *HMS Bruiser* hit her nearly square on, just forward of her bridge and rode up over her as she was designed to do, with her flat, landing-craft bottom. There was a horrible screeching sound of tortured metal and a cloud of spray and smoke mixed. The *Vauban* was rolled right over on her port side while the six thousand tons on her foredeck pressed her bow down. Her forward momentum at full speed carried her under the sea, like a submarine crash diving. Her starboard screw came out of the water, still revolving at high speed. Warwick had a view of her bridge officers in their white anti-flash gear, frozen in horror, clinging onto the sides of their open bridge, looking up at the huge, exposed, red-leaded bottom of *HMS Bruiser* as their ship rolled over and dived beneath the waves. It was the last sight they would ever see in this world.

"Stop engines!" ordered Warwick. "Yeoman, get the cox'n to sound the for'd ballast tanks; I suspect we've ripped the bottom out of her."

290

The stern of the *Vauban* reared up on their port side. Some men survived there, gradually dropping off it into the sea. After a minute or so, the stern sank with a swirl of water and a host of huge bubbles, leaving only an oily scum and numerous pieces of wreckage.

"Get Jack Watson to launch the duty sea boat and see if he can get those Frenchmen aboard," said Warwick to David. There wasn't much for David to do in the navigation department now.

HMS Bruiser came to a stop in the calm sea; well down by the head with the forward ballast tanks filled with seawater. Normally these were flooded up when beaching the ship, then pumped out when she was ready to be hauled off. Now she was floating on their tank tops. Warwick felt suddenly weak and tired. He'd lost a lot of blood, was quite badly injured, and the adrenalin was ebbing as the excitement of the brief action changed into the mundane work of clearing up. His face was white and drawn, and he swayed a little and supported himself on the jagged plating. David returned to the bridge, followed by the Yeoman of Signals. The bridge VHF was shattered; it had been where Jerry had been stationed.

"One officer and three ratings dead and four injured, one badly," reported David. "The forward ballast tanks are open to the sea and the ramp is set back about ten feet and will need shoring up and securing. There's a signal from *USS Hughes* congratulating us, and another from Commodore Troubridge. Shall I read that one out, sir?"

Warwick found his bridge chair and sat down heavily, holding his damaged left arm. "Go ahead David," he muttered.

"It's addressed to you personally sir, and reads; 'Heartfelt congratulations on your exemplary and highly successful action in sinking the Vichy French destroyer *Vauban*. Your conduct in unhesitatingly joining action with a much more powerful adversary in order to protect your landing craft and the progress of the disembarkation is worthy of the highest traditions of the service and I shall ensure that it is mentioned in despatches. Well done, Warwick.' Sir, you need to go below to Mitch!" David suddenly realised that Warwick was close to fainting and likely to drop off his chair. "We can look after things here, sir; you must go below."

David and the Navigator's Yeoman caught Warwick before he fell and laid him gently on the steel deck among the debris with his head pillowed on a lifejacket. A party from the sick bay had bagged up and removed Jerry Collins's remains and swabbed away the blood and now moved over to Warwick with a khaki, canvass, wooden-ribbed, Nielson stretcher. They lashed him in it, barely conscious, and carried him down the iron ladders to the sick bay on the main deck. Warwick noticed through the haze that seemed to be closing in on him that there was a big shell hole in the after deckhouse from which a small fire was rapidly being extinguished by Cox'n Blessed's damage control party. There were a couple more bodies laid out clear of the damage; whether they were alive or dead and their identities remained unknown to him.

"I ought to do something about that," he muttered to himself. "I've got to write to their next of kin. We'll have to bury them at sea, I suppose. We must stop the ship. Poor Jeanie; she's lost her Louisiana shrimp fisherman for good. I hope she's not pregnant. Poor Jerry, just when he was beginning to come good. I ought to have been nicer to him; now I've lost the chance forever. I'm a bad captain, that's for sure. Did we really sink that destroyer? I hope it wasn't an American one!"

His thoughts meandered as he gradually lapsed in and out of consciousness through shock and loss of blood. He started to shiver and his teeth to chatter. Suddenly, on that warm, Mediterranean day, he felt very cold.

Surgeon Lieutenant Ian Mitchell examined his latest patient. His assistant, Surgeon Sub-Lieutenant James Agnew, was fixing a drip over their most seriously injured casualty, Able Seaman Knowles, who was likely to need his leg amputated below the knee that evening. They had arranged to have him transferred to the hospital ship that afternoon, where the amputation would be carried out in their fully-equipped operating theatre.

"Now what have we here?" Mitch whispered more to himself than to his two attendant sick berth ratings. He checked Warwick's rapid pulse and temperature and noted his pale, clammy face. "He's in shock; give me some blankets and cover him up."

He saw that the shrapnel wound on Warwick's head, which extended from just inside his hairline to a few millimetres clear of his left eye, was only superficial and had already been sealed by an encrustation of black, congealed blood.

"As Nelson's barber surgeons used to say, 'A clean cut wound, bound up in its own blood, will often heal by first intention.' I think we'll leave this one, although if I was in the cosmetic surgery business I'd want to suture it as soon and as neatly as possible. I'm afraid our gallant commander will carry that scar for the rest of his life now. Just put a bandage round it to keep the dirt off and protect the wound."

He cut away the trouser leg and noted another wound below Warwick's left knee. This was still oozing a little blood, so, with the help of his sick berth attendant, he cleaned it off, painted it with iodine, put a couple of stitches in and bound it up as it was. They rolled Warwick over on his stomach very gently, ensuring he had clear access to breathe, and cut the clothing away from his left shoulder. There was a large gash in it still leaking a little bright, red, blood.

"The deltoid muscle has been badly torn," Doc dictated to Baby Doc who had joined him and was taking notes. "The scapula and clavicle appear to have been fractured in several places. I really don't want to probe too much to find out. Somewhere in there he's bleeding; some minor artery has been damaged, judging by the colour and amount of blood discharging from the wound. That will stop in a short while, so we can leave that pretty well undisturbed, too. Rig up another saline drip, Jim, and I'll just open up the entry area a bit and have a close look."

After a few more moments of visual examination he came to a diagnosis. "There's a lump of metal in there lying against the posterior rib cage. It's probably fractured a couple of ribs and may be resting against the upper spine. I can see the outer part of it; it looks like a bit of shell casing. It's deep seated and he needs an x-ray and more attention than we can give him here. There's no time to be lost; the whole of the left chest area will be infected in a few hours and he'll die of septicaemia unless we get him to the hospital ship and get that metal fragment out of him. Give him a shot of morphine and put a compression bandage on the entry wound. I'll see if we can have him ferried across as soon as possible."

CHAPTER THIRTY-SIX

Unconscious, Warwick was re-lashed in his rigid stretcher with his shoulder and arm immobilised by a sling and round body bandage and taken across by the hospital ship's LCI. The surgeon captain RNR, who in civilian life had been the Professor of Surgery in St. Thomas's Hospital in London, carried out the extraction of what proved to be part of the casing of a French 5. 5-inch shell.

"Put that in a jar in some surgical spirit, seal it up, and label it, please, nurse," he remarked as he and his assistant surgeon cleaned up the wound. "When he recovers he might want it as a souvenir to show his wife and children."

They took an X-ray and then spent some four hours realigning Warwick's rib cage, scapula, and clavicle. Part of his arm, as well as his shoulder, was supported by canvas bandages and wooden splints, leaving his arm immobilised from the elbow upwards. The whole upper arm was lashed in against his trunk. He was given another injection of morphine and settled down for the night. The hospital ship, originally a Cunard Line passenger ship which had recently seen service as an Indian-owned pilgrim ship and which dated from 1904, was carrying over two hundred seriously wounded casualties and it was decided that she should land them in Gibraltar and then return to the beachhead to take on the inevitable numbers of newly wounded army casualties.

By the morning of November 9, Oran was surrounded and its two airfields captured. The other two landing areas were already in Allied hands. Resistance ashore had been determined in places, patchy in others, and part of the French Foreign Legion had refused to oppose the American troops advancing on them, firing one rifle bullet into the sky as their token opposition, then happily surrendering en-masse. Obviously the joys of Nazi domination and the Vichy rule under Marshall Petain were entirely lost on them, and they seemed much relieved to be under Allied control.

The hospital ship had a good turn of speed in spite of her age, and came alongside the main quay, Gibraltar in the afternoon of November 9. Warwick and the other seriously injured men were landed and taken by army ambulance to the main hospital. Warwick was put in a clean bed and after a sound sleep he awoke in the early hours of November 10 to find a concerned and very attractive French nurse bending over him.

"My god; I'm in heaven," he exclaimed as her long sleeves brushed over his unshaven cheek, and her small, slim white hands rearranged his pillows and settled his left shoulder more comfortably. She had long, black hair under her nurses' cap. "What's your name then?"

"My name is Josianne, sir. Are you feeling better now?"

"Better for seeing you, that's for sure. Where am I?"

"You're in the recovery ward of Gibraltar Military Hospital, sir. You were landed from the hospital ship last night. The doctor said that you were to lie still to give your shoulder a chance to heal."

The following day, Warwick felt much better. He was a big, strong man in the prime of life and he recovered from his injuries and loss of blood more quickly than most patients would have done. The news came through to the wards that Vichy resistance had now ceased and that North Africa from Casablanca to Algiers was in Allied hands. General Anderson's forces were preparing to advance on Tunis, but were held up by the continuous cold winter rains which turned the countryside into a quagmire of sticky mud. Meanwhile General Montgomery and his Eighth Army were relentlessly advancing along the Libyan coast, driving Rommel and the Africa Corps ever westward toward the Mareth Line on the Tunisian border to the south and taking thousands of hapless Italian Army prisoners into the bargain. Within a few months, all North Africa would be in Allied hands, with a loss to the Axis of a quarter of a million German soldiers and huge quantities of war materiel, opening up what Winston Churchill had called 'the soft underbelly of Europe' for invasion.

He sat up in bed, reading his mail, which Josianne had just brought him.

"Are those from your wife, sir?" she asked as she saw two of the letters addressed in Sarah's neat, black script.

"Yes, indeed I'd know her writing anywhere. I hope she's still missing me." He dug a photograph of Sarah out of his bedside locker and showed it to Josianne.

"She's very beautiful," remarked Josianne in her sweet, French accent, perhaps a little wistfully.

"Thank you; I think so, too. She's expecting a baby sometime in April; it will be our first child."

There was also a letter from his mother, one from his sister Sally, and one from an old shipmate with whom he had sailed when he was a junior first officer in an old P&O passenger ship and who now had been sent to America to take command of a newly built Liberty ship. *Mr. Jeremy Smythe of the old WETB must have got hold of him when he docked in London, too,* he thought to himself.

Sally had been appointed Surgical House Officer and was enjoying her work immensely. Skilled surgeons were in short supply, as so many were serving in the forces, so she was taking on much more complex surgical procedures than would be normal in peacetime for someone only a few months qualified. His mother wrote that things were much the same in the Sussex countryside. The big news from her was that his father had been posted to the South-East Transport Command, serving under a Regular Army lieutenant-colonel of the Royal Army Service Corps. It was a much bigger job than he had held in Northern

Ireland and Scotland, as preparations for the inevitable invasion of France would come under his purview, in addition to the continuous transportation required for the supply of the southern RN, Army, and RAF bases. It also meant he was home much more often at weekends, as his office was only about fifty miles away, in the outskirts of Portsmouth. Sarah had been over for a happy visit to them the previous Saturday.

He had saved Sarah's letters until last. Sarah wrote at length. She trusted he was safe. It was too early for any reference to their success in Oran and the equal success of the other landings to find its way into letters from home, so she could only wish him well. Her second letter indicated that Robin King had spoken to her in confidence and told her that they had received classified signals to the effect that the fleet was approaching Gibraltar and had suffered no losses to date. She said that things were very quiet in that remote corner of Hampshire. She had mothballed the Packard, having got Mr. Alfrey to jack it up and put it on blocks in the stable buildings then cover it with a white dust sheet. It used much more petrol that she could possibly obtain. She had packed up their little boat, had the decorator rub it down and varnish it, then put it on bearers and covered it with a dust sheet, too. She had got Mr. Alfrey to drape the sails and ropes over the dry beams above to keep them from damp and mould.

She used the little Alvis but rarely, only driving down to the village to get shopping once a week and to the pub for a meal and chat to the locals each Saturday night. Otherwise she ate in the kitchen in the evenings with Mr. and Mrs. Alfrey who then repaired to their rooms above the stables for a chat and a cup of steaming hot Horlicks. Mostly she was in bed by eleven pm.

The Wray Optical Company had started making large licence payments monthly, as they had a huge backlog of orders for the special compass binoculars from all three services. She had a stack of money in the bank, and very little to spend it on, now that the house and outbuildings had been refurbished and redecorated. Mr. Pearson, their old solicitor, had found her a nice, young chartered accountant, a Mr. Childs, who had had polio as a child and so was unable to serve in the armed forces. He was keeping their accounts and advising her on their investments. She had bought another freehold house to rent in Newcastle, and her friend Shirley was looking after her property portfolio there and collecting the rents, as well as running the boarding house where they met. She was thinking of putting the boarding house and the Newcastle properties into a small, limited company and giving Shirley around twenty percent of the shares in it, with Warwick and herself holding the balance of shares equally between them. She was also considering buying some properties to rent in Southampton and Portsmouth and forming another little limited company to run them. She asked what her husband's views were on these proposals.

Doctor Williams was very happy with the progress of her pregnancy and had advised her that she should rest as often as possible with her feet up to relieve her slight oedema; her ankles were a little swollen. The baby was growing rapidly and starting to kick violently and she was sure it was a boy as it was showing the same energy as his father.

She ended all three letters by saying that she was very lonely, that she loved him more than life itself and would do so for all the rest of her life, and that she was lonely without him and was longing for him to come back to her.

He called for pen, envelopes, and paper and began to write back to Sarah, Sally, his parents, and his friend in America to congratulating him on his sudden elevation to command.

That afternoon they took the bandages off his left leg and his head, and Josianne gently washed off the crusted blood. After she finished, she handed Warwick a mirror. Warwick looked at his reflection for a long time and rather ruefully. There was a wide, red gash running from about an inch inside his hairline on his left temple, and finishing just below and close to the outer side of his left eye. If it had been sewn up within a few hours of the shrapnel hitting him, it would now only be a barely discernible white line that would fade with age. As it was, he was scarred for life, and to add to his rather morose inspection of his reflection, he noted that the hair around the upper end of the scar was growing back as white stubble, contrasting with the dark brown colour of his natural hair.

"I ought to go to Heidelberg University when this war is over," he said to Josianne. "With this scar, I'd be a big hit with the duelling fraternity"

Later that day, he was visited by Vice-Admiral MacDonald, now Governor of Gibraltar, with Warwick's friend from *Freshwater Bay* days, Lieutenant-Commander Jim Marsh.

"A fine job you've done, my son," began the admiral. "Your action in ramming that Vichy destroyer to protect the big Oran landing beach has gone down very well in London, I can tell you. Admiral Burroughs has passed on Commodore Troubridge's recommendation that you be awarded the DSC for it. I knew you'd do well when you first came here in that old steamer and promptly shook up the base ward master's department."

"I'm sorry about that episode, sir. I hadn't realised it had come to your attention. But a DSC? Surely I don't qualify for that."

"In 1940 Lieutenant-Commander Gerard Roope was awarded a posthumous VC for ramming the German heavy cruiser to try to prevent her raiding our convoys, and what you did has many similarities with that action Warwick."

"Well, I suppose I ought to be grateful that I'm not going to get anything posthumous; I'm pretty fit and well now, apart from a few chunks knocked off my profile and this great, itchy bandage all over my back and shoulder, sir." He felt a warm glow of pride spreading through him, noting that the admiral had used his Christian name for the first time.

"There's another thing that I want to thank you for that's a bit more personal, Warwick. My son David was with you on the bridge of your ship. Commodore Troubridge relied on him for a full report of the action between *HMS Bruiser* and the *Vauban*, as well as his general report on the entire landing, which Lieutenants Browne and Watson also contributed to. He has subsequently mentioned David personally in his dispatches and commended his actions to Admiral Burroughs. I can't thank you enough for all you have done for David in the year or so he has been with you. I really appreciate the care you have taken of him and so does his mother back in England.

Warwick thought of Jerry Collins and the fact that but for a difference of a few seconds of arc in the training of the *Vauban's* main armament, it might have been David lying on the bridge deck with his head blown off and not Jerry. They were only standing about ten feet apart when the bridge was hit.

"What's happened to my ship and her crew, sir?" he asked the admiral.

"Lieutenant Browne was recalled from the beach and took her to the dry dock at Mers el Kebir, just along the coast, for emergency repairs to her bow and bottom plating. He's a bit old for a command now, but he's been promoted to lieutenant-commander and will probably take her back to England with David and Lieutenant Watson. Then they'll all be sent on a fortnight's leave while Portsmouth Dockyard makes permanent repairs. I'll fly back for David's wedding to Monica Zeigler in Inveraray on December 10. There's a standing wedding invitation for you and your wife. I know David is so hoping you'll make it. He's asked me to ask you if you would consider being his best man."

"I'd be honoured, sir; please let him know that. Sarah will be so pleased; she loved both of the Ziegler girls; in fact the whole family. Any news of Jo Crowthorne, sir?"

"Jo is back with the US Army on General Fredendall's staff. He's a first lieutenant now, or so I hear. He's still in contact with Brigitte Ziegler and may yet become David's brother-in-law."

"Do we know what's happened to their son in Stalingrad, sir?"

"David has told me that they fear the worst. There has been no communication with him for several weeks now and they know from the BBC that the situation of the German Sixth Army is deteriorating by the day, with a huge backlog of casualties for them to try to transport out."

After the admiral left, he chatted with Jim Marsh for a while, talking about the time he was there last, less than a year ago. Jim was due for re-appointment in England any time now and hoped for a destroyer command. They arranged to have a night ashore together as soon as Warwick was allowed up.

"But I'm not going anywhere near the Red Shoes Bar and Madame Erica, and that's for sure!" said Warwick firmly, looking at Jim's grinning face and realising that they were both thinking of Warwick's last birthday run ashore.

"Don't worry, my lad, your girlfriend Esperanza's left. She married a US Marine master sergeant in Gibraltar Cathedral a couple of months back. Looked really demure in white, she did. Butter wouldn't melt in her mouth! Mind you, if you want to catch up and chat about old times, I expect my intelligence department can locate her for you."

"Don't even think about it, Jim! I'm a happily married man now, with a son who might turn out to be a future admiral on the way in a few months' time."

CHAPTER THIRTY-SEVEN

That evening, Warwick applied himself to his correspondence. He wrote to Sarah, telling her of the good news about his pending award for bravery and his long, friendly chat with the admiral. He wrote about David MacDonald's wedding to Monika on December 10, to which they were both invited and at which he would act as best man. Then he dealt with the less good news about his injuries, especially the big scar on the left side of his face, which he feared he would carry for life. He said he was likely to be discharged from the hospital in about ten days' time and would probably join a homeward-bound troop or hospital ship shortly after that.

He then wrote to his parents, congratulating his father on his new job with Southern Command and gave them the news about his recommendation for the award of the Distinguished Service Cross and his own injuries, both of which he played down.

He wrote to Jeanie Cameron, expressing his sorrow at Jerry Collins's death in action and outlining the development of the action from the bridge where Jerry and he were stationed, as well as praising Jerry as a fearless and capable officer who would be a great loss to the US Navy and whom he was proud to have had serving under him. He said that Jerry had spoken of her constantly while they were on passage to North Africa and that it was obvious that he had intended to ask her father for her hand on their return. It was not an easy letter to write, but when he was finished, he read it through and was satisfied with what he had written. After all, it was better for her to get such a letter from him than not to get a letter at all, even if someone else might well have expressed it more skilfully. His unexpressed hope was that she was not pregnant from that night in bed with Jerry while *HMS Bruiser* was at anchor, when he had taken a spin around the deck and peered through Jerry's cabin scuttle to see why the light was still on. That was actually less than a month ago but it seemed a very long time back now.

On 22 November, the supporting strapping on his left shoulder was removed and replaced by a sling. He was discharged from hospital and transferred with his kit to the wardroom accommodation of *HMS Raleigh*, the Royal Navy Base. His other injuries were completely healed, being more or less of a superficial nature. He received a letter from the Admiralty confirming his rank as Commander, Royal Naval Reserve. No longer was his rank to be prefaced by "Temporary Acting." The same letter said that this confirmation of his status as a senior officer at the early age of twenty-seven was in recognition of his exemplary service and his sinking of a powerful Vichy destroyer and the protection of the major Oran landing beach while the initial waves of troops and supplies were being put ashore.

He also received a handwritten letter from US Major-General Fredendall thanking him for his great efforts in protecting US troops and thereby facilitating the taking or Oran two days after the landing, especially after the sad loss of six hundred of his troops when the USCG ships *Walney* and *Hartford* were set on fire in Oran Harbour by the two Vichy destroyers and the shore artillery, which caused the failure of the initial direct assault on the town and the anticipated early capture of the town and its harbour. He had made a recommendation to Washington that Warwick be awarded the US Navy Cross for valour. Warwick suspected Jo Crowthorne, now on the general's staff, had something to do with this award and the letter, but appreciated the trouble the general had taken to write to him, especially as he was now engaged in preparing his green troops to face elements of Rommel's experienced and battle-hardened army that had arrived in Tunisia after their long retreat from el Alamein.

Later that month, Vice Admiral MacDonald presented Warwick with his DSC on behalf of King George VI at a small ceremony at Government House. He spent that night ashore with Jim Marsh to celebrate, but they kept well clear of Madam Erica's establishment and other, similar bars with bedrooms upstairs and pliant female staff massed around the bars on the ground floors, waiting to pounce on innocent sailors.

Belatedly, the news came through that the Russians had made a huge breakthrough on the Volga and had surrounded the German Sixth Army in Stalingrad. With the onset of the Russian winter, which had come early that year, the hopes of rescue for Colonel-General Friedrich Paulus and his Sixth Army grew daily more remote. Warwick thought the chances of survival of the Zeigler's son, seriously wounded there and refusing the offer to fly out to Berlin, were very slim indeed. He hoped it would not cloud the celebrations of David and Monika's wedding at Morag House on December 10.

Later that week, his orders arrived. He was to join the old Bibby liner *HMS Oxfordshire*, now requisitioned as a hospital ship and bound for Portsmouth, when she docked in Gibraltar. His kit was packed up for the second time and taken down to the main jetty where she was alongside, flying the Blue Peter to indicate her imminent departure for England. *HMS Oxfordshire* had been built as long ago as 1912 and had served as a hospital ship in the Great War before being released back into her owner's Far-Eastern passenger and immigrant service in 1919. She had four tall masts and a long, thin funnel amidships. She was an oil-fired steam ship with a maximum speed of thirteen knots. In spite of being clearly marked with a broad red line on her white hull, interspersed with large red crosses, it was decided that she should be escorted by two old, ex-US four-stack destroyers, *HMS Lancaster* and *HMS Richmond*. They sailed at 2300 on the night of November 30.

The passage was expected to take just over four days. Warwick helped his steward unpack into the small cabin near the bridge that they had allocated him. It was old fashioned to the extreme and reminded him of Cyril's cabin on *SS Freshwater Bay*. There were a couple of polished brass scuttles with deadlights hooked up above them, looking out over the wide, teak boat deck, a settee with a tropical cover attached, a strip of carpet, a washbasin with a wooden-framed mirror over it, a chest of drawers, and a single wardrobe. He had a bunk with a high washboard, making it difficult for him to climb into with his left arm still immobilised. There were a couple of upholstered mahogany chairs, and the bulkheads and deckhead were painted cream, which contrasted nicely with the dark wood of the furnishings. The whole cabin smelt of floor polish and was spotlessly clean. The communal showers and heads were just down the passageway.

All in all he was very comfortable and lucky to have a single cabin. He knew the army officers on board of the rank of major and above were sharing double cabins; with four berth cabins for the more junior officers. Down below on the ward decks, there were around two hundred and fifty casualties, confined mainly to metal beds, being brought back from the fighting in North Africa and the damaged and sunken ships which had taken part in the Malta convoys.

Before turning in, he wandered up the wooden stairs to the bridge, just one deck above his cabin. It was overcast with a freshening, icy, northerly wind and a steep, short sea. The lights of Spain were receding on the starboard quarter as the old ship headed on a north-westerly course out into the Atlantic. He could just see the two accompanying destroyers ahead, carrying out an Asdic search pattern of some complexity. The second officer was on watch; a pleasant broad-shouldered Old Conway boy who had just passed his Masters' Ticket, and was only a year younger than Warwick. The old ship had a steady, corkscrew roll with the seas on her starboard bow. Icy cold spray feathered across the foredeck, with the occasional plume hitting the bridge and making them duck down below the bridge dodger.

"The forecast looks bad, sir. The barometer has dropped half an inch in the last six hours. There's a big North Atlantic depression coming in from the west, right across our path. I think the Bay of Biscay will live up to its name on this trip. God help the wounded below if it does; they're in for a right shake up!"

"At least it will discourage any prowling U-boats," replied Warwick. "I know this is a hospital ship, but on a dark and dirty night, they may not make the distinction."

"We do have the ship entirely floodlit, sir. Even the dimmest U-boat commander ought to notice that as he looks at us through his wretched periscope."

The second officer, whose name was William Strong, boiled up the bridge kettle and made them both a cup of cocoa. He had a half bottle of dark rum in the bridge locker. He poured two capfuls into each mug and handed one to Warwick. "There's nothing like a bit of rum in the kye on a nasty night like this. I've been on the middle watch now for two years solid and I know what it takes to make the best of it."

"Doesn't Captain Lawrie object to you keeping a bottle of rum on the bridge?" asked Warwick

"Good god no sir; not old Annie Lawrie! Have you not met him yet? He's an old sailing ship man. He's well over sixty and as rough and tough as they come. He used to serve on West Country barques to Australia when he was an apprentice and a young officer. I remember once steaming into Fremantle. I was on the bridge, with him working the engine telegraphs. The local pilot was with us there, giving the helm and engine orders. He was a little, neat chap in whites; a born-again Christian or a Seventh Day Adventist or something like that. He asked the old man if he'd found Jesus yet. That was really not the sort of thing to ask Annie. I tried to be as inconspicuous as possible, hiding behind the brass engine telegraph where I was stationed. Annie was quiet for a moment, and then he said, "See that breakwater to port pilot?" "Yes indeed, I see it, captain," said the pilot brightly. "Well, pilot; I built that fucking thing, stone by fucking stone!" The pilot went very red and didn't speak a word to Annie after that."

"What on earth made him say that he'd built the Fremantle breakwater?" Warwick's curiosity overcame him.

"Well, apparently it was true. He told us all about it one night when we were alongside, having drinks before dinner. When he was a lad of sixteen and on his first trip to sea; their first port was Fremantle. They were a hundred and nine days out from Falmouth. It must have been in the early 1890s. He went ashore to a dance, met a local girl, and fell deeply in love, just like most first-trip apprentices do when they're away from their homes and mothers for the first time. Anyway, he couldn't bear to leave her when the time came for his ship to sail, so he jumped ship. He thought he'd join the Kalgoorlie gold rush to earn his fortune and then marry his beloved and settle down in Western Australia. They wouldn't take him on as a labourer in the goldfields as he was too young. He didn't have any money and eventually the police caught up with him, as he was a deserter from an English ship. They put him into Fremantle Gaol overnight and the following morning in court, the local magistrate sentenced him to two weeks' hard labour. He ended up on the gang carrying big rocks out to build the new breakwater. Then they deported him by putting him on a ship going back to England as a Distressed British Seaman. Don't mention I told you that, please; he's a bit sensitive about the story, especially when we've passengers or service officers on board."

The steward had left a tray of ham and cheese sandwiches for the middle watchkeeper, which William generously shared with Warwick. Warwick finished his cocoa and sandwich, and let William show him around the bridge and chartroom. It had not been thought necessary to fit a radar set, autopilot, or a bridge VHF to the old ship. Most of the rest of the equipment was from the original 1912 fit out, down to the huge brass-bound teak wheel with its steam steering telemotor chuntering away and the array of brass, whistle-capped voice pipes.

"This does rather take me back," Warwick remarked, remembering some of the old P&O ships that he had served his apprenticeship in, now nearly ten years before.

"They never thought a hospital ship needed much modern navigational equipment," explained William. "A lot of our time we spend anchored. Really, we're just a mobile hospital to be positioned where the current conflict is raging, or as near to it as we can get. We've been in Grand Harbour, Malta, for six months; a bit nerve racking that was, with the Luftwaffe coming over and bombing the town seven nights a week."

It was getting rougher and Warwick was having trouble moving about with only his right hand and arm available to steady him. He went slowly down the bridge ladder to his cabin, and with some difficulty, undressed and turned in to his bunk.

The next morning, the ship's motion was much more violent. Looking out the cabin scuttles, he could see great seas rearing up on the starboard side. The ship must have slowed down in the night; he could tell by the beat of her old steam engines. He judged they were down to around six knots and the wind outside was at least gale force eight, gusting nine.

With some difficulty, he got dressed and made his way down to the main dining saloon. It was very ornate, with dark wood and brass fittings and a somewhat worn, red, patterned carpet. The décor was in the grand Edwardian style. It was designed to hold five hundred passengers at a single sitting, but only three tables at the far end near the serving doors were laid up for breakfast, both with wetted down white cloths on them and the anti-roll battens around their edges raised to prevent the crockery and cutlery from falling onto the deck.

Captain Lawrie was at the head of one table, with the chief officer and a single army major, presumably the only soldier feeling up to breakfast that morning. There was a scattering of other ship's officers at the adjoining tables. Warwick sat next to the captain, after asking his permission. He was as William had described him; a large, beefy, red-faced man in his mid-sixties, with cropped grey hair and a nose that looked as if it had been punched hard and broken a while back and not been reset since.

"Welcome aboard, young man!" His voice was deep and stentorian but his face was kindly.

Warwick surmised that he didn't suffer fools gladly (if at all) but he would welcome those whom he thought were reliable, competent seamen. He hoped that Captain Lawrie had put him into that category.

"Nasty weather out there, sir," volunteered Warwick, "and I understand it's likely to get worse before it gets better."

That's right, commander; we don't get forecasts at sea in wartime, but from what we picked up in Gib, it's likely to get up to storm force or more in a few hours. If it gets much worse than this, I'll have to heave-to. She's an old ship and she won't take too much of this, nor will the wounded on the hospital decks." He turned to the chief officer who was quietly addressing himself to his eggs, bacon, fried bread, fried sausage, and baked beans, all covered in tomato sauce. He was in his late thirties, small and neat, greying at the temples and obviously an experienced seaman, completely unfazed by the conditions outside. Warwick found out later that he had been three years with Captain Lawrie as chief officer and had already lasted over a year longer in that position than any of his predecessors.

"Are you absolutely sure we're all secure on deck Mr. Mate?" Captain Lawrie enquired.

"Yes, sir," said the chief officer between mouthfuls. "I went round the decks with the bos'n, carpenter, lamp-trimmer and half a dozen ABs this morning. We've put double lashings on the derricks and clamps, and rope lashings across the tarps on the cargo hatches. The ventilators are off and their bearing pipes plugged and covered. The anchor cables have a wired lashing on them hove tight. All the topping lifts and wire hoists and their cargo blocks are stowed below. We've been right around the ship, and as far as I can see, we're as secure as we can be."

"Well done, Roger," said the captain warmly, eyeing the amount of breakfast the chief officer was still shovelling into his mouth. "Don't starve yourself, will you? Keep the old nourishment up; you may need it. It's cold and miserable outside."

Warwick ordered a similar breakfast to the chief officer's, plus some fresh orange juice and black coffee, from the white-coated, Maltese steward. He had some difficulty dealing with it with only his right hand, using his knife and fork alternately while steadying himself against the ship's motion with his legs. He enjoyed every mouthful; then he went back to his cabin to read. He didn't feel up to walking around; if he fell and damaged his partly-healed shoulder or broke something else staggering about or climbing up the gangways, he would be laid up for months. Inaction was not a prospect he relished much, especially on a ship at sea.

As predicted, the weather got worse, much worse. Later that morning, the wind was gusting to hurricane force twelve and the height of the seas, a quarter of a mile apart, increased to around sixty feet from crest to trough. Spray was continuously blowing off the tops of the waves, reducing visibility to a few hundred yards. Occasionally a gigantic rogue wave would sweep right over the cargo decks, and one such wave was high enough to sweep the boat deck and smash up the accident boat lashed in its davits. A considerable amount of sea water found its way down the engine room skylight, which was, of necessity, cracked open on the lee side. Low, black cumulonimbus clouds scudded before the wind, nearly touching the wildly gyrating mastheads, with frequent wild rain and hail squalls passing over the ship.

Captain Lawrie decided it was time to heave-to and carefully selecting a moment when the wind had eased slightly, he turned the ship downwind, setting the engine revolutions for a bare three knots. They were gradually drifting toward the French coast near La Rochelle, three hundred miles to the southwest. The two old, four-stacker destroyers followed suit after ballasting their stern double bottom tanks to keep them a little steadier. They both took position ahead of the *Oxfordshire*, which pumped out small quantities of oil to prevent the great seas breaking as they overtook the little fleet from astern. Warwick was very glad of the benefit of Captain Lawrie's experience and seamanship and realised that if things were this rough on the 13,000 ton *Oxfordshire* they must be absolute hell on those long, lean, and rather fragile old destroyers.

They had plenty of sea room and continued to ride out the storm. He had purloined a copy of Tolstoy's *War and Peace* from the ship's library and wedged himself, fully dressed, into his bunk, with a lifejacket under the outside of the mattress, pushing it up a few degrees and forming a V with the bulkhead. With his legs splayed out against the bulkhead on one side and the bunk board on the other, he managed to keep himself fairly secure. He had always meant to finish *War and Peace*; his previous attempts had seldom got past the second chapter.

CHAPTER THIRTY-EIGHT

For forty-eight hours the storm raged, and the ship headed slowly south-east instead of north, the direction of England. Warwick read, slept, and occasionally ate. The galley was reduced to providing hot soup in mugs, bread and butter, and the occasional bacon and egg sandwich, toasted.

He ventured up to the bridge once, to look at the awe-inspiring panorama of the huge seas marching in stately ranks down to the ship's counter and occasionally sweeping over the foredeck, but it was really too hard for him to hold on with one hand and, after a few words with the captain and William, who was the afternoon watchkeeper, he retired again to his bunk and *War and Peace*. He took to thinking of the welcome he would get from Sarah and their lovely, warm home in the beautiful Hampshire countryside. He resented this storm and the time it was wasting when he could have been with his wife.

After two days, Captain Lawrie judged the weather to have abated enough to set course again for England at an even twelve knots. They were forced to give Ushant and the Casquets a wide berth, remaining at least two hundred miles off the German-occupied Brittany coast.

Warwick, up and about again, prowled around the ship, visited the officers on the bridge and ate in the dining saloon, which, now that the weather had abated, was rather more populated by army officers. In the intervals, he progressed with his reading of *War and Peace*. He found it hard to concentrate on Tolstoy and his hero's delight and awe at his Masonic initiation in Saint Petersburg; he just longed to be home and cuddled up in front of the fire with Sarah.

He visited the sick bay to have his shoulder injury assessed. The surgeon lieutenant-commander in charge had him x-rayed and decided that his scapula had knitted sufficiently to allow him to take his left arm out of the sling with some care, and do some gentle exercises with his hand and arm to strengthen them up after their immobilisation. He advised Warwick to retain the sling whenever possible and rest his arm in it. Further, he was only to use his left arm and hand for light, non-stressful activities and not try to lift any weights or volunteer to take off tight jam-jar tops and the like, and particularly not to raise the arm up to or above the shoulder level. He told Warwick that although the scapula and collar bone had more or less healed, the places where they had been torn apart by the shrapnel would still be vulnerable, especially as the surrounding dorsal muscles had been badly damaged and were not yet supporting the bones as they normally would.

The ship entered Portsmouth Harbour on the afternoon of December 7. It was a grey, blustery day with a chill easterly wind. It needed two Navy tugs to push her alongside C Jetty, not far from *HMS Victory*. Warwick took off his sling and put on his smartest uniform, then moved to the boat deck rail to look out for Sarah on the dock. In spite of borrowing a pair of 7 x 50 binoculars from William, he couldn't see her anywhere among the girlfriends, wives, children, and parents gathered to meet the wounded men who would shortly be disembarked – on foot or on stretchers, depending on the severity of their condition. There were twenty or thirty army ambulances with khaki-clad WRAC drivers alongside them, behind the greeting party, but he couldn't see any sign of the Alvis among the few civilian vehicles parked there.

"Dammit, she might have turned up to greet her wounded hero of a husband," he muttered to himself. "Maybe she's run out of petrol coupons."

He knew this to be nonsense; she would have taken a taxi or managed to get a lift somehow, or even persuaded *HMS Victory's* transport officer to send a staff car in normal circumstances. Sarah was not one to let small difficulties stand in her way, especially when it concerned her greeting her husband on his return from active service. Then he caught sight of a little group of people, all of whom he recognised but who formed an unlikely conjunction on C Jetty on that cold and blustery December day. There was Commander Robin King, together with old Doctor Ian Williams from the village, and the local vicar, the Reverend Christopher Lovell. They were huddled together, talking something over. He wondered what on earth they were doing there. They looked very serious. Robin King was doing most of the talking so far as he could make out.

The lines were made fast, the gangways came down, and the customs and immigration officials boarded, followed closely by Robin King and his two civilian companions. They met with Warwick on the boat deck.

"Warwick, can we talk privately, please?" said Robin, looking down at the deck. Warwick noticed that neither the doctor nor the parson made any attempt to meet his eyes.

"Where's Sarah?" he asked urgently. "Has she had some kind of accident? Is the baby all right? Is she in hospital or something?"

"Let's just go below, please, Warwick." Robin put a fatherly arm around Warwick's shoulders.

The four of them made their way down to Warwick's cabin, where the steward was busy packing his gear.

"Please leave that for now, steward; we need to talk to Commander Hursey." Robin ushered the steward out into the passageway and shut the door. "Warwick, I won't beat about the bush. It's very bad news I'm afraid. Last night a Canadian-crewed Manchester heavy bomber on a night training exercise suffered an engine fire over Southampton. They only have two engines and those engines are prone to overheating and catching fire for no apparent reason. They had to take the Manchesters off front line service; they killed more trained air crew on ops than the Germans did. Anyway, the crew bailed out, leaving the pilot to try to get the plane clear of the town. He tried for Southampton Airport, but the wing was on fire and the plane became uncontrollable. He crashed into the outbuildings of West Lodge. The plane had a lot of fuel left, and burst into flames on impact. The stable block was completely destroyed. The main house was untouched; the port wing must have missed it by inches. The pilot died in the crash. Sarah and Mr. and Mrs. Alfrey were in the Alfreys' flat there. It was about eleven p. m. when the plane hit them. There were no survivors, I'm afraid; no hope of anyone surviving, really. I'm so terribly sorry, Warwick."

Warwick sat down suddenly and heavily, jolting his shoulder and causing him a violent stab of pain. He tried to take in what he had been told. His shoulder began to hurt badly and he wondered if he'd damaged it. The room went darker and the images of the three worried men standing over him blurred, with little points of light dancing about in the gathering gloom. He thought vaguely that he might pass out.

"The Lord giveth and the Lord taketh away; blessed be the name of the Lord our God." The Reverend Lovell proffered Warwick some spiritual comfort, "She was a wonderful woman; we all loved and admired her in the village. She had time to spare and a kind word for everyone, rich or poor. She put so much into the repair of the fabric of our church; I can't tell you how grateful we were to her. That church has stood in the village since the fourteenth century. She said she wouldn't let it fall down in her lifetime. She loved you, Warwick; she loved you more than her life itself. She came to me to pray for you when you were going south into action, and she came again to give thanks to her God when she heard that you had survived. Be assured that such love never dies; you will surely be reunited with her in heaven."

"Such love never dies." Warwick thought about that in a dull stupor. How could it; all the times they'd shared, all the little things they'd done and said together. How could it die just as quickly as a plane crashing?" He felt tears prickling his eyelids and put his head in his hands. His shoulder pain had reduced to a dull ache now. He hadn't cried properly since he was a fourteen-year-old cadet.

"We've done our best this morning to sort everything out." Ian Williams was speaking now. "We will only be able to identify the bodies by the dental records; there won't be much left after the fire. We'll soon arrange everything for the funerals; you can trust Christopher and me to look after that side of it."

It suddenly struck Warwick that if the Oxfordshire hadn't been hove to for fifty hours by the big storm, he would have been home last night and at eleven p. m. Sarah would have been in bed with him in the main house and not in the Alfreys' flat in the stable block. The Alfreys would have died with the bomber pilot, but Sarah and their baby would have been safe and well. Then he thought about the baby. The son he'd hoped for. The son he'd imagined that one day, half a century on, might have been an admiral. He'd have been perfectly content with a daughter, but he had convinced himself it would be a son. Now it wasn't anything but a fragment of unidentifiable charcoal amongst the wreckage.

"We contacted your mother and she contacted your sister, in her hospital in London," said Ian Williams. "They are both travelling down to Hampshire to live in with you at our house in the village. It's a big house; there's plenty of room for you all. They wouldn't let you stay at West Lodge while they are clearing up there. You won't be on your own tonight; there'll be me, my wife Betty, and your mother and sister in the house to keep you company."

"Thank you so much, Ian," said Warwick dully, thinking there wasn't really much left for him to live for. He might just as well book in at the distressed seaman's home in Portsmouth.

All he needed was a bunk, washbasin, lavatory, a bit of heating, and some occasional stew or something to keep him alive. He had no desire for comfort; no ambition, nothing. "But I do want to stop off at West Lodge first. I must see where she died; I'm sorry, I just have to."

He had a sudden thought. "Robin, can you do me a favour, please? Can you contact David MacDonald, my navigator in *Bruiser*, and the Zeiglers in Morag House, Inveraray? I'm due to act as best man at the wedding of David and Monika Zeigler in three days' time. If you could let Admiral MacDonald know, too, if you can. He's coming over to England from Gib for the wedding. Please give my apologies and tell them about Sarah and the bomber crash."

"No problem, Warwick; no problem at all," said Robin. "I'll get onto it right away."

They made their way ashore where Robin had laid on a staff car for the vicar, Ian, and Warwick. Having loaded his bags and suitcase, the driver headed for West Lodge. There was little enough conversation; they were all lost in their thoughts. Warwick's shock and despair had subsided into a dull ache. His arm felt better now and he supported it in his lap to let it recover. He thought again of the *Oxfordshire's* delay, but for which Sarah and he would have been safe and sound, tucked up in the big house in their bed last night.

Then he tried to think about life as it would be from now on. They'd only met thirteen months ago, but now, life on his own without her was almost unimaginable. Then he thought of all the unfinished business he'd have to sort out. Then of the funeral in a few days' time, and of the difficult and (to his mind) irrelevant things he would have to do. Then of the inevitable wake afterward. Who would come? Probably most of the village, plus some of his shipmates and ex-shipmates who were in the country, he supposed. And all the time, there was this dull, nagging, hopeless ache gnawing away at him from somewhere in his chest.

CHAPTER THIRTY-NINE

When they arrived at West Lodge, Warwick insisted on looking at the remains of the outbuildings before he went inside the main house. They were just an empty, burned-out shell now. There were many fragments of green-painted aluminium scattered about. Over the lawn were some larger lumps of the bomber's fuselage. A wrecked and a burned-out Rolls Royce Vulture engine had been carried on by its own momentum, and had fetched up against the border fence a hundred yards away. Of the other engine, there was no sign. The wreckage was still smoking and the local AFS truck was there with the auxiliary firemen damping down the site. The burned out hulk of the big Packard was clearly visible, but there was no trace of their little sailing boat. The Alvis two-seater had been parked in front of the stables, and had been crushed by falling brickwork.

A few men in white coats from the Hampshire Police Forensic Department were sifting through the charred debris with white, canvass bags at the ready, and some RAF personnel were there too, collecting parts of the bomber for the inevitable official enquiry.

Warwick thought of the two of them sailing in that little boat on the lake in the sun a few months back, and of Sarah writing to say that she was hanging the sails up over the beams to keep them fresh and free of mould, and felt a new wave of ineffable, bleak sadness welling up. He wandered through the cold rooms of West Lodge. In their bedroom, he opened the drawers of the old, bow-fronted chest and pressed his nose to Sarah's clothes. They smelt faintly of Chanel No.5.

Later, they drove to Ian and Betty Williams's big house in the middle of the village. Sally and his mother had arrived before the staff car got there. The heating was turned up and the house was warm and welcoming. Betty Williams had a brace of pheasants roasting in the oven and had found a couple bottles of Burgundy.

The time passed much more pleasantly for Warwick than he had expected. Ian and the women had been good company, and comforting, and had kept his glass well topped up with the wine and later some single malt whisky they had found in the cellar and decanted.

Warwick went up to bed at about ten thirty. He thought he would lay awake in that comfortable, big bed so like the one he had shared with his wife up at West Lodge, but dropped off to sleep within a few minutes.

Then the bedside telephone rang. He picked it up.

"It's me!" said Sarah's voice.

"Sarah! It's you, darling; you're alive! How wonderful!"

The line went dead; there was only the dial tone. Warwick was fully awake now, holding the receiver rather foolishly, and wondering if he had dreamed it or if it had really happened. He laid awake a long time after that, waiting for the phone to ring again, but it never did.

The days passed. Warwick had been granted compassionate leave on top of the fortnight's leave he was due. Sarah's funeral came and went a week later.

There was a good turn-out from the village and they were joined by Admiral MacDonald with David, his new wife Monika, Brigitte and Heimlich and Anne Zeigler. There was a small contingent from the USN; Captain Osmond, Fred Harden, and Alan Royle. Commodore and Mrs. Troubridge attended, as did Commander Ken Mills and his wife, as well as Robin King and his wife. They had all known and loved Sarah, and they all came to pay their respects to her and to Warwick.

They gathered at Ian and Betty's house afterward, where Betty, Warwick's mother, and Sally had laid out food and drinks, their joint rations supplemented by some supplies from the wardroom store of *HMS Victory*, thoughtfully organised by Robin. Warwick felt it was an ordeal that just had to be borne, and soldiered on, being polite and non-committal to everyone.

Admiral MacDonald took him aside. "Warwick, you've suffered a great blow and my family and I extend every sympathy possible; you know that. But there's one thing that I have to say to you. We're fighting a war now, and in war, people die. Jerry Collins died fighting for us off Oran; John Evered died in action at sea off Gibraltar and the Zeigler's son Karl in Stalingrad is almost certainly dead. They have managed to come to terms with that now. He was their only son, remember, even though he was fighting on the wrong side. You could so easily have been dead yourself, instead of being badly wounded. Time is a great healer, although I know that's hard for you to accept at the moment. My advice is for you to get matters settled here and then go back to sea as soon as you can. Never mind Christmas; wherever you spend it, it will be a sad and lonely ordeal for you, not the happy, convivial festival you deserve. I've spoken to both Commodore Troubridge and Admiral Burrough and I can assure you that we want you, as soon as you feel able, to resume your duties. There's an important and vital job awaiting you when you do come back. I don't want to sound too much like General Kitchener, but your country needs you, Warwick."

"I suppose you're right, sir. Everything I have to do just seems so pointless to me at the moment. It all seems like a nightmare, and I still haven't quite taken it in. I was always fighting for Britain, yes, but also for my dreams of a peaceful life with my wife and kids in this beautiful Hampshire countryside when peace came again. I'm sure I can get going again and, on the practical side, I need to have a meeting with our solicitors and accountants and also to find a reliable housekeeper and gardener to take care of this property. Then I've really no reason to stay ashore on leave. I'll spend a few days with my mother, but there's really nothing left to hold me here now."

The local garage had a 1936 Hillman Minx on the blocks in their workshop, covered with a dust sheet and stored for the duration of the war. Warwick arranged to hire it, and it was uncovered, the wheels put back on, serviced, its tyres inflated, and filled with petrol from petrol coupons thoughtfully sent by his father via his mother. He arranged a meeting with Mr. Pearson, the solicitor in Cheltenham, together with Nicholas Childs, the young chartered accountant that Sarah had retained. He drove down there in the Hillman on a cold and rainy December morning.

He was ushered into the warm, old-fashioned solicitor's office by a prim, middle-aged secretary. There was a big log fire in the Georgian fireplace, and Mr. Pearson sat behind a huge partner's desk in the window bay with the grey, December light behind him. The room was suffused with the smells of good pipe tobacco and burning apple wood.

Mr. Pearson started the conversation hesitantly, fiddling about scraping out, filling, and tamping down the tobacco in his big briar pipe while he talked. "I am so sorry, Commander Hursey. We had grown very fond of Sarah, and after her mother died, I felt myself almost to be her surrogate father – one of the family at least. Rest assured; Nick and I can look after everything for you. Leave it with us; your job is to fight for freedom and protect England and the free world and win this wretched war. We civilians left at home are here to do all your legal work and accounting."

He lit his pipe with a Swan Vesta, took a puff, and sat back. The secretary brought in a china pot of tea and three matching cups, together with a tray of shortbreads, tastefully arranged.

She made somewhat of a pantomime of pouring the tea and enquiring about the precise portions of milk and sugar they each required and then handed round the plate of shortbreads, Warwick first. Warwick, playing along with her performance, thanked her profusely for her efforts, at which she coloured visibly and simpered embarrassedly. Warwick, who had driven down in full uniform, as was the wartime custom, wondered if he ought to have put on a civilian suit instead.

"Now to business." Mr. Pearson shuffled a sheaf of papers in front of him and puffed out a cloud of smoke and sparks impatiently. The middle-aged secretary left the room in a hurry.

"Sarah left everything to you in the event that she predeceased you, which was, in fact, the case, so there will be no death duties chargeable as you are her widower and sole heir. My guess is that her estate is going to amount to nearly £70,000, with a considerable annual income from her father's patents and from her rented properties. It will take a little while to get probate granted, but I would hope that with a simple, single beneficiary and no question of any tax to pay, the whole thing should be cleared up in a couple of months. We will also contact your household insurers and the War Insurance Office. There should be a considerable sum due in respect of the damage, especially as it was caused by a RAF bomber with known defects. I know it's wartime, but they could be argued to be negligent. Those Manchester heavy bombers were withdrawn from front-line service after only six operational months and that was back last June. They should never have allowed them to be flown over populated areas, even for training purposes, with their Vulture engines so prone to overheating and catching fire. Apparently, they built over two hundred of them and they all should have been scrapped by now, wartime or not. They were a bad design, completely unfit for service."

"Thank you for all your help Mr. Pearson and you too, Nick. I don't want to get involved in a big legal case, but I am sure that the RAF will pay out for the rebuilding. Just one thing; I want to rebuild the stables much the same as they were, with a staff flat, two garages, storage space with some stabling for a couple of horses; only a bit further from the main house. Possibly you could get an architect to draw something up for me."

"That's not a problem, commander," said Mr. Pearson. "I know just the man for the job. He's a young chap with his own practice, and a client of mine."

"I mustn't hold you up any longer," said Warwick. "I don't know what I would have done without you two; I couldn't have asked for better friends in this sad, difficult time. Sarah was so good at looking after things and doing business and I used to leave it all to her. Anyway, now I've cleared most of the outstanding matters up, I've decided to go back to war again in the next few days. I'll notify the Admiralty that I'm available."

Warwick left the office after saying goodbye to the secretary, which made her blush again, and drove back to West Lodge. He checked that the heating was on and that the house was in good order. Most of the debris had been cleared from the stables at the back, and only low, blackened, brick walls and the outline of the floor tiles remained. He decided to move back in there with his mother. Sally had gone back to the Middlesex Hospital in London, where all qualified medical staff were urgently needed and were working in three shifts. His mother had located another couple in the adjoining village, Bert and Lilly Wicks, who were willing to live in West Lodge and look after it and the grounds while he was away. They didn't own a car or a have a driving licence, but she had arranged a standing order with the local taxi company to take them into the village to shop a couple of times a week at Warwick's expense.

A day or so later, after they had moved in, he drove down to the church to talk with Christopher, pray a little for Sarah with him, and attend the Thursday morning communion. He took comfort in the service and in the chat and prayer they had together. He sat for an hour or so afterward in one of the pews of the eight-hundred-year-old church, sniffing the slightly musty, dry air, reading the ancient plaques around the walls and the inscriptions on the tomb stones in front of the altar. He thought about the generations of villagers who had lived and died there, remembered now only by these inscriptions in the church and on the tombstones outside. He mused that living, personal knowledge of each and every one ceased about eighty years after they had died, when those who had known them died in their turn, and so on down the ages. Probably by about the year 2010, no one would be left who remembered Sarah. All these people whose remains lay here had had their loves, their triumphs, and their despairs during their time on earth, and now these were long gone and forgotten. He thought of Shakespeare's lines on Cleopatra's death. "Age cannot wither her, nor custom stale her infinite variety . . ."

"That would be Sarah," he mused to himself. "She'd have made a fine Cleopatra." He took a long, deep breath, "Well, I suppose the rest of my life started this morning, so I'd better get on with it."

When he got back to West Lodge, he found two suitcases full of Sarah's clothes in the hall. One case was yet to be shut, and there was a lingering hint of Chanel Number 5 in the air.

"I thought it best to pack it up and get rid of it all now, Warwick," said his mother. "You don't want to come back to an empty house with all the cupboards and wardrobes full of her clothes. That would be too sad. There are plenty of people who've been bombed out in London and who'll be grateful for them. I'll take the whole lot to the Salvation Army. I've put all her jewellery in the little safe in your bedroom."

The following day, a buff, manila envelope arrived by messenger with OHMS in bold, black letters on it, marked *Confidential*. He signed for its receipt and opened it. As he had guessed, it was from the Admiralty. It was short and to the point:

CONFIDENTIAL
BY MESSENGER ONLY
For the attention of Commander W. M. G. Hursey DSC, Royal Naval Reserve

December 18, 1942

On the understanding communicated to this office that you are fully fit and ready for further active service, you are hereby requested and required to attend at Admiralty

Buildings, Whitehall, on Tuesday December 20, at 1130 when you will be apprised of your next posting by Captain Fairclough, Royal Navy.

Should you be unable to attend at the date and time specified above, please contact the undersigned on the telephone number below.

I remain, sir, your obedient servant,
D. R. Griggs, MBE
Assistant Deputy Secretary
(Officers' Appointments & Posting – Admiralty)

Warwick packed his gear with the help of his mother and put it in the boot of the Hillman Minx. They arranged to thank Ian and Betty for their hospitality that evening and ask them to dinner in the Dog and Duck. Meanwhile, that afternoon they went to the church again, said another little prayer for Sarah, and waited in the pews for the annual, afternoon carol service to start. Warwick loved traditional carols. The service took him back to his childhood when, as a local schoolboy, he sat next to his mother and all the other children from the Warnham Church of England School at Saint Margaret's carol service, conducted by the austere Canon Farson-Smythe, some twenty years before.

THE END

CPSIA information can be obtained at www.ICGtesting.com
Printed in the USA
LVOW081724161212

311898LV00003B/575/P